REDEMPTION POINT

REDEMPTION POINT

CANDICE FOX

A TOM DOHERTY ASSOCIATES BOOK NEW YORK

3/19

This is a work of fiction. All of the characters, organizations, and events portrayed in this novel are either products of the author's imagination or are used fictitiously.

REDEMPTION POINT

Copyright © 2018 by Candice Fox

A Forge Book
Published by Tom Doherty Associates
175 Fifth Avenue
New York, NY 10010

www.tor-forge.com

Forge® is a registered trademark of Macmillan Publishing Group, LLC.

The Library of Congress Cataloging-in-Publication Data is available upon request.

ISBN 978-0-7653-9851-2 (hardcover)
ISBN 978-0-7653-9853-6 (ebook)

Our books may be purchased in bulk for promotional, educational, or business use. Please contact your local bookseller or the Macmillan Corporate and Premium Sales Department at 1-800-221-7945, extension 5442, or by email at MacmillanSpecialMarkets@macmillan.com.

Previously published by Bantam Australia in trade paperback in January 2018

First U.S. Edition: March 2019

Printed in the United States of America

0 9 8 7 6 5 4 3 2 1

For Nikki, Malpass, and Kathryn

REDEMPTION POINT

There were predators beyond the wire. I knew they were there, although in the months since I'd been released from incarceration I hadn't yet seen one. My evening ritual was to come down to the shore and look for the ominous rise of two dead eyes above the surface of the water, the flick of a spiky tail. Feeding time. Half a ton of prehistoric reptile lolling and sliding beneath the sunset-lit water, separated from me by nothing but an old, rusty fence. I looked for crocodiles every day, drawn to the bottom of my isolated property on Crimson Lake by the recollection of being one of them. Ted Conkaffey; the beast. The hunter. The hidden monster from whom the world needed to be protected.

I couldn't stop myself coming down here, though holding the wire and watching for the crocs brought up the comparisons, the dark thoughts, all those scary old memories of my arrest, my trial, my victim.

She was never far from my mind. Claire would come to me at the strangest times, more vivid than she possibly could have been when she first etched herself into my memory, standing there at the bus stop by the side of the road. Every time I thought about her, I saw something new. Gentle wind from the approaching rain tossing her almost-white hair over her thin shoulder. The glaring outline of her small, frail body against the blue-black clouds gathering on the horizon.

Claire Bingley was thirteen years old when I stopped my car beside her on the ragged edge of the highway. She'd stayed at a friend's house the night before. Her backpack was stuffed with pajamas, half-eaten bags of candies, a brightly colored magazine; little girl things that would in a few short hours be spread over an evidence table and dusted with fingerprint powder.

We had looked at each other. We'd hardly spoken. But on that fateful day, the backpack would stay by the side of the highway while the girl came with me. I snatched her right out of her beautiful little life and pulled her, kicking and screaming, into my depraved fantasy. In a single act, I ruined everything that she ever hoped she could be. If all my plans had come to fruition, thirteen would have been her last birthday. But she survived the fiend that I was. Somehow, she crawled back out of the woods where I left her, a fractured remnant of who she'd been when she stood before me at the bus stop.

At least, that's what everyone says happened.

Only half of that story is true. I did stand before the child at the bus stop that day, impossibly taller and broader and stronger than her, opening the back door of my car, watching her nervous eyes. But in reality, I'd only pulled over to shift my fishing rod off the backseat where it sat leaning against a window, tapping irritatingly on the glass as I drove. I'd spoken to Claire Bingley briefly, but what I'd said wasn't an invitation to come with me, a plea or a threat. I'd made some stupid comment about the weather. Cars full of witnesses had whizzed past us on the road, looking out, photographing us with their suspicious minds, knowing somehow that we weren't father and daughter, that something was wrong here. Premonition. I'd got back in my car and driven away from Claire, forgetting her instantly, having no idea what was about to happen to her. Or me.

Someone did abduct that little girl, just seconds after I'd been there. Whoever he was, he did take her into the woods and violate her, and he did make that awful decision, the worst a person can make—he decided to kill her. But she survived, too traumatized to know who the hell had done this to her, too broken to put anything much about the crime into words. It didn't matter what Claire said anyway, in the end. The public knew who'd done this. Twelve people had seen the child, seen me standing not far from her, talking to her, the back door of my car yawning open.

I'd heard the story of Claire's attack described to me so many times across my trial and incarceration that it was easy to see myself doing it. There are only so many times you can hear a lie before you start living and breathing it, actually remembering it like it was real.

But it was not real.

I'm not a killer or a rapist. I'm just a man. There are things I am, and things I used to be. I used to be a cop, a new father, a devoted husband. I'd been someone who could never imagine myself wearing handcuffs, sitting in the back of a prison van, standing in the queue for chow in a correctional facility food hall, a wife-killer in front of me and a bank robber behind. There had been only one little girl in my life, my daughter Lillian, whose existence on the Earth I was still measuring in weeks when I was arrested.

I used to read voraciously. I drank red wine, and I danced in the kitchen with my wife. I regularly wore odd socks and I often left beard stubble in the bathroom sink. I was an ordinary guy.

Now I was a runaway living on the edge of nowhere, looking for crocs, watching the sun disappear beyond the mountains across the lake. Wandering back up the hill, my hands in my pockets and bad thoughts swirling. When an accusation like that comes into your life, it never leaves. The story of what I had done to Claire Bingley played on and on, in the minds of my ex-colleagues, my friends, my wife, Claire Bingley's parents, and the barrister who prosecuted me before my trial collapsed; they saw it just as vividly as I saw it. An unreal reality. A false truth.

People passed the story on to each other in whispers as I walked into the court in cuffs. The media printed it. The television stations ran it. The story was so real that it came to me in flashes of light in the strangest moments—while I was showering, while I was sitting alone on the porch drinking Wild Turkey and watching the water. I dreamed about it often, woke sweating and twisted in my sheets.

I am not, and never have been, a pedophile. I don't find children sexually attractive. I never laid a hand on Claire Bingley. But that doesn't matter. To the world, I am a monster. Nothing was ever going to change that.

Working on my goose house seemed to drive out the darkness, so I went to the newly erected structure and stood before it, making plans. Around me on the sprawling, empty lawn seven geese wandered, plucking at the grass, muttering and clucking contentedly to one another. When one settled by my feet, her hunger apparently sated, I reached down and stroked the back of her soft gray neck, the feathers collapsing, weightless, until I felt the soft, warm flesh of her neck underneath. My geese don't think I'm a monster, and that's something, at least.

I never planned on being a goose daddy. I spent eight months in prison with no idea if I was ever going to see the outside world again, let alone what I might do if I was ever released. I didn't have a home to go to. Three weeks after my arrest, my wife Kelly had started to turn her back on me, the weight of the evidence against me and the pressure of the public opinion simply too much for her to withstand. I didn't make any plans for life after the accusation. I was taken to prison and I tried to survive each day there without going completely insane or getting myself killed. Then, without warning, three months into the trial proceedings, with my lawyer looking more strained and exhausted with every passing day, the Office of Public Prosecutions dropped the charges against me. The legal procedure, a motion of "no billing," meant that I was not technically acquitted. I was not guilty—but I was not innocent either. There simply wasn't enough evidence to ensure I would be convicted, so they decided to let me go until new evidence could be acquired, if any ever surfaced. With the knowledge that I could be re-charged at any time, I was sent out into a hateful city. I went home, packed my things and fled north on nothing more than the instinct to hide and terror of the public's revenge. Kelly wasn't at home when I left. She refused to see me. I had to borrow a car from my lawyer.

Not long after I'd arrived in Crimson Lake and rented this small, beat-up house, a mother goose with a broken wing had showed up and interrupted my sunset drinking, squawking and flapping on the other side of the wire—the croc side. It was the first time in more than a year that I'd laid eyes on a creature more helpless than myself. The three-foot-tall, snow-white *Anser domesticus*, which I named Woman, had six fluffy chicks trailing behind her, just begging something slippery and primordial to emerge from the dark waters of the lake and snap her up. Since then, Woman the goose and her babies and me had lived together on the edge of the water and tried to heal.

Her babies had grown up quickly, and these were the creatures that surrounded me now as I assembled their new living quarters, approaching at times, examining my bare feet in the lush grass or pecking at my pockets where I sometimes kept grain pellets. Watching, their beady eyes following my hands as I pushed the screws into the corrugated iron roof of the playhouse.

Yes, instead of a proper goose coop, I'd acquired a children's playhouse. Not the most sensible idea for a notorious accused child rapist living in hiding with no children at home. I'd found the playhouse online, free to whomever was willing to come and pick it up from the nearby town of Holloways Beach. I'd scrolled past it at first. It was a dangerous idea. Vigilantes and gawkers had learned of my presence not long after I arrived in town, and they still drove by my house every now and then, curious about the man who'd somehow escaped justice. And one in three times when I opened the front door to a knock, it was a journalist who greeted me, notebook and pen thrust out like guns. All it would take was for one of these people to spy the playhouse in the backyard to bring the press and the public mob to my front door, pitchforks in hand, once more.

But money hadn't exactly been in abundance, and the playhouse was free. A genuine goose coop cost anything from $1,200 upward, and all I really needed to do to the playhouse was remove the floor and replace it with wire, and build a ramp to the entrance for Woman and her young. Since I'd found them, the family of geese had settled on the porch of my small, barren house, and I liked to sleep out there on the couch sometimes when the night was hot and loud with the barking of crocodiles and the cry of night birds. More than once I'd been awakened at dawn by the sensation of a goose beak foraging for bugs in my hair. Sometimes the first thing I saw when I opened my eyes in the morning was a curious bird-face inches from mine, waiting for me to hand out the breakfast pellets. Something had to give.

I squatted in the grass and swept away some of the cobwebs from under the playhouse, tested the base with my fingers. I would cut it out with a jigsaw, staple a sheet of wire across the bottom, then fit a steel tray I could unhinge and spray out to keep the house clean. The construction of the cubby was solid and would protect the birds from the foxes and snakes that sometimes made guest appearances around the property, preying on waterhens down by the shore. I went to the front of the playhouse and opened the shuttered windows, tore down the moldy curtains that some kid had probably spent many years enjoying drawing against the outside world, closing their little house off in privacy for their games. Playing house. My daughter might have enjoyed a playhouse like this. She was going to be two years old in a week. I couldn't remember the last time I'd seen her in person, held her, warm and wriggling, against my chest.

"I'll tie these up for now," I said, pushing the shutters closed on the windows, showing the geese as the chipped wooden frames clicked into place. "But eventually I'll probably put locks on. You can have them open during the day. You lot are sleeping in here tonight." I pointed, stern. "You're not sleeping with me. It's getting weird."

Woman, the only white goose, wandered close at the sound of my voice and tilted her small head, eyeballing me. I reached out to pat her but she swung her head away as she usually did, muttering. She'd never been very affectionate, but I'd never stopped trying to win her over.

"Two shelves for roosting." I showed her, leveling my hands halfway up the house, mapping out my vision. "And I'll put in some of that straw you like. Snug and safe, the lot of you. It'll be grand—probably grander than you need, but I'm a nice guy. What can I say?"

I shrugged, looked for an answer. The goose looked away.

I talked to my geese all the time. Particularly Woman. I recognized that I had started doing it at the same time as I realized it was too late to stop. I talked to her like a wife. Updated her about things I'd seen while out and about in the town, chatted to her absentmindedly, let her in on my thought processes. I would talk to the bird through the screen door to the kitchen while I cooked dinner, throwing things into the pot on the stove, the bird settled on the porch just outside the door, preening. I'd heard that lonely people talk to themselves. I'm not sure I was lonely, exactly, but I sorely missed having a wife. Kelly used to sit at the kitchen table when I was cooking, drinking wine, flipping through magazines, as disinterested in my ramblings as the regal mother bird. You can talk to people in prison, of course; there are no rules against it. But the guards will invariably answer you in single words until you give up and go away, and I was housed in protective segregation because of the nature of my charges. The inmates in my pod were mostly pedophiles, and pedophiles rarely come into the company of others of their kind in the outside world. So they like to talk about what they have in common. A lot. The only feedback I ever got from the geese was questioning looks and indecipherable bird babble—but I never had nightmares about that.

I left the geese and went up the stairs to the porch and into the kitchen. There were cable ties in the bottom drawer beside the sink, left over from some running repairs I had done when I moved into the old house. Deciding I'd use them to secure the windows of the cubby, I crouched and rummaged around in the clutter for them.

I was just slower than my attacker had anticipated as I rose up. If he'd been on point, he'd probably have killed me. But the wooden baseball bat whizzed over the top of my head and smashed into the wine bottles lining the windowsill, spraying wine and glass everywhere.

Emotion whipped up through me, an enormous swell of terror and anger and shock that seemed to balloon out from under my ribs and sizzle down my arms and over my scalp. There wasn't time to shout out, ask questions. A man was in my kitchen and he was swinging at me viciously with a baseball bat, my own bat, a weapon I'd been keeping just inside the front door to threaten the vigilantes with. He swung again and got me in the upper arm. The pain blinded me. I put my hands up as a reflex. The bat was coming again. I couldn't see my attacker. It was happening too fast. Shock of blond hair. Dark eyes. I bowed and threw myself at his waist.

We crashed into the dining room table and chairs. Ridiculously logical thoughts started zipping through my brain, caught and pulled down randomly from the whirlwind. The geese were screaming in the yard. The lights were on, and I hadn't turned them on. There was blood on my hands. The man had hit me in the face and I hadn't even felt it. I was yelling "Fuck! Fuck!" and he was saying nothing, determined only to hurt me, to bring me down.

He wasn't bigger than me. Not many people are. But there was a fury in him so hot and wild, he had all the impossible strength of a cornered animal. His anger would trump my desire to survive in this struggle. I knew it, but I kept fighting, kept growling, kept trying to get ahold of any part of him, his shirt, his hair, his sweat-damp neck. He dropped the bat. I pinned him and he bucked and I fell against the cupboards. His fist smashed into the side of my head from low down, a full-arm swing up and into my temple. The floor smacked my face. Hands around my throat, a tight band of fingers crossing my windpipe. I didn't even have time to fear that I was going to die. I grabbed at his knuckles and then passed out.

———

The sound of the geese woke me. They make a peeling, squealing kind of distress noise, a screaming punctuated by deep, growling honks. I remember thinking as I lay on the floor of my kitchen and listened to them that the sound meant that they were still alive, and that was all that mattered, really. I was lying on my front with my hands at the small of my back. As I shifted, I felt one of the cable ties I'd pulled from the bottom drawer around my wrists let a little blood flow into my numb fingers. Prickling, stinging. A black boot passed near my face.

He was raiding my house. I've been raided a few times since all this began, my house turned over by Crimson Lake cops with a grudge. I've come to recognize the sound of it. A crash, the whisper of papers sliding across the polished wood floor. A drawer clunking as it's wrenched from the dresser. I looked around. All the kitchen cupboard doors were open, smashed cups and plates, Tupperware containers on the floor. Wine everywhere, running down the cupboards like thin blood. One of the chairs was broken. He'd started here, moved from room to room. I tried to shift upward, assess anything broken or bent inside me. Everything hurt in equal measure.

"Don't move."

The boot came back, emerged from the blur at the corner of my vision and shoved me back down onto the floor. I heard a goose's wings flapping on the porch. I watched the blond man as he disappeared again into the bedroom, came to the kitchen table and righted the remaining dining room chair. He sat, dumped my laptop on the table and pushed it open.

"There's nothing in the house," he said. "I didn't think you kept it online. Too traceable that way. But maybe I'm wrong."

He became distracted, clicking through the inner workings of my computer. I braved a covert, awkward shuffle into the corner of the kitchen. I pushed myself up, took a moment to look at my attacker. I was steadily growing hotter. My entire body boiling beneath my clothes. Recognition. I knew this man. I knew his thin, angular face and big, dark blue eyes.

"What are you doing?"

"What do you think I'm doing?" He clicked around the computer, glanced at me. Looking at my face brought him out of his frenzied search of the laptop. I shifted backward, but there was nowhere to go. "I'm looking for pictures. Videos. Documents."

He was looking for child porn. Whoever this man was, wherever I had seen him before, he was associated with my case. This wasn't a robbery, although I'd known that from the anger. This was personal. I felt blood running down my jaw, tasted it between my teeth. His shirt was torn. I hadn't made much of an impact.

"If you leave, I won't call the police," I said.

"Do the police respond when you call them?" He snorted. Bitter. "I wonder how far they'd have to come. Whether they'd make it in time."

"Look, I don't know who you are—"

"You don't?" The man's brow dipped just once. Genuine shock. "Really?"

He grabbed the baseball bat from the floor and came toward me. My stomach plummeted.

"Please don't."

"You really don't know who I am?"

"Please."

I squeezed my eyes shut. He grabbed my jaw and shoved my head against the cupboards until I opened them.

"Look at me," he snarled. "Look at my face."

I could hardly breathe. If I didn't get the picture soon he was going to kill me. I could see him losing control again. Twitching in the muscles of his tight, red neck. His heart was hammering—jugular ticking fast in his neck. I searched his face and cringed as it came to me.

"Oh, god. You're Claire's father."

The baseball bat was in his fist. I cowered into the corner, expecting another blow as he rose to his feet.

"That's right, shithead."

I'd hardly looked at my victim's parents during my trial. Not *my* victim. Claire. I had to stop thinking about her that way. The way the rest of the country was looking at her. Because I didn't deserve this. There were angry tears on my face as a brief swell of defiance prickled in my chest.

"What took you so long?" I asked. "I expected you to be out there with the mob when they televised where I lived six months ago."

"Yeah?" He sat down again. "Sorry. I wanted a more personal visit."

"What are you gonna do?" I asked. It wasn't a challenge. I was serious. Because whatever he'd told himself about coming here and finding child porn and having me sent back to jail wasn't going to pan out, and he was starting to realize that. He could do whatever he wanted to me out here, and no one would hear me scream. I wasn't sure a beating would satisfy him. If he was going to kill me, all I wanted was to be sure he wouldn't touch my fucking geese. I started working my way mentally toward an argument for them. Toward getting him to make me a promise. But it was hard to maintain complete consciousness. He'd really smacked me around, maybe even after I'd passed out. The lights above me weren't completely clear. I had the feeling I'd been kicked in the chest a few times. Things were crunching and rattling as I breathed.

He was back in the chair, ignoring me. Head in his hands, fingers gripping his hair, thinking, as I was thinking.

"I kept a picture of you," he said. He drew a long breath, let it out slow. "Since Claire picked you out of the photo lineup. I asked the cops to show me the lineup, show me who she'd identified. You. I asked if I could take the picture. I kept it in my wallet. I would look at it sometimes to remind myself that you were just a man. That you weren't some . . . thing. A ghost."

A car drove by on the road outside. I thought about screaming.

"I figured if I let myself get overwhelmed by the idea that you were more than you really were, then I'd start to see you everywhere," he said. He rubbed his hands together. Examined his skinned knuckles.

"Rose, my wife, she was seeing you everywhere even after you were arrested. Big men hanging around little girls. Fathers with their daughters, you know? No. I'd take out the picture and look at your face and I'd think to myself, *He's a man, and he's in prison, and he can't hurt her anymore.*"

His lip twitched. I saw a flash of teeth.

"But then they let you out of prison," he said. "And I didn't know where you were. And you kept hurting her. Even though you were nowhere near her. She hurts. Every day. Just . . . Just being alive."

I was shivering from head to foot. The new calm that had overtaken him was sending my terror into overdrive. This man had the capacity to kill me. Not as he had been before, blinded by fury. But like this. Calm, and methodical. No one would investigate my death very deeply. Any number of people all across the country wanted me dead. They'd have to leave my grave unmarked, so that the vigilantes didn't come to piss on it.

"Listen to me," I told him. "I didn't hurt your daughter."

"I thought about this for so long. It was the only way I could go to sleep at night. I'd think about buying a plane ticket, coming here, finding you." He opened his hands, gestured to my kitchen. The shattered glass and plates at my feet. The broken chair by the door. "I thought about all sorts of things. About cutting you. Hanging you, for a while. Shotgunning you in the face. I had all these fantasies. They were so real, I could feel them."

He was suddenly crying. Manic. He pulled his hair, scratched his scalp hard with both hands. Rubbed his face with his palms like he was trying to wake from a dream.

"And now I come here and I find you're just a fucking man," he said. "Just like I told myself. You're just a man."

I didn't know what he was talking about. All I could think of was my own survival. I'd heard men talk like this before, about their fantasies falling in a heap, their plans coming undone. In my job as a cop I'd listened to them on the radio, standing in the street looking up at them on ledges, standing just beyond reach of the negotiator. He was going to kill me. It was all he could do. My lips were so dry I could hardly form words.

"Please. Please listen. There's a yellow envelope among my papers," I stammered. "In the second bedroom. I've been . . . I was working with a partner. She found some things on the man who really did hurt Claire. Some leads. I haven't done—I didn't—"

He stood and I tried to scramble away, got nowhere, curled into a ball, thinking he was coming for me again. But he just turned down the hall and left the house.

There was a shoe by my face, but it wasn't a black boot this time. It was a dirty pink Converse sneaker with wet grass sticking to the shoelaces. A thin ankle covered with tattoos of yellow tigers and wet jungle leaves straining as she stood over me. I felt Amanda nudge me in the side with her other shoe. I made a sound of life.

"Ted! You *are* alive!" she said, but her jubilation plummeted quickly into grief. "Damn it. I just lost a bet with myself."

She leaned on me, and I felt her slip a knife or scissor blade into the cable tie at my wrists. My hands flopped onto the floor, numb and useless.

"Birds," I said.

"What?"

"The birds."

"Oh," she said. "Good point."

She walked away, through the porch door, letting it slam behind her. I lay on the floor and dreamed. I'd taken a few beatings in my time, in prison and out, and I knew the worst thing I could do right now was try to get up too fast.

Amanda Pharrell was my investigative partner, a strange tattooed pixie who could be brilliant in the throes of a case, but annoying as a poke in the eye in equal measure. I'd been working with her since I moved to Crimson Lake, my old life on the drug squad with the New South Wales police long forgotten. I guess you could say she "hired" me; I was technically employed by her private investigations firm, the only other person on the payroll. But our partnership had been more of a beautiful accident, the hand of fate pushing us together. When I fled Sydney, I'd stopped and decided to settle in Crimson Lake by chance. And by chance, there was someone in town who everyone hated just as much as me. It was my lawyer who had put us together, and somehow—I still struggle to understand how—it had worked.

Like me, Amanda was never going to be welcomed back into the loving circle of civil society. She'd stabbed a seventeen-year-old school-mate to death after the two sat in a car in the rainforest together, about to walk up to a party. It wasn't her fault, but like my crime hers was a one-way ticket out of the "normal" world.

It was Amanda who had brought me a yellow envelope one day shortly after our first case together, a package containing papers detailing exactly what she'd managed to find out about the man who really did abduct and rape Claire. I'd been too scared to look very closely at them. She hadn't pushed me on the issue. It was my decision what I did with the investigation of my own case, and in the weeks that had followed, all the envelope brought me was worry and terror at the possibilities. Maybe if I went looking for Claire's attacker, I'd never find him. Maybe I would find him, and he'd get away. Maybe I'd try to find him, and only further implicate myself somehow, or be unable to prove it was he who'd attacked Claire Bingley. Maybe I'd ignore the envelope altogether, and he'd do it again, and this time he'd kill someone, and that would be my fault. I didn't think any good could come of what was contained in the envelope, no matter what happened.

I heard Amanda thump back up onto the porch.

"How many geese did you have before?"

"Seven," I groaned, pulling my legs toward me slowly, easing my way up onto my elbows. "Six gray, one white."

"Yeah, they're all there." She sniffed, kicked the porch door closed behind her like she owned the place. "They're just puffed up. Cranky."

"I'm pretty cranky myself." I staggered to my feet. She slipped under my arm and tried to help me to the bathroom, but being so small, she wasn't very useful. I smeared blood on the doorframe, made footprints on the divorce paperwork my wife had sent me, still unsigned. In the bathroom mirror, my face was awash with blood, one-half swelled so that the eye was a slit between two purple lumps, patterned with a cross from lying on the kitchen tiles.

"What are you doing here?" I asked her.

"I figured something was up," Amanda said, helping me to sit on the edge of the bathtub. "You don't go to bed till ten. Weren't answering your phone."

"How do you know I don't go to bed till ten?"

"I'm a supersleuth. An investigative genius. A deductive savant."

"I might have been out. Had visitors."

She laughed as she wet a washcloth in the sink. She was right, of course. I went to bed at exactly ten. In prison, lights out had been exactly eight. So I'd extended my sleep time to normal adult hours when I was freed, but I kept to the exact timings because too much free will was still uncomfortable for me. I got up at six. Had breakfast at six thirty. Lunch at midday. I went to my room to go to sleep at exactly 9:45 p.m. and played with my phone until lights out. Nothing else felt right.

"This will need stitches," she said, touching my face. Amanda had a dozen or more strict rules about working with her, and one of them was that I never touched her. But the longer I'd worked with her, the more she touched me. She seemed to be holding part of my cheek up. "You want me to call that quack?"

I craned my neck and looked in the mirror again. There was a curved five-centimeter gash under my eye, hanging open, revealing raw red flesh. "That quack" was a coroner I'd befriended who saw to all my medical needs. I couldn't see regular doctors, attend regular hospitals. Even to buy groceries I had to go two towns over, wear sunglasses and a cap pulled down low, and make sure I didn't talk to anybody. In and out, breathing deeply and sweating, like a man on a bank heist. Once, I'd been the only face on the cover of every newspaper nationwide. When people recognized me, there were a range of reactions. Men sometimes tried to punch me. Women tended to go all cold, walk away, ignore me until I left. Old ladies shouted and pointed at me. I was terrified of having to see a dentist.

I took the washcloth and pressed it into the wound.

"It's fine. I've got to go. I'm going to catch him before he leaves."

"Who?"

"The guy." I looked at my partner. "It was Claire Bingley's father."

"No way!" She slapped me in the chest. I winced.

"Way."

"What are you going to do? You going to bash him? I'll come." She punched her palm, her jaw jutted. "I like a bit of argy-bargy."

"I'm not going to bash him, I'm going to talk to him."

"Talk to him?" Amanda balked. "About *what*, exactly? The dude just KO'ed you on the kitchen floor. Seems like he might have got his point across. Or are you confused by his message? I can spell it out for you, Ted—he wants you *dead*. He wants to *shred* your oversized *head*. Grind your bones to make his *bread*."

"I got it," I said. "But I think I have a right of reply."

She looked me over, took in my injuries, seemed to assess my chances in another tangle with Mr. Bingley.

"You're not in a good way."

"I'll be fine."

"Your employee health insurance doesn't cover suicide missions."

"Amanda."

"Can you even walk? Did he get you in the nuts?" Amanda cringed in expectation of my answer.

"I don't know. Everything hurts." I stood.

"If I finally got hold of the guy who'd raped my daughter, I'd have gone right for the nuts," she mused. "I'm not sure I'd have used a baseball bat, either. Pair of scissors, maybe. Icepick."

"This isn't making me feel better."

"I don't know why you'd want to go anywhere near that guy again." She shook her head. "You got something to say, send an email."

"I'm going. Help me get cleaned up and get me to my car, would you?"

"You're stranger than pie, Ted Conkaffey. If you want to go get yourself murdered, fine, but you're not going anywhere with half your face falling off." Amanda took me by the shoulders and pushed me back onto the toilet. "I'll fix it. Have you got any fishing line?"

"Forget about it. I'm not letting you anywhere near my face, with or without fishing line."

"What, you think I'm gonna mess it up? You're not a pretty man, Ted Conkaffey."

"Yes I am."

"You don't need to be a doctor to stitch a guy's face," she said, lifting my chin, examining the wound. "I'll do it. It'll be great. It'll be very erotic. Like when Val Kilmer cuts his face in *The Saint* and Elisabeth Shue stitches it for him. Urgh, Val Kilmer. *Val Killlmerrr.* I'm sorry. I need a moment." She sighed and hung her head back, her eyes closed, remembering. Gave a warm, wide smile.

It turns out that a lot of women have stitched men's faces in movies. Amanda told me all about them, straddling my lap in the bathtub, where the light was best, her breath on my face as she fed the fishing line through my skin with a sewing needle and ignoring my whining. Aside from Elisabeth Shue and Val Kilmer's soulful interaction in *The Saint*, Rooney Mara stitched up Daniel Craig's brow in *The Girl with the Dragon Tattoo*, and Mary Elizabeth Winstead put some stitches in John Goodman in *10 Cloverfield Lane*.

It wasn't all that odd to have Amanda sitting on me, crotch to crotch, jabbering excitedly about erotic moments in movies, neither of us feeling anything remotely sexual. There was nothing erotic about us. In fact, Amanda seemed to have little concept of regular emotions. She was exactly as bright and cheerful about me not being dead as I imagined she'd have been about finding my corpse. She used weird expressions like "stranger than pie" as if everyone should know what they meant. Her social-emotional barometer had certainly been bashed around by her murder conviction, by her decade in prison. But I wasn't exactly sure it had been firing on all pistons before that.

She helped me out to the car and I got on the road, my hands locked on the wheel, everything pulsing with pain in protest to the movement. I should really have been in the hospital. But then, I hadn't been where I was meant to be or doing what I was meant to do in a very long time.

I was working on a hunch that Claire Bingley's father had flown into Cairns to confront me, and that it wasn't the kind of mission that would be extended out so that he could go sightseeing, maybe catch a jumping crocodile cruise. I figured he'd have left my house and gone right back to the airport to catch a plane home. The whole mission seemed badly planned, spur-of-the-moment. He might have seen a reflective feature story mentioning me and snapped. Might have just been thrown out by his wife. Maybe something had happened with Claire. He'd acted out of rage, and now that the deed was done and the dream was broken he'd be running, wondering if I'd called the police, if they'd answer, if they'd be waiting for him at the terminal.

I drove to Cairns airport, speeding all the way, now and then scratching at my bruised nose as blood dried inside my nostrils. I didn't know if I'd find him. It was a terribly long shot. But I'd been too terrified to say what I needed to say at my house, and the man had been too angry to hear it.

I parked in the short-term parking lot and walked across the front of the long, squat buildings, looking in the windows at the empty check-in counters, receiving worried looks from the red-jacketed receptionists as I passed. The front of my shirt was splattered with blood, and I limped heavily on my left side, one arm hugged close to my body to brace what were probably cracked ribs against the jolting of my steps.

When you've been beat up a few times, as I have, you learn that the best way to manage the pain is to keep moving if you can, even if very slowly. The first time I'd been smacked around in prison—a misunderstanding over some newspapers in the rec room—I'd gone to the infirmary and curled up in the nice, soft bed and surrendered to the blessed desire to sleep. I'd been in general population until my segregation was approved. It was safer to sleep in the hospital there than it was in my cell; the beds were better, the place was cleaner, and there were more guards around. It was so quiet that I'd been able to delve briefly into a fantasy that I was free, outside, in a regular hospital. Big mistake. All my muscles seized up and all the fluids in my joints settled, and I woke up in more pain than when I'd arrived.

When I found Mr. Bingley, he wasn't inside the airport at all, but sitting in a rental car in the hire lot. I spotted the white-blond hair, his head buried in his hands, defeated, just as I'd seen him in my kitchen. I stood nearby for a while waiting for him to lift his face, but he didn't. I went to the passenger-side door and opened it, and when I got in he shuffled violently against the driver's door, grabbing for the handle.

"Wait," I said. I held my hands up, palms out. "Just wait."

He froze, staring at me, wild-eyed. I pulled my door closed slowly, its weight agonizing for my bruised arm. We were sealed in silence, closeness. I fancied I could hear his heart beating, a smashing rhythm that reverberated through the car around us—but maybe it was my own. I carefully pulled the folded yellow envelope out of my back pocket and held it between us, a peace offering wavering over the handbrake.

"You forgot this," I said.

"I don't want anything from you." His jaw was twitching, teeth clamped together. "I need you to get out of this car. Right now."

"This is what my partner has been able to find out about—"

"Get out of my car!"

"—about the man who raped your fucking daughter!"

Our voices swelled against the roof of the car. Neither of us could look at the other. We sat staring ahead, panting, two passengers in a vehicle going nowhere.

"I did not rape your daughter," I said after a time, chancing a glance in his direction. "I don't expect you to believe that until you've looked at this." I threw the envelope into his lap. "I hope you'll look at it. But I don't expect you to do that, either."

He didn't move.

"Why did you come here?" he asked eventually. "Why did you follow me?"

"Because I want him caught too. Can't you understand that?" Suddenly I was on the edge of shouting again. Thumping my sore chest. *"I. Didn't. Do. This."*

He was stiff, the muscles of his neck pulled taut, eyes locked on the dashboard. His hands were in his lap, under the envelope, one raw, bloody knuckle visible. It was my turn to put my head in my hands.

"I don't even know your name," I said.

"How the hell do you not know my name?" His voice was a low, dangerous monotone. "How did you not recognize my face?"

"Because from the moment I was arrested I was in terror for my fucking life," I said. "I lost my family. I lost my job. I lost my house. I was put in chains and thrown in prison with a bunch of psychopaths. My own colleagues interrogated me. My *friends*. The whole world was upside down. My brain didn't have room for you. Or your wife. Or your daughter, for fuck's sake."

He shifted at the mention of the child. I took a breath and continued carefully.

"I saw Claire for a few seconds on the side of the highway that day, and *I never saw her again*. You understand? I had no idea who she was. I didn't even remember seeing her, in the beginning. All this has been just a fucking *idea* to me. It never actually happened."

I stared at the side of his head. I wasn't sure he understood at all, or if he even should. Long minutes of silence passed.

"My name is Dale," he said eventually. "Now get the fuck out of this car."

I got out and shut the door, stood there wondering if there was anything else that I could or should say. But there wasn't. I walked away and left him.

Dear Diary,

Is that how you start one of these things? Dear Diary? *I've never had a therapy journal before, and to be honest I'm feeling a bit stupid about it. The whole "dear" thing makes it feel like I'm writing "to" someone, but Dr. Hart assures me that no one will ever read this. Not even him. The whole point is that I use it to be aware of my illness, bring my addiction out from under the shovelfuls of dirt I've been habitually heaping onto it for the past decade. Uncover it. Hold it in my hands, so that I can understand it somehow, maybe one day find the strength to put it aside. The whole problem is, I guess, that he thinks I'm uncovering and holding up and examining something relatively harmless here. I'm starting out my "therapy journey" with a lie. I've told him I think I am a sex addict, which he's surprised by, me being twenty-five and all. He doesn't see anything wrong with a guy my age thinking about sex all day long. He was confused by my deep shame, my terror at even coming to see him. But, in truth, Dr. Hart has no idea of the nature of the thing I'm really talking about. The thing that follows me, the friend I made when I was about fifteen, who I didn't know would be right beside me for the rest of my* life. I'm not sure he would treat me if he knew what I really was. There's doubt in the psychological world that you can even treat people like me at all.

My first therapist wouldn't even try.

I went to my mother once and asked her to take me to a psychologist. She was standing in the kitchen stirring a pot of stew, losing herself in the motion of it, her eyes downcast and cheeks rosy from the steam coiling all around her, pretty and slim in her nightie. I'd been floating around for a little while thinking I should ask the question. Loitering, trying to work up to it. I picked some bacon out of the rice in the pot next to the stew and Mum glanced at me, cheeky, told me there wouldn't be any left if I kept going. It was hard to bring her down from the dreamy place she went to when she cooked, created things. She used to sculpt back then. I'd watch her for hours in silence, her slick fingers moving over the slimy gray clay.

In the end, I just filled my lungs with air, counted to three, and did it.

"I think I need to talk to someone," I'd said. "A counselor."

"Kev." Her brow had dipped, eyes shooting to mine from the work before her. "What? What do you mean?"

Her face was a picture of confusion, flickering with panic, the sculptor who sees a wet vase leaning, sliding, who can't understand why it won't hold its body like the rest of the identical vases she'd spun, sitting straight on the kiln shelf like soldiers. She was the chef who smelled burning but couldn't see it, the expectant mother who feels an odd twinge in her belly, the baby shifting suddenly as though stung. What's wrong with my creation? Or, more accurately, what have I done wrong here? It hurt, to both tell her and not tell her, to make up some tale about being depressed and sit silently all the way to the cold, quiet psychologist's office without any explanation for her about what she'd not given me, what she'd not said, which moment she hadn't been "present" that had left me in this state—unable to share with her at all why this clay pot had cracked.

I'd sat in the shrink's office gnawing my fingernails and examining the certificates on her walls while she stood out in the hall with Mum, reassuring her that prepubescent depression was normal and that she'd probably be able to find the cause of my distress within a couple of sessions. That it wasn't likely I'd need to be medicated, but it was an option. There'd been some talk of statistics. Of limiting my TV time and increasing my vitamin intake, making sure I got to sleep at a reasonable hour. When the psychologist had come in and shut the door, I'd watched her carefully as she walked to the other side of the desk, smoothing down the sides of her neat black bob, as though she couldn't possibly chat without knowing every hair was in place.

"Kevin, why don't you tell me a bit about yourself?"

I'd told her exactly that. A bit. I'm looking back on myself now, on my teen introduction, and smiling. I'd told her about the books I was reading and the video games I was playing, and about my best friend Paul and our bikes. She'd asked me if I was being bullied. How my grades were going. If I was drinking. All the normal sources of a young person's despair.

I'd been just about dripping with sweat by the time I got up the courage to tell her. She was leaving me long, gentle silences, trying to build me up to it, letting the ticking of the clock on her desk mark the seconds that I had left in the session to spill my guts. I licked my lips and looked at the floor, and when I spoke it was over the top of her as she was posing her next question to me.

"I think I'm a pedophile," I said.

Her mouth was still formed in a small, tight O from saying "Do you . . ." the way she'd been saying "Do you . . ." since we started the session. Do you enjoy getting outside the house? Do you spend much time with friends? Do you ever get angry? But now there she was, stuck on the edge of that "Do you . . ." because I'd done all the things she'd asked me if I'd done, and now she realized it wasn't about what I did at all. It was about what I was. She sat back in her seat and looked at me, and her mouth for a moment turned downward, making the muscles in her throat pull tight.

"What do you mean, Kevin?"

The words were tumbling out of me now. I was hardly drawing a breath between long, rambling, stammering sentences. I could feel the heat climbing up my chest, into my neck, a burning rash that lit the rims of my ears on fire. She listened, hands hanging by her sides, lips slightly parted. I was panting like I'd been running.

"What sort of pictures?" she asked. "How did you find them?"

I'd told her about the pictures. My very first foray into my addiction that was not entirely contained within my brain, actual images I'd been sent from someone in an AOL chat room. How I'd clicked from picture to picture, link to link, video to video down a dark staircase into the bowels of the internet, to places most people didn't even know about. I told her what the pictures were of, described them all in details I knew perfectly from lying in the dark staring at them on my laptop screen beneath the blankets of my bed, terrified that someone might come in and see me with them if I wasn't covered up. I told her how terrifying and exhilarating it had been to see the images of the things I had been thinking about on the screen, like I'd somehow opened a window into my own mind. The things I'd been imagining, that I'd been sure were impossibilities, depraved fantasies, had actually happened somewhere in the world and someone captured it and now I could see it whenever I wanted, as many times as I wanted. I was Dorothy opening the door on Munchkinland, everything suddenly in color. I told her about how great that made me feel.

And I told her about how awful that made me feel.

How sick and wrong and vile a thing I knew I must be to think about these things and feel relief that they weren't just inside me.

"I don't want to do those things," I said. I was hugging myself now, trying to stop myself from shivering. "I . . . I don't know what's wrong with me. I don't know why this is happening. I've been wanting to ask someone like you what I should do, you know? I mean, should I be looking at these things? If I'm looking at these things being done to these kids, that kind of means I don't have to do them myself, right? I mean it's not like what those people did was okay. But . . . But it's like, if they do it, then I don't have to."

I was rambling, pleading, and she could see that. But as I kept talking, her face was becoming redder and redder, and a thin sheen of sweat was starting to pop up at the edge of her hairline, on the short, fine hairs that receded to fluff on her brow. And then she did the last thing I thought she would do.

She got up and went out into the hall and brought my mother into the room.

And I sat there and listened as she told my mother everything that I'd just said.

I promised my mother as she sat in the car crying and thumping the steering wheel that I was going to stop looking at the pictures, stop thinking about little children, stop doing those things to myself in the dark and wondering what the hell was wrong with me. Because yes, there was something wrong with me. I knew that. I knew it was wrong. And I was finished with it. I'd got it out of my system, talking to the therapist. It didn't matter that the therapist wouldn't see me anymore, had said that she couldn't treat me. I reassured my mother that there wasn't a problem anymore.

Lies.

It has been ten years. My problem has never been worse.

I acted on my desire for the first time.

I got awkwardly out of my car at the crime scene, the faces of four or five uniformed officers turned toward me, and each was completely unreadable. The police in Crimson Lake had mixed feelings toward me. For all they knew I was guilty of attacking Claire Bingley, a dangerous pedophile running wild on their beat, an imminent threat to the children of their town. To them, I'd thumbed my nose at the justice system—every breath of free air I took was a personal insult. And then there was the fact that I worked with Amanda Pharrell, who'd been cheeky enough to get herself approved for a private detective's license despite the killing in her late teens. She'd been a juvenile when she stabbed Lauren Freeman and, having served her time, she'd successfully convinced a panel of experts that she could and should be approved to investigate crimes on a private contractual basis. To the Crimson Lake cops, Amanda moving in on the law enforcement game in the very same town where she'd committed the murder of one of their high school golden girls was just rubbing salt into the wound. No one here was ever going to accept Amanda Pharrell, or me. We were utterly alone together.

Police and private investigators are always at odds anyway; people only hire us because they believe, however truthfully, that the cops aren't doing their job. It also didn't help that I actually used to be one of them. I had spent five years as a drug squad detective back in Sydney. Pictures of me in uniform had been circulated by the newspapers during my trial, smiling broadly when I graduated the academy, frowning sternly as I put a pimp into the back of a police car. I was a traitor to the force. The ultimate insult.

It should have been all-out war between the Crimson Lake cops and Amanda and me, but things were not that simple. On our first case together, Amanda and I had solved a murder. This put one of the Crimson Lake police department's only unsolved homicides back in the black. The Crimson Lake cops hated us—but they also owed us.

They stood now beneath the sprawling branches of a two-hundred-year-old fig tree dripping with Spanish moss, immaculate uniforms, shining boots. The Barking Frog Inn had been almost completely consumed by the rainforest at the edge of the creek. A tangle of poisonous vines with furry sprouts crept up over its wood-paneled walls and across the corrugated iron roof, a blanket of green making it seem as though the bar had popped up from beneath the earth, a trapdoor spider's lair exposed with glowing window eyes peering out. Some brave spirals of native wisteria had joined the fray along the porch rail, but its cheerful purple blooms were struggling under the grip of the weeds and were browning at their tips, thorns piercing new branches, dripping sap onto the boards.

The officers attending the scene had festooned blue and white police tape across the entryway to designate the inner cordon. There was an older, gray-haired man pacing the edge of the outer cordon, head down, watching his feet. As I crossed the dirt road and ducked under the tape of the outer cordon Amanda appeared from the side of the bar in denim shorts and a faded cotton singlet. Her only forensic efforts were a pair of cotton booties over her sneakers and a cap of the same material pulled down over her shaggy black and orange hair. She'd called me that morning and given me the address, waking me from a painful half slumber on the couch on the porch. She came to me and inspected the work she'd done on my slightly less puffy and bruised cheek. In the dim light of the cloudy morning her scars were obvious, running down her arm and shoulder, along her lean legs, crossing hundreds and hundreds of individual tattoos, slicing through inked faces, cutting objects in half. A crocodile had tried to make her its evening meal once, and now her colorful body was cracked with these baby pink lines and cracks. She was fun to look at, Amanda.

"Did you catch up with the prize fighter?" she asked.

"I did." I walked with her to where her yellow bike was leaning against another ancient tree. "I gave him the leads you gave me. He can do what he wants with them."

"That was pretty ballsy."

"Well, I've still got 'em. Might as well use 'em."

"He didn't try to thump you again?"

"I think he might have, if I'd pressed any harder," I said. "What's this all about?" I gestured to the officers under the tree, the shadows of more inside. I didn't think there were this many cops this side of Sydney.

"Happened this morning, about three, they think, though we don't have any ear or eye witnesses. Last text message from one of the victims was at two forty-seven a.m. telling Dad he was just about to head home."

One of the victims. All Amanda had told me that morning was that people were dead inside a bar, not how many. I could have been about to walk in on a full-scale massacre or a lover's spat gone wrong.

"Who's hired us?" I asked. Amanda nodded over my shoulder at the stocky man with gray hair standing by the outer cordon, looking at the bar. As we walked toward him I recognized the stranglehold of grief on his otherwise powerful frame, the shoulders hanging and arms limp by his sides, all the effort he could muster going into keeping him upright. I knew the feeling, the incredible weight on the back of the head, as though the hurt has lodged there like a lead ball in the back of your skull. I put my hand out.

"Ted Collins," I lied.

I got the impression that this man's handshake would usually have been firm, masculinity-driven. It was limp and cold now. He had hard hands and a trucker's build, hours lifting and sitting, the shoulders strong and the belly round. His eyes were puffed from crying.

"What happened to you?" he asked dimly, offering no name of his own.

"Car accident," Amanda covered for me. "Ted, Michael Bell here has brought us in—his son is inside."

"I'm so sorry," I told Michael. I looked around the empty parking lot. "Isn't there anyone who can come and be with you right now?"

"My whole family is at the house." He glanced away, distracted. "I can't . . . I can't be there. Not while Andy's inside. I just walked off. There's too much crying. Too much . . ." He trailed off, rubbing his beard, the thoughts swirling. "They called me this morning, to confirm I was home. Six o'clock. You get a phone call from the police and you don't know what they want and then they come to the door . . ."

He drew a shuddering breath. I wanted to hug the big man but I didn't know how he or the cops nearby would react. Now and then, flashes of rage crossed his features, lightning cracks there and then instantly gone. I knew from delivering the news of deaths to loved ones as a cop that the rage could leap out at any moment, bursting through the grief like a fireball.

"I saw the stories about you both, the Jake Scully case," Michael offered. My stomach twisted. He must have known then who I was, what I had been accused of. That I wasn't "Collins" but "Conkaffey": the notorious. "I need . . . I want everyone on this. I need to know what happened. The cops, they fuck this kind of shit up all the time. You see it on the news. Missing evidence and corrupt officers and . . . and . . ." He gestured uselessly, hand flopping by his side. "Whoever has done this, I need to know. I just . . ."

"We'll do everything we can," I said. I didn't know what exactly had happened inside the bar, but what this man needed now were assurances. "But I've got to warn you, Michael, that hiring private investigators this early—you run the risk of putting too many cooks in the kitchen. We're not going to trample all over the police investigation." I looked at Amanda, making sure she knew I was telling her also, not just Mr. Bell. "Mate, I really suggest you go home, or you call someone to be here with you."

"I'm fine," the father said, shifting from foot to foot, already beginning to retrace his pacing path at the edge of the cordon. "I'm not leaving Andy."

I followed Amanda under the police tape to the door of the bar. The large room was packed with people, most of them looking in on the empty bar and kitchen area, a forensic staff–only zone. As I appeared, most eyes turned toward me, examined my bruises, the dried blood that I couldn't seem to fully expel from the rims of my ears. Everyone had donned a Tyvek suit from a pile on a table by the door. I stopped and grabbed one, pulled it on, my face burning with the quiet scrutiny of dozens of people.

There were officers around who looked like they wanted to come and stop us entering the scene. A woman in a suit approached and pulled back her hood. I braced myself for the speech from the lead crime-scene officer about how Amanda and I weren't wanted there, about how insulting it was for a victim's family to bring in private detectives without giving the police half a chance to fuck it up. But I was surprised by a familiar face. Officer Philippa Sweeney had been Holloways Beach police when I first met her, a beat cop tasked with watching over my house six months earlier when a mob had assembled outside it, shouting and carrying on over my arrival in their town. She turned a heart-shaped face up toward me, and I was glad to see it wasn't creased with jurisdictional fury.

"What happened to you, Conkaffey?"

"Slipped on a banana peel."

"Right." She smirked. "I'm the lead on this case. Detective Inspector Pip Sweeney. I was on protection detail at your house a while back."

"I remember." I shook her gloved hand. "That's a swift upward turn in the career trajectory."

"Yeah, well. Seems there were a couple of openings in Crimson Lake for sergeant suddenly." The corner of her mouth tightened, just slightly, with a smile. She didn't want to thank me. Couldn't. "I took the exam and they rushed me through."

"Nice work," I said.

"Mmm."

"Look, it's very unusual, us being hired this early," I said. "I've already said as much to Mr. Bell. But I'm happy to go and talk to him again, tell him that you guys need to lead and we'll come in afterwards if there is anything we think we can assist on."

"He's in shock," Sweeney said. "It's been three hours since he learned his son is dead. He's grabbing at straws. I've seen it before. You tell someone the news and before they can do anything else they go hang the washing on the line. I'm not insulted. I think he's had a kneejerk reaction."

"Right," I said.

"But I'm not going to tell you guys to shove off right away," she said. "Get a look at the scene. Make some calls if you want. If it makes Michael Bell feel better to have you here I'm not going to argue."

She turned and pulled her hood on. I did the same, gave Amanda a quizzical frown. Sweeney's attitude was far beyond what I had expected. I'd expected to be turned on my heel and shoved right back out the door, but instead I found myself following Sweeney to the edge of the bar area where the crowd was thicker and a photographer's flash was bouncing off the walls. Sweeney was letting us in, but she clearly didn't trust me. She had the restless eyes of someone trying to decide whether they can turn their back on a dangerous animal, constantly searching my face when she didn't think I noticed.

There were two bodies visible from the door to the kitchen. A brown-skinned woman had been lying on her stomach when she was shot in the back of the head, her jaw still resting against the dirty tiles. Her hands were flat, palm down, sitting either side of her head, which was turned away from me. A man I assumed to be Michael's son Andrew had been shot multiple times just before the entrance to the back door and had dragged himself a little way, painting the floor in jagged streaks as he went for the exit and was shot again. There were footprints in the blood, one set, it looked like, but this could have been from whoever discovered the bloodbath. A photographer was getting a close-up of the woman's face.

"That's Keema Daule, twenty. Over there is Andrew Bell, twenty-one," Amanda said, looking at her notes.

"Christ." I winced. "They're just kids."

Hearing me say the word "kids" sent a ripple of uncomfortable looks around the people in earshot. There are certain things I can't mention as an accused pedophile. Children, toys, schools. I've talked about cartoons in public and made people shift uncomfortably in their seats. It never wears off.

"Are they a couple?" I asked.

"No," Sweeney said. "He's got a girlfriend. Local girl, Stephanie. Keema here is over from the UK recently, been backpacking her way around the country. Mum's of Indian heritage but Keema's lived her whole life in Surrey. We're making calls liaising with the Surrey cops. They're going to go around there and give them the news."

"Who found them?"

"Delivery guy coming in with frozen chips." Amanda looked at the ceiling. "Terry Hill. Local guy. Andrew is usually here to let him in in the morning. He knocked at the front, no answer. Came round the back, looked in the back window and saw a foot. Called the ambulance. Thought someone might have fainted."

At the back of the kitchen beside a shelf full of blackened pots and pans there was a tiny barred window, greasy from the kitchen air. The angle looked right. Around the side of a bench, the delivery man would have been able to see only Andrew's splayed foot and nothing of Keema.

"Someone interview him?"

"Yep."

"So what are the current theories?" I wondered.

"Most popular vote is it's a stickup," Amanda said. "Someone comes in, trying to hold up the bar. Tells the pair to lie flat on their stomachs like she's doing." She pointed to the dead girl. "Keema and Andrew think they're going to be tied up while he raids the safe, probably. Instead he executes her. *Bang*. Andrew freaks out and tries to make a run for it. He gets it next. *Bang, bang*. He doesn't go down right away. Keeps trying for the door. He cops the rest of the clip for his troubles. *Bang-bang-bang-bang-bang!*"

Amanda had her fingers out in a pistol shape, pointing at the body by the door, one eye closed for aim. People were staring at us. I pushed her hand down.

"What do you think?" I asked Sweeney.

"The setup works," Sweeney said. "Cash register and safe are empty. Safe was full from the week's takings, about to be emptied today. So it was a hell of a convenient time for someone to come in and knock it off. We're rounding up all current and ex-employees."

"Bit of an odd thing to do, kill them both, if it's just a robbery." I looked at the girl's limp, inward-turned feet. I ducked to get a better view of her face. There was a flashy necklace in the blood at her throat. "Why shoot them? Did they recognize the robber?"

Neither woman answered.

"Anyone weird hanging around the bar before closing time?"

"We're bringing in the last customer, Darren Molk, a Holloways Beach postman. His was the last transaction on the readout of the EFTPOS machine, and he says he was the last to leave. We're going to see if he saw anything strange. He's a regular. Apparently it was just Darren for the last half an hour or so before closing. Usually went like that."

"What time did Darren say he left?"

"About two a.m."

"Two?" I said. "That's odd."

"Why?"

"I worked in bars while I was at uni," I said. "Tough work. Takes a long time to close a bar down for the night. You've got to wash and polish all the glasses. Do the mats. The kegs. The fridges. Put all the chairs up. Do the floors. It sucks. You think the night is over when the last customer leaves and then you're there for ages trying to get the place cleaned up."

"What's your point?" Sweeney asked.

"Well, if they'd only had the one customer since one thirty a.m., why didn't they start the closing process then so that when the guy left they could just about walk out?" I shrugged. "Why hang around for forty-seven more minutes than you have to?"

"Maybe they had staff drinks," Sweeney said.

"What? Just the two of them? Together?"

"Men and women can be colleagues without being romantically involved," Sweeney offered.

"We better hope so." Amanda nudged me in the arm.

"I'll talk to the owner," Sweeney said. "They might have been partway through cleanup. We'll see what the routine was, how long it usually took. Whoever was waiting to hit the place might have been thinking the girl would leave and Andrew would stay behind to lock the door. Got a surprise when it looked like they were going to walk out together."

It could have been a robbery, easily. Guns were right for robberies. If both had been stabbed, I might have thought differently. Just because they were both dead, that didn't mean it was something personal. One of them might have seen the robber's face, or recognized his voice.

I'd had a few murder-robberies in my time on the drug squad, rival gangs going into each other's houses and blowing each other away, stealing their stashes. A few times it had been over women, or territory, or insults. The good thing for me had been that as soon as my team walked in on a murder, we walked right back out again. Handed it over to homicide. Sometimes I didn't even see the bodies, didn't bother entering the scene in case I messed up evidence. So bodies and death were still foreign to me. I hadn't worked up the desensitization I was obviously going to need as a private investigator, and I wasn't blessed with Amanda's empty toolbox of emotions. I was feeling a little upset at the sight of the dead young people, so I moved off to check out the rest of the place.

I walked along the bar and into the small staff office where another forensics officer was taking prints from the safe. The roster for the night showed Keema and Andrew were the only people on for the evening. It was a Tuesday night. That seemed about right to me. A chef named Ben had left at nine. I noted where he had signed out for the evening. Amanda was correct—Keema had clocked off at 2:45 a.m. Andrew hadn't signed off at all. The register would give the police a picture of how many customers they'd served. There was a CCTV system, but it was old. I pushed open the flap with a gloved fingertip and found the video tape slot empty. The fact that they were still using VHS to tape the bar's goings on wasn't a surprise to me. The bar was ancient, with running repairs visible everywhere. A piece of wood kicked off the bottom of the bar, replaced with a strip of ply. The cracked corner of a mirror held in place with sticky tape. If it wasn't broken, these people didn't replace it, and if it was broken they fixed it cheaply.

There was a photograph pinned to a corkboard of a bunch of young people hanging out on the porch of the pub, back when the wisteria was in its infancy. There didn't seem to be anyone over the age of twenty-five who worked here, spare for an old woman with heavy jeweled earrings who I guessed was the owner.

Two young people dead on the floor of a shitty dive bar, their faces in the grease and grime of a tiny kitchen. Their deathbed was run by underqualified short-order cooks who'd left after dinner service without so much as a sweep up of the dead cockroaches under the sticky counters. It was such a waste.

Bartending had been a tougher job than I'd thought it would be when I started out in the industry as an eighteen-year-old. I'd been sucked in by the apparent glamour of the pubs and clubs in Sydney's CBD, the thumping music and the drunk girls flirting with the fit young guys behind the crowded counters. The illusion wore off pretty quickly. I finished work in the early hours exhausted and reeking of cigarette smoke, my feet sore and my ears ringing with the same soulless tunes thrumming out from the DJ's stand over and over. The girls flirted with me, sure, but they were half as charming when I was tired and sober as they seemed when I was on the serving side of the bar. For every long-legged beauty who tried to get free shots from me there were four angry men who felt overlooked in the line and let me know it in no uncertain terms. The vomit and piss all over the bathrooms, swimming with cigarette butts and used condoms, were suddenly my responsibility.

No one was supposed to work in places like this for very long. It was a place for backpackers to drop in and grind out some cash to fund their way north toward Thailand, a place for locals to dwell for a while before they laced up their boots and got out into the real working world. This filthy, rotting place was supposed to be a launch pad only, a rest stop on the way to better things. The only people who were supposed to dent its benches and bar stools would be the local drunks and long-haul truckers who'd already given up on young people's dreams. The small ghosts of Andrew and Keema would be out of place here in the silent hours. They'd be confused, bright-eyed spirits still wiping the counters and changing the kegs, so unprepared to be dead that they didn't even know that they were. I held the photo of the young people drinking on the porch and felt sad.

Sweeney appeared beside me, her face still quizzical.

"How's your case?" she asked. I remembered her trying to ask me questions about my arrest back when I first met her. I didn't want to be interrogated on it now, standing by the cooling bodies of two kids. So I just shrugged.

"Is that what this is about?" She looked at the gash in my cheek. "Are vigilantes still messing with you?"

"No," I said. "It was just a pub fight over something stupid. A snooker table. It's fine. It's all fine. Thanks for asking."

I tried to move away, went to the front porch and stood looking at the wall of rainforest across the road behind my car, a tall, impenetrable tangle of green. Someone had finally come to join Michael Bell, another graying, rough-edged man who was trying to cajole him into a car. Sweeney followed me, pulling off her latex gloves.

"Amanda will be your only contact from our end for a couple of days," I said, gesturing back inside to where my partner was raiding the bar for cigars. "If you decide to let her interview victims, don't leave her alone with them for too long. She's about as subtle as a kick in the face. I wouldn't leave, but I've got to head down to Sydney for a couple of days. It's my daughter's birthday. I can't cancel."

Sweeney nodded gravely. Whenever I mention anything to do with my daughter, people do that, nod gravely, like she's dead. There were press vans turning up outside the bar now, officers directing them away from the parking lot, where they were trying to photograph tire tracks. I prepared to do the old duck-and-run to my car before they cornered me for an interview I couldn't give.

"I've been listening to the podcast," Sweeney said suddenly.

I stopped. Exhaustion swept over me.

Toward the end of my first case with Amanda, a group who believed in my innocence had formed. It had started with a journalist named Fabiana Grisham, who'd come to Crimson Lake to pursue me for her newspaper. She'd expected me to be the sniveling, bent-backed, hand-wringing child predator of her nightmares, but she'd been struck by how normal I was, as most people are. She'd started asking me questions about my alleged crime, and I'd had answers for all of them. After a while I turned her around.

Fabiana had gone back to Sydney and started an organization called Innocent Ted, which had a website, a podcast that chronicled the crime and speculated over the evidence, and a few videos on YouTube. As the group grew, the media took interest in it and they insinuated that Fabiana and I had been romantically involved.

She'd been punished for it pretty badly in the court of public opinion. People were calling her a pedophile sympathizer, a traitor, a conspirator. The more sympathetic of Fabiana's detractors mused that she probably had hybristophilia, a fixation on sexual partners who have committed violent acts like murder or rape. She'd had a few bricks through her front windows, like me. But much of the backlash went to her social media profiles, where people threatened and stalked her, sent her obscene photographs, hacked into her personal accounts and published her correspondence.

I did not need to drag someone else into that kind of mess.

"Have you listened to it?" Sweeney asked.

"No."

Of course I hadn't listened to it. The podcast was the last thing in the world I wanted to listen to. It had real audio from Claire Bingley's interviews with police, which I'd heard during the trial and sometimes heard even now in my nightmares. The podcast contained recorded snippets of my own interrogations, my desperate pleas with my colleagues. It had detailed reports from the doctors who'd examined Claire, cataloguing the injuries she'd suffered. It had audio from the frantic, tearful public appeal Dale and his wife made the evening of her disappearance. It made me sick just thinking about it.

"It's pretty good," Sweeney said.

"Pretty *good*?" I asked. She didn't notice my disdain.

"I'm up to about episode five, I think. They've gone all the way through the crime, the witness accounts, the interviews. They're pointing out the inconsistencies. They have some pretty compelling theories."

"Uh-huh."

"It's the number one podcast in Germany, you know," she said. "They have eight million subscribers over there. Do you interact with *Innocent Ted* at all?"

"No." I cleared my throat in what I hoped was a dismissive way, trying to end the discussion. "The woman who started it copped some real problems, so I don't . . . I don't want to encourage it."

"You don't want to encourage it?" Sweeney squinted at me. "But these people think you're innocent."

"I know," I said, trying to resist the anger swirling up from the pit of my stomach. "And that's great. Really. But I don't want to draw any more attention to myself, if it's all the same. I'm sure the podcast is very entertaining. But as long as I'm free, I just want to live my life quietly and try to get past everything that's happened. People going around wearing *Innocent Ted* T-shirts and commenting on the website isn't going to give me my marriage back. Or my job. Or my relationship with my daughter. It's not going to replace the time I spent in prison. Or help Claire Bingley recover from the attack. Or give her parents *their* marriage back. Or . . ."

"I get it," she said.

"Or convince people who have already decided that—"

"Okay, okay! I get it." She touched me on the shoulder. I found that my fists were clenched. When I unclenched them, my knuckles cracked. I kept my eyes fixed on the rainforest. It was getting scary, my desire to go off on long rants like this, my words speeding up, slurring into each other.

The anger had been a long time coming. When I first got out of prison, I'd been too tired and relieved to be angry. But these days I was angry at everyone, even people who sympathized with me. My goose-wife didn't mind my bleating on and on about my problems, but I'd have to tone it down in front of humans if I wanted to maintain the few people I had who were willing to listen to me at all.

After a time Sweeney spoke, and her voice was small. Uncertain.

"It might help catch the guy who did it, though, all this," she said. "If you really didn't do it."

Dear Diary,

I guess I'll do this. Write it out. Go back to when it started and try to understand what I can do. Writing about telling someone for the first time what I am deep down inside, the real me, that felt really good. Maybe if I can write about what I did, I can prevent myself from doing it again. Because I don't want to do it again. I feel bad. Of course I feel bad.

It might take a few entries. But I want to understand it. There's so much I need to say.

See, it's like this:

I'm a normal young man. I make sure that I do absolutely everything that twenty-five-year-old, heterosexual, part-time employed men do. It's not hard. We're not complex beings, full of mystery and intrigue. All I've had to do to construct my disguise is play a constant game of mirroring. I hang around other guys my age, at uni or the bar where I work, and I listen to what they say. I say the same things back.

I go to "the club" and stare at "bitches" and talk about how bad they want me to "put it up" them. I can tell by their lips. Their big, plump "booties." When women turn their backs on Pete and Dave and Steve and me, one of us makes a gesture, grabs our crotch or something, makes a pained noise like dogs howling after their mates trotting across the other side of the pound wire. When we're not scoping bitches I complain about my work, my boss, keep one eye on the rugby on the screen in the corner. Moan as the ball fumbles out of someone's hands. I've got the guys covered. They believe I'm one of them.

My therapist, I've got him fooled. No real hardship there. Chloe, she was a little harder to convince, but again, it's not unachievable. If you're a red-blooded Aussie bloke who's half-decent looking, you've got to have a girlfriend. So I picked her up in sociology class. I'd moped around a few dead-end jobs in my late teens and decided I'd do a bachelor of arts, keeping my head low, trying to keep up with the normal crowd. I found Chloe there, struggling with the material and needing pointers. I'd had a couple of girlfriends before her, but nothing serious, and I needed to get into something serious before people started wondering why I kept leaving these perfectly good girls. We've lived together in our soulless little rental property in the sun-scorched suburban hell that is Blairmount for five months now. Vinnies furniture. She vacuums a lot. Insists on the kitchen benches being empty, me not leaving my wet towels on the floor. She wants a cat, but I'm not big on pet hair all over my clothes. I fuck her about twice a week. To maintain my disguise, I think a lot about what she'd say if I was ever arrested. If they ever found me out for what I really am, what I've done. How was your sex life? Normal. Did you ever fight? Now and then, about inconsequential things. How were his university grades? Fine. Did you get on with his friends? Yes. Did he ever express any strange desires? Say odd things in the bedroom? Leave questionable material on the computer? No. No. No.

If I were a chameleon, my color would be gray. Depthless, calming gray. I'd be a slow-moving, bug-eyed creature creeping along in the gray world, taking hand-holds of storm-colored branches, sliding my round belly over steely leaves. The hardest part about it all is how boring it is.

But I do get my color. About a year ago, when I'd first met Chloe, I took her to a café for lunch. Comfortable, getting used to being around each other, the supposedly easy intimacy of young lovers. She blathered on about something. Trying to tell me all the time about her childhood, so that I could really appreciate her for the woman she was becoming, bond with her, intertwine her history with mine. In my memory, the street outside is gray. Then, a flash of coral pink in a window across the street.

A group of ballerinas prancing across a polished floor. Ten or fifteen brown-limbed girls, preteen beauties hurling themselves through the air. I watched their heads bobbing and thin arms flailing as they fluttered into a corner, formed a huddle, burst away from each other, a pink flower blossoming. I was mesmerized.

Chloe was scanning the newspaper. I'd stopped listening, had no answer for her question when it came. I'd dropped the mask. I could feel the color flooding through me, blood surging in my face, dangerous flashes of the beast inside trying to penetrate the surface, alert her. Alert the waitress setting our coffee on the table. Alarm pulsed in my neck and eyes.

But Chloe didn't see it. She's stupid. I chose her because she's stupid.

It starts with a frown. Sometimes the cocking of a head, the pursing of lips. They watch me, even as I look away. I can feel their gaze on me, taking in the shape of my jaw through the beard, my nose, the big hand raised to my brow trying to disrupt the viewer flipping through their memories until they find my face wherever they saw it. On the news, in the papers, on the internet, on someone's Facebook feed. Maybe all of those places.

When they get it, their mouth drops open. They stop what they're doing. Maybe they're sitting across the plane aisle from me, pulling the lid off their tiny container of milk, a steaming paper cup on the tray just inches above their knees. An elbow juts into someone's ribs. There's pointing. A sort of sixth sense ripples out through the people around us, other people noticing the recognition, the whispering, starting to recognize for themselves. At first there's a sort of stiff, confused calm, the same sort that causes people to pretend they haven't seen mega movie stars sitting in the café near them, walking along the same Florida beach. Everybody act normal! The same way they flipped through their memories to find me, they flip through their emotions for the appropriate reaction, and they all find the same one.

Rage.

Most of the time, people turn away from me. If they're a little more adventurous, they talk loudly about my case, glancing over to see if I'm listening. "They should bring back the death penalty in this country for pieces of shit like him." Sometimes, people loiter menacingly, follow me to my car, write down my license plate. People sometimes take pictures of me, video me for citizen news. Now and then physical confrontations arise, but they're usually half hearted. Someone shoves past my table at the bar, knocks my beer over. Blocks me from entering the supermarket, chest puffed, saying nothing, daring me to push past.

If I'm recognized and things become hostile, I leave before there's a fight. The last thing I want to do is challenge a member of the public. The people of Crimson Lake did me a massive favor simply by not running me off the way a number of towns did with Dennis Ferguson. After his conviction for the abduction and sexual assault of three young children, Dennis attempted to resettle in Bundaberg, Toowoomba, Murgon, Ipswich, Miles, and Ryde before angry mobs chased him out each time. He was eventually discovered dead in a flat in Surry Hills. No one found his body for several days. A mob had come to my door in Crimson Lake, with all the fanfare Dennis had been treated to—the placards and the chanting and the TV live-crosses. Police officers standing outside my door. I hadn't left, and the panic and anger had died down.

As my plane landed in Sydney, I thought about these dangers, sitting stiffly in my seat at the back of the plane, a magazine clutched high around my face. It was enclosed situations like this that frightened me the most, because there was nowhere to run if something violent kicked off. It had taken some serious self-talk in the toilet cubicle at the airport gate to even get on the plane. I'd brought prop glasses with heavy frames for the occasion and slicked back my hair. But the black eye and stitches were drawing gazes.

I knew that the public was barely okay with the idea of me living in an isolated marshland far away from big cities, where they could lose track of me. But no one would be happy about me coming back to Sydney. People would wonder if I was going to resettle here, and that was a great scary headline for the papers. I was expecting news of my movements to spread fast and generate excitement. The more savvy reporters would have noted my daughter's birthday, and would be watching to see if I visited. There might also be those who'd got word that I'd agreed to appear on *Stories and Lives*, and would be stalking the front of the TV studio waiting for me to arrive.

I was just beginning to feel the relief of having not been recognized, walking through the airport with my backpack slung over my shoulder, when I noticed the two men following me. I stopped and looked at them in the reflection in the window of a brightly lit stationery store, pretending to peruse the pretty gold- and silver-trimmed diaries and letter sets. All I could see were two enormous shapes loitering across the broad walkway in front of a men's fashion outlet, one with his hands clasped in front of him, the other talking on a mobile phone. I surveyed my options, but there were few. Passengers were being shuffled like cattle down the walkway toward the baggage escalators, or up toward the gates. I thought there was a chance I could lose the men in the food court. But when I got to the top of the stairs and looked at the crowd before me, I noticed a small huddle of press at the entrance to the Flyaway Bar, almost all of them with their eyes on their phones.

Sweat began to tickle down my bruised sides. The breath only seemed to reach the top quarter of my lungs. I kept my eyes down and walked quickly past the baggage and taxi crowds toward the rental car lot, dashing through the traffic. The two men following me sped up and were close behind me when, just before the glass doors to the Hertz office, another man stepped out from behind a pylon, stopping me in my tracks.

"Oh fuck." I gripped my chest, took a couple of steps back from Khalid. "Oh, Jesus, fuck."

"Gave you a scare, eh, Coffee Cup?"

Khalid's two thugs stepped up behind me, boxing me in. Relief was rushing over me like warm water, deepening my chest, easing the pain in my ribs.

I'd met Khalid Farah for the first time as a young patrol officer responding to a domestic dispute at a small property in Camden, long before Khalid became one of Australia's biggest drug dealers. Back then he'd been a proud, neatly dressed foot soldier of one of the drug crews in the city, the fancy car and the huge watch indicators that he was a good earner, that eventually he'd probably get to the top of the scrum if no one killed him first. My partner Rylie and I got the call that Khalid's sister Jima and her husband Mahmoud were having an all-out shouting match, and the neighbors had seen Khalid arrive and called the cops, thinking things were about to turn violent. It had been a standard domestic. Khalid and Jima and Mahmoud all shouting in Lebanese in the kitchen. Sweat, popping veins, puffing chests. A baby screaming somewhere in another room, forgotten.

My partner Rylie had taken Mahmoud while I took Khalid and Jima off into the living room to give them a stern talking-to about communicating with calm and empathy—all the sort of stuff the academy teaches you to say. Everything had seemed to be under control. But Rylie and I were both fresh graduates. We were supposed to be partnered with more experienced officers, but staffing didn't always allow it. We broke the first rule of working in domestic disputes in a closed environment. We didn't keep in sight of each other. The last time I saw Mahmoud and Rylie, Mahmoud had gone to the other room and grabbed the baby and was pacing with it, joggling it to try to stop the crying while Riley followed him, talking. Second rule broken. You're supposed to sit the suspect down and keep him in place while you talk it out. I refocused on my pair, until I heard a yelp and a thump, and by the time I got back to the kitchen Rylie was on the floor. As I came around the corner, Mahmoud was putting the infant girl into the microwave on the kitchen counter. I drew my gun just as he slammed the door. It was the first time I'd ever drawn my gun, let alone pointed it at someone. Mahmoud put a finger less than an inch from the "Quick Cook" button on the microwave and told me to take my radio off and put my gun down.

I didn't put the gun down, but I did pull the radio off my belt and gave the three rapid blips that would signal to the patrol frequency that we were in trouble before I put it on the table. I told Mahmoud that if he pushed the button on the microwave I'd shoot him dead. I was terrified. Khalid and his sister stood behind me, screaming and crying in horror until I told them to shut up. Rylie was unconscious at my feet. It looked like Mahmoud had simply punched her square in the nose and knocked her out cold.

The three blips got the patrol frequency's attention. They called back, wanting to know the situation, but of course Mahmoud wouldn't let me answer. The baby actually calmed down in the microwave, stopped screaming and just lay there grizzling quietly in the dark box, with no clue her father was threatening to cook her alive. For five minutes I held the gun on Mahmoud and tried to talk him down. Ten minutes. Fifteen minutes. My arms trembled with the weight of the gun and sweat poured down me. Mahmoud wanted Khalid to give him some money. He wanted Khalid's sister to promise she wouldn't divorce him. They of course agreed to all his demands, but still he didn't budge, his finger now gently resting on the "Quick Cook" button.

After twenty-one agonizing minutes, patrol cars arrived silently outside, and a scout looked through the kitchen window and saw what was going on. My arms were numb by the time they cut the power. The second the lights went out above us, I leaped forward and smashed Mahmoud in the face with the butt of my pistol, threw him on the floor, and cuffed him. Khalid Farah had shaken my hand hard outside the little house in Camden, his eyes full of young, naïve admiration, no idea how sick and horrified I'd felt throughout the whole ordeal.

"Conkaffey?" he'd said, looking at my nameplate. "I'll remember that name. It's a weird name. What kind of name is it anyway?"

"I think it's Irish," I'd said.

"Conkaffey. Cankoffey. Canned coffee." He'd looked at his sister, who was hugging the baby tightly nearby, too upset to appreciate Khalid's humor. "We should call you Captain Cappuccino."

The coffee-related names had spread through the drug community like wildfire. I'd had corner dealers calling out to me from across the street a few days later, "Yo! Frappuccino!" The story about the baby and the microwave did the rounds as well, becoming wilder and more elaborate at every turn. I heard once that I'd picked up a chef's knife from the kitchen table and flung it across the room into Mahmoud's eye socket to save the baby.

Khalid Farah was immediately grateful to me for saving his niece's life, but I couldn't accept much more than his thankful words. He'd tried to offer me money on the scene, but I'd refused. He'd sent a Rolex watch and a bottle of champagne to headquarters, but I'd had to send them back. Eventually his thankful advances drained away, but not before I'd suffered plenty of jeering from my colleagues about the drug dealer with a crush on me.

As predicted, Khalid had climbed the ranks and developed his own crew of foot soldiers. I'd run into him a number of times over the years. We'd formed a weird relationship. Not exactly a friendship, but a sort of forced camaraderie brought about by the sheer number of times we'd encountered each other, and of course my "heroism" in his sister's kitchen. It was always awkward, bursting into his lavish Elizabeth Bay mansion in a flak jacket and boots, trailing a squad behind me, acting on orders to turn the place upside down. I'd participated in raids at Khalid's nightclub, his grandmother's place, the houses of his cousins and lieutenants, their laundromats and rug shops. A few times, over the years, my colleagues had brought Khalid up on drug or murder charges, which he'd always traded out or thrown high-priced lawyers at. If I'd ever actually managed to put Khalid in a jail cell for a decent amount of time, he might have forgotten about the whole thing with his baby niece and started hating my guts. But he had always been just too slippery for me, so he had remained there, my indebted admirer, for more than a decade.

"Bin a long time." Khalid smiled at me now in the airport rental car lot, his hired goons an intimidating wall of muscle at my back. "Haven't seen you since all your shit blew up, bro. 'Cept on the news, a'course. Man, you neck-deep in some crazy shit. I got no idea how you beat that rap. No clue."

"Yeah, well, I did beat it. So now I'm trying to keep it on the down low," I said. "I'm only here in Sydney for a couple of days and then I'm off again. I don't want to ruffle any feathers. In and out."

I didn't know how Khalid felt about what I was supposed to have done to Claire Bingley, but I wasn't game to hang around and find out. I made some short steps to the side, out of the triangle of men, but they shifted around me, kept me at their center like a rabbit surrounded by wolves.

"How you bin? How you holdin' up?"

"It's hard." I shrugged. "But it's over now."

"Over? I don't think so. People are still upset down here about what you did. I heard fools talkin' 'bout takin' your head off, they see you out and about in your old stompin' grounds. Looks like some might feel the same up where you ran away to, even." He gestured to my face.

"It's fine. Really."

"Maybe you thinkin' it's fine and it's over is what's gettin' you messed up so often." He adjusted the cuffs of his shirt, a tough-guy pop of his chest, like the discussion was over. "Listen, Coffee Man, I bin watchin' all this shit about you and the kid they say you grabbed. And I'm here to tell you that I know it's not true. You didn't do it. You're not that type. I seen that type, and you're not it."

"Thanks." I nodded. "That's kind of you to say."

"So when I heard you was comin' down, I thought I'd catch you before you go all white ninja on me."

"Who told you I was coming down?"

He waved my question off. "Doesn't matter. I just wanted to tell you, in case you were worried about what I thought about it all, that I only got love in my heart for you, man. Anything you need, my people are here for you."

"Great," I said. "That's great. Listen, it was so nice to see you. But I've got to get going. I've got somewhere to be."

"Uh-huh. That's why my boys are here." Khalid jutted his chin at the lumbering goons behind me. "This your protection detail while you're Sydney-side."

"What?" I almost laughed, which made the goons bristle indignantly. "Oh, no. I don't need a . . . a protection detail."

"Really?" Khalid snorted. "You know you ain't walkin' straight right now, motherfuck."

I looked at the goons. They were oddly well-dressed for men in that kind of service. Glittering cufflinks, intricately woven shirts beneath the tailored jackets of very expensive suits. You don't usually see thugs dressed like that, because thugs don't tend to make a lot of money. People generally only take up the profession of enforcer because they want to get close to the powerful people in organized crime and maybe one day take over their position, so they're commonly strapped for cash. Aside from that, the moment they perform their intended duties they're likely to get blood on anything pricey. I turned back to Khalid, who was examining his manicure.

"I can handle my own personal safety."

"Oh." He laughed. "I believe you. You *real* convincin' with a face all fucked up like that, lookin' like somebody's leftovers."

The goons snickered.

"Nobody's askin' you what you can and can't handle," Khalid continued. He put his ring-adorned hands up in surrender. "But bro, takin' you down would earn some dogs around here some proper respect. You know nobody likes a kiddie-fucker. I got kids, man. Lotta dangerous people do. Takin' out some baby-rapin' piece-a-shit would be a real favor to the world, and some people think it might be their duty, you know what I'm sayin'? With the police havin' fucked it up and all. Just let my guys do their thing, okay? Think of it as a favor to me. So I don't worry about you all night. I don't sleep well, you know. Plus, I never got to pay you back over my niece, Sammy. She's fifteen now—you know that?"

"No, I didn't know that."

"She wouldn't have been anything if not for you."

"I was just doing my job." I tried to sidestep away again. "I don't need to be paid back."

"Yes, you do." Khalid sighed and shook his head like I was being an idiot. "And besides, you'll probably be havin' a look around while you're down here, maybe tryin' to see if you can find the guy who *did* do that to the kid. Well, I want that guy. You understand? If anyone's gonna get him, it should be me."

I understood. This wasn't just about old favors being repaid. This was also about the criminal hierarchy. Criminals hate criminals who commit worse crimes than them. Fraudsters reassure themselves that they're not, in fact, bad people because they look at burglars and say—well, at least I don't commit my crimes face-to-face. Men charged for hurting men look down on men charged for hurting women. Killers look down on rapists, and rapists look down on pedophiles, and on and on the pecking order goes, each criminal justifying their life because they have someone who's "badder" than them. Pedophiles and child killers were the lowest of the low. To kill them in prison is a heroic act. To find one and kill him in public would have been a criminal badge of honor for Khalid.

"When you come across the guy," Khalid said, "you just hand him over to my people. We'll even let you watch, maybe. But you don't give him to the police, or I'll be very upset with you. I mean it."

"I'm not looking into my own case while I'm here."

"What?"

"No."

"The hell not?"

"Because I . . ." I was too tired to explain it all again. "It's just easier if I don't."

"Huh." Khalid raised his waxed eyebrows.

"Khalid, I can't have your people escorting me around," I said. "This is all very kind, and I don't want to sound ungrateful, but things are very bad for me already. I can't draw any more attention to myself."

"Linda and Sharon are very professional." Khalid put his hand on his heart. "I promise." I looked at the men. The one named Linda cracked his knuckles.

"Linda and Sharon?"

Sharon spat on the ground.

"White ladies' names," Khalid said. "They don't get the boys in blue excited when they hear them on the wire taps."

"I see," I said. "Ingenious. What have you instructed these guys to do if any trouble does arise?"

"Be effective." Khalid shrugged. "Be discreet. Just what I always tell them."

"I can't have this," I said.

"Look, you just do what you're told, Cappuccino," Khalid said. "All right? Everythin' will be fine. You're gonna follow Linda and Sharon. They're gonna take you to the car, and you tell 'em where you need to go. That's it, brother. End of discussion."

One of the goons took my bag off my shoulder, while the other gave me an encouraging shove toward the north lot. My resistance failed. I felt exhausted. The last thing I needed was to visit Kelly and Lillian at the Department of Family and Community Services offices with a couple of hairy thugs in tow. But on the other hand, looking at these two, I felt the tightness in my shoulders easing. Their wide hips bulged with guns under their suit jackets, and each stood a good foot taller than me, which was saying something. I had accepted so much about my new life. A helping hand from a murderous drug dealer and his crew wasn't the weirdest thing I'd adapted to since I was released from prison.

"I'll check in with you, bro," Khalid said as we parted, taking a set of keys out from his pocket. He pushed a button, and the taillights of a black Lambo at the back of the lot flashed. He winked at me as he turned to go. "Stay frosty."

Amanda stood at the door of the Barking Frog and looked down the road at the edge of the rainforest, to where it curved left toward the highway. Hours had passed while the bodies of the fallen bartenders were taken away and the scene was processed, every stray napkin and discarded straw bagged and tagged, every surface polished with print powder, every sheet of paper categorized, labeled, and hauled away in boxes. Some of the family and friends of the deceased had arrived to huddle at the corner of the outer cordon and cry, some of them pacing back and forth, looking wonderingly at the gray sky. When police officers came near the family, the officers approached with their hands up, like they were being taken hostage. The family talked in high, near-hysterical voices. Amanda sucked on her cigar and looked up, tried to see what they all kept looking at, what it was about the meandering steel-gray clouds that they thought might give them answers. She didn't understand grief much at all. The grimacing faces of the families bewildered her.

During her murder trial, the family of her own victim had been very aggrieved indeed. The emotion itself had many facets. One moment the grief seemed heavy and sluggish, making the mother and father of the girl Amanda had stabbed seem like they were walking through water. The next moment it seemed to sparkle through them like electricity, flaming behind their eyes, twitching in their legs as they sat staring across the courtroom at her. Amanda's lawyer had instructed *her* to look aggrieved throughout the trial, so that the judge would understand that she was sorry for what she had done. Amanda was sorry. But she didn't know how to *look* that way. Should she jog her knees? Should her mouth be downturned? What kind of grief was the right one?

She hopped down the porch stairs of the Frog and wandered to the edge of the building, peeling off her forensic booties and leaving them on the verandah. Beside the squat wooden building, the grass had been flattened by cars rolling in and out the night before, fresh, resilient grass that, like all Cairns flora, could spring up overnight with hope of life only to be crushed down by humanity. There were more defiant things growing behind the bar; twisted tomato plants born from a single rotting fruit that had rolled out of the garbage pile, and sunflowers, the seeds of which had probably been spat there by birds flying over from the suburbs. She went to the back door of the pub, where more forensics officers were taking casts of footprints in the mud. The ground here was littered with cigarette butts by the bins, each of which was being carefully lifted with tweezers and slipped into paper envelopes. She watched the activity for a while, then walked down the small hill to the creek. Something slippery slithered away from her and into the water as she approached.

When the big rains came they carried crocodiles down the back channels of water like this, between the lakes and rivers. Tree-change city families who bought McMansions in the suburbs closer to Cairns were the prime victims for fat-bellied predators who used these smaller waterways as their secret alleys. The city families with their city dogs and cats didn't heed the croc warning signs. They wanted unhindered waterfront views and pretty, bougainvillea-laden gazebos a stone's throw from the creek bed. Missing-pet posters littered the supply store windows.

Across the creek, fifty meters from the back door of the Barking Frog, was a wooden fence with a single odd paling, a new blond plank of wood boarded over an old one that had fallen down, a bright tooth in a stained row. Amanda stepped carefully on three big rocks that created eddies in the creek, exhaling cigar smoke over her shoulder as she made her way toward the little house.

She walked along the side fence, heard a bubbling sound and peered through the cracks. In the back corner of the small, neat yard there appeared to be a goldfish pond outlined with large sandstones, the surface of the water almost covered with huge green lily pads. Orange flashes of life in the depths.

She reached the open front yard. There was a car in the driveway covered by a protective tarp—an old Chevy, it looked like—the shiny vintage hubcaps barely visible. She found a young man pulling the bins from their little latticed cage in the manicured garden. Amanda stood smoking and watching his lean, tattooed frame until he got the first bin free and turned to wheel it toward her.

"Oh, hello."

"Hi." Amanda smiled. "This your house?"

"No." The man had been working. His hands were dusty and worn. "My grandmother's. My brother and I are here renovating for a few days. Are you one of her neighbors?"

"Nope," Amanda said brightly and followed the young man to the roadside, where he aligned the bin with the curb. "I'm here about a murder."

"What?"

"Some murders, actually," she said, struggling to make herself plain. The man stared at her.

"The murders I'm here about happened at once. Last night."

"Okay."

"Back there, at the Barking Frog Inn."

"The bar?" The man looked over where Amanda was pointing with her cigar, toward the tops of the trees, as though he'd see some sign of devastation like smoke on the light wind. "Jesus."

"No, not Jesus. They solved that one a long time ago. This one is unsolved. Couple of kids. Bartenders. Somebody went into the bar last night, popped 'em."

"What?"

"Yeah. *Bang!* Killed 'em *dead* before they could get home to *bed*, filled their families with significant *dread*. The kitchen floor's *red*, and the killer has *fled*, and . . ."

Amanda thought. The man stood wide-eyed, waiting.

". . . and now the forensics guys are casting his *tread*!"

"Um," the man said.

"That was a good one. Made that up just now. Pretty clever, the forensics bit. It just came to me."

"Who did you say you were?"

"I'm a private investigator. Amanda Pharrell. I was wondering if you were here last night. If you heard anything that might pertain to the case."

"Ah, no." The man dusted his hands. "I mean, no, we weren't here. We just came in this morning. My brother Eddie and I. Ed! Let me get him." The man walked up the steps toward the house, opened the screen door and let it slam behind him. Amanda followed to the door and looked in, saw an old black and orange recliner chair near the entrance to a living room. A cup of tea sat there on a small side table, a pair of pink-rimmed glasses. There was a wrinkled elbow resting on the arm of the chair.

"Hi." Another lean, dust-coated man appeared in the doorway, bristly and handsome, all edges, looking concerned. "I'm Ed Songly. This is Damo."

"Yeah, Damo, sorry." Damo was still frowning. "I didn't introduce myself. I got . . . distracted."

"I'm Amanda. Do you reckon Nanna heard anything last night?" she said softly, glancing warily toward the elbow on the chair. "Was she here? Is she asleep?"

"She's got Alzheimer's," Ed said, pushing lanky black hair behind his ear with a dusty hand. "I'm not sure she'd be any good to you, even if she did. We're doing up the house to sell it. She's about to go into aged care. We haven't been so happy about her living here anyway, you know, with the bar back there. Sometimes she gets yahoos down by the creek, people chucking stuff over the fence."

Amanda nodded, glanced the other way down the hall. There were drills and cords littered on the floor. They appeared to have started only recently—some of the items were still in packets, new boxes broken down and stacked against the wall. The two men watched Amanda across the threshold, not inviting her in, not asking her to leave, Damo still apparently markedly disturbed by Amanda's rhyming skills.

"I think the bar gets a few bikers visiting," Damo suggested, leaning against the wall. "Drug deals, that sort of thing. Was the place robbed?"

"Possibly," Amanda said. "I'll keep most of that sort of thing under my hat for now. My metaphorical hat. I don't have an actual hat right this minute. Not with me, anyway."

The two men looked at each other.

"If no one here heard anything, that's all I need to know."

"There's another house not far down," Damo said, pointing. "A young family, I think."

"All right, I'll check it out." Amanda saluted with her cigar and closed the screen door carefully behind her.

The people of Cairns sure were antisocial, Amanda thought. Between the houses on the other side of the creek lay thick tangles of rainforest, impenetrable by the eye, walls of crossing vines and elephant ear leaves wet and dripping. She was forced to walk out and along the isolated street to reach the next property, another neat dwelling with terra-cotta potted plants lining a rocky garden path. As soon as she set foot on the grounds a chocolate brown lab rushed to the flyscreen over the front door, barking madly and pawing at the wire. From the front door of the house, no other properties were visible. She might have been in the middle of the Amazon. She stubbed out her cigar in some kind of bird's nest–looking plant and smiled at the frowning young lady who answered the door.

"Do you know the bar?" she asked after explaining the situation, gesturing toward the back of the property. "Have you been there? Noticed any murderers hanging about looking devious and lethal?"

"My standards are a bit higher than that." The young woman, Lila, rolled her eyes. "I went once. It smelled like possum pee and the bathrooms were filthy. I didn't go back."

"You didn't hear anything last night? Gunshots? Screaming?"

"This one barks," she said, trying to hold the dog back by its collar as it lunged repeatedly in Amanda's direction. "I don't hear anything. She goes all night. We haven't been here long and she reacts to the night creatures. Place is alive from about five o'clock. Crawling with things. Bugs. Bats. Frogs. Urgh. I don't know why we moved here."

"I don't know either," Amanda said, wincing as the dog erupted into barks again. She pointed a finger at the dog's face. "Quiet, you!"

"She's just expressing herself," Lila said. "Talking about her environment in her own language. When animals are in distress they have to verbalize things. She'll adjust in a few weeks. That's what her psychologist says, anyway. He suggested the tree change in the first place."

"Your dog has a shrink?" Amanda said.

"Everyone needs a shrink," Lila said knowingly.

On the other side of the Songly house, Amanda approached a property that had once been neat, and might at some time have had a manicured garden, but was now more battered and overgrown than the other two dwellings closest to the bar. A pair of officers were just leaving, their notebooks in hand, treading Amanda's path in reverse.

"Don't bother with the other two," Amanda said, jerking her thumb toward the houses through the forest behind her. "Deaf old lady was asleep, and the yuppie girl's dog barks too much."

"Fuck off, Pharrell," the female of the two officers said. "We're trying to solve a murder, not commit one, so we don't need advice from you."

Amanda was used to this kind of disdain. Everyone in the town knew who she was, what she had done, and each generation of cops passed on to the next that she was not to be trusted or befriended, no matter how friendly she seemed to be. She didn't take it personally. Not a lot of exciting things ever happened in Crimson Lake, so the murder she had committed more than a decade earlier was one of painfully few talking points. While people were frequently mean to her, she knew having a murderer in town was a source of interest for some. Being angry at her for what she had done, even though they never even knew the girl she'd killed, made some people feel good. Amanda didn't mind. She liked people to be happy.

She shrugged and went on past the officers to the older house. An obese woman in a floral nightie was just closing the door after the officers but paused when she saw Amanda. She gave the small investigator a suspicious once-over, noting the tattoos with disgust. The woman was covered with a fine sheen of sweat, and seemed only just roused from bed. Amanda glanced at the sun through the trees. She heard a television playing an infomercial loudly somewhere inside.

"Hi," she said brightly. "I'm—"

"I got nothin' else to say," the woman snapped. "Me shows are on."

The woman slammed the door in Amanda's face, and that was that.

A yuppie, an old woman, and an obvious recluse. Amanda decided that the strip of residences behind the Barking Frog Inn was a typical Cairns street. Nothing particularly noteworthy.

She retrieved her bike and rode through the backstreets, between the towering fields of cane, only just managing to dodge a brown snake making its way across the baking asphalt on her way into town.

———

At the Shark Bar, Pip Sweeney was just noting how much the place looked like a police station mess hall, patrol officers lounging in the booths cooling their heels, some of them talking on phones, making notes. Many of the men around her had been shipped in from other districts, a kneejerk reaction to the horror of a rare murder in the otherwise sleepy region. They would thrash out the case's initial leads for forty-eight hours, traditionally the most critical stage in the hunt for a killer. One by one they would then be called back to their own cases as the pursuit cooled. Sweeney's colleagues were tracking down witnesses, CCTV, bank accounts, and criminal records. They were a hive of hornets stirred by the killings. Under a sprawling painting of a pink hibiscus flower Sweeney sat wedged into a booth across from two large detectives. She had just begun to feel at ease directing the two older detectives to lead their teams over search grounds in the area when Amanda Pharrell appeared out of nowhere, leaning her bike against the front windows of the café.

"You're in my spot," Amanda said as she reached the booth. Sweeney and her colleagues looked up from the pages spread before them, the policewoman still clutching a phone to her ear. One of the male detectives looked Amanda over, gave her a sneer.

"Fuck off, Pharrell. This café is headquarters now."

"Everybody is telling me to fuck off today!" Amanda threw her hands up.

"Maybe you should take the hint." The detective smiled.

"Look, you guys can use this place as headquarters, but not that spot." Amanda pointed to the seat beneath the bulging man. "That's *my* spot. I own it."

"You don't own a seat in a public café."

"Yes I do."

"No, you don't."

"Yes," Amanda said, "I do."

"She does," Vicky the waitress said, breezing by the table, collecting stained coffee cups as she went. "Amanda did a deal with

Keith, the owner, maybe a year ago. She owns zero-point-zero-eight percent of these business premises. Specifically, the seat you're sitting on."

Sweeney slowly put down her phone. The men in the booth with her stared after the waitress as she moved on, wiping nearby tables, seeing to officers across the room with their hands raised for more drinks.

"Detective Sergeant Hanover," Sweeney said carefully. "Would you be so kind as to move for Ms. Pharrell?"

The detectives shifted awkwardly out of the seat, muttering obscenities. Sweeney watched as Amanda slid neatly onto the bench before her, the twitches in her neck and jaw momentarily out of control with apparent revulsion at the warmth of the bench after the detectives' presence.

"If someone had told me police headquarters was going to be here, I'd have warned you guys about my seat," Amanda said.

"I didn't purposefully exclude you from that information," Sweeney said. "I guess I just forgot about you. I apologize."

"Apology accepted." Amanda smiled.

"Amanda, I'm not sure if you're aware . . ." Sweeney shifted uncomfortably ". . . but I'm brand new on the Crimson Lake beat. And I'm new to the rank of Detective Inspector. I was promoted and shifted over after Damford and Hench were arrested."

Sweeney remembered walking to work that fateful morning six months earlier and seeing the front page of the newspaper being flung into every yard, Amanda's picture sandwiched between mug shots of the two policemen who were now behind bars. Amanda's murder committed a decade ago was now back, sprawled across a four-page extended feature, the harrowing self-defense story that had exposed officers Damford and Hench to be monsters. One teenager had been slain, another sexually assaulted in secret and then stuffed into prison. It was fuel for nightmares. Sweeney was indebted to Amanda now for her job, but she couldn't ever say so. Nothing Amanda had gone through had been worth her new stripes, her pay upgrade.

"Well, look at you." Amanda grinned, her eyes wandering appreciatively over the woman before her. "Out of the uniform and into the detective's duds. Has someone bought you a deerstalker and a calabash yet?"

Amanda reached over and gave the other woman a celebratory punch on the shoulder. Sweeney felt blood rush into her face, looked around the café at the other officers, who were all watching with hardly an effort to disguise their gaze.

"Uh, no." Sweeney cleared her throat. "And there's no time for congratulations. My chief, Damien Clark, seems to believe in baptism by fire."

"Oh, I know Damien Clark." Amanda nodded. "Or I know of him, anyway."

"Well, look, Amanda, Chief Clark has made me lead on the Barking Frog murders."

"And you've never dealt with a murder before," Amanda concluded.

Sweeney cringed. Again she looked around. Though no other officers were near enough to hear their conversation, she felt inescapably as though they were all listening.

"Did someone tell you that?"

"No. But Holloways Beach is hardly murder central," Amanda said. "Rich foreign bankers in their big white mansions on the sand, stealing from shareholders and avoiding taxes. Their bored wives having too many semillons over lunch and yanking one another's hair extensions out, plowing the Beemer into a palm tree. I'd be surprised if you'd dealt with anything more exciting than that."

"You may be close to the truth."

"Well, this is exciting then." Amanda bounced in her seat. "Your first bloodbath! Congratulations again!"

"Mmm." Sweeney winced. "I'm not going to lie. It's pretty tense. There are officers around who consider themselves to have been more worthy of the position. And it has caused further tension that Michael Bell has hired you."

"Oh, come on. If someone had popped my kid I'd go straight to C&P Investigations, too." Amanda jutted her chin smugly. "We've got a brilliant track record. No case we ever pick up is going to slip between the cracks—all Ted or I would have to do to get some publicity would be to stick our faces in front of a camera and tell the world what we're working on. Every time I do my laundry it's national news, and Ted's everyone's favorite pedo."

"Amanda, please keep your voice down."

"And as an added plus," Amanda continued, "mine and Ted's physical differences are very reassuring to the potential client—Ted's the lumbering lughead, the basher and bruiser of villains, and I'm the spritely spider monkey, scaling back-alley walls in pursuit of baddies on the run." She made a ferrety face and scratched at the air. Sweeney nodded, but concluded from her advertising spiel that it was likely Amanda had no idea why Michael Bell, then sitting in initial interviews with some of Sweeney's officers, had jumped the gun and brought in private dicks.

"There's also the fact that he believes you lot killed his dad," Amanda yawned, waving dismissively at the room full of cops.

Sweeney choked on her coffee.

"Uh, *what?*"

"Well, not that you killed him yourselves, but that you were responsible for it," Amanda said. "Michael Bell's father was Christopher Layot."

"The biker guy?" Sweeney said, shocked. "Why was I not told this?"

"Different surnames. I think Michael changed it to distance himself from dead ole daddy. He's legit. Or so he says."

"Christopher Layot was—"

"A Los Diablos man." Amanda nodded. "Down in Taree. Police were surveilling the Taree Satan's Saints gang and knew there was a hit out on Christopher Layot for some offense or another. Didn't warn him. The police botched a stakeout—the Angels crew slipped right out from under the noses of their watchers, killed Michael's dad and slipped back in beneath the radar again. Well, that's what Michael believes, anyway. He was eight."

"Oh, great." Sweeney put her face in her hands.

"Could be he's wrong," Amanda continued. "Layot's body never showed up. Could be he just blew town and is in the Philippines spearfishing lobster and tanning his arse." She shrugged. "I dunno."

"Jesus." Sweeney rubbed her eyes. "Michael Bell told you all this? This *morning*?"

"Yup."

"How did you . . ." Sweeney trailed off. She glanced around, wary of trying to learn anything from Amanda in front of her colleagues.

"We've got the same tattoo artist in Cairns," Amanda offered. "And I'm a talker. What can I say? Sometimes people talk back at me just to get me to shut up."

"This is just what I need," Sweeney said. "An uncooperative family member and . . ." She trailed off again, but the additions to her concerns didn't warrant listing aloud. Her first major case as a detective. A double homicide. A biker connection, and the town's two most hated people smack-bang in the middle of it trying to assist. Sweeney looked at Amanda, who was carefully tearing off a corner of a napkin, which she rolled into a ball and began to chew. A table of male police officers nearby weren't even pretending to work now—they stared in obvious contempt at the tattooed investigator as she worked through her napkin snack.

"Amanda." Sweeney took a deep breath. "I'm not going to tell Chief Clark that you and Ted are on the investigation."

"Oh?" Amanda raised an eyebrow.

"No," Sweeney said. "He'll find out, of course, from one of my fellow officers. And he'll berate me for not telling him. And he'll insist that I get rid of you. But before that happens, perhaps you can come up with a few leads for me."

"You sneaky, sneaky detective." Amanda smiled, waggling a finger. "I like your style. And I like being in secret relationships. Ooh, dangerous liaisons. Undercover partnerships. Covert alliances. I feel like I'm on an episode of *Survivor*."

"So," Sweeney broke in. "Maybe you—"

"Being *hush hush* gives me a *rush*." Amanda was talking to herself now. "Makes me *gush, flush, blush* like I've got a *crush*—"

"Amanda?"

"—*plush*—"

"Amanda." Sweeney leaned forward, taking up her pen again. "In the spirit of cooperation, maybe you could fill me in on anything else you have already, anything as significant as your biker connection."

"Ah, yes, I could."

Sweeney set her pen to the page, but Amanda stood, brushed flecks of napkin from the end of her shirt. "But you're going to have to bide your time, Sweeney McBeany. I'm a lady. I don't go around giving it all away at once the first time someone expresses interest. I'll be in contact."

Sweeney watched in horror as Amanda turned and left the café, winking to the nearest table of officers as she went.

Dear Diary,

I'm sorry. That should count for something. I'm sorry that I am this way, and I don't want to be this way, and when I do the things that I do and think the way that I think, I feel bad about it. You know, you see a lot of pedophiles on TV shows. They're happy, smiling guys. They're not sorry. They're confident, nasty. I watched an episode of Law & Order one night, Chloe with her head in my lap, half-asleep, the light on her face. It's terrifying to see pedophiles on-screen, even fictional ones. This pedophile guy, the leader of a child sex ring, he was telling a young boy that it was okay, he didn't need to worry—he was into little girls. He and the little boy's father were friends. The boy needn't recoil from his touch, needn't feel uncomfortable beside him at the table.

It would be so great if my life was like that. If I was so callous that I could tell a small boy, as casually as I would report the weather, my darkest, secret shame. Say it as a consolation. Imagine if I had a "ring" of friends who shared my "predilection." What bullshit. I wouldn't dare go looking for someone like me. It would be too risky, even online.

Maybe if I had friends like me, they'd have been able to talk me out of Penny. Convince me that she wasn't all that I thought she was.

I caught sight of Penny the day Chloe and I moved in to the Wish Street house. She was sitting on the porch steps digging holes in the lawn with a stick, poking the tip deep down into the rain-pregnant earth while she waited for her mother to come out. Weirdly, I didn't experience the usual stomach-collapsing thump of desire, the one Dr. Hart had told me to be wary of. Penny was wearing a little sky-blue tunic, something expensive, Charlie&Me maybe. Tiny heels. I notice children's fashions. Try not to let people know I do. I see that mothers are getting into heels for little girls these days, and I'm all for it. Handbags and sunglasses. Gorgeous. I saw Penny as I was moving boxes into the house and I thought: "There's a pretty girl." That was it. Maybe the therapy was working. Maybe I was distracted. A bit depressed. I'd seen a newspaper article that morning that bothered me a lot.

Camden Park residents are being asked to assist police with information about a man frequenting the area who may have engaged in inappropriate contact with children. There are reports a man has approached children near the Angela Leigh Dance Academy and spoken to them inappropriately. The man is reported to be 20–30 years of age, Caucasian, with shoulder-length dark blond hair.

I'd cut my hair, given Chloe some shit about wanting a change. But I couldn't shake off the guilt. It had happened before, when I was a teenager and got a bit handsy in the surf one day after "accidentally" getting swept into a group of little blond nippers. Had a couple of lifeguards chase me after a mother made a complaint. The idea that someone was going to come knocking was never far away. My life is like that. Whenever the phone rings and it's a number I don't know, or there's an unexpected rapping at the door. Or one of my mates has to confide something, or Chloe tells me we "need to talk." I think, This is it. At least once a day I think This is it. It's exhausting.

I'd been standing by the barbecue in the backyard, listening to Chloe inside unpacking the kitchen, nesting, when the girl I'd seen at the front of the house next door suddenly popped her head up over the fence. I was still a little self-conscious about my newly shaven head and found myself rubbing a hand over it, trying to hide it. So I suppose I cared, maybe liked her, even then. She was white-haired, around ten. A bit old for me, but I returned the curious smile anyway.

"Hi."

"Hi."

"I'm Penny."

"I'm Kevin."

A little tingle in the belly. I went about setting up the barbecue. Didn't want to look too keen. She watched me, picking at the top of the fence palings with her chipped, pink painted nails.

"Have you guys finished moving in?" she asked.

"We've still got to unpack the boxes," I said, screwing the gas bottle in. "But that won't take too long."

"I knew the guy who lived here before," Penny said. "Mr. Byles. He was grumpy."

"Well," I said, "we're not grumpy."

"Is that your wife?" She could see Chloe at the sink through the kitchen window.

"My girlfriend."

"She's pretty."

"So are you," I said. She didn't blush. Didn't respond. Didn't giggle, like someone younger might. Probably heard it all the time. She was switched on, this one. I was feeling a heat creep up my neck, a familiar feeling. Chemicals colliding. The shame is an instant thing with me. I feel sorry. That's what people will never understand. That's why I will never tell anyone. Because normal people don't know these feelings, these intense, sickening, prickling sensations rushing over my skin. I know it's wrong. I know I'm wrong, I'm—

"How old are you?" she asked.

"I'm twenty-four," I told her.

"That's old." She smiled. Knew she was being sassy. Cheeky little bitch. I laughed. Her mother called her from the house.

"How old are—" I began. But she was gone. Disappeared. A mystery girl who might never have been there. When Chloe touched my arm I jumped. I'd been listening hard to the slap of Penny's shoes up the steps, the crash of the screen door as she left my life.

My adult girlfriend asked me something, I don't remember what. I responded, I guess, because she went away. I crouched on the bricks and cut the cable ties we'd secured the barbecue shut with, all the while deafened by the painful, relentless ringing of Penny's name in my brain.

Three or four weeks after I was arrested for Claire Bingley's sexual assault and attempted murder, my wife gave up on me. She surrendered to the relentless pursuits by *60 Minutes* and gave them an interview distancing herself from me, stopped visiting me as often in remand, stopped appearing in the audience at my committal hearings. She still called and wrote and came to meetings when my lawyer summoned her, but she could hardly look me in the eye, and she called me Edward, when for fourteen years it had been Ted. I lost sight of my daughter, Lillian. She'd been just beyond the visiting room glass, and then she was only a wailing sound in the background of Kelly's cold phone calls. Soon, she was just an occasional picture on the phone, soundless, foreign. The ghost of a child whose tiny body I had once held in my arms, whose tired eyes I had smiled at, as she blinked slowly, refusing to sleep. Whisperings in the dark at 3 a.m.

The few people who believed in my innocence couldn't understand Kelly's actions, but I could. It was safer, emotionally, to give up on me. My incarceration wasn't a slow and drawn-out thing. I went to work one morning and never came back, and suddenly this man appeared in Kelly's life, always at a distance, worn out and terrified and not allowed to kiss or touch her in the prison. A man who everyone was telling her had done a vicious thing that they were certain they could prove. We haven't ever talked about it, but I imagine that to Kelly, the Ted she knew died that day. I know what that feels like. He kind of died for me, too. I knew myself as a sort of happy-go-lucky character, an easygoing bloke who loved his family, his job, the warm, sunlit corner of the living room on a Sunday afternoon, book and beer in hand. I can't imagine ever being that Ted again now. To me he seems naïve and tragic, a figure eternally waiting for the rug to be pulled out from under him.

All this terrible history with the dead Ted and his ghost child and his icy wife accumulated into a swirling nervousness as I stood in the lift of the building that housed the Department of Family and Community Services on Macquarie Street in Parramatta. Kelly and I had texted about meeting somewhere public with plenty of distractions, but with the press after me and the threat of vigilantes, we thought it would be safest for our daughter to meet deep in the bowels of the soulless but decidedly inaccessible building for my first supervised visit. Under my arm I carried a soft, badly wrapped package. Linda and Sharon shuffled uneasily behind me in the tiny elevator like two restless bulldogs, detecting my rising trepidation with their tightly wound protective senses. As I watched the electronic numbers counting off floors Sharon startled me with a thump in the shoulder.

"From Khalid."

I looked at the tiny box he thrust toward me, as long as my index finger and wrapped in thick gold paper. A tiny silver bow slightly crushed by Sharon's jacket. When I didn't take it, Sharon jerked it at me, impatient.

"What is it?"

"A present, fuckhead. What do you reckon?" He snorted. Linda sighed in agreement.

"I don't want a present."

"It's for the baby." Sharon palmed the box into my chest, knocking the breath out of me. "Jesus."

I slipped the box into my pocket as the doors opened. Kelly was standing there. I should have known. The more worried about me she was, the further out she always stood from home, trying to meet me at the earliest possible opportunity. Sometimes, when I'd had a dangerous shift on drug squad, or failed to answer my phone, I'd turn into our street and find her standing on the corner, watching for my car as it appeared in the night. It surprised me how good she looked now. I guess I'd unconsciously thought she might be as physically battered by the past year as I was. But she was fit, athletic. When we were together she had liked to run for stress. She must have been pounding the pavement like a mad person.

"Kelly," I said, smiling. "Hi."

"Hi." She backed away to let us all out of the elevator, seemed to suffer the impulse to hug me before correcting herself. She wrung her hands at her chest. "How are you." A statement, not a question.

"You can hug me," I said. I don't know why. Maybe she didn't want to. I knew I was cringing but couldn't stop myself. My throat hurt. This was all so awful. "It's . . . It's okay."

Kelly danced forward and put her arms around me like I was hot to the touch, only made contact with her palms on my back. The gesture seemed to exhaust the very last vestiges of any goodwill she'd managed to gather over the time since we'd last seen each other. She examined my face the way she used to when I'd copped a stray elbow during a raid.

"What the fuck happened to you?"

"Oh, shit." I touched my face, remembering. "I, um—"

"And who are these guys?" She took another step back so she could take in the enormous spectacle that was the two men behind me. "Sorry, do you mind?"

"They're with me." I tried to take Kelly's arm, consolatory. She shifted away. "I'm sorry. They're sort of . . . my escorts, I guess."

"Are you fucking serious, Edward?" Kelly marveled at me. "You turn up here on your daughter's birthday with your face half bashed in and two . . . two . . ."

She flung her arm at Linda and Sharon. Tried to find a word. I didn't have one to offer.

"Are these guys associated with your drug dealer friends?" Kelly was really on the warpath now. I remembered all her little gestures, how they'd come on like lights in a sequence as her anger grew. The squinting eyes. The vein down the side of her neck.

"Lady, if we could get going . . ." Linda gestured with his big palm toward the hall behind Kelly, like a nightclub bouncer showing a crazy drunk woman the door. "People need to use the elevator."

"Don't." I shook my head at him. "Don't tell my wife what to do."

"I'm not your wife!" Kelly snapped. "This is bullshit!"

I could hear Lillian crying down the hall. The sound of it cut through the argument like a fire alarm. We all stopped, Kelly making little upset sounds as she panted, wiping her sweating brow.

"Let's just go," I told her. "Can I please—"

She walked off on me. I followed her, the goons close at my back.

"I need you guys to back off a bit, huh?" I told them as I walked. "This is my family."

"We know."

"So cut me some fucking slack. I haven't seen them in a long time. I'm making an attempt to enjoy myself here."

Any enjoyment I might have expected or hoped for dissolved when I turned the corner and found my two-year-old daughter standing in the waiting room of the office, surrounded by adults.

Lillian took one look at me and started screaming.

Kelly and I were not divorced. We'd had a run at it and failed. The problems had occurred first on her end, with Kelly asking a judge to put a supervised visitation order in place after my release and then refusing to answer my or my lawyer's calls. She'd hired her own lawyer and decided to take me for everything, and then fired the lawyer without explanation and backed away. After months of silence, we'd reconnected gently and drawn up a settlement, but just as we were about to proceed, it was me who stalled, telling her I needed time to think about the fairness of the settlement. Really, I'd just been terrified of signing the final papers. But she hadn't pushed me to do it. All the paperwork was still split between my house and hers, filled with little yellow tabs showing where our signatures needed to go.

The indecision about the divorce played out in my indecision about my wedding ring. The first time I'd taken it off had been on the car ride up to Cairns, Sydney in my rearview mirror. I'd stashed it in the car's glove box, but put it back on soon enough, my finger feeling bare and weird. Over the months, I proceeded to furiously take it off and slam it down, sheepishly pick it up and put it back on, usually drunk for each. I had it on now, twisted it around and around my finger as I walked around the corner, following Kelly.

There were two social workers and some dude Kelly had brought with her, perhaps her new boyfriend, I didn't know. Kelly crouched and swept Lillian into her arms, took her away from me, left me and my goon squad standing there with her emotional support network. The social workers were the typical kind I'd encountered many times before in my job, diving into meth dens and sweeping twitching, withdrawn newborns and stinking, scab-covered toddlers out of the dark depths. Hard faces. Long skirts. Lanyards with swipe cards and ID hanging around their necks.

I reached for the dude first. It didn't look like anyone was going to introduce him.

"Ted." I put out a hand.

"Jett," he said, shaking my hand hard. No explanation of who he was. I could tell he was Kelly's man. The handshake was clearly a big gesture for him, something he'd decided on well in advance. He looked around to make sure the ladies noticed it, him being the bigger person. He was much shorter than me, but fit, wiry, the way Kelly had become. Something about the outer ends of his eyebrows wasn't right. Were they waxed? A lot of him seemed oddly, unnaturally hairless, in fact, now that I was getting close to him. The angry Ted deep inside was causing me to posture like a cop, chest out, looking down the nose, tight mouth. *Don't do that,* I scolded myself. *Don't be a dick. This guy might end up your daughter's stepfather.* I smiled awkwardly instead.

I introduced myself to the FACS ladies. No one seemed willing to commit beyond hellos. I went the way that Kelly had gone and found a large playroom smelling of disinfectant. Kelly was sitting on the floor with a snuffling, sighing Lillian, trying to coax her into conversation with a pink teddy bear. I sat on the floor nearby, not too close. It was hard to get down that low. My ribs moved in shockingly painful ways. Linda and Sharon went to the other end of the playroom, Linda picking up a fire truck, examining it.

"Do we have to have those guys in here?" Kelly asked.

"It wasn't my decision," I said. "Khalid Farah put them onto me."

"Khalid Farah!" Kelly's eyes widened, mortified. "Jesus, Ted!"

I waved at her. "Keep your voice down." There are drug lords, and then there are drug lords who appear in the media on murder and extortion charges often enough they become household names. The social workers and Kelly's dude didn't seem to have noticed. They had seated themselves at a plastic table nearby, the ladies already making furious notes. I took out the small boxed present and handed it to Kelly.

"It's from him," I said. "For Lil."

"I don't want it."

"Well, you're going to take it."

"No, I'm not."

"Please, Kelly." I glanced at the FACS people. "Please just—"

Kelly snatched the box from me and shoved it into the pocket of her cardigan. "Ted, you can't be hanging out with people like that." She leaned in, threatening. "You just can't."

"I have a lot of bad people in my life right now, Kel." I gave an icy smile. "And you know, it's weird. None of these thugs, drug lords, and murderers have ever questioned my innocence. Not even for a second. My wife, on the other hand . . ." I shrugged.

Kelly said nothing. I rubbed my bruised eyes.

"I'm sorry," I said. "That was nasty. I'm sorry. I'm sorry."

"It's okay." She watched Lillian on the floor before her, the child's back to me, fiddling with the teddy bear's eyes. "Lil, look who's here. It's Daddy. You remember Daddy, don't you?"

Lillian turned and looked at me. Her chin trembled.

"It's Daddy." I smiled. "You know me, don't you, Boo-Boo?"

Lillian turned away from me. I pretended to scratch my temple, kept my hand up and ready in case I lost it.

"She'll come around," Kelly said.

"I know."

I picked up my present and offered it, but Lillian didn't want anything from me so I started unwrapping it myself. She watched from the corner of her eye. I extracted a green plush toy dinosaur from the paper and made him walk up and down the mat beside me. After a while I covertly shuffled sideways so that I was close to Lillian, maybe a foot or so away. I was painfully aware of the clock on the wall, ticking away the seconds of my two-hour supervised visit. My mission in those two hours was to hug my kid. I was going to get a genuine, panic-free hug if it killed me.

"I guess I'll just play with this guy here if no one else wants to play with me," I said casually, walking the dinosaur in a circle before me on the ground. *"Oh, I'm a happy dinosaur. I'm such a nice guy. Very green, very handsome."*

Lillian was interested, but still cautious. It was my black eye that scared her, the bloodshot whites. The haphazard fishing-line stitches. I lay down on my side, ignoring the pain, propped my head on my hand.

"I'm such a happy—"

"That's mine," Lillian said, taking the dinosaur from my hand. Our fingers brushed. I sat up again and shifted closer.

"That's cool. You can have it."

"My dino-sorb," she said, making him walk around, as I had. She looked up at me, a little twitch of a smile. The tiniest flash. *"I'm a green guy. I'm a green guy."*

"She's so big," I told Kelly. "I can't believe how big she is. She's turned into a little girl."

"They grow up fast," Kelly sighed. "We're onto potty training at the moment. That's . . . interesting."

I wondered if she meant "we" as in she and Lillian or she and the dude. Was this guy living with my wife, giving my daughter lollipops when she used the potty? Tucking her into bed at night, singing her songs? I looked up, found Jett giving me a stare-down. I gathered up a little plastic mouse to fiddle with. Lillian took it from me, pushed me in the chest.

"That's mine," she said.

"You can have it." I smiled, took a chance and patted down her soft black curls. She didn't twist away from me. I was getting closer to that hug.

"Can they have physical contact?" Jett winced, looked to the FACS ladies for help. "Is that allowed?"

"She's my daughter," I said.

"Hey, I'm just being cautious." Jett shrugged stiffly. "If there was no cause for concern, I'm sure the court wouldn't have ordered supervised visits."

"Jett," Kelly said.

"Physical contact is fine," one of the FACS ladies said. "Whatever the custodial parent is happy with."

The custodial parent. What did that make me? The accused parent. The charged parent. The non-custodial parent. The parent who touched his child like she was made of tissue paper, wary not to shock or horrify anyone, including the girl herself. And what did that make Jett? The stand-in parent? I wondered how long he'd been with Kelly that she would bring him here to such a tense meeting, that he would be so concerned with being the good guy in front of the FACS people. It must have been serious between them. And yet she hadn't mentioned it at all, just landed me with it without explanation. I wondered if a warning would have made any of this easier. I didn't want to ask Kelly about her relationship with Jett. Didn't want to give her that; make it look like I was surprised or upset. For all she knew, I also had a girlfriend. I briefly considered pretending I did. Pathetic games.

His protest complete, Jett settled back in his chair, eyes locked on me. I tried to focus on Lillian. After another ten minutes, she'd held my hand, laughed at me, and poked me in the neck. I was getting so close to that hug, the urge to just throw caution to the wind and do it was pulsing in my arms and chest. I was afraid if I grabbed her and squeezed her the way I wanted to do, I might not only terrify her but perhaps injure her in some way. My body longed for her, a heavy hunger that set my teeth on edge. I could smell her. Baby-smell of milk and soap and something plasticky—Play-Doh, maybe crayon—trapped under her fingernails. Linda and Sharon were in the corner intent on a game of Connect Four until one of them thumped the table with a fist after losing and scattered the coins everywhere, shouting in Arabic.

I got pretty close to my hug, but when I opened my arms and offered it, Lillian threw herself at Kelly. My wife gave me a half hearted, conciliatory smile. I think that, after the initial novelty of seeing me when we'd been so long apart, Kelly had refocused herself and remembered that it was because of me that we were here, that because of me, whether I'd intended it or not, everything she'd thought she had lined up for her future, for her daughter's future, had been destroyed. If I'd just left the house slightly later that day. If I'd just pulled over a little further up the road. If I'd just tried harder, found something definitive that would prove I was innocent, something that would blast the case open, something that would assure everyone, even her, that I hadn't attacked Claire Bingley. But I hadn't done any of those things. To Kelly, this was all my fault.

When the second hand came around to the end of my two hours, Jett got out of his seat. He scooped Lillian up off the floor before me just as the minute hand clicked into place.

Everyone prepared to leave, Linda and Sharon taking last longing looks at the toy box in the corner. Kelly sidled up to me. I thought she was going to say goodbye.

"That girl you work with now," she said instead. "Amanda Pharrell. The killer."

"What about her?"

"What's she like?" Kelly searched my eyes.

"Amanda is a wonderful person," I said, finding myself in my cop pose again, shoulders back, chin high. "She's a very good partner. An absolute crack investigator. A very good friend."

"Oh," Kelly said. "You're friends, then."

I dropped my shoulders, confused. Was Kelly asking me if my "killer" friend was dangerous? Or was she asking if we had feelings for each other? What the hell did that mean? I looked at my wife, trying to make sense of her now, a woman who I'd thought had completely reassembled her broken life after me. She had a male friend who she obviously trained with, who she seemed to keep close enough company with that our daughter was quite happy to be picked up by him, lugged around on his hip. Why did she give a damn about the women in my life?

"We've gotta go, Kel," Jett said, coming close to us. I took a chance and reached up, patted Lillian's warm head, tugged on her velvety soft ear, the way I used to when I was the only man who could hold her without upsetting her.

"See you next time, Boo-Boo," I told her. "I love you."

Lillian let go of Jett's collar and put an arm out to me. Jett took a step back. I felt my teeth lock.

"Let her go," Kelly told him. "She wants to go to him."

Jett's neck and jaw flushed red, a blossoming rage color creeping up around his cheeks. He let Lillian lean out. I took her into my arms.

"Oh, my baby," I found myself saying. I turned away from them. From confusing Kelly and her fury-filled boyfriend and the stares of the FACS women. I walked to the window and held Lillian, trying hard not to squeeze the air out of her. "My baby. My baby. My baby."

I stood there, faced away from them all, feeling her tiny arms around my neck, her chin on my shoulder. I rocked her. Smelled her. Cradled her head in my big hand and tried hard to hold on to the thrilling sensation that perhaps when I turned back around we wouldn't be in a stale office in an ugly building, surrounded by hostile faces. That perhaps when I turned back around, I'd find I'd been standing at the living room window of my home the whole time, looking out on the yard, my happy baby in my arms, my loving wife at my back, alone.

"I love you, Lil," I told my child. Her fingers were in my hair, playing with a curl at the nape of my neck.

"I love you, Daddy," she said.

In the elevator, riding toward the ground, Linda and Sharon at my back, I wiped the tears that were falling safely now that the doors had closed on my family. Soundlessly, discreetly, so the two monsters accompanying me wouldn't be tempted to make fun. I was surprised when Linda spoke, his voice high above me, deep, like the growl of a god.

"You want us to crush that guy?" he said.

"What?" I turned briefly. "Who?"

"That faggot with the eyebrows," Sharon said.

"Wha—No, I—No, I don't want you to . . . to crush him." I cleared my throat. "But thanks for the offer. Really."

One of them gave a disappointed sigh.

Pip Sweeney had seen many households in crisis. She knew the signs. All usual maintenance activities were arrested immediately. Dishes piled up in the sink. Plants sagged in their pots, thirsty. Dogs wandered aimlessly between the people squeezed into every conceivable corner, confused by the universal sadness, the occasional flicker of rage. When she arrived at Michael Bell's home in Redlynch, the scene beyond the rickety screen door was exactly as she expected it. The kitchen to the right of the small living room was acting as a base camp for a young woman hiccupping with desperate tears and two plump, middle-aged companions, maybe her mother and aunt, trying to rub and smooth the distress from her. There were pizza boxes on the corner of the counter, hasty sustenance that would soon delight a trail of ants creeping in from the window frame. A peace lily on the windowsill beginning to wilt, its long green spears slowly turning south. It was surprising how a dozen hours of grief could trash a place, leave the aftermath of a party that never happened. People wandered through, treating themselves to coffee, food, beer, bringing with them the supplies they thought a father would need as he progressed through the horror of losing a child. Takeout containers of leftovers beside the overstuffed fridge. Bags of bread. Pamphlets for counselors and psychologists. No one opened the front door for her, she simply walked in. The ritual of knocking and waiting to be permitted was abandoned in the case of a death—all doors to the house opened, all privacy washed away. If news of a death could not be contained, then there seemed no point in containing anything within the household.

To her left, Andrew's bedroom door stood open, tossed for evidence by detectives she had sent over hours after the death notice. Sweeney glimpsed tangled sheets, a Sepultura poster on the wall—skulls and torn flesh. It was an unopened packet of cigarettes on the cluttered desk that caught her eye. Andrew would never smoke them. The simple fact of his having bought and left them there seemed desperately unfair. He had not known in that moment, handing over the cash, taking the small box, that his last hours were ticking by. Becoming mere minutes. Seconds to the end.

She paused inside the front door and hugged her folder of papers to her chest, briefly filed through what aspects of the investigation were already in action. She had officers reviewing traffic cameras to see exactly which vehicles had been on the highway near the Barking Frog in both directions, chasing down those drivers, receiving explanations for where they were going at such an ungodly hour and checking those explanations. The forensic examination of the crime scene was well underway, and all the samples taken from the bar would be rushed through analysis—there would be a team of specialists to separate out biological matter from what was collected and try to connect that matter to people who had reasons for being in the bar, particularly in the back kitchen area where the murders had taken place. There were an extraordinary number of samples to be taken. Sweeney had assigned officers to take DNA samples from every employee at the bar, including the owner, Claudia Flannery, and any maintenance or delivery personnel who might have walked through the kitchen area in the course of their duties. Then there were the friends and lovers of the staff who might have hung out in the kitchen area during the evening while the boss was away, young people coming through to grab a free snack and a chat.

She had assigned officers to the analysis of the bloody footprints found at the crime scene, in order to obtain the type of shoe worn by the assailant, the size, any interesting foreign material transferred from the sole of the shoe to the kitchen tiles as the killer walked through. Her phone bleeped as she was about to walk forward into the Bell family living room—a constable reporting that they had visited the house directly behind the bar and found the old lady there was the only one home the night before and that there was nothing unusual to report.

In the living room, Michael Bell sat in silence, surrounded by the hairy, burly kinds of men who could only be brothers or workmates. There were beers everywhere. In hands. On the carpet. Being used to drown cigarettes. People stopped speaking as Sweeney entered. She cleared her throat, standing by the end of the couch, snapping the grieving father from his daydream.

"Mr. Bell?" she said, straightening the front of her crisp white shirt, a garment she'd bought as part of a suit for her first day out of uniform.

"What's happening?" the heavy man on the couch looked up, anxious, mouth downturned. "Did you catch him?"

"Not yet," Pip said. "But we will. May I sit down? I'd like to ask you a few quest—"

The screen door of the house slapped open, startling the men around her. She felt her heart sinking as she recognized the familiar squeak of sneakers on the floorboards.

"I'm here!" Amanda announced triumphantly, throwing her tattooed arms up as she reached the end of the hall. "Don't panic, everyone. I've arrived."

"What the fuck have you been doing?" Michael twisted, watched Amanda stride through the living room. "You haven't been answering your phone."

"Oh, mate, I've been running around like a mad chook," Amanda puffed. "Making calls, chasing up leads. You're way down the list. My last priority. I assume if you had any good ideas you'd have told me when you hired me."

Michael and Sweeney watched her, speechless.

"What the fuck have *you* been doing?" Amanda looked around the room, the mess on the counters. The washing basket at the foot of the couch, full of clothes that looked fresh from the dryer. "This place is trashed! It's a disgrace! My god, it's like a bomb hit!"

No one spoke. Sweeney felt sweat running down her ribcage inside her pristine shirt. Amanda dropped to the floor beside the washing basket and plucked out a pair of boxer shorts, folded it neatly into quarters and placed it on the carpet beside her. The men nearest her exchanged looks.

Sweeney took Michael hesitantly through what was being done on the police side of investigations, watching Amanda folding and stacking the clothes, pairing socks. Michael listened, his jaw set.

"I have to ask you about Andrew's mother." She looked at her notes. "One Silvia Bell? We haven't had any luck finding a current phone number or address."

"She's probably not a Bell anymore." Michael waved dismissively. "Good luck finding her. I haven't seen her in seven or eight years. She ran off with some arsehole from down south."

"Jeez, you're not having much luck, are you?" Amanda snorted from the floor, folding a T-shirt. "Dad dead, son dead, wife run off with a southerner. You're cursed, mate."

"Hey." One of the men nearby frowned at Amanda. "Take it down a notch."

"Can we talk about the weeks leading up to Andrew's passing?" Sweeney interjected. "Did he tell you about any problems he was having? People who might have wished him harm?"

"Andrew was a good kid." Michael glanced around menacingly, in case any of his cohorts decided to challenge the notion. "He had a few rough mates, but everyone does. Some of his friends were into the drugs'n that. But not Andy. Not in this house. His bedroom is the front one there, so I have to pass it every time I come in, and every time I go out. Nothin' but cigarette smoke and bad music has ever come outta that room."

"The autopsy will probably show that," Amanda said. "They'll do a tox report."

"Amanda, please," Sweeney sighed.

"What?"

"What about . . ." Sweeney turned her body toward Michael, tried to keep her breathing even. "I understand that, um . . . As Amanda mentioned, your father . . ."

"See?" Michael was suddenly red-faced, giving dangerous eyes to the men nearby. "Not twelve hours in and they're already onto it. The biker connection. Yes. My father was a patched member of Los Diablos, okay? And you fucks in blue didn't do a thing about his being knocked off by some Malo Sicario boys."

"I thought you said they were Satan's Saints," Amanda said.

"Malo Sicario!" Michael snapped.

"Sorry." Amanda returned pleasantly to her folding. "Sometimes I don't listen."

"I've been legit my whole life." Michael fixed his eyes on Sweeney. "I told the cops this morning in the official interview. I'm telling you again. I do not, and have never had, anything to do with bikers."

"You look like a biker," Amanda said. Michael reeled around to face her. "What? You've got the body for it. Big chest, thick arms. You look like you've been in a few pub brawls. That nose is flat as a pancake."

"I drive trucks," Michael Bell growled. "I don't own a bike, have never owned a bike. My criminal record speaks for itself. Yes, I've been in a few pub fights. But I'm legit. Andy was legit. We're all legit." He motioned to the men around the room.

"What about the pub," Sweeney said. "Did Andrew enjoy working there?"

"He had other things in mind for the future but he seemed to like it fine."

"I bet he loved it," Amanda chipped in, folding a shirt on her lap.

"Free booze. Free staff meals. Working side by side with your sexy chicky babe? Who wouldn't love that?"

"No." Michael cleared his throat, the big, angry men suddenly uncomfortable. "Stephanie in the kitchen there is Andrew's girlfriend." He gestured to the girl with the eyes puffed from crying, still being patted by her companions.

"*I'm* his girlfriend," Stephanie confirmed, tapping her chest, the women comforting her looking very nervous at her side. She was on the edge. Sweeney felt a pull, a restless desire to go to the girl, to wipe a hand over her tear-stained cheeks. Amanda's voice broke through the fantasy like a car horn.

"You were *a* girlfriend," Amanda corrected, a finger in the air. "Keema was seeing Andrew also. That makes two girlfriends." She raised a second finger.

"What?" Stephanie burst forth, stopped short by the kitchen bench that announced the start of the tiny living room. She seemed to hesitate, not committed to walking around it to confront the investigator on the floor. "What are you talking about?"

"Amanda," Sweeney warned.

"Oh, Schweppes! Should this have come out later?" Amanda grimaced at Sweeney. "Were you guys holding that information back?"

"We don't have any information about—"

"Holding what back?" Stephanie pushed at her sweat-slick hair. Her neck was reddening. "There's . . . There's nothing—"

"Andrew was sleeping with Keema." Amanda shrugged. "It likely has nothing to do with the murders. I assumed you knew, Sweens. I assumed you all knew. Did you not know? I mean, it's so obvious." She looked around the circle of men, every face turned toward her, some darkening with skepticism, insult. Others confused, curious. "I mean, the cars. The necklace."

"What are you talking about, Amanda?" Sweeney snapped. Her patience was gone.

"I'm gonna lose it." Stephanie's chin was trembling. "I'm just—I can't."

"Let me explain, for everybody who's apparently had their heads stuffed in the sand." Amanda rolled her eyes. She reached into her back pocket, glanced at the notebook she extracted. "Keema's British, right? She hasn't been in Cairns very long. Four weeks. She arrived in Sydney, stayed there for two weeks. She did two weeks in Byron, two in Brisbane and then she settled here. For a month. Must have liked the weather."

"Would you get to the point?" Stephanie inched nearer, her fingers closed into fists.

"When she died," Amanda continued cautiously, "Keema was wearing an opal necklace. It's in evidence now. It was a hell of a necklace. Not the dodgy little opals you get in those little clear plastic boxes in the tourist shops. The cheap ones. This was a biggie, and the setting and the chain were genuine. Real deal. Authentico. What does it mean? It means she was sleeping with Andrew."

"What the fuck?" Michael growled at Sweeney. Amanda was building momentum, almost rambling, her words slurring together, fast as machine-gun fire.

"It's an expensive necklace. You don't bring it over from England. Not when you know you're probably going to spend most of your travels in backpacker lodges, leaving your shit around for anyone to pick through while you go to the shower or go out for the night. Not when you know you'll likely be picking fruit on big farms, or working a stop 'n' go sign at the roadside for cash while you get around the big Down Under. She got the necklace here in Australia." Amanda drew a long breath. "It was *given to her* here. By someone who didn't foresee her picking fruit and working at the roadside and staying in crappy hostels. By someone who thought, or hoped, she'd stay in town. Which she did. For four weeks. Double the time she spent in any of her other stops around the country."

"This is all bullshit," one of the men said. "This is—"

"You don't wear a big-arse rock like that to work," Amanda continued, folding shorts and shirts, stacking them and pushing on their flattened surfaces like she was trying to stamp down creases in cardboard. "Not when you're leaning over bins, changing them and lining them, the pendant dangling down, threatening to be lost in all that junk. Not while you're wearing a pair of faded black jeans and a Kmart T-shirt, an outfit that will be soaked in beer and reek of cigarette smoke by the end of the night, a functional outfit strikingly ill-matched to your big fat expensive necklace. You'd only wear a rock like that to work because you knew you'd see the guy who gave it to you there, and you didn't want him to think you didn't like it."

"Some customer could have given it to her," a man by the hall said.

"Nope," Amanda said.

"Why not?"

"Because it was an opal," Amanda said. "Not a diamond. Not a pearl. Not—"

Stephanie stormed out of the room, ripping herself from the hands of the women in the kitchen as she went. There were filthy glares among the curious glances now, everyone in the room besides Michael Bell trying to stare Amanda down. Michael Bell looked curious. Thoughtful. No one spoke. Sweeney stood and gestured for Amanda to follow her out.

Outside on the lawn, Amanda stretched in the waning sunlight, rolling her lean, tattooed shoulders. Sweeney followed her to the sprawling poinsettia tree at the side of the unmarked road and watched as she picked up her yellow bicycle, pushing the tires with her thumb to test their pressure.

"Okay," Sweeney said, "I'll bite. Why does the fact that the necklace was an opal stone mean Andrew gave it to Keema?"

"Because Australians don't buy opals," Amanda said.

"Why not?"

"I don't know, I'm not a bloody geologist." Amanda snorted. "Aussies just don't buy them. They haven't been popular in jewelry here since the 1980s. Foreigners buy them because you can't get them overseas, and around here we have them coming out of our ears they're so common. Tourists love them. That's why they're only for sale in the shop windows of the tourist strips in Cairns," she said. "That's why they sell them for cheap in the little plastic containers. Keema was a tourist, so she would have seen the opals, and she'd have liked them. She'd have mentioned how much she liked them to Andrew at some point in their conversations. Yes, *conversations*. More than one. Because you don't mention a thing like that the first time you meet someone, a customer maybe, across the bar. Whoever gave her that necklace, it was someone she worked with, because she wore it to work, and it was someone she talked to a lot because she was fucking them."

"Why not someone else she worked with?"

Amanda swung a leg over the bike, reached into the back pocket of her shorts and pulled out a strip of pale pink lace with all the pomp and ceremony of a magician feeding silk handkerchiefs through his fingers. She stretched it between her index fingers and let it spring at Sweeney. Sweeney caught it against her chest.

"From the washing basket?" Sweeney unfurled the G-string, marveled at it in her fingers. "It could belong to Michael's girlfriend."

"Michael? Oh please. That man hasn't got a girlfriend, or she'd be here comforting him in his hour of need. And you don't have one-night stands in Crimson Lake. You'd go through every woman in your age-range in two weeks. He's a trucker. He gets his rocks off on the road."

"It could be Stephanie's," Sweeney said, not sure what to do with the G-string, looking self-consciously back toward the house.

"Wrong again, Sweeney Todd," Amanda said. "Not Stephanie's size." She kicked off and pedaled the bike away.

I don't know what I thought a television studio might be like. It's possible I'd developed a preconceived idea from Hollywood that it would be all flashy sets, glossy floors being crisscrossed by enormous cameras on wheels. People sitting in folding chairs yelling through megaphones at beautiful people under gold lights, the occasional Pomeranian waiting patiently to appear atop a mountain of brightly labeled cans. Plenty of security to protect the frighteningly young and pretty actors fondling each other on couches in fake living rooms or sitting down in fake kitchens to serious cups of tea.

The Channel Three studios I found when I arrived the next morning had none of the glamour of my brief, naïve expectations. We rolled into the sunbaked parking lot before soulless brick buildings stacked like stairs along a featureless hill. The reception area was poky, sterile, the walls pocked with hooks and nails that once held framed television show posters, now long gone, replaced with other hooks and nails, other posters. The goons and I were given lanyards and buzzed through a heavy, dented door not unlike some thresholds I'd traversed in prison.

I had concocted plenty of fancy, emotional excuses for accepting the *Stories and Lives* interview offer in case anyone questioned my decision. This was my chance, for example, to put the record straight in my own words about Claire Bingley's abduction and assault, to finally assert my innocence and vindicate anyone who might have been halfhearted about supporting me for so long. There was a chance her attacker might be watching, might finally be confronted with the effect of what he had done on my life, something that could perhaps persuade him to hand himself in or at least seek help for his problems. Lillian would grow up and eventually learn of her father's apparent crime, and a testimony from me of my innocence might lend some weight to her accepting the horror I'd wrought on her life, on our family, even before she was old enough to know it.

Those were all nice ideas. But at the end of the day, when *Stories and Lives* contacted me about an exclusive public appearance, they'd been offering $300,000. I'd held off, sought my lawyer's advice, and in the interim the offer had been bumped to $450,000. I took it. Yes, it was more than likely I was going to have a terrible time on the show. There was a chance I would do more damage to my reputation than I intended if I didn't handle the questions carefully enough. And to a certain extent, public interest in me had been dying down since it had peaked six months earlier with the mob outside my door and every television station in the country trying to cover my possible lynching. But those risks guaranteed a reward of almost a half a million dollars. I said I'd do it. I planned to purchase the beaten-up house on Crimson Lake. I would tuck a little away for a rainy day, and the rest I would put into a trust for my daughter.

It appeared my arrival for the interview was highly anticipated. I'm at least fifteen minutes early everywhere I go—a leftover symptom of time in the police force—so I caught a group of producers or executives having a powwow just inside the glass door marked with a huge blue book, the logo for *Stories and Lives*.

"Oh my god." Someone popped their head out of the huddle as I opened the door. "He's here."

"Ted." A small woman wearing a red power suit turned toward

me, slicked back the side of her already very slick hairdo. "Erica Luther. We've spoken over email."

She reached out to shake my hand. Everyone in her group balked slightly at the gesture, little tightenings of the corners of mouths and roundings of the eyes. It's a big deal to shake my hand, apparently. I gave her a firm grip.

"Nice to meet you."

"This is Lara Eggington." Erica presented an extremely slender woman in a taut cream dress. "She'll be running the interview this morning."

I'd seen Lara on-screen putting the daggers into people like me. She was even narrower, sharper about the face in real life than she was on the show. I shook her limp, soft hand, a collection of bird bones in a satin bag.

"You've been in an accident," she said by way of greeting, turning those eagle eyes on my face.

"Uh, an accident. Yes. I'm fine."

"And these are your friends. Did we approve this?" she asked no one in particular. She looked Linda and Sharon over. "I was sure we only approved your lawyer to be on set."

"Where is my lawyer?" I glanced around the studio, where cameramen and sound recordists were trying not to stare. "He said he'd be here."

"He's running a little late." Erica smiled. The panic swirled. Sean Wilkins had been the only person to stand by my side through every minute of my ordeal, from the day I was arrested. He'd come to me in my holding cell at my own police station, a calm, collected island in the swirling, treacherous waters of my life. Suddenly I was the kid at the first day of school and my dad had left me to fend for myself, to follow instructions from people I didn't know. To trust that they'd take care of me.

The goons and I were led through the studios to a small sitting room–style set, comfy wingback chairs and a phony fireplace. Linda and Sharon arranged themselves like mighty birds of prey on a nearby bench, preening their jacket cuffs and sniffing. I was examining the boom mic above my head and listening to instructions when the clopping of frantic footsteps down the hall made Lara stiffen in her seat across from me.

"Oh, shit," someone said. Lara massaged her impossibly smooth brow as my lawyer emerged into the light, puffing.

"I knew you'd do this." Sean was right up in the little producer's face, Erica Luther backing into a camera stand, almost knocking it over. "I fucking knew it. You said ten a.m. You said ten. Ay. Em." He tapped his expensive watch manically, making it rattle on his wrist.

"Sean?" I stood.

"There must have been some kind of miscommunication," Erica sneered. "I don't know who you've been in contact with, but—"

"They do this," Sean told me, grabbing my arm and tugging me away from the chair like it was booby-trapped. "They tell the lawyer the wrong time so it'll be far too late when I arrive. Look at you. You're a fucking mess. You were going to put him on like this, weren't you? You look like *shit*, Ted."

I'd never seen Sean this flustered. Not in the courthouse, not in the prehearing meetings. Never. He was sweating into the collar of his shirt, his silk tie askew. "Where's hair and makeup?" he demanded. "Get them in here, now."

"Hair and makeup was never part of the agreement," Erica said. "You should have—"

"Right." Sean yanked my arm. I was suddenly walking with him, Linda and Sharon hurrying down the hall behind us. We jogged past an empty news desk and a row of sound booths, turned down a narrow passageway and along a set of fire stairs. Sean seemed to know where he was going. We emerged into a gold-lit dressing room where a beautiful Asian woman was waiting by a row of shirts.

"Ha!" She laughed when she saw me. "You were right, Sean. He looks terrible."

"I really don't think I look that bad." I pushed down the front of my neatly ironed shirt, my black tie.

"Get in the chair." Sean shoved me before a huge mirror lit by several white bulbs. I got a proper look at myself. They were right. I looked terrible. My black eye was stark, a deep blue brushstroke curving out from beside my reddened nose. I smoothed down my beard. It didn't help.

"The beard's coming off," Sean was telling the woman as he shoved shirts aside on the rack, examining each one. "Make sure you get the sideburns."

The lady searched around on the counter, moved bottles of lotion and canisters of powder.

"When Cali is done with you, you put this on." Sean tugged a rich royal blue shirt off the rack and showed it to me in the mirror.

"Is it my size?"

"Yes." Sean put a hand on the woman's shoulder. "I called Cali yesterday. She works on the teen dramas. I knew—I fucking *knew* the *Stories and Lives* crew would get up to their usual tricks. The white shirt and black tie is a classic example." He flipped my tie in disgust. I smoothed it down.

"They told me to wear this!"

"Of course they did. You look like you're on your way to court."

I looked at myself in the mirror. He was right. I looked like a thug heading to a court appearance. How had I not spotted this? I'd escorted plenty of cokeheads on the bad side of a binge to court and seen their public defenders thrust plain black cotton ties at them, plucked from a drawer full of identical ties. Plain black cotton—the cheapest choice—over plain white cotton shirts—the safest choice. The shirt on the rack, a deep royal blue, looked interesting. Expensive. It made me look like I had an opinion about my appearance. Like I had a personality. Like I was human.

Cali the emergency makeup artist shaved my face, trimmed my hair, brushed it back and did something to it with a comb and some gel that made it seem like it had some kind of deliberate shape. She stood between my knees and lifted my chin and dabbed foundation on my bruises.

I tried to hide it, but I was in extreme physical pleasure at being touched. It was not a sexual pleasure, but a warm, heady feeling of having affection and attention applied to me, the kind I imagined dogs felt when an owner who'd returned from a long time away scratched them just right, rubbed down their ears, whispered gentle affirmations of their goodness. Since my accusation, people didn't touch me, not the way they had before I was marked by that fiery curse that was pedophilia. Sure, there were very heroic handshakes. Carefully considered, rigid hugs. Linda and Sharon tended to shove me around like a staggering drunk, and Amanda was as likely to pat my arm as she was to punch me. But this woman I didn't know was smoothing a cold, soft makeup pad over my nose and jaw, her thumb on my chin and fingers on my temple, directing my head this way and that. I felt safe enough to close my eyes as she worked the makeup gently as close as she could to the base of the stitches Amanda had put in my face. She talked absent-mindedly about makeup jobs she had done, special effects gigs, my skin, the colors she was using. When I looked at myself after she was finished, I jolted in my chair. I reminded myself of the Ted who appeared in my wedding photographs, that smiling young man who'd somehow managed to snag a wonderful woman before anyone else had. Who, against all odds, convinced her to marry him.

When I settled again into the wingback chair across from Lara Eggington, she looked up from the pages resting in her lap and scowled at me, gave the heavy, worn smirk of someone who had lost a battle. People fluttered around us, adjusting mics and lights, touching our hair, doing checks. I sat quietly, remembering Sean's brief.

"Her main aim will be to get you upset," Sean had reminded me. "She'll try to make you frustrated as fast as she can so they can have you looking edgy and dangerous on-screen. She'll call you dirty names. She'll change up the questions so you don't go too far down a certain track. Remember, you're the monster here. They're going to paint you as the monster in the ads. In the commentary. Don't smile or laugh but try not to be too cool or despondent either. Stay human, Ted. At all times, try to stay human."

Lara arranged her legs now at an uncomfortable-looking angle, her knees together and glossy hairless shins reflecting the light like chrome. She put the heels of her stilettos side by side and sighed, whipped her hair, an apparent signal for her people that she was ready to begin.

"We're rolling," someone said.

Dear Diary,

It was her fault, a lot of it. The way it began. I mean, obviously I was attracted to her. That first day, when she'd popped her head up over the fence, Penny had dumbfounded me. Her cheeky, sassy nature. Her big, dark eyes. But I know what I am, and I knew the girl next door was off-limits. I'm not that dumb. But that's what they make you, I guess, those special loves in your life. They make you dumb. You slip into fantasies about them, in which they become too perfect, so attuned to everything you've ever desired that when you see them again some sparkle of that fantasy is still lingering around them, and they're like fairies, angels, walking in the everyday world. The next time I saw Penny, we were having a long-awaited backyard barbecue Chloe had been whining about, the "housewarming," our uni friends getting drunk and covering our pathetic little yard in cigarette ash and fallen sausages. Chloe was talking about getting a dog. I was thinking about throwing myself off a bridge. And then Penny was there, her pale face rising over the fence like a perfect moon shining hopefully, soothingly, on a sailor lost at sea.

"What are you guys doing?" She caught my eye, jutted her chin. I

went over and the crowd around the plastic chairs hardly seemed to miss me.

"Having a stupid party," I said. Rolled my eyes. "It wasn't my idea."

"Is it a birthday party?"

"No, just a housewarming."

"It'll be my birthday soon."

"When?"

"March fifteenth. I'll be eleven. I'm almost a teenager."

"You sure are getting there." I smiled. I heard Chloe somewhere behind me telling our guests I was "great with kids."

"What's that?" Penny reached over with her milk-white arm and pointed at my drink. I had the almost uncontrollable desire to grab the arm before it slithered away. Nibble the impossibly tender flesh. See if I could resist hurting her.

"It's rum and Coke."

"What does that taste like?"

"It's great," I said. I took a sip, glanced back toward the people at the table. Chloe was regaling them with tales of her latest bare scrape through the first round of assignments. "You want to try some?"

"Sure!" Penny grinned.

"You can't tell anyone, though." I gave her the serious eyes, a devoted friend offering her a test, something to weigh our future interactions upon. She wanted to be my friend. She wanted me to like her. This was serious business—whether or not she could be trusted. "Can you keep secrets?"

"I'm the best secret keeper," she huffed, affronted. "Of course I can."

I rose up on my tiptoes, trying to shield the exchange with my head and shoulders. I passed the drink over the fence, swift, keeping an eye on my guests. Penny took an awkward gulp and coughed.

"Urgh! That's weird."

"Kind of burny, right?"

"I think it's in my nose." She coughed, pinched her little nostrils. "Why do you drink that?"

"I don't know." I looked into my drink. "It's fun, I guess?"

"Not for me." She made a vomiting sort of noise and hopped off the fence, disappearing into the twilight green of her backyard. I rose up and tried to see where she went. My little earth angel wisping away from me again.

LARA: Good evening. I'm Lara Eggington. Tonight, *Stories and Lives* brings you an exclusive interview with Australia's most hated man. Ted Conkaffey is an accused violent pedophile, recently charged with the abduction and attempted murder of a thirteen-year-old girl. He's never spoke publically about the arrest and court case that stopped a nation—the sudden, unexplained withdrawal of charges by the director of public prosecutions that sent members of the Australian public reeling. Tonight, you'll hear what he has to say about the crime, as well as a bombshell that threatens to blow this case wide open. Ted, welcome to the program.

TED: Thanks, Lara. But what's this bombshell you mentioned?

LARA: Don't worry about that. That's just promo stuff.

TED: Sean, do we . . . <inaudible> Okay. All right. Yep, we can go on.

LARA: Ted, why don't you start by telling us a little bit about yourself?

TED: Well, my name is Ted Conkaffey. I'm a father. I have a beautiful daughter, Lillian, who just turned two. Um. I used to be a drug squad detective with the New South Wales police, and now I work assisting a, uh, a private detective.

LARA: But that's not why we're here today, is it?

TED: No.

LARA: Why don't you go on?

TED: Well, I . . . Last year I was arrested and charged with a terrible, terrible crime that I did not commit. That I had nothing at all to do with.

LARA: You seem to be having trouble even saying out loud what that crime was, Ted. Is that because you're ashamed?

TED: No.

LARA: You're not ashamed?

TED: I guess it is hard to say it out loud. It's a horrible thing. But, I mean, sure, I'll say it. The crime that I was charged with was the abduction, rape, and attempted murder of a thirteen-year-old girl.

LARA: Claire Bingley.

TED: Yes. Claire Bingley.

LARA: Ted, you told police you were, as the old saying goes, just in the wrong place at the wrong time. That somehow, on the tenth of April 2016, at exactly 12:45 p.m., you pulled over into a bus stop on the side of the Hume Highway for some obscure reason, and that—

TED: I'm not sure the reason was completely obscure.

LARA: Just let me get this out for the sound bite.

TED: Sure. Okay.

LARA: And that you saw and spoke to thirteen-year-old Claire Bingley at the roadside. You were witnessed there, talking to the child, by no less than twelve people driving by on the highway. You said that when the coast was clear, when the highway became empty, you simply drove off, leaving the girl untouched.

TED: There are a few problems with what you're saying there, Lara.

LARA: Are there?

TED: Yes.

LARA: Why don't you set the record straight for the people of Australia, then, if you can.

TED: I pulled over that day because there was a noise in the back of my car. A tapping noise. I wanted to stop it. And that's a fairly reasonable thing to do, I think.

LARA: Uh-huh.

TED: I didn't even see the child standing there.

LARA: Claire Bingley, you mean? She has a name, Ted.

TED: But *you* just called her "the child." Earlier, I mean.

LARA: Please, go on.

TED: I didn't even see Claire. One of the witnesses said that I turned off the road suddenly, suggesting that I pulled over because I saw her. I never saw her. I was just trying to fix a noise. I got out of the car and I spoke to her, yes, but, I mean, I hardly even remember what I said. The whole thing was just nothing. It was all very casual.

LARA: What happened to Claire was "nothing"? It was "casual"?

TED: No, Lara. Jesus. My pulling over my car was casual. My intentions toward Claire were nonexistent. Nothing.

LARA: And then you just drove away. At the exact same time she was abducted.

TED: No, just before she was abducted.

LARA: It seems like an incredible tale, Ted. Some people would say "unbelievable."

TED: People say all kinds of things, Lara.

LARA: You must be the unluckiest person in Australia.

TED: I . . . No. Nice try, but we both know that what has happened to me pales in comparison to what happened to Claire Bingley.

LARA: Still, you've lost everything. You lost your job. Your wife left you.

TED: I'd appreciate it if we left Kelly out of this, actually, if you don't mind.

LARA: She left you rather suddenly.

TED: I don't think—

LARA: Did Kelly know something about you that Australia didn't? Was she surprised by what happened? By your arrest?

TED: Of course she was surprised!

LARA: Because there are some things we know about you, Ted. Some disturbing things we've uncovered during investigations into your life.

TED: Um.

LARA: You have a penchant for pornography featuring extremely young women. You and your wife, Kelly, fought on the morning of the incident.

TED: See, those two things are not related. You're trying to make it sound like they're related.

LARA: I think I'd be upset with my husband if I found he was addicted to pornography.

TED: Addicted! I'm not. I wasn't *addicted*. I owned a couple of DVDs.

LARA: Why?

TED: Because . . . I don't know. Men watch pornography, Lara. Hundreds of thousands of men. When you're married, sometimes you're tired or your wife is tired and your sex life starts to suffer a bit. Kelly and I were both working, and we had a newborn baby, and life just gets like that sometimes. Look, this isn't relevant to the case. It's not relevant to anything.

LARA: You don't think it's relevant that your sex life was "suffering," as you call it, and you argued with your wife the day of Claire's abduction? That you left the house in an agitated, aggressive state—

TED: I was not aggressive. I don't get aggressive when I'm angry. I never have.

LARA: You don't?

TED: No. If anything, I sulk. Ask my wife. She'll tell you.

LARA: Your ex-wife?

TED: The divorce is—we're still doing the paperwork. Do we have to put that in?

LARA: But you can become aggressive? You're lying when you say you're not aggressive.

TED: What are you talking about?

LARA: Wouldn't you have been trained in your job as a drug squad cop to be aggressive? Isn't your job all about kicking down doors and roughing people up? Manhandling people? Reacting with violence?

TED: This is ridiculous. You're drawing some pretty bizarre parallels here.

LARA: Bizarre? You were arrested, Ted. You were charged. These ideas aren't bizarre. They were convincing enough to compel the police to arrest you.

TED: <inaudible>

LARA: Your case, and the amount of attention it has received, has brought some very interesting characters out of the woodwork. There's a podcast that has gained subscribers from all over the world that expounds on various theories about who Claire's attacker might be.

TED: The *Innocent Ted* podcast has been very good to me.

LARA: Including its founder, one Fabiana Grisham. How did you meet Fabiana, Ted? What was the nature of your relationship?

TED: Platonic.

LARA: Really?

TED: I don't have anything juicy or titillating to say to you about Fabiana and I. She was a reporter investigating the case. She founded a podcast about it. She believes in my innocence. Her support for me has made her life very difficult, and I don't plan on making it any more difficult here. She's a good reporter. A good person.

LARA: A good reporter might be stretching it. I have a list here of some of the theories mentioned in the podcast for your innocence. That you were framed by your colleagues in the police. That a serial killer was responsible. That—

TED: I haven't listened to the show.

LARA: Why not?

TED: The whole thing is rather distressing to me.

LARA: I guess you might feel like the podcast just spreads information about your case further and further across the world, when you just want to forget it. Move on.

TED: Mmm-hmm.

LARA: Because you never know who might pop up out of the woodwork next, right?

TED: I suppose.

LARA: Well unfortunately for you, Ted, someone has popped up.

TED: Excuse me?

LARA: I'd like to play you a small section of video on a laptop here, and I'd like you to comment, if you can.

TED: What is this?

LARA: Just watch.

TED: Okay.

MELANIE: *My name is Melanie Springfield. I dated Ted Conkaffey in high school. I was fifteen when we met.*

TED: Oh my god.

MELANIE: *Ted and I had a strange relationship. I guess you always do, when you're kids. Like, it's never normal. You're trying to figure out what real relationships are all about, how to navigate them, I guess. But at the time, almost from the beginning, I knew what was going on with Ted was very wrong. I'm ready to tell the world what really happened with him and me, and my little sister, Elise. Ted Conkaffey had a predatory relationship with my younger sister. He used me to get to her. She was eight years old.*

TED: *Oh my god.*

LARA: Ted, do you have anything to say about what you've just seen?

TED: I . . . I don't. I can't believe this. Sean? Can we—

SEAN WILKINS: <inaudible>

LARA: Just ignore them. Answer my questions. Do you remember Melanie Springfield and her sister Elise?

TED: I remember Melanie. The sister, no. Not . . . not really. I mean I knew she had a sister. Sean, should I? I don't know what to say. Jesus. *Jesus.*

LARA: Can you explain Melanie's allegations?

TED: No. I can't. Absolutely not. I don't know what she's talking about. I don't know why she would say these things.

SEAN WILKINS: Stop the interview. Stop it right now.

LARA: It's fine. It's fine. Let's go back to the day Claire was abducted.

TED: What?

LARA: Ted, let's—

SEAN WILKINS: Turn the cameras off. <inaudible> Right now.

TED: Sean?

LARA: You agreed to an interview in full. You're under contract.

TED: Why would she say that? Why would she say that?

Pip was fifteen when he died. She remembered the feeling of the afternoon sun on her narrow shoulders as she stood at the doorstep, looking at the slim enameled door handle waiting for her grip. The trigger of a starting gun on her evening nightmare. Pip had been doing everything she could to stay at school later and later as his drinking grew worse, offering to clean up the classroom after the last period, chatting to the reception staff as they saw the last buses off from the front gates. On Monday that week she'd picked a fight with her math teacher and scored herself a detention that took her to seven in the evening, when her father was already well into the sleepy phase of his drinking ritual, when he would stop rattling around the kitchen, kicking things over in the backyard, yelling about the neighbors. When he would sink, like an angry guard dog, into the safety of his chair.

This afternoon, there'd been no cleaning to be done at the school. The receptionists had all brushed her off, and her math teacher had been in too good a mood to do more than roll his eyes at her taunts. She'd wandered the local parks throwing stones in the ponds and scratching up the dirt with her shoes. She couldn't avoid him forever.

So at five o'clock Pip walked into her house and heard him inside, slamming the door of the fridge.

Into the dark, cold cloud of his presence.

Pip put her bag on the hook in the hall and called out a greeting. He didn't answer. When he was out of the recliner by the television he was at his most dangerous, so she held her breath, went to the bedroom, shut the door quietly.

She wasn't naïve. Pip knew she had it lucky, as far as arsehole fathers went. One of her friends at school had told her how her father had dragged her into the backyard by her hair and kicked her in the ribs after he caught her stealing from his wallet. She'd read newspaper articles about fathers who sold their little girls to the sex trade, burned them with cigarettes, wiped them out one night after being sacked from his corporate job. Pip's father didn't do any of those things. He just grabbed her and squeezed her every now and then. Squeezed her until her muscles ached, growled something in her ear so low she barely heard it or so loud her eardrums pulsed. He shoved her sometimes. He'd left a bruise on her hip this week knocking her out of the way of the back door. She had a three-stripe purple band around the top of her arm from him yanking her out of the corner of the kitchen. It wasn't much on the scale of things. And it hadn't been happening long.

Her mother had only been gone a year. Pip had been spending her lunches at school touring the internet, trying to find her, like a detective. She saw glimmers of the drawn, pale woman she knew mentioned in the comments of her friends and workmates on MySpace, but never the woman herself. She'd scanned pictures of men and women at parties or on the beach for the outline of her, the long wispy hair, her pointed features. Pip didn't know what she'd say if she ever found her. She supposed her first question might be why she never said goodbye. Why she didn't take Pip with her. Why she left her here with him. They'd been wandering in the fog of anger and sadness that surrounded him all the time, holding hands, hoping, rather than knowing, that somewhere just beyond their reach the fog would clear and there would be a safe haven. Pip's mother had dropped her hand and dissolved into the mist without warning. Without, it seemed, regret.

The questioning pulsed in her mind all the time, suddenly stopping time, causing her to sometimes find herself standing, staring at the floor, feeling the loss of her mother. Trying to make an absent limb move and function again, failing silently.

She snapped out of her dream. Pip knew she couldn't lock herself away in the bedroom for too long. He'd feel neglected. She changed into a T shirt and shorts and opened the door again, stepped back into the cold fog. He was at the window looking out, sunset lighting his bristly face. It was one of the last times she would see him alive. Red in his irises. Reflections of clouds.

"I don't feel good," he said.

"What do you mean?" she asked, taking the empty brown bottles from where they stood lined like soldiers along the back of the sink.

"What the fuck do you think I mean? I mean I don't feel good. I don't feel well."

"It's been hot today," she offered, wincing. There had been back-burning across the nearby national park. Cutting back, thinning the rainforest. Trains and trucks trying to shift the cane before the fire season began. She'd smelled smoke on the wind walking home.

She started on the washing up. Felt her father watching her. The memories of the first time he had grabbed her wouldn't fade. He'd been standing by the table, reading the note her mother left, and Pip had come crashing through the front door of the house into his upturned world like a happy puppy. A year had passed, and she still remembered the feel of the bones in his fingers pressing into her flesh like it was happening in that very instant.

"You don't fucking care," her dad concluded when she had nothing more to add about his being unwell. She tried to think what her mother might have said if she were there, but came up with nothing. She was the child. She was the one who was supposed to go to him unwell, needing care, solutions, sympathy. The world hadn't righted itself after her mother left. It was still backward, her father throwing a tantrum, she trying to focus on the dishes.

When he went to the recliner, she exhaled with relief. Rainbows on the bubbles at her fingers. His sudden yelp was like electricity, made her skin break out in little sparkles of pain.

"What is it?"

"I said I don't know!" He rubbed his chest. "I don't feel good!"

"What can I do?"

He seemed to be hiccupping. Or coughing. Grabbing at his ribs. She stood with her back to the kitchen counter and watched, frozen, every muscle taut. Pip knew what it was before he did. The confusion blazed in the whites of his eyes.

Only two weeks earlier she'd sat with her friends on the floorboards in the school hall while the PE teacher wrestled with the old television and DVD player, trying to make the blue screen flicker with life. She'd watched, halfheartedly picking rubber from the soles of her shoes, as cartoon people pumped on cartoon chests and breathed into gaping mouths, lips locking perfectly over lips while numbers flashed on the screen. The training video's voice-over was strangely cheerful as its characters tried desperately to save the lives of children pulled from pools and elderly men fallen from treadmills.

NEXT, observe if the patient is breathing. It's important to LOOK! LISTEN! and FEEL!

The cartoon people in the CPR training video had remained pretty and happily smiling, even through unconsciousness. Pip's father was not happy. He twisted toward her, out of the chair, still making those little hiccups of breathless pain, loose strands of his dirty hair shivering. His eyes went to the cordless phone on the counter beside her. The words wouldn't come. Pip didn't look. She knew what he wanted. Knew the phone was there. Knew she should grab it and dial.

But she didn't.

Pip didn't move. Her father crawled unsteadily toward her across the living room floor to the edge of the kitchen, reaching, the pain seeming to make him want to curl his body into a ball. His face flushed purple, then white, the dark cloud now inside him, swelling up and out through the surface of his skin. He collapsed within centimeters of her. Hand grabbing, fingers extended, for her foot.

She slid down the kitchen counter and looked at the top of his head. The bald spot. The unfamiliar shape of his face from above, still brows and dots of sweat on the bridge of his nose.

Seconds passed. Minutes. She imagined herself leaping forward, rolling him into the recovery position, checking for a pulse as an inappropriately merry voice narrated, *Now Pip's applying her hands to the STERNUM REGION!*

She did not apply her hands to the sternum region. She had, in time, reached up, pulled herself into a crouch, her whole body suddenly heavy with fatigue, shaking as she moved. She took the cordless phone, fell back against the cupboards, clutched it at her chest.

Still, she didn't dial.

She watched her father die of a heart attack on the floor of their little kitchen, and didn't perform CPR, and didn't call for an ambulance. Switches and dials inside him flipped off, one at a time. The lights going out along wide, empty hallways, death walking from room to airless, soulless room, shutting the windows and doors. Pulling the curtains. Closing time. Pip clasped the handset to her chest like a child's doll and did nothing. A last red slice of sunlight lingered on the ceiling in the living room, narrow and long like a finish line. It faded and disappeared, and sometime after it was gone she pushed the spongy buttons on the phone and said the words she was supposed to say.

When had he stopped breathing? the operator asked.

Only moments ago.

Did Pip know CPR?

Yes.

Had she tried it?

Yes.

Would she continue applying it now while the ambulance came?

Of course. Yes.

The dispatcher hung up. The ambulance left the hospital. Details were entered into a computer somewhere. Alerts and signals appeared on screens. Pip imagined these things happening as she sat and clutched the phone and looked at her dead dad and didn't do CPR. Didn't touch him at all. Didn't even pretend.

When Pip got older and became a cop herself, she learned what she'd done wrong that evening. She'd told the ambulance dispatcher on the phone that her father had died only moments earlier. That she'd tried CPR, but he hadn't responded. That she'd try again. It would have been obvious to the paramedics when they arrived that those were lies. Pip's father had fallen on his front and remained there. The purple patches rapidly spreading over his chest and the undersides of his arms and the side of his face as his blood stopped circulating and headed downward told as much. He'd died and he'd lain there, untouched. Pip had obviously not attempted CPR. Her father's shirt was still buttoned. His body temperature, and the pale, gray, waxy finish to his skin would have told the paramedics that he had been dead at least an hour before the call was made. Probably two.

There should have been consequences. Probably not criminal ones. But failing to render assistance to her dying father, and then lying about the fact that she hadn't, were not the actions of a mentally healthy teenager. Someone might have insisted an official file be created for this child. A legal caution entered. Someone might have enforced a psychological assessment and entry into a counseling program, brought Pip's actions to the attention of the Department of Social Services. In all, someone might have marked this moment in fifteen-year-old Pip Sweeney's history. Made sure she never forgot it. And that it never forgot her.

But instead, preparing at any moment to be handcuffed and dragged off to jail, Pip silently accompanied her father in the ambulance to the Cairns Base Hospital and then waited in a long, empty hallway while someone tried to track down her mother. She stared at her shoes and listened to the clicking and beeping of machines in the rooms around her and rehearsed what she would say when they finally asked her why she had let her father die. She hardly noticed when an old woman in a white coat came and sat down beside her and spoke to her for ten minutes, not about her father but about her school life, her friends, idle chatter. The small encounter with the old woman with the big wet eyes and purple painted fingernails had hardly recorded itself on Pip's brain.

When the police did finally come, Pip had burst into tears at the sight of the cuffs on their belts, the police car visible through the distant glass sliding doors to the hospital. Once she had started, it was hard to stop. The tears had been so panicked, so desperate, that the two officers had looked at each other, concerned. They'd got in contact with her uncle, they told her. They were taking her there to stay with him until further arrangements could be made. Pip had risen shakily, assisted by the tall, wiry female of the police pair. The woman's warm hand had slid down into hers as they walked down the corridor together, and for the first time in a long time Pip felt like she was in the presence of her mother.

Pip was thinking about her father now as she signed in to the visitors' log at the medical examiner's reception desk at Cairns Hospital, just two floors below the corridor where she had sat all those years ago. He would have come through these doors then, down the long green hall and into the tiled rooms beyond. It was Dr. Valerie Gratteur who had sat and talked with the teenage Pip for a short while, who had ignored the blotches on her father's arms and chest and face, left them out of the unexpected death report. She'd ruled that she believed CPR had been performed to no avail to save the man's life. Years later, when Pip was newly graduated as a young constable, she'd come here and tried to ask the old woman why she had done what she'd done. Val had brushed her aside, trying to say at first she didn't remember the case. When Pip insisted, she'd said only that her job didn't involve just looking at the body. "I see everything," she said. Dr. Valerie Gratteur had disguised Pip's failure.

And yes, that's how Pip thought of it now, as a failure to save him. She should have understood his downfall better. Should have helped him recover from her mother's loss. Should have called an ambulance. Should have flipped him, ripped open his shirt and pumped on his chest, and given him another chance.

She tried to shake these thoughts away as she opened the door to Lab One.

There were two bodies on tables in the center of the room. Pip hadn't been ready for the sight of them lying there, stark beneath white sheets, toes pointing upward, making peaks in the spotless fabric. They looked absurdly like stage props, Halloween decorations, the obvious curves and dips of the human form illuminated by bright light from above. Two young lives destroyed. Dr. Gratteur was nowhere in sight.

Pip waited, fiddled with the badge on the chain at her chest. A sickly curiosity pulsed in her. She went to the nearest corpse, tried to see the face through the tiny holes in the fabric. Closed eyes. Dark hair. Pip glanced toward the double doors at the end of the room and reached out.

The body surged upward.

"DON'T TOUCH THE BODIES!" Amanda screamed.

Amanda thrust the sheet downward, ripping the fabric from Pip's fingers, springing into a seated position like a jack-in-the-box. Pip's yowl of horror ballooning up against the ceiling, the tiled walls, seemed impossibly amplified. She fell back against the bench at the side of the room as Amanda's laughter cracked through the air, maniacal hacking.

"You fucking bitch," Pip snarled, feeling heat rush up from her chest into her face. "You fucking little bitch!"

"Oh god," Amanda was gasping. "Oh, I got you good. I got you so good. Oh Jesus. Oh my god that's funny. Oh. Oh." She covered her face, rocking back and forth, a grotesque puppet of a dead body on the mortuary table, lamenting its own death. The laughs seemed impossible to suppress. Amanda struggled for breath.

"What exactly is going on in here?" Val Gratteur had pushed through the rubber double doors with a steel gurney, a body covered in a sheet, the rightful corpse to complete the duo of murdered bartenders. "You two are screaming blue murder."

"I got Sweeney so good," Amanda gasped, thumping her own chest with her fist, trying to drive out the giggles still rippling up from her belly. "She just about shat her pants. Didn't you, Sweens? Didn't you? Oh god, that was funny."

"The old animated corpse gag." The doctor gave Sweeney a sympathetic look. "I haven't played that one in a long, long time. We used to get the trainee nurses down here on their first shifts and give them the terrors with that one. Really, Pip, you might have expected it, knowing this idiot here was coming along today." She nudged Amanda off the slab.

"This *hilarious* idiot," Amanda corrected.

"You two know each other?" Sweeney straightened her clothes, trying to take the focus off her own humiliation.

"She knows my handiwork." Amanda winked at the doctor. Val shook her head.

"I have dealt with cases involving Amanda in the past," Val said. "We met for the first time at Ted's. I care for Ted's geese when he's away, and Amanda was there last time, making a nuisance of herself."

"A *hilarious* nuisance."

Sweeney kept her eye on Amanda as Dr. Gratteur uncovered the bodies of the two murdered bartenders. The petite investigator stood with her lower back leaning against the table, her arms folded, wearing the wandering look of someone quietly sinking into a daydream, her mind floating off somewhere else. All over Amanda's body, little itches and twitches seemed to flicker, a shift of weight from her right to left leg, a finger tapping restlessly against her bicep, the gentlest of tics of her head to the right. When the bodies were uncovered completely, Amanda looked up and yawned. Sweeney felt her stomach tightening at the sight of the girl's jaw clicking back into place.

There was no emotion in there. Amanda might have been looking at mannequins, rather than the bodies of two young innocents.

"All right," Dr. Gratteur said, pushing back the sleeves of her blouse. She pulled a pair of pale rubber gloves onto her fingers. "Here they are. The lovers."

"Amanda told you her theory?" Sweeney piped up. "About the affair?"

"No." Dr. Gratteur dropped back on her heels. "Why? Was this a secret?" She pointed to Keema, Andrew.

"Yes. He's got a girlfriend. *Had* a girlfriend." Sweeney cleared her throat.

"Well, Keema's saliva was on Andrew's penis," Dr. Gratteur said. "So unless there's some fantastic explanation for such a phenomenon, I'm going to assume they were having a sexual relationship."

"I told you so!" Amanda yelled, startling Sweeney. The girl's grin was spread wide. "Urgh. I love to say that. I was right. Every *night* I'm *right*. I'm *right* because I'm quite *bright*, out of *sight*, filled with intellectual *light*."

"Trite," Val said.

"The affair puts Andrew's girlfriend Stephanie up on the suspect list," Sweeney mused. "She might have come in and shot them as an act of revenge for his infidelity. We'll look at her alibi again. See if Keema was involved with anyone, also, who might have been upset by the relationship."

"This one." Dr. Gratteur moved around the gurney that held Andrew's body. "He might hold some clues for you. Come closer, both of you."

Amanda skipped over into position beside the doctor. As Sweeney approached, she felt the tightness in her stomach increasing. She had managed to barely glance at the bodies of Keema and Andrew before, but now there was nowhere to look but at the young man's pale, limp form, his flaccid penis and dark pubic hair, thick thighs flattened against the polished steel. The cavity in his chest and abdomen where Dr. Gratteur had cut into him to investigate his internal organs, to be sure beyond question that it had been the gunshot wound to his head that had killed him, had been neatly closed. But Sweeney knew that the organs, returned to their place in his body, were not sitting right. His stomach was strangely deflated. The mussed, sleepy look to his face she knew was caused by the sagging of tissue and muscles no longer being pumped with blood. He looked like a bad clay replica of himself. Impossibly smooth. Slightly pudgy.

And the wound at the top of his head. A mess of flesh and hair and bone. Sweeney exhaled and looked away.

"There was dirt," Dr. Gratteur said, lifting the corpse's palm. "Here, in the webbing of his fingers. Caught up beneath a silver ring he was wearing. None under the nails."

"Dirt," Amanda said. "Huh."

"What's a bartender doing with dirt on his hands?"

"Well, he must have been outside the bar. In the rainforest," Sweeney said. "He must have . . . I don't know. Picked something up? Picked up a dirty rock or a stick?"

"Was there any dirt on his clothes?" Dr. Gratteur asked. "I didn't get the clothes. They went straight to forensics."

"I don't know. I'll check."

Amanda was examining Andrew's hands. She smelled the fingers, held them against her cheek. Spread the palm and looked at the lines there.

"Maybe he fell," she said suddenly.

"What makes you say that?"

"Well, the dirt was in the webbing." She spread her hands before her, fingers wide. "If he'd picked something up, the dirt would have been on the palm. On the outer surface of the ring. If he fell, though, he'd have spread his hands out to stop himself. Scooped up the dirt in the forward motion, getting it in the webbing, into the gap between the ring and the finger. He'd have dusted his hands, maybe, when he got up, but the dirt in the webbing would have remained unless he washed his hands."

"That's what I was thinking." Dr. Gratteur smiled. "So he fell outside the bar. Didn't have time to wash his hands before he was killed. Why did he fall? What was he doing out there?"

"Maybe he saw the attack coming," Sweeney said. "Maybe he was running. Trying to get away. The earth is moist. Fallen leaves everywhere, wet. He slipped."

"If he was running, why run into the bar?" Amanda asked. "Why not run away?"

"Maybe he was running in to grab a weapon," Sweeney mused. "Warn Keema."

The three women looked at the bodies before them. Amanda was still holding the dead boy's hand, like the family member of a coma patient, trying to give the lifeless body strength, trying to warm the limp fingers. Sweeney watched her. Her face was still cold. Nothing behind the eyes.

Total mental shutdown. I recognized the sensation from my time in prison processing, those red-hot minutes between incarceration at my own police station and internment at Silverwater remand center. I was moved about, herded like a mindless cow, my wrists in chains. Onto the bus. Off the bus. Down a corridor to the back of a queue of men waiting to be seen by the medical officer. Being given my physical, standing naked in a room filled with prison guards with batons. Only complete emotional detachment could have got me through it, through this absurd transition from police officer to criminal. I went where I was told to go. Lifted my hands, turned, bowed my head, signed pieces of paper thrust before me. Took the stack of folded clothes and toiletry items and went to my cell. Sat on the bed. Focused on continuing to breathe.

The interview with Lara Eggington actually went on after my old girlfriend Melanie Springfield's revelation. I was aware that Sean had tried to bring it to a halt. That the crew had filmed him arguing with the producer. That there had been threats. Talk of contracts. I'd answered more questions. The focus had turned away from the new accusation. I had no memory of the rest of the interview when the lights above me clicked off.

I stood and relinquished all control again, all emotion. Sean and the goons argued in the hall. I looked out the windows at the street, where a crowd of press was gathering. They'd got wind of the fact that I'd be appearing on *Stories and Lives*, probably had people camped out, waiting to see when I would exit the building. Word had spread fast. The driveway of the Channel Three offices was crowded with people, cameras.

"He's coming with me," Sean was saying. "I'll have my colleague come over. We're going to work on a strategy. We're going to sue. We're fucking suing. Ted? Ted? Come on, mate. You're coming with me." He grabbed my arm.

"Khalid says to take him to the house," Linda said. "So he's going to the house."

I guess the goons won out, because hands directed me, and voices propelled me, and I found myself in the huge, lush car again, two enormous silhouettes in the front seats, motionless, cameras flashing at the windows. I had vague memories of them pushing through the crowd, one ahead of me, one behind, slapping cameras away from me. Sharon palming a cameraman in the chest, almost knocking him off his feet.

I looked at my phone as we drove away. I googled myself without realizing what I was doing, without making the conscious decision to do it. Already, the page was filled with links.

BREAKING
New Conkaffey accusations revealed on upcoming
Stories and Lives exclusive.

BREAKING
Stories and Lives producers tight-lipped on new
Conkaffey developments.

BREAKING
Speculation hidden Conkaffey victim will speak.

Breaking. Breaking. Not only had someone leaked that I'd be at the Channel Three building giving an interview, but someone somewhere had let it slip to the world that there were new allegations. The news was spreading lightning fast, rushing through layers of cyberspace like bushfire. I gripped my head, hid my face in my palms. I could almost feel my mind splitting, falling apart. Logical thoughts ceasing to come to any conclusion, an impossible tangle of disconnected impulses.

How could she—I never—I didn't—I don't even know—What if she—Why didn't she—

I lost time. Suddenly I was following the big men through the huge double doors of a mansion somewhere, wincing at the light bouncing off the water of an oversized fountain embedded in the manicured lawn. There were voices inside, a clatter of dull sounds punctuated here and there by the sparkle of female laughter. Khalid Farah's house. I realized I had been here before. I had kicked down these very doors, seated the immaculately dressed man on these very cream couches in the front sitting room while my colleagues crashed through his belongings, looking for drugs.

There were drugs here now, on a coffee table surrounded by tattooed men. I glimpsed them lounging in the dim light as I walked past the door. Dark eyes rimmed by long black lashes, snarling lips, silver chains. The front room guards. A team of men with greased, shining haircuts, patterns shaved into the stubble above ears. I kept walking. Almost ran into a woman carrying a plate of little meatball-y looking things in through the double doors to a huge kitchen. There was a table of people in another expansive room off the foyer, sitting down to lunch. Children. Old people. Lots of red wine.

"Cappuccino!" Khalid's voice came through the French doors to the balcony. We emerged into the day again. I remembered walking out onto the sweeping, empty space during the drug raid, looking at the glimmering harbor beyond, peeking between similarly oversized houses. The young prince was leaning against the stone railing now, a glass in hand. It was cold out here. Or was I still in shock, still reeling from the interview hours earlier? My phone was buzzing in my pocket. I noticed a group of ladies further down the huge patio, sitting crowded around deck chairs, wineglasses in hand.

"Now there's a face." Khalid smirked, jutting his chin at me. "I've seen that face on little boys headin' off to the can for the first time. You look sick, bro."

"I don't feel good."

"I seen it on the news. You're fucked."

"Mmm." I rubbed my stomach, felt a burning in my throat. I'd forgotten how to put words together. They were like marbles in my mouth, clacking against my teeth. "It's not okay. Things are not okay."

"Who's this girl? Why's she saying these things? Tell me what's goin' on."

His tone had changed. The "tell me what's goin' on" was a command. For the first time, I realized how dangerous this situation might be. I was in the house of one of the country's most dangerous drug lords, a person who had stuck his neck out for me, believing in my innocence from the outset. His men had been protecting me when a second accusation came down. I knew exactly what he was thinking. It was what the entire world would be thinking as news of the interview spread. What were the odds of an innocent man being accused of the same thing twice? I looked away, again at the women all the way down the other end of the balcony. They were not family members. This group was like the group of men in the front room—Khalid's soldiers, tolerated by his family members because his work and his involvement with these types had paid for the exorbitant roof over all their heads. These women were exotically, unnaturally beautiful, tanned and toned and glittering with expensive fabrics. Heels that looked dangerous to walk in. As I looked back at Khalid, I found him gazing at me skeptically. Was he trying to decide if I found them attractive?

"The woman, she's a girlfriend I had in high school," I said. The words, once trapped, now came spilling out. "Melanie Springfield. She was fifteen when we met. I was eighteen. We went to the same school. It wasn't even a real relationship—it was two kids saying they were together and kissing and going to the movies. It must have lasted . . . I don't know, a couple of weeks? A month?"

"You fucked her?"

"No."

"Come on." Khalid snorted, humorless. "You were eighteen!"

"I was shy," I admitted. "I was . . . I don't know . . . A late bloomer, I guess. Is that even true? When do boys have sex? Urgh. Jesus. I wasn't very popular. I hung out with the nerds."

"So she wasn't your first?"

"No, no. My first wasn't until about a year later, a girl I met at university."

"Well, what's all this bullshit about the little sister then? You didn't even sleep with her? How could you have slept with the little sister?"

"I don't know!" I thrust my hands out. "You tell me! I don't know why she would do this. I can't explain it. I don't even know her. We didn't talk after high school. I didn't really keep up with any of my high school friends. Once I joined the cops, you know, you get a whole bunch of new friends who do what you do, and you don't have time."

Khalid said nothing. He leaned against the balcony rail, watching me, a bored cat. Dangerous, with the potential to spring and slash me to pieces. Waiting for me to explain why he shouldn't.

The memories were flooding back. Embarrassing, self-conscious teenagers, never looking at each other's eyes. "I remember that the little sister, Elise, used to hang around Melanie and me a bit while we were at her house. Melanie hated it. She used to chase the girl away. Those are about the only interactions I had with her. She was the annoying little sister of a girl I barely dated."

It couldn't possibly have been as cold on that balcony as it felt. I gritted my teeth to stop them chattering. I didn't have anything else for Khalid. Any further assurances that I hadn't pursued this child I hardly knew many years ago for underage sex. He glanced at the women at the end of the balcony. Then at me. There seemed to be a specific girl that interested him. A long-limbed brunette in a flowy gold dress.

"You like her?" he asked, tipping his glass in her direction.

"Oh come on, Khalid."

"You can have her, if you want. I think she likes you. I've seen her look over here at you a couple of times."

"And what exactly would that prove?"

"I don't know," he said, knowingly.

"I was with my wife for fourteen years," I said. "Offering me one of your girls isn't going to convince you I'm not what people are saying I am. You just have to believe me or not believe me."

He smiled. I was right. Now was the time to decide. And it seemed he did decide, his eyes wandering over my face, our every interaction perhaps playing through his mind. In time the man straightened, shifted his glass to his other hand and took a sip.

"You want me to make it go away?"

"No," I said. "I certainly do not. I want it to go away, definitely. But I do not want you to do anything about it. You need to be one hundred percent clear on that, Khalid. I know you think you know what's good for me, but that would be very, very bad for me right now."

He shrugged a shoulder, clicked his tongue, disappointed.

"I'm serious," I stressed.

"I got you, bro."

"I've got to go home." I glanced at the horizon. The city skyline, sharp and imposing. "I might have people targeting my house again after this."

"What are you goin' to do 'bout it?" he asked.

"I don't know. Nothing? It might blow over. I'll talk to my lawyer. Maybe . . . Maybe we'll sue? Force her to admit she's lying. Why would she do this? I don't understand. What could she possibly gain from this?"

"Lawsuits," Khalid sighed. "Bro, you oughtta start thinkin' 'bout which side you're on."

"What do you mean?"

"This chick has lied about you," he said. "Whatever the reason. Whatever she gains from it, man. Doesn't matter. She lied. It's a lie that could bury you. Literally put you in the ground."

"I know."

"So you're, what—" he scoffed, sneered. "You're gonna get your fuckin' lawyer onto it? You're gonna see her in court? You fuckin' serious?"

"Maybe?"

"You're dealin' with people on the bad side, Conkaffey." He put a hand on my shoulder, squeezed. "This guy that raped that kid. This chick who's telling lies. They're from the bad world. You gotta treat bad world problems with bad world solutions."

The small, lethal man before me stood strong and proud as a lion. But his eyes were appealing to me. Pleading with me to let him out of his cage. There was, indeed, a bad world, and I'd let myself be led blindly right into its brilliantly lit, lavish town hall: Khalid Farah's mansion. I glanced at the figures behind me in the house, moving shadows clinking glasses and shifting chairs on plush carpets. An endless party in a perfectly decorated hell. I went to the balcony rail and Khalid leaned against it, mirroring me, his arms folded on the cold stone, eyes searching the distant shore.

"You fell off the good ship, bro," the drug lord said. "You're in the water now, and they ain't turnin' back to get you. There are black sails on the horizon. You gonna grab on, or you gonna drown?"

Ships. Boats. Big white planes with huge sail-wings bearing me home to my geese, to the case I should have been working on, the things that were supposed to matter. I walked through the tunnel to the plane with my head down, certain the people walking behind me were talking about me. There were pictures of me on the television screens beside the lists of planes departing and arriving. The public didn't know what *Stories and Lives* was going to reveal about me on the upcoming episode, but one thing was for sure—the entire country would be watching. The show had that kind of pull, and so did my downfall. I needed to get home.

I made eye contact with no one as I headed to my seat, my boarding pass crumpled in my hand, an unconscious gesture. I stopped and unfolded it, glanced at the seat to my right, 10D.

There were children on the seats beside mine. A young boy in the window seat, sixteen maybe. His sister, maybe thirteen, was texting in the middle seat, thumbs dancing over the keys. Two redheads, a pigeon pair. I grabbed at the pain in my throat and looked around desperately for help.

"You right, mate?" said the man behind me, sighing.

"I can't sit here."

The girl in the seat was looking up at me. The unfair perfection of youth. Impossibly soft skin. Her T-shirt had some high-cheekboned rock star with bad hair on it, a celebrity not much older than her roaring into a microphone on her narrow, featureless chest.

"What's the holdup?" Someone further back in the queue.

"I can't sit here," I said. Panic was creeping up my arms, hot liquid rolling into my chest. I looked beyond the line of people behind me, twisted too fast, bashed my bag against the nearest seat. There were red-blazered flight attendants at the end of the plane. I headed down the length of the aircraft to where they stood fiddling with things in the storage area.

"I'm sorry. I can't sit in my seat," I blurted. There were two of them, a man and a woman. The woman turned to me, pursed her red-painted lips and adjusted her immaculate bun like my words might have knocked it askew.

"I'm sorry, sir." She composed a smile. "All passengers have to take their assigned seats, at least for takeoff."

"I can't do that."

"Why not?"

I pulled at the skin at my throat, told myself to stop. Didn't stop. "I just can't. Trust me. You're really going to want to move me."

The male flight attendant had turned around, two bags of small muffins in his hands. He actually stumbled backward a little at the sight of me.

"But, sir—" the woman was saying.

"It's okay, Sheree." He grabbed her shoulder. "It's okay, sir, we'll move you. I've got this."

He wriggled past me in the tight space between my bulk and the thin doors on either side of us leading to the toilet cubicles. I felt the heat draining from my face as he presented a seat in the back row. He took my bag from my fingers, physically and metaphorically lightening my load. I sank into the seat and let myself be dragged mentally into a magazine I found tucked into the back of the seat before me, my heartbeat slowly returning to normal.

I didn't question why the young male flight attendant had saved me. It was easy to assume that upon recognizing me, he'd been quick to act simply because he knew that if someone snapped a picture of me on the plane, regardless of who I sat beside, it would make waves on social media. People might boycott the airline because they'd accommodated me. They might question whether I was properly supervised while in the air, whether I'd lurked menacingly by the toilets, waiting for girls to pounce on. Certainly, seating me beside a teenage girl was business suicide. I was safest tucked away, out of sight, out of mind.

But then, when we had reached cruising altitude, the male flight attendant tapped the top of my magazine and I brought it down from around my face to find him unclipping and pulling down my tray table. He glanced behind himself, secretive, as he put a small plastic bottle of red wine, a plastic cup, and a little packet of cheese and crackers down on the table before me.

"Hang in there, Ted," he murmured, before ducking away again.

It was the best wine and cheese I'd ever had.

There was nothing for it. I needed a bathroom party.

The bathroom parties had started when the geese were very small, so fragile that a stiff breeze could send them rolling helplessly across the lawn like fuzzy gray tumbleweeds. With humidity-cracking storms frequent in Cairns, sometimes it was just too harsh out for the baby birds, so I'd fill the bathtub with a few centimeters of water and drop the lot of them in under the watchful eye of their skeptical mother, still lame, hobbling in the hallway. In the beginning I'd simply sit on the toilet lid and watch the birds ducking and diving in the tepid water, paddling their little feet and exploring the emptiness of the white porcelain towering above them with their beaks. They always seemed like happy creatures to me, because I remembered them gathered at the bottom of the cardboard box when I'd rescued them, squealing in terror on the sandbank where I'd found them. My parental instinct was to try to make them happier, all the time, an inner drive to ensure every possible experience was as enjoyable as it could be. It wasn't much of a leap to grab a couple of plastic bath toys from the supermarket the next time I was doing one of my undercover shopping missions and toss them in with the birds, something interesting to peck at and squabble with on the tiny waves. Then one day I'd brought a book in with me and sat reading as they paddled around. On another occasion I'd played music. Before I knew it, I was lounging in my bathroom while my feathered family played, a glass of wine on the vanity and Neil Diamond in the air. They seemed to like Neil.

When I got home to Crimson Lake I dumped my bag in the doorway and headed straight out the back to where the geese had been locked away in their playhouse overnight. Dr. Valerie Gratteur, my close friend and occasional goose babysitter, had left a note on the fridge, which I barely glanced at in my haste to get to the birds. I recognized a painful yearning in my chest not dissimilar to the kind I had felt when I'd stood in the elevator waiting to see Lillian at the FACS offices. My loves waiting for me. Daddy's home. Everything's okay now.

I don't know much about the intuition of waterfowl, but as I unlatched the playhouse doors they spilled out, a parade of fat, waist-high waddling soldiers all shivering, the dainty feathers of their lean necks aquiver as though from cold. Geese shiver when they're excited. They knew somehow that a bathroom party was imminent.

The geese had long ago become far too big to all fit into the tub together, so I led my posse of followers through the kitchen and into the bathroom and started filling the tub with cold water as they waited in the hall, talking in their strange language to each other, a low gaggle of pips and squeaks and stuttering. I turned on the shower and pointed the stream at the empty tiles. Sometimes they all rush at me, but there seemed to have been some consensus this time about order. Three gray geese went for the tub and three waddled into the shower, shaking and bristling as the water hit their glossy feathers. I lifted the birds one at a time into the tub, wincing as the third got impatient and flapped its huge wings at me.

"All right, all right, all right!"

Their mother, the only snow-white bird among my flock, never seemed very interested in the festivities. The slower-moving creature stood in the hallway looking in, the regal, beak-up glare of a woman superior to such frivolity. I passed her, got my wine and started the music, and by the time I'd returned she'd taken up her usual spot at the front door, investigating my travel bag for signs of goose pellets, watching out the screen door for trouble.

I called Amanda, taking a long sip of wine.

"Conkaffey and Pharrell Investigations, Yvonne speaking," Amanda said.

"It's me," I said.

"Ah, you must be looking for Amanda. I'll just put you through."

Amanda sometimes pretends to be her own secretary. I understand that—it probably makes the business sound bigger and more official than it is. Why she carries the ruse on with me, I have no idea. I sighed as a bunch of tones came through the receiver, Amanda uselessly punching numbers into the phone.

"Good evening, Conkaffey and Pharrell Investigations, Amanda speaking. How can I help you?"

I drank more wine.

"I need the lowdown on the Barking Frog case, egghead," I said.

"Should I be sharing details of our company's active investigations with someone of such grotesque repute?" she said stiffly.

"Oh Jesus. You see it online?"

"No, Sean told me the news. But now I've been watching it on Twitter. This is one of those occasions the young people call 'breaking the internet' I think."

"Mmm," I said. "Well, I'm trying not to think about it."

"Denial. Good strategy. My favorite, in fact."

"Can we talk about the Barking Frog?"

"I may have to put you on hold while I get my notes."

"Don't put me on hold," I said.

"Oh, come on! I've got new hold music now. It's better than the last lot."

"What is it?"

"It's a pan-flute rendition of 'Advance Australia Fair.'"

"Don't put me on hold."

"All right. Ballistics have had a look at the shell casings and the stippling on the bodies and they think the gun used was a nine millimeter. Nothing fancy. Did the job. Unlikely the neighbor across the way would have heard it over her dog." I heard her shuffling papers on the other end of the line. "And Andrew was indeed cheating on his girlfriend with the backpacker, Keema. Saliva tells no tales, Ted. It *never* lies."

I wasn't near drunk enough to get into what that meant.

"What's Stephanie's alibi?"

"At home, asleep, with no one to confirm her whereabouts, of course."

"Let's get into Stephanie's accounts. Bank, phone, social media. See what the phone towers have to say about the whereabouts of her phone during kill time. Same with Keema and Andrew. Did she have plane tickets back to England or was she planning on staying longer? How serious was it? Has she had any other relationships since she's been here?"

"Aye aye," Amanda said. "We got the readout from the till, also."

"Oh yeah?"

"Only a couple of beers on the EFTPOS. Twelve hundred and change in cash."

"I thought it was the week's takings."

"It was," Amanda said. "Two lives lost for twelve hundred schmackos. Six hundred bucks a pop. Hardly seems worth it. Hey, is that Neil Diamond?"

A notification buzzed and I looked at the phone. Kelly. I reached into the tub unconsciously, stroked one of the geese paddling and swirling around there. Found comfort in the damp feathers, the bird nibbling at my fingers. I got off the phone with Amanda and dialed my ex-wife.

"It's not true," I said by way of greeting.

"Of course it's not true," she replied. Kelly told me she had learned of my new accusation from Sean, who'd probably called to warn her about the possibility of increased hostility toward her in the coming days. I was momentarily stunned by her words. I had expected a barrage of anger, maybe those old exhausted tears I'd got so used to hearing on the end of the line while I stood gripping the phone in jail, a lifeline slowly fading.

"That's an odd thing for you to say," I said.

"Well, it's clear this woman's lying. I mean, was she even your girl-friend? Do you even know her?"

"I dated her in high school. A kid thing. It was a few weeks."

"Why would she bring it up now? Why after all this time? And telling it to *Stories and Lives*, of all places? She wants a piece of the limelight. She's probably hoping for hush money or something. Maybe a magazine deal."

"Huh," I said. There was a chilly silence while Kelly analyzed the sound, the tone of surprise.

"What?"

"Well, it's just—I don't know. Three weeks into my incarceration you turn away from me. Your partner of fourteen years. You believe a child when she says that I raped her. Now an adult is saying something along the same lines and you're scoffing at it."

"I never believed you were guilty, Ted," Kelly said. It was the first time she'd said anything like that. I felt my jaw tighten, almost pain-fully, my back teeth locking together. For a long time, I didn't know what to say. I drank the wine.

"It's very hard for me to hear you say that, Kelly," I said eventually.

"What are you trying to tell me? That you didn't believe the accusations, but you abandoned me anyway? Was the whole fiasco just an excuse for you to dip out of our marriage?"

"Oh, fuck you, Edward."

I bit my tongue.

"I didn't believe you did it," Kelly said. "I just wasn't sure why they'd say you did. I was confused. I'm still confused."

"Good to know," I said.

"Don't be an arsehole."

She was right. I was being an asshole. She was, too, but that wasn't an excuse. The whole "abandonment" line had been a low blow. I'd been about to replace it with "left me to rot in jail" but had thought it was too dramatic. It was the bitterness of a man scorned, a jealous man fresh from looking his wife's new boyfriend in the face. Still bruised from being tossed aside. I was above that most of the time.

One of the geese was treading water at my end of the tub, eyeballing me. I smoothed down her neck, gave her a scratch under the beak. The geese believed me. Innocent Ted members believed me. Gangsters and murderers and thugs and random flight attendants believed me. I pinched the bridge of my nose.

"Was there anything else, Kelly?"

"That present," she said. "From Khalid Farah. It's a diamond bracelet. Like, real diamonds. Big ones. Twenty of them. On a child-sized bracelet."

"I thought it was probably something like that. He's a flashy guy."

"What am I supposed to do with it?"

"I don't know." I shrugged. "Give it to Lillian."

"She's two!"

"I mean when she's older. She can sell it. Or you sell it. I don't really care what you do with it, Kelly. The man gave it to me to give to you. I did my job. It's between you and him now."

"It's between *me* and *him*?" she scoffed. "He's a bad person, Edward. I'm not like that."

Bad people. Black sails on the horizon. The taste of salt water in my lungs, panic gripping at my heavy legs, trying to pull me down beneath a death cold swell. Grab on or drown.

"No, you're not," I said. She must have interpreted something in the tone, a conclusion of her own with a thousand possibilities, evidence of my contempt to take back to her new boyfriend. She hung up on me.

My body shot up in the bed before my mind had awakened, warm air rushing into my lungs, driving out dreams of pressure there, dark depths and the sandy bottom of the ocean rushing up toward me. I heard my own yowl of surprise. My mind scattered. All I knew was that there was a man in the doorway of my darkened bedroom and I couldn't move my hands fast enough toward the gun on the nightstand.

"Jesus!" I was yelling. "Jesus! Jesus! Jesus!"

"You really don't have enough security here," he said, leaning on the doorframe. "I mean, you don't even— You don't even . . ." Words failed him. He gestured down the hall.

I was pointing the gun at him in the dark while bewildering realizations pulsed through me. My brain was trying to bring me calm, but nothing about the seconds that followed was calming. As my eyes adjusted to the dark, I picked out the lean profile of Dale Bingley in the doorway, matched it to his slurred voice. He was drunk. Really drunk. As I recognized the slouch, I remembered the slur in his words, smelled bourbon in the air all at once.

"No cameras." He found the words, gestured down the hall again.

He was holding something against his leg. A dark, rectangular shape. I clicked back the hammer on my gun.

"Drop it," I said.

"Drop what?"

"Whatever you're holding."

"This?" He lifted something. I squeezed the trigger, not tight enough to fire, but deathly close. Felt the metal slide on well-oiled metal, the springs compress. He dropped the envelope on the floor at the end of my bed. I barely heard it fall over the thumping of my heartbeat in my ears.

"Whatever," he said, and walked off down the hall.

I couldn't catch my breath. I was already drenched in sweat, causing the sheets to latch on to me, grip at my waist and legs like vines. I made my way out into the hall in my boxers, still holding the gun, thought about more clothes. The envelope. I went back for it, then found my victim's father sagging in my remaining unbroken kitchen chair, his fair hair slick with sweat.

"I nearly just shot you," I said, turning on the light. I showed him the gun. "Do you understand that? You can't walk into my house in the middle of the fucking night and stand at the end of my bed like a ghost. I . . . Oh god. Imagine if I'd shot you just now."

"Imagine that." He stifled a burp. "How many questions there'd be. The press would love it. Just the fact that I was . . ." He lost his words again, twirled his hand. "Why don't you have any cameras or anything? Why don't you lock your windows?"

Because I spent enough time behind locks and bars, I thought. And locked windows and locked doors wouldn't be enough, not once I started going down that track. I'd have to put up CCTV. A taller fence at the front with a chained gate. Alarms I'd punch a code into when I arrived home and when I went to sleep. I knew if I started adding these things to my home, little by little I'd create my own prison. The lack of security was an act of defiance, a rejection of my past. I could hear the geese outside screaming up a storm. I hadn't been able to hear them from the bedroom. I was too angry to speak.

I went to the fridge and pulled out a beer, held it to my face. Condensation.

"I don't know what you're doing here," I told Dale. "But if you come at me like you did the first time, I will put you on your arse."

"Tough guy." He snorted, laughed to himself. He was hanging an arm over the back of the chair like a bored card player in a saloon. Now that I had time to look at him, I could see he was in a very bad way. He smelled, not just of bourbon but of days without a shower. His knuckles were still grazed from the attack on me. They hadn't been treated, and some were infected. I couldn't fathom why he was here, but I didn't care. My geese were upset. I went out, letting the screen door slap shut behind me, hoping that when I returned the ghost of Claire Bingley's father would be gone.

I opened the door. Seven sets of wild eyes peered at me from the dark. They stood, crowded forwards. I pushed at the soft, puffy chest of one, my fingers disappearing into an armor of flustered feathers until I found warm bone.

"No, no, no, don't come out. I'm fine. I'm . . ."

A goose slipped by me and waddled down the little ramp. Then they all spilled out, an angry parade, bristling and shivering, picking at the grass in the night.

Dale Bingley was at my side. I smelled him before I saw him, and stepped back out of his swing range. I drank the beer and watched the birds form a crooked row foraging in the gold light from the porch, now and then stopping to glare at my visitor or chase off a restful cane toad. As I turned I noticed Dale had snagged a beer from my fridge. I examined his high cheekbones and pointed nose in the glow from the house, my chest still tight with confusion.

"This might seem like an odd question," I said slowly, watching him put the beer to his lips. "But if you aren't here to bash me, what . . ."

"What the fuck am I doing here?"

"Mmm."

He shrugged. We watched the birds.

"I looked at those papers you gave me," he said. "The ones in the envelope. That's why I'm here. I guess. I don't know. To be honest, the year or so I've just been wandering from place to place, and it's anyone's fucking guess why I do anything. Maybe I was hoping you'd shoot me. Maybe that's why I didn't knock."

"So you either have a death wish or you want to discuss your daughter's case with me?" I summarized. He sat on the grass by way of an answer, his legs flopped out in front of him.

"I don't have anything to say about those papers," I said firmly, edging closer. "I haven't even looked very hard at them. I don't want anything to do with the case. I'm trying to live a quiet life here, so that maybe, if I'm lucky, people will forget about me and leave me alone. I can't help you, Dale. Maybe you could talk to Amanda about those leads. But I don't think she's gone much further with them, either. I think she—"

Dale flopped onto his back. The beer bottle toppled over. I watched him fighting sleep as one of the geese neared him, picking the grass warily beside his pockets, hoping to catch a glimpse of pellets in the fabric folds.

"Christ," I sighed.

Dear Diary,

I was stalking her. There was no doubt about it. Not that I tried to fool myself very much. When you're constantly squinting through the gaps in the back fence to see if she's there, your ears pricked for the sound of her, a giggle or a squeal on the wind, you know you've turned. I followed her to school a couple of times, watched her mother walk her there. It was exciting, trying not to be seen, not to be noticed by other parents, lurking in the shadows in the car a hundred meters down from the gate. I considered buying a child-sized mannequin and propping it up in the passenger seat so that just the top of the head was visible through the window. But try hiding that from Chloe. Having a girlfriend is a real necessity when you're like this, but it does have its downsides.

I guess the only thing I was kidding myself about Penny was how far it would go. I'd never offended. I thought I could control it. I thought all my wicked little games were just that; a bit of fun.

The easiest person to convince of anything is yourself. I stood in the TechWare store holding the teddy bear nanny cam and looking at its plump, cheerful face, and told myself what I was planning was a compromise. If I had to have these predilections at all, mental impulses that I didn't ask for and that I never encouraged, I was at least allowed to compromise so that I didn't end up doing the worst of bad things. Being too hard on yourself doesn't work. I was born this way. I was working with what I had.

I'd tried a less invasive strategy, of course, if only out of sheer laziness. Someone online, one of the ghouls with magic fingers from deep in the dark web, had taught me how to hack into the family computer next door and switch on the camera on the desktop without turning on the little red light indicating it was operating. Absolutely thrilling, this kind of stuff. I'd seen images online captured secretly from a hacked family computer—someone undressing unknowingly before an open laptop, someone thinking they were using a private webcam line to sex-talk their long-distance boyfriend. But when I turned the camera on, all I got was Penny's mother Andrea sitting there night after night, clicking away at shopping sights, her face flabby, an unhealthy blue in the reflections on the screen. Unlucky.

So I bought the teddy bear nanny cam at the tech shop and then I went down the street and bought some colorful wrapping paper.

Placing the bear was the hardest part. I'd listened to Penny talking about her upcoming birthday party through the fence and learned that her mother planned to place the present table up against the side fence, our fence. But when the day came and the yard next door was filled with squealing, running, shouting kids, I peeked over and saw that the present table was at the back of the yard. It was almost a full-on disaster, but as the evening descended I walked around the block and spent some time scouting the house behind Penny's. The occupants weren't home. No sign of security cameras. I went along the side of the house to the back fence, waited for an ideal moment, and dropped the present over the top, hearing it land with a soft, crumply sound on the pile.

I don't think I've ever sweated so much in my life. By the time I got home I was drenched in it. I told Chloe I'd gone for a run, but I was still sweating as I sat in the yard with a beer listening to the party next door drawing to a close. Penny's tinkling voice wishing everyone goodbye. Her excitement as she and her mother went into the yard and began carting all the presents back to the house, including one tightly wrapped, adorable teddy bear. No card. No sign where it had come from.

I wanted so badly to turn the camera on. To hear her confusion through the microphone, her delight when she prized the paper open. A mystery present. It was a high-end bear. Mohair fur—none of that acrylic shit. She'd love it, I was sure. Something traditional for a girl who appreciated the finer things. But every time I tried to open the app on my phone and activate the bear, Chloe came fluttering around me like a fat, needy moth.

I would bide my time. I was good at that.

Detective Inspector Sweeney sat stiffly in one of the chairs before the desk in Amanda's "office," looking about her at the place. It was hardly the dry, professional environment she'd expected from the private detective novels she had enjoyed in her youth. She'd anticipated a bare space, a filing cabinet with the proverbial whiskey bottle stashed in the bottom drawer, a map filled with colored pins, and stacks of files. But the office was more like the slightly messy living room of an elderly eccentric. Plush red lounges to the left of the door, bathed in sunlight, a shag carpet beneath them hosting three cats curled like scattered circular cushions. There were framed certificates, as one might expect, but they were not of an academic nature. One qualified Amanda in horse husbandry, another in the use of a soldering iron. They were issued by Brisbane Women's Correctional Centre during her incarceration. A bookcase crammed with books, many of them technical manuals, the upper shelf home to another of the cats, its striped tail hanging over the ledge, curling back and forth. To the right of the L-shaped desk, a small kitchen, the sink manned by used novelty coffee mugs, one sporting what looked like a human ear in place of a handle, another clearly swiped from Brisbane Women's Correctional, possibly during Amanda's incarceration.

The investigator herself had left Sweeney waiting for a long while, appearing at the door at nine in a Batman-themed satin bed robe, half-comatose from sleep. Sweeney had sat and listened to her padding around the upper floor, yawning loudly, groaning, swearing, showering. She'd glanced at her watch after a while and told herself not to bother seeking Amanda again before the clock struck ten.

Ted Conkaffey seemed to know the drill. She watched through the window beside the front door of Amanda's office as Ted parked and locked his car, glancing up and down the street like a man on the run. He had a nervous, low-headed kind of walk, a tall and broad-shouldered man who would be taller and broader if he weren't so weighed down by his circumstances. The beard was gone, and he wore a stark white shirt with jeans. Clean, as though he'd tried to scrub off some of the trauma of the past year and now his skin squeaked. Before he could reach for the handle Amanda appeared, inexplicably, and thumped into him from the side, a shoulder barge that almost sent him tumbling onto the grass. Amanda must have seen him pull up and snuck down the stairs and around the back of the building.

Pip watched them talking, the tall, world-weary gentleman and the petite, buzzing garden sprite who had confronted him. Amanda made a grand gesture about something with her arms and Ted rolled his eyes. Sweeney couldn't fathom how their relationship worked. Why it worked. Surely there was something about Amanda's murderous past that struck a raw chord with Ted, even if the killing had been in self-defense. Or had Ted's accusation opened his mind to people like Amanda, the ones society rejected? Sweeney wondered what Ted might think if he found out she had let her own father die on the kitchen floor like an animal, help the mere push of a button away. A valve in her father's heart had ruptured that night. It was probably one of the most painful things a human being could experience. Pip had watched and done nothing. She didn't have the luxury of Amanda's self-defense claim—Amanda had seen and known what the men in the rainforest had wanted to do to her. She'd been in the midst of the danger. Pip had only seen the flickers of danger in her father's eyes. She'd guessed, assumed, what he might have become. But she knew, deep down in her heart, that there was a chance he'd have stopped hurting her, stopped the drinking, cleaned himself up and become the father she'd wanted and needed him to be.

She'd denied him that chance.

She'd looked into his eyes as he died and judged him.

As Ted opened the door, a fat orange cat leaped from the floor at him like a round, furry cannonball, colliding with his chest. He winced at the impact, barely caught the animal.

"Can I come around here just once without being assaulted?" he moaned, trying to pull the cat down from his neck. "I'm getting it from all angles here."

The cat was meowing loudly and repetitively, a desperate and insistent noise. It seemed to want to scramble back up his chest, against his face. Ted flipped the animal and held it like a babe in his arms. Pip found herself trying to suppress laughter.

"Six is Ted's girlfriend," Amanda mocked, gesturing to the cat trying to maul her partner. "She *loves* him. She's *obsessed* with him. She wants to *marry* him."

"I'd shake your hand, Inspector Sweeney, but I'm in a bit of a tangle." Ted took a seat beside her, trying to wrestle the mewling animal down into his lap.

"It's fine."

Amanda narrated the cat's voice, a high, anxious titter. *"Oh, he's here. My soul mate. I thought he'd never return!"* She switched to her own voice. "You can't marry him, Six, he's a human being!"

"How are things?" Ted glanced at Sweeney's notebook, which was sitting on the desk. "I'm sorry I've been distracted. I'm here now, ready to focus. This is what's important. Everything else will sort itself out." He seemed to be assuring himself more than her.

"Are you sure?" Sweeney said. "You're headlining every online news site."

"My lawyer's onto it."

"How did the new allegation come about, exactly?"

Sweeney listened as Ted explained, his eyes lowered to the cat in his lap, a big hand stroking the creature. It had finally settled, but its purring was loud and deep, like the hum of an old air conditioner. Amanda was leaning on the desk, watching her partner. Sweeney noted a new kind of warmth in her face, perhaps an affection for him, a sorrow at Ted's obvious pain. But just as Sweeney noticed the look, it seemed to have disappeared. A flash of rare connection.

"I spoke with the lawyer this morning," Ted continued. "I'm sure when we get in touch with Elise Springfield she's going to put all of this to rest. But she's refusing all media requests at the moment. I haven't looked at the *Innocent Ted* website. Are they saying anything about it?"

"There's an emergency podcast out tomorrow, I think," Pip said.

"Right."

"Have the police called you?"

"Not yet."

"If you get arrested in the middle of our case, Ted, you still have to make my cake." Amanda pointed an accusatory finger at her partner.

"Her cake?" Sweeney looked to Ted.

"We made an agreement that whoever solves the next case wins a cake," Ted said. "The loser has to make it. When I say we 'made an agreement,' of course, Amanda came up with the idea and I wasn't really listening and suddenly it was a done deal, which is how most things work around here."

"This guy—" Amanda flopped a hand in Ted's direction. "He makes out like it was all me, but he had quite an elaborate cake in mind and he had it straightaway, as soon as I asked, like he'd thought of it before. I was happy with a no-bake Mars Bar slice but he wants a black forest gateau."

"With hand-tempered chocolate shavings." Ted scratched his wife-cat behind the ears.

"Hand-tempered." Amanda leaned over the table, fixed Sweeney with a glare. *"Chocolate shavings."*

"Getting back to the very serious accusations against your good name . . ." Sweeney said.

"I don't know anything about the accusations," Ted sighed. "All I have is a clip played during my interview that talked of me having a 'predatory relationship' with Elise Springfield when I was eighteen and she was eight. I don't know what that means. I don't know if Melissa is talking to the police. I . . ." He threw up his hands. "Maybe we should just focus on the case before us and let my life sort itself out."

"Whatever you like." Sweeney shifted uncomfortably, opened her notebook and spread the papers before her. She extracted a forensic report. "Here are the autopsy reports for Keema and Andrew. I've got the print and DNA analysis of the scene. In my opinion, there are three key elements to the crime scene itself that we should note. The safe was wiped clean after it was emptied. The gun was most likely a Browning Hi-Power nine millimeter."

"How do we know that?"

"I've used our local ballistics guy from Cairns, but he's referred to an expert from Macquarie down in Sydney," Sweeney said. "A real gun nut. He reckons he can tell the type of weapon not only from marks scored into the bullet as it was fired through the barrel of the gun but also from tool marks made on the casing as the bullet was slotted into the chamber. These days they seem to be able to tell which gun a bullet came from even if you never fired it."

"People are so clever," Amanda mused. "What do we know about Browning Hi-Power nine millimeters?"

"They're easy to obtain," Ted said. "They're a common law-enforcement gun. So some cops, correctional officers, security guards have them. They became the standard handgun of the Australian army in 1935 and haven't relinquished the position since. They'll be one of the easiest pieces to get hold of on the street. All someone with a standard-issue weapon has to do is go to their boss and tell them they need to replace a part of the weapon, and get a friend to do the same a few weeks later. Pretty soon they've assembled a totally new weapon from ordered parts, which they then sell on the street."

"Great," Amanda sighed. "Nothing special, then. Nothing memorable."

"Aside from the weapon, we know that the victims were ordered to lie facedown next to each other with their hands on the back of their heads, fingers interlocked," Sweeney said.

"That's no amateur," Ted said.

"No. The fingers interlocked—that's experience speaking." Sweeney nodded.

"So you put the safe robbery, the gun, and the directions given to the victims and what do you get?" Amanda said.

"Someone with forensic knowledge," Ted said. "Enough forensic knowledge to think, even in the heat of the moment, of wiping the safe clean of DNA traces and prints. The same someone in possession of a knockabout, commonly used police and security gun. And someone with enough training to know how to subdue people calmly and efficiently, to place them in a position that would make it difficult for them to move around, to plan their escape."

"I hate to say it, but this sounds like a police officer," Sweeney said.

"Or a security guard," Amanda offered. She was doodling a curly mustache on the autopsy photograph of Andrew Bell. "Ex-military. The army, navy, or air force. Reservists, also."

"What else does the scene analysis tell us?" Ted wondered aloud, watching Amanda's doodles with an expression of quiet horror. "Do we have footprints?"

"We have the bloody set. That's a standard Blundstone work boot, newish, men's size ten," Sweeney said.

"Oh good," Amanda said. "So every man in Australia's got a pair."

"I've got two," Ted said.

"What size are you?" Amanda squinted at her partner. He rolled his eyes.

"We can't tell if he came in the back door, but he definitely went out the back door after the murder. There are a lot of other footprints," Sweeney pressed on. "The chefs and the bartenders would all traipse back and forth out the rear door on smoke breaks. The earth is quite moist out there. Black soil. It was the bartender's duty to do the floors before they left for the night. Very last job on the closing checklist, according to the owner. Evidence suggests they were just about to do it."

She explained the dirt on the webbing between Andrew's fingers and what Dr. Gratteur had said about it, picking up the autopsy report. Ted leaned in close, followed her finger across the page.

"Something's not right," Ted said.

"What?"

"I don't know." He smoothed his cat-wife's head. "I can't quite get a picture of the assailant in my mind."

"His behavior doesn't make sense," Amanda said, putting her feet up on the desk. "The killer is cool, calm, and collected enough to take over the joint and subdue two fully grown human beings. But on the way in he's unprepared and clumsy enough to alert Andrew, standing out the back of the bar, to his intentions, causing him to run back into the building, to slip and dirty his hands on the way. So which is it? Is the killer a fully prepared assassin, or is he a dumbass who almost messed the whole thing up?"

Sweeney made some notes in her notebook. Then it struck her, suddenly, that neither Ted nor Amanda were taking notes. The thought hit her like a punch in the stomach. Ted had been a drug-squad detective when he was arrested. In fact, were he still in the force, he'd likely have outranked her. She was sitting next to someone who had far more experience in the job than she did, and then of course there was Amanda, who had a kind of experience of criminality she would never be able to obtain—the perspective of the perpetrator, the killer accused, tried, and incarcerated. There was neither experience nor worldliness on Sweeney's side. Intimidation picked at her, so that she almost shrunk in her seat, watching uneasily as Ted and Amanda bounced ideas back and forth.

"Two assailants?" Amanda wondered.

"Could be. Everything is not as it seems here," Ted said. "I feel like there's something right in front of us that we're not seeing. We've got to find that gun. There's something about it being such a cheap and boring gun that's bothering me."

"How so?" Amanda asked.

"I'm just speculating," Ted said. "But if this whole idea started out as a robbery—was always meant to be a robbery but ended up as an execution—then why get yourself such a throwaway gun? You're not going to throw it away. From the kind of experience this person is demonstrating, it's like they've robbed before and they're going to rob again. Why not get yourself a proper gun?"

"Something reliable," Sweeney caught on, straightened in her seat. "Something big and showy that's going to scare your victims."

"Maybe it was a one-time-only thing," Amanda sighed. "And they couldn't have been bothered spending big bucks on a proper gun."

"A one-time-only, go-out-with-a-bang robbery of twelve hundred bucks?" Ted asked.

"Maybe they expected there to be more in the safe," Sweeney chipped in.

"Based on what?" Ted said. "You've seen the Barking Frog. Place looks like it's on its last legs. If it was a one-time robbery, it was a gross overestimation."

"We need a new perspective," Amanda said, leaning over, trying to turn her head upside down while still sitting in her chair, like an owl. She disappeared under the desk. "Find the gun. Find the answers."

"Well, of course, I'm already on that," Sweeney said. "I've had teams of men going up and down the sides of the road looking for it. And another team dredging the river on either side of the nearest bridge."

"Ooh, treasure hunt." Amanda perked up. "We could help."

"You're not going to just wander in and find anything they haven't already found, Amanda," Sweeney said.

"It would be terribly annoying for everyone if I did." A smile spread over Amanda's face. "Almost sounds like a challenge."

"You're due to meet the owner there anyway, right?" Ted said.

"Yeah." Sweeney glanced at her watch.

"Good." Ted got out of his seat. "Let's go back there and get a new perspective."

I was so distracted by the thought of Dale Bingley at my house that I completely zoned out for most of the ride to the bar. I'd given Pip Sweeney a lift so she could give her patrol car to another officer who wanted to run out to Cairns hospital and have a look at the bodies again. She sat in the passenger seat asking me questions about Amanda, looking at me in that quiet, quizzical way, like she was trying to read sins written on my face. I knew she still hadn't decided if she could trust me, whether I was the hidden monster the entire world had made me out to be. Every time she interacted with me, Pip Sweeney was crossing a new line with herself. She'd spoken to me. She'd agreed to work with me. She'd got into a car with me. That was how it had been for everyone in my life since my accusation. My own ex-wife had been unsure whether hugging me was something she was prepared to do.

I'd helped Dale Bingley up onto the couch on the porch and left him sleeping there, unsure of what else I could possibly do with him. There'd been no chance of sleep after that. I'd cleaned the kitchen, though it was spotless, as always. Prison had left me with a strange affection for housework, for scrubbing and wiping and dusting. If you've read your weekly ration of books, there's not much to do in your cell in remand but clean, arrange, and rearrange your few precious items.

As I'd prepared to leave the house at half past nine, Dale had still been asleep. I'd stared helplessly at him for a bit, listened to him snore, but that didn't solve anything. I couldn't decide whether it was more inappropriate for me to tell him to go away or to allow him to stay. When I tried to predict what might happen when he heard about my new accusation, if he hadn't already, there were far too many equally likely possibilities. He might disappear, leaving all my possessions intact and closing the front door quietly behind him. He might burn my house down and kill all my birds.

Alerting Amanda to the situation outside her office hadn't gained me any useful advice, either.

"A sleepover!" she'd cried. "Can I come?"

I realized Sweeney had asked me a question, and I'd been watching the walls of green rainforest on either side of the road sail toward us, flashing by the windows, trying to figure out why Dale Bingley had come to my house. He'd said it was because of the envelope, the evidence Amanda had collected about Claire's attacker. Was he here to confront me because he didn't believe it? Or did he believe me, and want my help pursuing it? Which was worse?

"Do you think it made her the way she is?" Sweeney asked.

"What, sorry?"

"Amanda." She seemed a little frustrated. "Her crime."

"I'm sorry, I've just had a terrible morning." I rubbed my weary eyes, straightened in the driver's seat. "Can't sleep. I haven't been listening to you."

"I wondered whether you thought Amanda's crime formed much of her personality." Sweeney's tone softened. "She's so . . . cheerful."

"Yes." I laughed. "A murderous little forest fairy."

"Is it a deflection thing, do you think?" Sweeney persisted. "The cheerfulness. Her . . . inability to show grief. Is it an act? Does she refuse to have any complex emotions because they'll drag her down into those memories again?"

"I'm not a psychologist," I said. "But if I had to guess, I just don't think Amanda *has* very complex emotions. I mean, I've seen her less than chipper. I've seen her angry. She does feel things, just not very often. Or, not in public. I think there's a whole lot that goes on with her that we never really get to see."

"Maybe she has Asperger's," Sweeney said.

"Everybody thinks everybody's got Asperger's these days. It's very fashionable."

"Well, it would explain her inability to read other people's feelings," Sweeney reasoned. "She carries on like the whole world's full of daisies in front of the victim's family." She told me about Amanda dropping a bombshell about Andrew's cheating ways in the middle of the meeting with his loved ones.

"I don't think it's useful to diagnose her with anything." I shrugged. "Maybe she has Asperger's. Maybe she's a sociopath. Maybe she's just chocko-bananas."

"Chocko-bananas?"

"One of her terms." I smiled. "She rubs off on you after a while. Point is, she solves a mean crime. And that's really all that counts for me."

"I'm just interested to know if she's genuine or if it's an act. How can you be around someone day in and day out without knowing if they're lying to you?"

"I don't think it's an act," I said. "Amanda is genuinely amused by her own antics. She thinks she's hilarious. Ask her—she'll tell you. Most of the time I think she's just going around entertaining herself."

"But how can we tell what kind of person she is if she doesn't show us anything?"

"What does it matter what kind of person she is?" I frowned.

"Well, she killed someone. That's got to do something to you."

"Like what?"

"I don't know. Make you a bad person."

"I don't think so," I said. "Just because you've killed someone, doesn't mean you're bad."

"If it's in self-defense, I guess."

"Or not."

"You think?" She shifted closer.

"Sure." My dark thoughts were pulling at me again. Worry about my house. My geese. I was only half focusing. Talking as the thoughts popped into my mind. "People kill. Normal people. I don't think it makes you evil, if you do it. There are plenty of reasons why people do it. I think I know some fairly generous killers."

She fell silent. We rolled over a wooden bridge lined with police officers on either side, divers in the brown water, their hooded heads bobbing just a few meters out from the shore. The search teams had cleared the section beneath the bridge and set up nets twenty meters out on either side to protect the divers from crocs, but I was relieved to spot two men on the bridge with rifles just in case, their eyes fixed on the divers, jaws set with tension. There were more men up ahead sweeping the sides of the road with metal detectors. As I watched, Amanda careered out of the rainforest on her bike, startling two of them as she swerved onto the side of the road. She knew all the shortcuts through the forest and fields of cane, often beating me to destinations as though by teleportation. She was like that, slightly supernatural, able to appear seemingly by will exactly where she needed to be, her senses heightened, aware on another plane of people's thoughts and intentions unspoken. She might have annoyed me with all of her deeply unfair extraordinary abilities if I didn't like her so much. If I wasn't so grateful to her. She'd appeared in my life when I arrived in Crimson Lake, exactly when and where I needed her, exactly *who* I needed, like she'd already known I was coming.

"Does Amanda annoy you?" I asked Sweeney.

"Oh no," Sweeney said without hesitation. I was surprised. "She's . . ."

Exactly what I need, I thought. I don't know why. Sweeney never finished the thought.

"I find her fascinating," Sweeney said.

"She'd probably love to hear you say that."

"I'd never tell her." Sweeney gave a guilty little smile. I thought there was a hint of sneakiness to her face, a covert kind of joy. But I wasn't sure. I glanced over, trying to see if I could catch a flash of it again, some clue to her tone. But she was lost in her thoughts. I took her lead and retreated into mine. The old car rattled around us.

The burly, gray-haired Michael Bell stood with a lean, young blond woman outside the Barking Frog, off to the side of the crime scene tape, their arms folded. I parked behind them and the big man dropped his arms and took in the sight of me, probably measuring me against my infamous images in the morning's newspapers.

"They've fucked it up," he said, gesturing angrily to the bar.

"Mr. Bell," I said calmly. "I'm sorry I haven't been here. I was—"

"You." He ignored me, pointed a stubby finger at Sweeney as she arrived. "Your people should have been here to stop this kind of bullshit from happening."

"What are you talking about?"

"The owner," the blond woman said. She was thin and pale, small-eyed, the kind of absurd Queensland resident who couldn't take the harsh sun. "She's turned on the sprinkler system. It's doused the whole bar. Those police scientist guys, they said they weren't done in there yet."

"Oh Jesus. Why didn't anyone call me? Oh, Jesus!" Sweeney breathed, running and ducking under the tape. I stood at the edge of the cordon, feeling like I should do more to assure my clients before I went inside. But there were no pleasantries. Mr. Bell turned on me like a disturbed guard dog.

"Have you got any leads yet?"

"It's only been forty-eight hours. We've just got our feelers out. We're searching—"

"Feelers?" Mr. Bell snapped. "Feelers! What are you, a cockroach? I don't need a fucking cockroach on my son's murder. I need a bloodhound."

"We—"

He stormed off toward the edge of the road. I scratched at my scalp, thinking I should probably get away from the woman beside me before any press turned up. Photographs of me beside petite young blondes always sold well, no matter the woman's actual age.

"I'm Stephanie Neash," she said. "Andrew's girlfriend."

"Right." I turned to her with renewed interest. "My apologies for Amanda's tactlessness at your first meeting. She's not the most sensitive person who ever lived."

"She was right," Stephanie said. She pursed her lips, tried to drive out encroaching tears with a hard frown. "He was cheating with Keema. We were talking about getting engaged soon, you know. All our friends knew about our plans. We'd even picked out a wedding venue. And there he was. With her. There was a G-string . . ." she trailed off. A couple of sobs, a humiliated cringe. "I logged into his Facebook account. It was all there. The messages. I can't believe I was so stupid."

She bit her lip hard, her face reddening as she fought to hold back the tears. I thought about hugging her, but it was too risky out here in the open, where someone could snap a picture, sell it to the press. I looked at the treetops, the dirt beneath my feet, anything.

"You weren't stupid," I submitted, and put a hand on her shoulder, squeezing the top of her arm.

"It took some weirdo investigator lady to tell me he was cheating, and she knew from taking one look at a necklace, for Chrissake."

"I wouldn't base the obviousness of Andrew's affair on what

Amanda saw," I said. "She sometimes sees things no one else could possibly see. She balances out her occasional genius by being excruciatingly impractical the rest of the time, believe me."

"I wish I could ask him why he did it," Stephanie said. One tear was caught in her eyelashes. I wanted to wipe it away, but didn't dare. "I'd just need five minutes. What did I not do? What did I not say? What about me wasn't enough?"

"It wasn't you, Stephanie."

"Then what was it?"

I struggled to offer something. This woman I didn't know was young and fragile, and looking to me, an impartial stranger, to tell her what she needed to hear. I didn't know anything about the ways of cheating partners—I'd never cheated, and no one, to my knowledge, had ever cheated on me. Of course, there were obvious theories to grab at. Andrew had probably been her first serious relationship. Maybe she was his, and he got scared or bored or seduced by the beautiful and exotic Keema, and the distant, fantastical life she represented. Maybe Andrew was just mean. A narcissist. A sex addict. But there again the rabbit hole yawned before me, diagnosis and the shallow comfort it offered. There was nothing I could do for Stephanie—even if I consoled her about the cheating, she was stuck in the middle of the mother of all bad breakups—the death of a partner. I felt like a fraud even as I began to speak.

"You're allowed to hate what he did," I said. "Even if he's dead. You can still love him and hate what he did."

Stephanie didn't seem to know whether to believe me or not. How could I tell her that I still loved my wife and hated that she had left me to bear the horror of the past year alone? That I thought nightly of going home. Of pretending it had all been a dream. That I actually fantasized about opening the door to my house and finding her there waiting for me the way she had done in the old days, even though I was so consumed with resentment for her that I felt like a hole had been burned in my stomach.

Andrew's father returned from the roadside. It seemed he had been crying, the rims of his eyes red. He made a sad figure walking back across the barren dirt toward us, trying to drive out the emotion with hard eyes, a tight mouth.

"Do you still think it was a burglary?" Michael asked.

"We're looking into that angle. Sweeney has officers checking up with suspects of that type in the area. People with past convictions."

"If they catch him and you guys make out like it was a robbery gone wrong at trial, he might get less time. Voluntary manslaughter, not premeditated murder." Michael Bell took a deep breath, seemed to struggle to let it out without it catching in his throat. "This was not a robbery gone wrong. It was a cold-blooded execution. My boy and that girl were on the ground. They were *helpless*."

Stephanie hid her face in her hands.

"Maybe there was a robbery afterwards," Michael snarled. "But it was *murder* first. I hired you and that woman, Amanda, so you could be here from the start. You better make sure there are no illusions about what this crime really is when it comes to trial."

"Try to put thoughts of a trial to the back of your mind," I said. "We need to think about catching the guy now. Don't get ahead of yourself. Right now it's time for—"

"For what?" he snapped.

"For being sad." I shrugged. Stephanie was crying into her hands. We both watched her, unable to help. "Right now, you and your family, you just need to be together and be sad. Leave the rest to us."

The big, burly man submitted, took his dead son's girlfriend into his arms. Sweeney appeared on the porch of the Barking Frog and I excused myself from them to meet her there. She was speaking with an old woman dripping in jewelry, huge sapphire earrings pulling on her furry white earlobes, her hair an orange tangle pinned here and there with jeweled clips.

"This is Claudia Flannery." Sweeney gestured angrily at the woman. "The owner. Ms. Flannery has taken the extremely helpful measure of activating the bar's fire sprinkler system, so that we've now lost anything forensically useful that might have been remaining after the murders. I have to tell you, Mrs. Flannery, that this is a deeply suspicious act."

"You think I did this deliberately?" Claudia raised a penciled orange eyebrow. "You actually think I deliberately flooded my own establishment? Unbelievable. Unbelievable! Why would I want to add water damage to the already substantial mess your officers have made of my business?"

"Because you want to sabotage our investigation?" Sweeney asked.

"What exactly are you insinuating?" Claudia asked. "That I murdered two of my young staff with a gun? I've never so much as *seen* a gun in real life. Young lady, I'm seventy-eight years old."

"You think because you're seventy-eight I'm just going to exclude you from our inquiries?" Sweeney said.

"It would be sensible, in my opinion." Claudia looked at me as though Sweeney was mad.

"How did the system become activated?" I asked.

"No idea." Claudia shrugged, pulling her light kaftan up at the shoulder where it had sagged, revealing spotted brown flesh. "I came here last night to check everything was in place, and the system just went off. It might have been activated by my cigarette. Who knows? I didn't bother smoking outside. The place is already trashed. What harm could a little ash do?"

"You weren't supposed to access the scene at all!" Sweeney's neck had become red with fury, tendrils of color threatening to creep up her cheeks. "We specifically told you to stay out until our investigation was through. Don't you want to catch the person who did this?"

"Of course I do." Claudia gave an indignant snort. "But those children are dead. They're gone. We might learn something from their spirits, if they've chosen to linger. But you're not going to catch who did this by scraping up gunk from between the tiles in the kitchen and spreading your harmful chemicals all over my walls."

"Their spirits?" I ventured.

"I'm a certified medium." Claudia's tone softened. She took my hand and squeezed my knuckles. "Hospitality is just a means to an end for me. My true interests lie in spiritual guidance."

"Oh Jesus." Sweeney put her hands up, surrendered, and walked off.

"What happened here two nights ago was a dark act," Claudia continued, rubbing her thumbs over the back of my hand. "A slaughter. The man who did it brought the most extreme kind of negative metaphysical forces into this place when he killed those children. The sprinkler system was probably just a reaction of the building's forces."

"The building itself has . . . forces?" I asked.

"Of course it does." She gestured to the moldy roof above us, dripping with wisteria. "This place is older than me. You think it hasn't learned a thing or two in its time sitting here, taking human souls into its belly every evening, spitting them out every morning? It knows what happened to those kids. It's not going to tell you unless you treat it properly."

Claudia treated me to a wide, yellow grin. I extracted my hand slowly from hers, thinking I'd go and have a crisis meeting with Sweeney where she stood huffing with anger at the end of the porch.

"While you're here." Claudia grabbed me again, entangling my hand and forearm again like an ancient, glittering octopus. "You seem like a warm, gentle kind of man. A very perceptive man. The kind who listens."

"Okay," I said.

"I've been trying to get your law enforcement colleagues to do something about the noise from Victoria Songly's house." A hard look came over her features, pinching the corners of her eyes. "And no one is heeding my call."

"Victoria Songly?"

"She lives back there." Claudia thrust an arm dramatically toward the back of the bar. "Having renovations done, it seems. She's complained about the noise at night in the bar here on dozens if not *hundreds* of occasions. She gets away with it because her husband was Tom Songly. The commissioner. And now she thinks *she* can have jackhammering going on outside council-approved hours. Well, it's not fair.

Don't we want things to be fair around here, Mr. . . . I'm sorry, I never caught your name."

"Collins."

"Mr. Collins?"

"How long has it been going on?" I asked.

"I only noticed it this morning."

"Maybe it's just a short-term thing," I reasoned. "I mean, the bar's not even open."

"I'm sure I don't need to tell you, Mr. Collins, that it's the principle of the matter." Claudia smiled. "You seem like a principled man."

"I'll check it out." I pulled my hand free of her tentacles again. "No problem, Ms. Flannery."

Walking to the edge of the porch, I began to perceive a faint jack-hammering noise coming from the direction of the back of the property, somewhere beyond the tangle of rainforest at the side of the building. Sweeney reeled around to face me as I approached, almost sticking me in the face with an angry finger.

"The sprinkler system didn't just *come on*," she snapped. "She *turned it on* so that she could open the bar back up. She's losing money, the old cow. All that spiritual guide bullshit is so completely fake."

"Whoa." I held my hands up in mock surrender. "Your aura is *so dark* right now." The joke bounced off her.

"My mother was one of those 'spiritual' people," she sighed, staring at the people gathered by the side of the road. "She fluttered off like a mystically liberated butterfly when I was fifteen, never to be seen again."

"Oh. I'm sorry."

"It's fine," she huffed.

"It seemed like a bit of a desperate measure for a bar that doesn't make a lot of money," I said. "The week's takings were only twelve hundred bucks."

"She has to make more money than that here," Sweeney said.

"She said she was a certified medium," I suggested. "Maybe she does psychic readings."

"What garbage. How do you *certify* a medium? What's the test for that? Guess your star sign? Guess your credit card numbers, more like it."

I shrugged, not wanting to push it.

"There are rumors far and wide the place is a biker hangout," Sweeney said. "They probably make drug exchanges here to the truckers heading up and down the coast dropping packages. I mean, we said it, didn't we? That if this was a robbery, it was a gross overestimation?"

"Have your people checked out the biker angle with Michael Bell?" I asked. "Amanda told me his father was—"

She held up a hand to stop me. "We've looked into it." Her voice had dropped low. "He says he's legit, and there's nothing in his criminal record or his bank accounts that would suggest he has any kind of unsavory connections. I have a couple of officers tailing him to see if he meets with anyone in the next few days who we can connect to anything drug or biker related, but if he finds out about that he's going to lose his fucking mind."

"Right." I glanced back at Michael, who was ranting to Stephanie, pointing at the bar. I changed the subject. "Who's Tom Songly?"

"What? Oh, Songly—he's the ex–New South Wales police commissioner, mid-1970s. The house is back there." She waved a hand toward the back of the bar. "I sent officers around there too. Old lady didn't hear or see anything."

I nodded. "I thought I knew the name. Songly. Everybody flees north, huh? He was involved in all that seventies stuff."

The mid-1970s in Australian policing was a dire time for corrupt officers who had spent decades handling crimes with a less-than-professional approach. Cops were heavy-handed in their interrogations, free and easy with their violence toward criminals, and sticky-fingered with evidence, particularly of the paper kind. The center for this dark style of policing seemed to be New South Wales, but underworld wars in Melbourne marked the reach of the infection there. An inquiry revealed many cops were being paid off by criminals in the drug and prostitution trade in exchange for turning a blind eye to their occupations, and the reek of corruption climbed throughout the ranks. I didn't know if Commissioner Tom Songly had copped any heat during the royal commission, but making a break for it to the tropical north in his retirement years had probably been a sensible move given all the blame games in New South Wales.

"Does the old man still live there?"

"He's dead," Sweeney said. "Died of an aneurism a couple of years ago. What's the interest?"

"She's making too much noise for our resident spiritual goddess."

"She's complaining about the noise in the middle of our murder investigation?" Sweeney let out a long, heavy sigh, massaging her brow. "I'm so annoyed, I'm giving myself a headache."

"I'll deal with it," I told her.

I left her to make the necessary phone calls about the ruined crime scene and wandered around the side of the building to the back of the bar, where the rainforest gave way to a lush creek bed. It was wet here. The air was alive with clouds of fruit flies feeding on a wild passion fruit vine draped between enormous eucalypts. The jackhammering grew louder, an inconsistent grinding sound that echoed down the green tunnel of forest spreading out on either side of me, accommodating the creek as it trickled toward the river. Further downstream there was a group of cops sweeping the bank with metal detectors, one walking slowly in waders through the creek. I walked down the slope and hopped across some big rocks and up the other side, and was about to turn around the side of the house when I noticed a movement through the fence.

"Hello?"

"Hey," someone answered. I put a boot on a big rock and rose up, holding on to the triangle points of the top of the fence. There was a lean, black-haired young man in the backyard making a pile of broken concrete shards and splinters of wood.

"How are ya?" He smiled.

"Yeah, good." I reached over and shook his dusty hand. "Ted Collins. I'm with the police back here at the bar."

"Oh, yep."

"What you guys up to?"

"Just rippin' out a bathroom." He nodded toward a darkened living room. "It's my nanna's place. We're making moves to sell it."

Through the glass doors to the living room I could see a couch, the lap of an old lady sitting there, her feet in socks and pale blue terrycloth slippers. The television in the corner was on, a news update wrapping up, thanking the people who dressed the hosts in a roll of credits. In the corner of the yard I spotted a fishpond. It was a cute little place. I hoped the renovations weren't going to destroy its charm.

"Nanna doesn't mind all the noise?" I asked.

"She's deaf as a post," the man said.

"Funny. Our bar manager seems to think she's made a bunch of complaints in the past about noise from the bar." I jerked my thumb behind me at the bar. "The two seem to have an old-lady rivalry happening. She's asked me to come have a word with you about the jackhammering."

"Oh, right." He stopped with the concrete pile and stretched his back. "I guess it's not about the noise for these lot, though, is it?"

"No, it never is."

"They just like to stir up trouble. Get bored in their twilight years."

"Yep," I said. "I've seen it before." Most of my first years as a young copper were spent going around parties and worksites, passing on noise complaints and writing citations where they were needed. A lot of the time it wasn't about the noise. It was about a perceived insult that happened years earlier, maybe someone's dog crapping every morning on the neighbor's front lawn. The amount of dust a worksite caused in someone's living room. Noise complaints were just the simplest and most anonymous form of neighborly vengeance. All it took was a phone call.

"Try to just keep it to the council hours," I said. "Eight to five."

"You got it, chief." The young man saluted. "How's everything over there? You catch the guy?"

"Not yet."

"The coppers came round but we couldn't help." He glanced at the old woman in the chair. "Should she be concerned, do you think?"

"I wouldn't worry her," I said. "Just keep the doors locked at night. All the usual stuff." He stood back and squinted as he spied something over my shoulder. I followed his gaze and saw Amanda walking carefully across the rooftop of the Barking Frog, setting her feet between vine-covered tiles before taking each step.

"Amanda!" I ran back across the creek, shielding my eyes from the morning sun. "Jesus Christ, what are you doing?"

"Getting a new perspective," she called, then pointed. "Oi, there's a snake up here! A big green one!"

"Get down before you kill yourself!"

Sweeney arrived at my side. Amanda wobbled as a clump of vines gave way under her foot.

"Uh-oh!" She grinned. "Close one!"

"What the fuck is she doing?" Sweeney groaned.

"Probably looking for the gun," I said. "Did you send anyone up onto the roof?"

Sweeney blushed. I guessed she hadn't. I looked down the creek to where the officers were picking through the rocks with sticks. If Amanda brought down the gun right now, it would be a real coup. Typical Amanda.

"You find the gun?" I called.

"Nope."

I felt disappointment tug on my shoulders. Amanda came to the edge of the roof and leaned over. "But here. Catch this."

She hefted a cloth bag down toward me. I caught it against my chest.

"What is this?"

"I found it up here." Amanda pointed to the corner of the roof. "There's all sorts of stuff up here. Look! A bunny!" She held up a stuffed toy bunny, filthy and dripping. "I might wash this and give it to your cat-wife!"

"What's in the bag?" Sweeney asked, leaning over. I loosened the drawstring and opened it.

"It's cash," I said. I drew a wad of yellow fifties tied with an elastic band out of the bag and showed it to Sweeney. Her eyes grew wide. "The bar's takings."

Dear Diary,

I learned about her. I learned more than my mind could contain, so that for the next few days I was wandering around in a dream, trying not to count off the seconds until she got home from school and came back onto my screen, my little telephone pet appearing again from outer space. I did the best I could to hide it from Chloe, but of course she noticed me glued to the thing, smiling to myself, holding it up to my ear so that I could hear Penny's mumblings as she narrated the dismal lives of her dolls.

I learned that Penny was just on the cusp of giving up on those impossibly long-legged beauties. Sometimes, in the midst of play, she'd stare fixedly at their painted eyes, give their rubber faces an experimental push. I knew how she felt. I'd stood and watched Chloe in the bathroom mirror caking on her evening war paint before a night out with the girls, smearing over pocked skin, an instant tan that made her older and harder at once. Penny's dolls were dying in her hands, withering and wilting the way real women did. I lay in bed and listened to Chloe coming home, snickering with her friends, filling the house with the smell of smoke. Using words Penny wouldn't even know. Blistering assessments of their lecturers, their parents, their bosses. The oppressors. When would the little girl next door become one of these cracked, sagging dolls?

Through the nanny cam, I watched her dress. I watched her sleep. One night, in sickening joy, I watched as she took the bear from the shelf and brought it into the bed with her, her mouth blurred, too close to the bear's eyes, falling open as she drifted away, her breath fogging the camera. I'd long since given up any hope of not finding myself in love with Penny. I was in deep. Not sinking but sunk, consumed by the weight of the ocean, the pressure squeezing my brain. I wasn't fooling myself anymore—I knew that I was watching, wide-eyed, straining to listen all the time, every moment, for my way in.

Nothing had worked so far. I'd picked up tiny details about the boy band she liked, and her favorite shows, and the girls who were picking on her at school, and bounced them back to her over the fence during our little conversations. She must have thought I was ultra-cool, being into all the things she was. I was turning the dial, microscopic movements, trying to find the right signal all the time. Now and then there were flickers and blips, but she remained distant from me, a wary bird who'd come to peck a few seeds before fluttering away.

Life was excruciatingly mundane without her. I didn't know how I'd survived it before she arrived in my world. Bills had to be paid. Sports games watched and beers drunk. The car died. I should have gone and bought another one without Chloe, but she wanted to spend quality time with me, turn the whole thing into an adventure. I spotted an old white van, and I wanted it. I told myself and Chloe that it was because of the extra space—it would make our next rental move easier. I tempted her with the escapades she so loved—we could throw a mattress in the back, go camping. Hooray! What a nightmare. A van would make shopping easier too. Practical lies. We fought. It was all I could do to hide my passion for the idea. Stay hidden. Stay hidden. Force it down. We compromised on a ute bought from an ad in the paper. Pale blue. I put it in her name, just in case.

The air seemed full of tumult. Penny had got the idea from her mother that there was a puppy in store for her birthday, and though her birthday had come and gone she was convinced still—must have overheard something about a surprise and misinterpreted it. She'd drawn a bunch of pictures of herself to try to move the puppy-surprise along, cheeky suggestions, a pointy-eared thing she couldn't bear to waste time coloring in before she presented them to her mother. I paused the feed on the image of her, stick-figured and grinning grotesquely, a red lead encircling the neck of the equally ecstatic-looking hound.

When Penny had had enough of her not-so-subtle games she'd asked her mother. Mum said no. She'd entertained the playful suggestions long enough. There would be no dog—there had never been plans for a dog. Penny protested, said she'd heard her mother talking on the phone to another mother about a surprise. She was wrong, and was scolded for listening in on private phone calls. The hurt. It was almost unbearable to watch. I knew what it was like to take something small and whip it into a huge, all-consuming, deeply convincing fantasy, only to be let down. I'd sat in the bathroom with my headphones plugged in and listened to Penny crying on her bed, watching the sobs racking out of her on the screen, making her small body shudder.

This was it. I'd found my way in.

I didn't stay away from home for long. A heavy dread had settled in my chest. I needed to know what Dale Bingley wanted from me, if anything at all, and make decisions about the problem when I had more information. Compartmentalizing. Coping by overanalyzing the situation, micro-focusing. I'd done plenty of it in drug squad. Trying to cope with difficult or traumatic cases by thinking of one thing at a time, dealing with one small problem and ignoring the tornado swirling around me. See to the Barking Frog investigation. Now see to Dale Bingley. Later, think about all the other horrors. The Melanie Springfield allegation. The press. The vigilantes. The old, weary hurt that came from missing my family. All that could wait.

When I walked into the house and found it quiet and empty, I felt a rush of exhilaration. He was gone. Then a crushing downward dive as I spotted the top of his head through the kitchen window, his daughter's white-blond hair turning as he heard me walking through the house.

I grabbed a beer from the fridge, resisted the temptation to take the Wild Turkey bottle on the counter by the neck and sink it all.

He was sitting on the couch where I'd left him. There was a glass of whiskey at his elbow, the crumpled papers from the envelope in his lap. The geese had all gathered in the shade at the very end of the property near the fence, seemingly more comfortable sitting within meters of croc-infested waters than wandering anywhere near the stranger on the porch. I followed their lead, stood in the corner of the porch furthest from him, the beer tasteless and painfully cold.

Neither of us spoke. I watched him shuffle the papers, settling on each for a second or two before putting it at the back of the pile. I got the impression he had been sitting there doing this for hours. I knew the papers by glance.

A photocopy of an ad from a Mount Annan newspaper, advertising a white dog free to a good home.

A screenshot from CCTV footage of a blue ute not far from Claire's abduction site on the day she went missing.

A screenshot from CCTV of a man with a blue ute and a white dog outside the Yagoona RSPCA.

"Claire spoke about a white dog," Dale said suddenly, jolting me from dark thoughts. He sipped the whiskey. "I heard it, in the beginning, mixed in with all the other stuff she was saying. The gibberish. She said it again in counseling afterward. And she drew a picture of it. When they made her do those . . . those art therapy sessions."

"Did she ever . . ." I cleared my throat. "Did she ever say what it meant?"

"No," Dale answered.

We fell silent for a long time. Leads about the white dog had always been perplexing for me. Claire talking about a white dog in the days after her attack was the only thing that connected the man with the blue ute and the white dog to what had happened. Maybe it was nothing—coincidence. Claire talking about whatever fluttered through her traumatized brain, and a man, a random, unconnected man, simply obtaining a white dog from a pair of British people on the same morning of the abduction. Except that the man had injured the dog somehow, accidentally or intentionally, and then dumped it at the Yagoona RSPCA. His actions seemed unusual and cruel. But maybe they were not connected at all to Claire's abduction.

Or maybe they were. Maybe the man obtained the dog with the specific intention of luring a girl with it somehow. Inviting her to pat it, or asking her to help him find it, telling her it was in the area somewhere, lost. When Amanda had presented me with the white dog angle I hadn't wanted to do anything with it. I had passed on information about the blue ute and the dog to *Innocent Ted*. But I had not told anyone the dog was injured when it arrived at the RSPCA. It seemed one of those strange details that I needed to keep to myself, in case we ever found the man who'd dumped the dog, or a man saying he was him.

I still didn't want to do anything with the lead. I'd passed it on, and it was now someone else's responsibility. I drew a breath and prepared to tell Dale in the politest way possible to leave my house.

"I don't believe you're innocent," Dale said, before I could speak.

I didn't know what to say to that. So I said nothing.

"I can't believe in your innocence," he went on. He shrugged a little, helplessly. "It's not something my brain is ready for, I guess. I've hated you for so long, so intensely, that I can't . . ." He glanced at me. Wary. "I can't . . ."

"I understand," I said.

"But I have to know what this is about." He lifted the papers. "If this man has something to do with it."

"Okay." I realized I'd finished the beer. I was waiting for him to tell me that he was leaving. That he'd take the papers to the police, maybe involve Amanda, get her to explain in detail everything she'd learned about the man with the white dog, point investigators down in Sydney in the right direction. But he didn't move. I became aware that he was waiting for me to speak. Then, with a shock, I realized what he wanted.

"I can't help you," I said.

"Yes you can."

"I don't want anything to do with this." I held my hands up. "I'm trying to put my life back together here. I've got new problems to deal with. I mean, you've heard about the new accusation . . ."

"Yes," he said.

"Well, then, you understand, my life is *shit* right now," I struggled for words. He hardly seemed to be listening. "I mean, this woman is saying that I—"

"I can't think about that." He shook his head. "I need to think about this." He lifted the papers again. Compartmentalizing. Trying to get through it, one problem at a time.

I held my head. Reminded myself that I was dealing with someone very traumatized. Maybe not in his right mind.

"The police will—"

"I'm not going to the police." He took a long sip of whiskey. "If we find him, I don't want them getting in my way."

I scoffed. I shouldn't have. He looked at me, and I felt a stab of pain in my chest, my body recognizing the pain this man had inflicted on me, the power and strength his rage had inspired in his body the night he attacked me. *This is a dangerous, unhinged man,* I told myself. A man on the edge. There was a right and a wrong way to get him out of my life. If I didn't handle this situation carefully, he might hurt someone. Himself. Me.

"Where do we start?" he asked.

I struggled to answer. Leaned on the railing and tried to focus on my geese, my safe zone, the mottled shade where they sat preening themselves and snoozing, beaks tucked into feathered backs. As I stood watching, their corner of the property seemed further and further away. I was being sucked back into the horror of my past. Into the wild, painful world of what had happened to Dale's child, the storm brought down upon her that had accidentally swept me up.

"There are things you could do," I reasoned, trying to sound as noncommittal as I could. "I mean, I could start you off, and then you could go. Go pursue the case by yourself. We could try to find out the make and model of the car in the picture. Get a list of registered vehicles that match the color, the type. Check it against a known sex offender list. Look for cars bought or sold around the time. But I'm not taking it any further. I give you some stuff and you go away and you don't come back . . ."

My words trailed off. I wasn't convincing anyone. I'd opened the door a crack on a world of half thoughts I'd tried not to pursue as I lay awake, night after night. I was a detective. I knew how to pursue Claire's attacker. I'd always known. I slammed the door shut on those thoughts, closed my eyes and tried to drive them away. I couldn't do this. I couldn't go backward into my case. There was too much at stake. If I failed to catch the guy, I'd never be free of the accusation. I'd never get my life back.

But who was I kidding, thinking I could ever get my life back?

I didn't realize Dale had stood until he spoke.

"Where's your computer?" he said, almost to himself, opening the door to the kitchen. He was moving quickly. Invigorated. He'd left the whiskey on the arm of the couch. "I'll get the computer."

"You can't stay here," I called. "You'll have to get a motel room."

He didn't answer me.

In prison, I'd met a guy who was charged with the crime of prostituting a minor, his fifteen-year-old nephew. The guy and his nephew used to sit in the hallway of a local motel and wait for men to inquire over a website about meeting with the boy and paying for his services, at which point they'd go up to one of the motel rooms and prepare to meet with the client. Though of course I'd not wanted to hear stories like this, sometimes people talk at you in prison and don't care whether you're listening or not, and moving away from the conversation can be seen as an aggressive act. The guy was remorseless. He'd been complaining to me about what a waste of his time this activity had been. He only regretted that he'd sat in the hallway for hours upon hours with the boy, days upon days, just waiting, staring at the bare wall across the hall from where they sat.

"And now I sit in here," he had said, gesturing to a wall near where we sat. "And I stare at *this* wall. I wasted my time on the outside. I should have . . . I should have . . ."

He'd struggled to articulate his dismay. I'd waited, watching, trying not to imagine what depraved activities he missed about the outside world. When he finally reached a decision, I was surprised.

"I should have walked," he said.

I didn't get it at the time. But I understood soon after my release. On the inside, you know exactly how far you can walk anywhere. Five steps to the end of the cell. Fifty steps across the cell block. A hundred and fifty steps from the cell block to the chow hall. You walk far enough and you'll run into a fence. There are limits all around. The cage is only so big. It took me a while to realize when I was released that I could traverse the country on foot if I wanted to. No one could stop me. There were no bars anymore.

Not long after I'd moved to my home on the edge of the lake, I'd looked out across the water through the diamond wire and spotted a point on the west side of the lake, a long bar of rocks and gray sand jutting out toward the center. If I squinted, I could make out a twisted, bent-backed tree right on the end of the point. I don't know why, but the tree spoke to me, the way it grew defiantly on the end of the sandbar, on the furthest rocks, far away from the edge of the forest. Some bird had probably dropped its seed out there, or the wet season had caused it to drift and wedge itself between the rocks. Rather than dying for being dragged away from where it belonged, it stayed put and grew. I didn't know what kind of tree it was, but it was not one of the proud, straight-backed gums thrusting their way out of the rainforest canopy nearby. It was not one of the plump, pale mangrove trees reaching out uniformly toward the water. Its trunk was hunched like it carried a great weight, and its top was flat as though beaten down. I thought it might have been a poinsettia, but I'd never seen it flower.

Maybe the tree was a symbol for me. Of defiance, resilience, re-growth. Of a twisted, flowerless, removed life—but a life nonetheless—possible with only the bare minimum needed to carry on.

I decided one day that I would walk there.

It wasn't as easy as it seemed. Most of the edge of the lake is im-penetrable rainforest cut through with the faintest of animal trails. I tried and failed to find the point a bunch of times, following the trails, sometimes setting out from the roadside and not even succeed-ing in finding the water. Losing myself. When I finally did find the point after a couple of months, I'd walked out over the rocks, wary of croc movement in the water, and put my hand triumphantly against the gnarled tree. Not only was the tree growing here, but the tenuous roots that clasped the rocks had played host to other seeds. A thin strangler vine was slowly working its way up the trunk, a plant I knew would thicken, if allowed, and kill the tree. I pulled it down and tossed it into the water, vowing to return, a kind of guardian for the brave tree.

I discovered eventually that the little arm of land reaching out into the lake had a name. Redemption Point. I liked the sound of it.

Walking, whether to Redemption Point or not, became a kind of therapy. An act of protest against all the steps I'd taken in prison that had been halted by bare walls, iron grilles, stern-faced guards. I loved walking. Sometimes when I left the house, saying goodbye to the geese before one of my journeys, I fantasized about taking a dog with me. Chatting to the creature the way I chatted with Woman at home.

I left Dale Bingley and started out for Redemption Point. My house on the edge of the wide, mangrove-tangled Crimson Lake was very isolated. I didn't have any neighbors. My property cut into the im-penetrable bush and ended on the wet gray sand before the murky water, a strange choice for the tropical north, where crocodiles as big as limousines lurked in the depths.

When I'd moved to the north after being freed from prison, I'd found the heat oppressive, the humidity a choking fog that infected every minute of my day, relieved only in the early hours after I'd sweated through my sheets and lost any hope of sleep. Frequent storms came and broke the heat briefly, rain hammering the corrugated iron roof of the porch. The rain drew up from the hidden depths all manner of amphibians; geckos appearing on the roof beams and fat, glistening frogs lolling on the lawn. After a few months, I'd acclimatized. As I walked, head down and thoughts churning, the thick air brought a kind of safety bubble down around me, so that I calmed as I focused on the taste of it, the rainforest smell of earth and moss a natural remedy.

My phone shattered my newfound content. I recognized the number, stopped walking and gripped at my sweating throat, trying to encourage words.

"Hi," I wheezed, finally.

"Hi, Ted." Detective Inspector Francine Robertson cleared her throat, she too struggling to send words across the painful emotional space between us. "It's Frankie."

My arrest had been heartbreaking for my colleagues in the drug squad. We'd been a team. A family. Of course, they had to trust our counterparts in homicide and sex crimes when they made the decision to lock me up. They had to know what a difficult decision it had been, something not taken lightly or made in haste. I'd lost contact with Davo and Morris, my squad brothers. Last time I'd spoken to them, the vitriol on the other end of the phone had been poisonous.

"You must be calling about the new accusation," I said, trying to help out.

"Yes."

"I didn't do it."

"Sex crimes has asked Melanie Springfield to come in for an interview," Francine said. "She hasn't . . . ah. She hasn't done that yet."

I looked at the green wall of forest before me. Dark depths. A bird cry somewhere in there, high and pained.

"What does that mean?"

"They gave her a call about the statements she made to *Stories and Lives*," Francine said. "Asked her to come in so they can, you know, uh, see if criminal charges are warranted."

I crouched by the side of the road, put a hand on the ground to steady myself. I'd known this was coming. But my mind had pushed it back, forced it down into a dark corner of my psyche where it couldn't be heard through the screaming of my other problems. My legs were tingling, numb.

"She was supposed to come in this morning," Francine said. "But she hasn't shown up. Isn't answering the phone."

"So what now?"

"We don't know."

"What about the girl?" I said. "Elise. The younger sister."

"They're trying to get hold of her. The family seems to have closed ranks."

"Why did you call me?" I said. "You're not on the case. You're . . . Are you still in drug squad?"

"Well, I knew you," Francine said. "So I sort of . . . volunteered."

"You still know me," I said.

She sighed. I covered my eyes, tried to hide in the dark.

"They wanted me to ask you to come in," Francine said. "You're not being charged at this stage. No one's going to, um . . . It would just be appropriate, we think, if you made an official statement."

"I'll have to speak to my lawyer," I said. I hadn't spoken to Sean since the ambush at the *Stories and Lives* studio. He'd left me a voicemail, but I hadn't picked it up. Part of me was disappointed in him for not seeing their delicious accusation bombshell coming. I hadn't seen it coming, either, but during my trial I'd got used to the idea that Sean was smarter than me—that as my savior and protector, things like that didn't get past him. I was the drug squad thug and he was the satin-clad scholar. He didn't make mistakes. Of course I knew, deep down, that he was capable of mistakes. Entitled to them, even. But I'd needed some time to be unreasonably angry.

"It would be good to see you," I told Francine. "When I come down."

She made a noise, a word badly chosen, failing as it met the air. It sounded like it was going to be a "Yeah." But it couldn't be. It couldn't be good to see me.

"That's all I had to say, Ted," she said.

I thanked her, and she hung up. I started walking again, and got the air into me. After a couple of minutes, I called her back.

"You called me because you wanted to help me," I said.

"I wouldn't say that," she answered carefully.

"I would." I turned around, started walking back toward my house. "You said yourself, you volunteered to make the call. You did that because you knew it would be easier on me. Less stressful than being called and asked to come in by a stranger in the sex crimes department. There's a part of you that wants to help me, Francine, even if you're not ready to fully believe in my innocence."

She didn't answer.

"There are more things you can do to help me," I said. "If you want to."

Dear Diary,

It was risky business, but the window of opportunity was small. I told Chloe I was going to bed, left her watching one of her ridiculous shows and snuck out of the house. Penny's mother had put the bins out, right on time, as always. I crouched by the family car and waited, looking out at the street, checking every house to make sure the coast was clear. I took the top bag and rushed off with it, back down the side of our house into the yard. Chloe was totally consumed with the show when I checked on her through the living room window. Mouth open, practically drooling. Some idiot was handing out red roses to glamour models wearing sparkling dresses on the screen. Girls wiping at mascara running down immaculately made-up cheeks.

I opened the bag under the light in the backyard and rummaged through it. Lots of papers. Electricity bill. Used prescription. Receipts. Pages of a notebook. I seized on a scrap slightly damp from the juices of an empty can of asparagus spears. Penny's picture. The girl and her mother and the happy, smiling dog.

I was so excited I hardly slept. In the morning I was up and out of there in the ute, stopping at the RSPCA in Yagoona first to see if I could find the dog. I knew of course that the dog in the drawing was only white because Penny had been so desperate for her mother to confirm or deny she was getting a dog that she hadn't bothered coloring it in—but still, I wanted to stay true to the picture. That's what you do when you love someone. You pay attention to the details. You go the extra mile. You be poetic. I examined the picture closely, walking along the concrete aisles, bowing and squinting at the hounds barking at me from behind the wire in individual enclosures. Penny's dog had a classic long snout and tall, pointed ears. I found a white Chihuahua. A host of Maltese terriers. But they weren't right. I had to get the perfect dog, the one the girl had envisioned. I wanted her to see it in my arms as a thing plucked straight from her dreams. Her dream guy holding her dream dog.

The RSPCA was a blowout. I googled and found a dog and cat shelter near Liverpool, drove there almost panting with anticipation. The only white dog there was a scruffy little teacup poodle with smeary, dirty marks beneath its eyes. My frustration was building. I sat in the ute and googled another shelter. Mount Druitt. Half an hour one way. The morning was wasting away. Chloe called and I pretended I was at work. The man looking at me in the rearview mirror was not a happy guy. Dead eyes as he blew kisses through the phone.

My internet browser had picked up on the fact that I wanted a dog. When I opened my Facebook page, there was an advertisement squeezed into the feed that seized my breath in my throat. There she was! Sitting proudly before the camera, tongue lolling out of a pink-lipped mouth. I laughed aloud, thumped the steering wheel. I was almost shaking as I tapped through to the advertisement on the Trading Post website.

I started the car and drove like a madman, no idea where I was even heading, just wanting to be in motion when I got the address. The British couple met me outside their house with the dog sitting beside them, wagging its thick, furry tail.

Princess. What a perfect name. A princess for my little queen. I gave them the song and dance about my daughter and what a responsible *pet owner she'd be, showed them a picture of Penny I'd covertly snapped during our over-the-fence conversations, pretending to browse while we talked. How could they resist her? That face. They looked at each other, seemed to come to a smiling consensus. I started fumbling for my wallet, but the couple told me she was free to a good home. I could have cried. They were crying, hugging the animal around the neck, saying their goodbyes.*

I opened the door to the ute and Princess jumped right in. Everything was so perfect.

Why couldn't it all have just stayed that way?

Pip had reinterviewed Stephanie Neash at the Crimson Lake police station, her chief superintendent sitting in this time to ensure absolutely all the right questions were asked. There wasn't anything new that could be derived from the girl's story. The last time she had seen her boyfriend, he'd been leaving her house to go to work at the bar that night. She'd stayed in, cooked herself dinner, texting him now and then, receiving the usual kinds of loving responses. She knew he'd finish late, probably around 3 a.m., and go home to where he lived with his father. She signed off at 10 p.m. with smiling emojis and hearts, not realizing, she claimed, that she was saying goodbye forever. Pip had watched across the barren plastic tabletop as the girl struggled through her story again, pushing exhaustedly at frizzy strands of her unwashed hair that wouldn't stay in place behind her ears.

Stephanie's story lined up with her phone records. Her phone had stayed at her house near Crimson Lake all through the night, pinging off a tower nearby on a mountaintop in Cattana. Michael Bell's records indicated he had been home all night as well. Pip was skeptical that either was involved. Whoever Andrew had seen coming toward him as he stood outside the bar, they had caused him to run and fall. Neither his girlfriend nor his father, Pip assumed, would make him do that. Unless of course, she reasoned, they had said something threatening. Or they were holding a gun.

On a corkboard above her desk, Pip had pinned photographs of the two secret lovers. Andrew, steadily growing barrel-chested like his dad, grinning and holding a foaming schooner on some sunny balcony somewhere. Interviews with his colleagues had revealed a cheeky party animal who could be relied upon to pull stunts to amuse a loving crowd. Many recalled him climbing an enormous palm tree in a friend's backyard, slurring drunkenly, to rescue a cat that the noise of the party had scared up into its highest branches. The cat had leaped onto the roof of the house and Andrew had fallen into the backyard pool, inspiring his friends to jump in with him fully clothed. He was a big-hearted guy. He would have been Keema's larrikin Australian dream—sun-bronzed and grinning, gentlemanly and antiauthoritarian at once.

Being the "other woman" was not like Keema. She'd been the good girl at home in Surrey. Her photograph, taken from her Instagram page, was a typical traveler shot—lean arms thrust out before a huge waterfall, embracing the world. Her travels were well deserved. She'd finished school in the top three of her form, spent a year volunteering with humanitarian efforts in Uganda, and was taking this year before starting university to let her hair down. She'd had a boyfriend in high school whom she'd professed to everyone she wanted to marry one day, only to find the Ugandan trip strained the relationship too far. If she'd been hurt by the breakup, she didn't let the world know it. Her Instagram was full of wide-smiling selfies before towering landmarks and packed nightclub dance floors. She was the independent girl now traveling on her own, spreading maps across café tables and marking out her path.

Pip sat and looked at the pictures in her spare moments and found herself forgetting that the two young people were dead. Her mind naturally wandered forward in their lives, sought out careers and partners for the two of them. Keema would return to England and become a nurse. She had the kindly face for it, the resilience. Strong hands and big, welcoming eyes. Andrew would be sad when she left; wary of giving away his heart again. He'd move south, go to school, do something outdoorsy—engineering maybe. Pip could see the sun glinting off his hard hat, his hand at its rim, trying in vain to ward off the Outback sun.

But no. Neither of them would continue on. Someone had cut their paths short. And "cutting" seemed the right word for it; slashing through taut, colorful ribbons, a severing. Pip stared at the photographs and tried not to be dragged down into exhausted sadness at how wasteful it all was.

It wasn't a robbery. They knew that from the bag of money hurled up onto the roof of the bar, probably from behind the establishment. A proper search of the contents of the bag had revealed $1,247 and a stack of signed receipts, the count form Andrew had filled out as he shut down the till not long before he died. Pip sat at her desk and puzzled over the bag, sealed inside a plastic evidence pouch on the desk before her. The suspect had taken the cash out of the bar to make it look like he had gone into the bar with the intention of stealing it, while, in fact, he'd been there to kill Andrew and Keema. Pip understood that. What she didn't understand was why the suspect didn't just take the cash. The bills were unmarked. The killer might have simply transferred the money into his wallet and thrown the bag away. Why throw the bag on the roof of the bar? Why not dump it elsewhere?

Had they intended to come back for the cash later? Pip made a note to herself to order a second interview of Claudia Flannery and the rest of the staff who worked at the bar. Her mind swirled with possibilities. Pip's chief had said it was incredibly lucky the bag had been found at all. Pip knew it wasn't luck. It was Amanda Pharrell's upside-down view of the world. Her new perspective. Pip wanted to know more about Amanda's ways of thinking. If she could just get a handle on the strange woman's psyche, maybe she could take something, some slice of her apparent genius, and use it for her own purposes. It seemed a betrayal to be trying to learn something from Amanda, a person so loathed by Pip's colleagues. She was sleeping with the enemy.

Pip told herself it was these insistent questions, this new hunger for Amanda's secret view of the world that drew her back to the private investigator's office-residence that evening. It was only as she stood in the abandoned main street of Crimson Lake that she questioned her intentions at all. What would Amanda think of her turning up at night? And what if her colleagues saw her? The sun had recently set, the distant green mountains silhouetted black against an angry red sky. Soon, storm clouds would creep from behind them, spread their ghostly arms over the cane fields. Pip had changed her mind, was turning for home when the front door opened and Amanda stepped out.

"Whoa!" Pip actually reeled at the sight of the tattooed detective. Amanda's lean, angular frame was strapped into a spectacular silver dress Pip could never imagine herself pulling off, the entire garment hung with an expensive array of sequins and beads. Amanda turned on her enormous sparkly heels and took in the sight of Pip standing there in the jeans and shirt she had changed into at the station. Amanda's makeup was impeccable. Pip wondered if she was hallucinating.

"Whoa yourself," Amanda said, locking the front door and slipping the key into a black sequined clutch. "What do you know, Sweeney Todd?"

"I'm, uh, I just—" Sweeney pointed absurdly down the street as though the answer lay that way. "Where the hell are *you* going?"

"Out." Amanda shrugged. "The pub. I was thinking of going to Holloways Beach, maybe. I don't know."

"You don't know? You mean you're not meeting anyone?"

"Nope."

"But"—Sweeney gestured to Amanda's dress—"you . . . you look . . ."

"What?" Amanda frowned.

"You look a million bucks," Sweeney admitted. "You're just going to the pub? In *that*?"

Amanda glanced at the dress. "What do you go to the pub in?" she asked. Genuine confusion. Sweeney looked at her jeans, her boots. "This?"

Amanda assessed the other woman's outfit, her chin jutting out. "You can come in that." She nodded, the outfit passed.

"Oh, I wasn't asking to—"

"Let's go, Sweeney-Weeney." Amanda waved her arm. "Before all the goons get there."

When I was in prison, I was segregated to a block housing inmates who would be endangered if they were accommodated with the thieves, drug dealers, and murderers who made up the general prison population. I knew from my time as a cop that there were a number of offenses that could get you segregated. General population boys were expected to "bash on sight" anyone who'd committed a violent crime against a woman or child, so around me were pedophiles, wife killers and baby killers, rapists and child-porn distributors. There were real and suspected snitches, transgender inmates, and former corrections officers. There were also high-profile people, rich folk who might be extorted in the general population, and ex-cops or lawyers who might run into old quarries out there in the yard. Celebrities would appear briefly. Their hearings usually went through the system faster, and they more often than not made bail.

The "don't ask, don't tell" policy applied there, so for the most part no one knew why anyone else was in remand. The policy was supposed to keep violence down within segregation, but the effect was the opposite. Like all humans with more time than things to do, the inmates would spread rumors. Rumors, once born, grow quickly on the inside. One day someone might be whispering to me that a man on the other side of the unit had thrown his wife off a bridge to her death. The next day, it was his six-year-old daughter, and he'd raped her and tortured her first.

Whispers. Meaningful looks. Signals passed across a room and quiet conversations conducted in huddles in corners. Sometimes I'd longed for the crashing, clattering, catcalling noise of the general population. Segregation was the quietest, tensest place on Earth. The air hummed with malignant potential. It was hard to breathe. When fights broke out there was no warning, no shouting or scrabbling in the lead up. The sound of playing cards sliding and slapping on the concrete table would be exchanged for a scream. Then sirens. The shouts of guards.

As I sat across my kitchen table from Dale Bingley, I felt that old segregation tension pulsing in the air for the first time since my release. I'd dragged a chair in from one of the other rooms and set up an old laptop, having given him the new one I'd purchased when I started working with Amanda. He was consumed by his work, sifting through online databases of images of cars, now and then glancing at the screenshots of the blue ute on the table beside him. I felt his eyes on me every now and then as I worked through Andrew Bell's Facebook chat history, every movement of his body making my muscles tense. The sudden sound of his whiskey glass hitting the tabletop as he put it down sent a jolt of pain through my chest.

What was he going to do if we didn't find Claire's attacker? I wondered. He'd said he didn't believe in my innocence. Was he planning on killing me?

If we found Claire's attacker, would he kill us both?

I couldn't focus. I'd been struggling with a heavy sense of guilt over the lack of attention I'd been paying to the Barking Frog murders as my own life imploded. At the end of the day, Amanda was paying me for my services on the case. Michael Bell was paying her. The first days after a homicide were the best time to follow leads and catch the killer, so whatever I could contribute was precious. And yet, even when I was working on the Barking Frog case, a part of my mind was absent. Half listening, I turned over and over my new situation, sought out potential solutions, tried not to dream of potential scenarios. Whenever I thought I was fully focused on Keema and Andrew's case, my thoughts would wander back to Melanie. Kelly. Claire. Dale.

It was hard to forget Dale sitting there in my very kitchen. I gave up for a moment and went to the sink and poured myself a large Wild Turkey.

"Does your wife know you're here?" I asked him. Dale took a while to answer.

"We're separated."

I drank half the Turkey.

"I've been hard to live with," Dale continued. "She was planning to pick up Claire from her friend's house the day it happened. I said she could catch the bus. I thought she was old enough."

I'd been catching buses by myself at thirteen. I thought about saying so, but I didn't know if it was appropriate. I looked out the kitchen window at the dark, listened to the squealing of bats in the trees at the edge of the rainforest. Feeding time.

"Where is Claire?" I asked.

"She lives with her mother."

"Is she . . ."

"She's being homeschooled. She has trouble going outside the house. She's getting therapy. Lots of therapy."

He was standing behind me. I stiffened as he grabbed the Wild Turkey bottle from the counter beside me and sloshed some into his glass, went back to his seat.

"I think it's this," he said. I looked at the laptop screen. There was a photograph of a Ford Falcon ute in a sunlit field, a wire fence in the background. I edged closer, compared it to the screenshot of the blue ute outside the RSPCA at Yagoona. It certainly looked like a match for the car in the CCTV footage. Two-seater cabin, low, flat bed, and the angular lines typical of an older-model car. "Ford Falcon XF,

1988 or thereabouts. I don't think this blue would have come as standard, do you? You don't see too many pale blue utes."

"Might have been sprayed at some point," I said. "If it was sprayed commercially, that could be a good lead. We find out what kind of car it was, then check the mechanics, I guess."

"You go to a mechanic to get it sprayed? Or a specialist?"

"I'm not sure," I said. "I'm not a car guy."

"Neither am I."

"Well. I guess we're just two whiskey-drinkin' single dads who don't know anything about cars," I said. He stared at me, trying to figure out why I'd said that, something I was trying to figure out myself. I poured more whiskey, drank it. Probably a poor choice.

My computer blipped. I looked at the screen. An email.

"I've just got an email from the couple who may have given the perpetrator the white dog," I said. "I asked them again for a description of him. Give me your email address. I'll send it to you. I've also got access from a colleague of mine to a database of car sales and registrations. Hang on a second and I'll—"

"I've got it," Dale said.

I looked up.

"Are you in my email?"

"Yes." He clicked away. "You're friends with Khalid Farah? How interesting."

There was an email from Khalid wanting to know when I was coming down to Sydney next. I didn't know how he'd gotten my personal email address, but Khalid was like that. He had his fingers in everything, everyone, a connection here and a snitch there. Somebody that owed him, somebody that wanted to curry his favor. It was an essential part of being a criminal overlord, being able to slither under closed doors like smoke into police stations, rival meetings, homes, and businesses. He was all seeing, all knowing. He had to both know when danger was coming and be the danger seamlessly infiltrating all protective boundaries.

I frowned across the table at Dale.

"Could you maybe get out of my personal fucking email?"

"You gave up your right to privacy when you got yourself accused of abducting my daughter."

"Are you serious?"

"Deadly." He glanced at me. "You're upset that I'm all tangled up in your life? Too bad. There's nothing you can do about it. Not until we catch this guy. Or we find out that he never existed."

I exhaled hard. My face felt tight, the stitches in my cheek pulling at my skin. I cracked my knuckles.

"You know, I'm doing my best here, arsehole," I said.

"So am I," he replied. "Arsehole."

The bike was a rickety blue racer, older than the one Amanda rode, the chrome brake levers spotted with rust. Sweeney gripped the handles with white knuckles, glancing now and then at her riding companion. Amanda looked absurd in the extreme in her glamorous dress, her bare feet straining on the pedals, the ridiculous heels hooked over the handlebars. It was all so incredibly unnecessary. Beautifully, whimsically unnecessary and unexplained, a long and mysterious expedition out of the town and along a bare dirt road between cane fields, their tires making patterns in the clay. Sweeney felt a weird sense of joy. Warm air fluttered past her, channeled down the alleyway between the walls of cane. Amanda's dress caught the moonlight as her legs pumped the pedals.

"Have you thought about training yourself to get back into a car?" she asked, drawing her bike closer. Ted had told Sweeney about Amanda's refusal to ever travel in cars. He'd warned her against trying to trick or coerce Amanda into one, saying only that it was a bad idea.

"Training myself?" Amanda raised an eyebrow.

"You mustn't get into them because you're afraid, right?" Sweeney said. "Because of what happened to you. In the car. That night."

"I'm not afraid of cars," Amanda snorted. "Cars can't hurt you."

"So why don't you get into them?"

"Because I haven't since that night."

Sweeney tried to form an answer. It was like talking to a computer. The logic was at once completely present and completely absent.

"But wouldn't your life be easier if you could drive?" she said, gesturing to the road before them. "For stuff like this?"

"Are you having a hard time?" Amanda asked.

"No," Sweeney admitted. The moon blazed above them as they rolled up a sudden, small hill. She glimpsed the fields reaching out on either side of them, dissolving at the bottom of the faraway black mountains. "Not at all."

Amanda pulled ahead, guiding Sweeney into an almost invisible crack in the wall of rainforest lining the road where two cane fields met. They were suddenly bumping over the struts of an old train line snaking through the bush, a sugar cane delivery system upgraded and abandoned, grown over with flowering vines. Sweeney kept her eyes on her companion, ducked her head when Amanda ducked under low-hanging branches. She was too slow, copped a slap of wet fingers, the smell of golden penda or something like it. They emerged and skidded to a halt in the lights of a roadside bar almost identical to the Barking Frog, this one free of the grip of the forest, its front porch crowded with people.

Snap, the sign above the door read, with a faded painting of a happy crocodile. Sweeney stood by Amanda as the tattooed investigator pulled on her enormous heels. Amazingly, there wasn't a drip of sweat on her, despite the uncracked Cairns humidity, the bike ride through the dark. Sweeney was conscious of her own body odor. Amanda, somehow, smelled faintly minty up close.

"You'll love this place," Amanda said.

"How do you know?" Sweeney asked.

"I know everything," the woman answered.

"A young guy," Dale read the email from the British couple, sat back in his chair and scratched at his throat. He looked at me, but I wasn't in the mood for talking to him very much. I had escaped into the online conversations of the dead bartenders, Andrew's lengthy interactions with Keema after work.

ANDREW BELL: I think you were flirting with me that night. In fact, I know it. You might think you've got this subtle, refined British way about you, but I caught you a couple of times checking out my arse.

KEEMA DAULE: LOL as if, mate!

ANDREW BELL: It's been so long since I felt this kind of excitement about someone.

KEEMA DAULE: I'm excited, too. I think we're great together. I was smiling when I woke up this morning. I'd been having a dream about you.

ANDREW BELL: Oh really?

KEEMA DAULE: Yep!!!

ANDREW BELL: You should tell me all about it. Maybe we could act it out.

I scrolled through their flirting, their longing early-morning goodbyes, slightly guilty at the intrusion into their private conversations. It wasn't all sexual. They were on their way to something meaningful, it seemed. She talked about how her parents' expectations while she was at school had driven her into a deep depression only alcohol seemed to relieve, how she'd reached rock bottom when a friend dragged her out of a weekend party and berated her in the street for being a "drunken slag." Andrew wasn't the expressive type—couldn't see fit to confess his vulnerabilities to her the way she did, with her long, flowy messages. He carefully selected ready-made pictures from the internet and sent them her way. Two kids standing on a mountain top holding hands, their hair swept by wind. A pair of dogs running free through a field. You lift me up. You help me see the way ahead. I'd be hopeless without you. They were cheesy, but they were him. He'd been a greeting-card kind of guy.

A strange interaction had caught my eye in the lists of dated message streams. Two weeks before the murders, Andrew had logged into his Facebook account at five in the morning and sent Keema a single message that read "who this?" It was odd for a couple of reasons, the foremost of course that Andrew clearly knew who Keema was, had been flirting with her intensely via chat since she began working at the bar. But I was struck by the lack of a capital letter for "who" and the missing "is" between the two words. All of Andrew's dialogue prior to this single late-night message had been perfectly grammatically correct, perhaps an attempt to impress the British girl. A 5 a.m. interaction was also out of character for the two young people. Their usual pattern was to chat before and after work, at seven in the evening as they prepared to meet and briefly at 3 a.m. when they finished up, saying goodnight, exchanging smiley faces and hearts, making promises.

Had the "who this?" message come from someone other than Andrew? And why had they asked who Keema was when it was clear from the previous messages what she meant to Andrew? Was it possible that Stephanie had taken Andrew's phone in the early hours and sent a message, trying to chat to Keema? I was viewing the messages through Andrew's Facebook profile. The messages were plain to see. But were Andrew's messages to Keema deleted or hidden on his mobile phone, where the "who this?" author accessed them?

Keema hadn't answered the "who this?" message. She might have been asleep, and Andrew might have explained away the question when he saw her in person. I raked a hand through my hair, tried to stave off the sinking feeling I had about Stephanie and her knowledge of Andrew's affair. She'd told Amanda that she had no idea he'd been courting the pretty British girl before his death. I'd seen shock and confusion still lingering in her eyes as she stood at the roadside outside the bar with the boy's heartbroken father.

Was that all an act? Had she known? Was she shocked and confused not by the affair, but by what she had done to the young lovers?

"'A young guy,' I said," Dale repeated, slapping the table beside my laptop.

"What?" I slurred. My whiskey glass was empty.

"Look, here." He didn't show me the laptop, just pointed. "The description of the guy who adopted the dog from the British couple. *Young man, maybe twenty-five. Neatly dressed, brown hair. Polite.*"

"Yeah, that's the one," I said. "So if you look back in my email, you'll see a message just now from a woman named Francine Robertson. There's a list there of convicted sex offenders who lived in the area of Claire's attack. See who's in the age range and we'll have a look at the mug shots, see if they have Ford Falcons registered under their name."

"How can he be twenty-five?" Dale threw up his hands.

"Huh?"

"These people are telling me the guy who raped my daughter is twenty-five years old."

"I guess . . ." I went to the counter, poured more Turkey. "I guess it's kind of amazing that someone so young could do so much damage to so many people's lives."

"I can't . . ." Dale gripped his neck, seemed flushed suddenly, out of breath. "I can't understand it. Why do that? You're twenty-five years old and you grab some kid off the side of the road and you—"

"You seem particularly shocked by the single fact of his age."

"Aren't you?"

"I was housed with a bunch of pedophiles at Silverwater." I stared at the lights reflecting in my drink. "They were of all ages, colors, shapes, and sizes."

He said nothing.

"Mate," I said. "Look. You can't be getting stuck up on the details here. You're getting all emotionally fucking tangled up. You can't do that. You've got to put that aside and push on. You can cry about it later, when you've caught the guy."

He looked at me. I finished the bourbon, poured another. He gulped his, winced.

"Have you checked on Ford Falcon utes in the area?" I asked.

"No."

"Go back to that. Finish that, then move on to the next thing."

"You're trying to teach me how to be a cop?" he slurred.

"You're trying to be a cop!" I shrugged. "I'm not trying to teach you anything! Maybe how to get out of my house? I'll teach you that. You wanna learn that? Here. It's that way." I pointed down the hall toward the front door.

"I should punch you in the head," Dale sneered.

"You already did that." I touched the stitches in my cheek. "Look. See? *I* should punch *you* in the head. It's my bloody turn, isn't it?"

We watched each other. I put down my glass. He pushed the laptop closed.

The bar was hot and red, the throbbing internals of an enormous beast, groups of people standing around tall tables or lined in pairs along the bar, heads down, concentrating on intense conversations or stacks of playing cards at their fingers. In the corner, a jazz band squealing and writhing, shining brass cast pink in the overhead light. Sweeney had never been a big drinker, which had probably isolated her from her police colleagues over in Holloways Beach. The expectations of the pub scene filled her with dread. The few times she'd been out with groups of cops she'd cowered under the stares of men from the pool tables and the gaming room, tried to loosen up by hitting the spirits early and made a fool of herself shouting awkward responses to conversations that ran too quickly for her. She was always just slightly too loud or too quiet to fit in. No one turned to her for contributions. She never knew when it was polite to leave.

This place was different. No one looked up as they walked in. The bartender seemed to recognize Amanda and nodded as he took up a glass for what must have been her usual.

"And for your friend?"

Amanda looked. Sweeney felt the air catch in her throat.

"What are you having?" she asked Amanda.

"Chivas."

"Chivas? Christ!"

"I drank prison hooch for ten years," Amanda said. "Whatever I drink, it can't be fruity."

"I'll have the same," she told the bartender. They took stools at the bar, Sweeney wincing as someone's elbow jutted into her ribs, an order shouted over her head. The bartender put two glasses of neat Scotch and a pack of cards before them. Amanda didn't move to pay. Sweeney followed her lead.

"What are we playing?"

"Snap!" Amanda laughed. "What else?"

Sweeney hadn't played Snap since she was in primary school. Amanda shuffled the cards over-hand like an old-school hustler.

Cheers erupting all around them. Groups watching the cards fall, eyes glued to dancing fingers. Sweeney took her deck and started flipping the cards onto the pile in turn, Amanda's hand restless, hovering, the twitch in her neck ticking rhythmically.

"So what's the surveillance turning up on Michael Bell?" Amanda asked, clenching and unclenching her fists.

"For a rough, plain sort of guy, he's got a huge support network," Sweeney said. "The tail is bored out of their minds. People are doing everything for him. Bringing him food, beer, mowing his lawn. He sits at home mostly, seeing visitors. We've identified every visitor and conducted background checks."

"Anyone interesting?"

"Nope." Sweeney peeled and flipped her cards slowly. "Nothing questionable in his bank account, either. He doesn't own, and has never owned, a bike."

"You don't have to own a bike to be a biker these days," Amanda said. "It's all about your weight. If you can prove yourself a good earner you don't even have to know how to ride."

"How do you know this sort of stuff?"

"Ted and I went out to see an old swamp monster named Llewellyn Bruce on our last case."

"Llewellyn Bruce!" Sweeney said. "Jesus. You're brave."

"Anyway, I've been out there a couple of times since just to say hello on my rounds. It's good to keep up these kinds of connections."

When the pair came Amanda slammed her hand down on the stack with a triumphant howl that made Sweeney's ears ring.

"SNAAAAAAP!" she roared.

"Oh my god." Sweeney looked around, blushing.

"Come on, Sweens. You're going to need to be faster than that."

"You ought to be careful going out to those swamps." Sweeney's face was taut as the cards started flipping again. "Don't go by yourself."

"Why?"

"Because something will happen to you."

"Like what?"

"Like you'll be raped and fed to a crocodile, Amanda, that's what."

"I have dealt with both of those particular predicaments rather effectively before, I'll remind you," Amanda said. Sweeney felt her neck rush with heat. Amanda didn't seem to notice her embarrassment and carried on. "So back to Bell. We're not concerned about him. What about the girlfriend?"

"She's a wholly different creature," Sweeney said. "She's very alone."

"She lives alone?"

"Yes, but I mean she's alone in the rest of her life." Sweeney had to yell over the music. "Her parents are interstate. And aside from Andrew I'm not sure she really has any social connections."

"That's what happens when you let your first love consume you," Amanda said. "You get lazy. You don't need friends. You've got him. And then by the time he's gone you've never developed the ability to make friends. That's how old ladies end up dying in perfectly arranged houses and no one notices for three months."

"Huh." Sweeney tried to shake off encroaching dark thoughts, but they rolled over her quickly. She was alone. She hadn't been consumed by a first love, but by a first loss. She'd never developed the ability to make friends as an adult—hadn't noticed the lack in her life until it was too late. Now she was wandering, as her surveillance officers were reporting Stephanie was wandering, walking with her head down to the shops, buying nothing, walking home.

"My round," she said, pointing to Amanda's glass.

By her third Scotch, Sweeney felt warm and happy. Sweat was rolling down her neck into her bra. Everyone in the bar was sweating. Red demons doing their pleasant time in hellfire.

"Have you always had that twitch?" she asked suddenly. She regretted it instantly and squeezed her eyes shut as memories of awkward liaisons with her colleagues flashed before her. Amanda didn't even look up. She was watching the cards fall with the intensity of a cat watching goldfish swimming inside a tank.

"It started the morning after the murder," Amanda said.

"See, this is it. This is what I don't get." Sweeney kept flipping cards.

"What don't you get?"

"You. I don't get you. At all. You simultaneously will and won't talk about the murder." She heard the frustration in her own voice. "You say 'the morning after the murder' like you might say 'the morning after the wedding.' Like you're talking about nothing. It was so damaging to you that you're actually physically traumatized. And yet you go fluttering around your life like this invincible cartoon character, having a great time, solving Scooby-Doo mysteries."

"What exactly am I not telling you about the murder, Teeney-Weeney-Sweeney-Bikini?" Amanda asked. "What do you want to know so bad?"

"Do you regret it?"

"I regret getting the wrong person, that's for sure." Amanda laughed suddenly, absurdly. "I was going for Steven Hench. He'd been right there, outside the car door. But then when I opened my eyes it was Lauren Freeman. The old switcheroo." She glanced up at Sweeney. "Who knew, huh?"

"Yeah," Sweeney said. "Who knew."

"And now Steven Hench is in prison. And that annoys me. Because I loved prison, and maybe he does, too. I don't know."

"But going back to Lauren . . ." Sweeney said.

"She's dead."

"Yes." Sweeney edged closer to Amanda. "Doesn't that make you feel sad?"

"People die all the time," Amanda said. "An airplane engine could fall off a 747 and smash through the ceiling of this bar right now, crushing us both to death like juicy little cockroaches. You ever think about that? I do." She glanced toward the ceiling.

"We leap directly from the murder to airplane accidents," Sweeney said. "It's like being on a treadmill, just trying to keep up."

"Faster, faster." Amanda waved impatiently at the cards.

"Your attitude doesn't match with your behavior." Sweeney slammed her hand down on the stack automatically as a pair of queens appeared. Amanda howled with laughter, rocked back on her stool.

"That was a good one!"

"Are you guilty?" Sweeney persisted.

"Honey, is all this about my guilt?" Amanda asked. "Or yours?"

Sweeney reeled. The Scotch had gone right to her head suddenly. She wondered what the hell she was doing here with this strange woman, pursuing underlying signs of murderous guilt, trying to find a whisper of what she felt. Because yes, she felt it, that cold, dark shadow slithering and sliding around the recesses of her brain, now and then appearing and staining the bright white thoughts she dared to have about happy times in a bar with a real friend, someone who would understand her. She had the sense suddenly that Amanda knew all of it. That knowledge of what Sweeney had done—or what she hadn't done—had somehow escaped the locked box in her mind and Amanda had seen it all. Her father on the floor. His hand reaching. Eyes pleading.

"Oh shit!" Amanda exclaimed suddenly, and hopped off her stool. She was gone in a flash of glitter and beads. Sweeney stumbled after her, took the edge of the bar too closely and bumped her arm painfully on the mahogany trim. There was a big, heavy-shouldered man at the end of the bar, a rocks glass looking tiny in the nest of his tattooed fingers. Gray stubble grew to an equal length over his rugged jaw and skull.

"Oh shit," he said when Amanda slapped his bicep.

"It's the Spruce Caboose—Llewellyn Bruce! I was just talking about you! I didn't know you hung out here!"

"What the fuck do you want?"

"This is LB!" Amanda explained to Sweeney, slapping the big man's arm again in some kind of aggressive-affectionate greeting. "Ole mate! The big cheese of dogs with fleas!"

"I see you haven't grown any tits since I last saw you." Bruce leaned over, peered skeptically into the tiny gap between Amanda's small, hard breasts, pushed together by the dress. "You two on a date?"

"No," Sweeney said.

"This is my partner, of sorts. Sweeney McSweenface. We're on the Barking Frog case together. Not officially." Amanda jerked her thumb and almost got Sweeney in the face. "Hey, it's great to see you here, Bruce. Because you must know Claudia Flannery, the Leathery Queen. She'd be a hundred million years old, like you."

"I know Ms. Flannery." Bruce's eyes wandered over Amanda lazily. "I've known her a long time."

"People tell us the Frog is a biker hangout," Amanda said. "Drug den."

"Not to my knowledge."

"I thought that wouldn't be right," Amanda said. "I told 'em you're the Grand Poo-bah of drugs in the Far North."

Bruce raised an eyebrow in response, shrugged a shoulder. Amanda was about to press on, but stopped herself midsentence and announced she needed to pee, sprinting away into the crowd. Sweeney dropped her eyes from the ancient drug dealer's glare and noticed in doing so a gathering of dogs lazing around the bottom of the man's bar stool. They were not any particular kind of canine, but an assortment of ragged, misshapen things. One creature's neck bulged with a lumpy pink growth that threatened to creep up the side of its face. Another was missing both eyes, the cavities grown over completely with caramel fur. On the counter beside her, Bruce's big fingers took up his glass again, drawing her attention away from the beasts. The fingers of his hand were tattooed with the word "Skin" in mottled blue ink. She looked to his other hand. "Bone."

"I can see what you're thinking," Bruce said when she dared to meet his gaze. "You're thinking—Amanda and me are connected. So maybe she can help you get to know me. You can squeeze in there between us as the new detective in town. We can be one big cooperative family."

"Well," Sweeney struggled to say. "I wasn't, uh . . . assuming anything."

"Let me set you straight." Bruce leaned over. "We ain't no family. Yes, I was glad to see those pricks go. Your predecessors. And I tolerate that little freak fluttering around my place." He waved in the direction that Amanda had fled. "But I don't do cops. Never have. Never will."

"That's okay." Sweeney tried to look nonchalant.

"Oh, I know it is." He appreciated the new detective. "And while I'm handing out advice, you want to watch that Pharrell girl. She's a trouble magnet."

"I can believe that."

"Born under an unlucky star."

"What exactly does Amanda *do* out there at your place?" Sweeney asked.

"Nothing much." Bruce shrugged. "Shows up unannounced. Cracks terrible jokes. Plays with the dogs. I think she might be eyeing off a bike. Crappy old Harley. Doesn't like cars, you see. She never stays long. Zips in. Blathers on for a bit. Zips out."

"So why do you tolerate her hanging around? You want to sell her the bike?"

"I couldn't give a shit about the bike," he snorted. "You make room for your own kind."

Sweeney didn't know what he meant, at first. But then she saw it, flickering in the downward turn of the big man's mouth as the bartender, heading toward them to refill Bruce's glass, got distracted and turned away. A sparkle of malice. Killer instinct. Though she was sure it wasn't on a criminal database anywhere, or written in any court filings, Sweeney knew this man had killed. He made room for his own kind. Amanda, a fellow taker of life.

Amanda was back among them before Sweeney could ask more questions, faking a slow-motion punch to the side of Bruce's round gut.

"All right, spill it, Brucey. The Barking Frog isn't just a bar, is it?" Amanda pushed. "We're trying to figure out why someone would rob the place. It doesn't make any money. There's something we don't know, right?"

"You mean you don't know what goes on there?" Bruce sighed. "Jesus. I thought you were supposed to be some kind of supersleuth."

"I am!" Amanda looked appalled.

"We don't know what goes on," Sweeney said, leaning in. "Can you help us out?"

Bruce looked at his watch. Glanced at the clock above the bar, where a tiny slot in the cream-colored face showed the date.

"Why don't you go back there?" Bruce suggested, his voice light. He grinned, showing a collection of yellowed and gold-capped teeth.

"It's closed tonight," Sweeney said.

"Is it?" Bruce asked.

It wasn't a good fight by anyone's standards. Some cops like to fight, and will deliberately get in scraps with drug dealers and mules in their houses just for the satisfaction of landing a couple of shots to vent the many frustrations of the job. Put a foot through the enormous TV bought with the profits of some young person's life. When I was a drug squad cop, though, my size made me more of a battering ram. Drug dealers, invariably small, wiry people, ran from the sight of me. Kelly also tended to yell at me if I came home with too many bumps and scrapes, so I tried to be careful.

I'd got into a few fights in prison and knew how to defend myself, but even then I liked things to be over quickly. You never knew who was going to jump into the fray with a shiv because they thought they might get away with a quick murder in the chaos.

Dale and I were plenty drunk by the time we lunged at each other, although neither of us might have admitted it. I picked him up and threw him clean through the screen door to the porch. He rolled down the stairs onto the grass and I followed, picked him up and sucker punched him in the guts, copped his palm in my jaw for my efforts. We scrabbled on the lawn, swearing and growling, fighting the sloppiness and breathlessness that too many drinks bring. His nose was bleeding and my lip was split by the time we gave it up. That was about the worst of the damage.

We'd upset the geese again. Dale sat panting on the lawn while I went and hushed them, the light of the kitchen making the blood pouring down his lips and chin a rosy, beautiful shade of red. When I returned to the porch he was sitting with his back to the weather-board wall, carefully inserting a tissue into each nostril. I sat down against the wall nearby and drew my legs up and hung my hands off them, felt strangely satisfied. At the end of the property the water was shimmering as distant sheet lightning flashed over the mountains. The humidity had already surrendered in anticipation of the coming storm. The tension between my enemy and me had also cracked.

I must have drifted away into my thoughts, because when I came to myself Dale had stretched his legs out and the laptop was resting on them. He'd put a fresh glass of bourbon on the boards between us. I didn't know if it was supposed to be his or mine. I drank from it anyway.

He was scrolling through the pictures of cars again, the tissues hanging out of his swollen nostrils now red. I spat blood on the porch and watched the cars rising as he assessed and dismissed them, vehicles shifting up and disappearing off the top of the screen. I watched as he flicked over to the database Frankie had provided access to and started crosschecking the cars with vehicles registered in suburbs around Mount Annan.

We said nothing to each other. We were even, for now.

They rode in silence, heads down, a light rain beginning to fall, pattering warm on Sweeney's cheeks. She kept alongside Amanda, falling back as they penetrated rainforest blocks divided and separated by slick clay roads.

She remembered expressing her theory to Ted that the Barking

Frog made more money than it appeared to, that it was a rumored drug checkpoint for dealers distributing up and down the coast. If they were about to make a big drug bust, Sweeney didn't know how Amanda would go bursting into the bar unarmed, wearing that impossible dress and those ridiculous heels. Then again, she had pranced up to Llewellyn Bruce like she'd known the man for decades, slapped the old criminal overlord on the arm, a cheeky niece trying to rev up her ancient, war-scarred uncle. Bruce, Sweeney knew, was not to be toyed with. His camp of runaways, bikers, and degenerates out in the marshes was known for disappearing local dogs who had lived past their prime, and she suspected they fed more than that to the local crocodiles. Amanda apparently wasn't only guiltless, but fearless too. Fearless people were that way because they knew something most people didn't. Or because they had nothing to lose.

As they came into view of the bar, Sweeney was relieved to see that no lights glowed through the tangles of trees at the side of the road. But there were cars parked further along the road in the distance, the outlines of some visible through the trees, parked bumper to bumper along a narrow dirt road strip in the rainforest. Sweeney noted an old black limousine among the collection. The two women rolled to a halt outside the bar, trying to decide if, through the roar of the night insects all around, any sound was coming from within the building. Amanda kicked the stand down on her bike with her bare foot and Sweeney did the same, watching her partner in the dark.

"What was that old caboose going on about?" Amanda wondered aloud.

"Maybe he was just trying to get rid of you," Sweeney suggested.

"No, he doesn't mind me," Amanda said. "A lot of people do. But he doesn't."

Amanda pulled on her heels and walked to the bar, up the wisteria-coated porch. Sweeney followed at a trot.

"What are you doing? Is this a good idea?"

Amanda bashed on the front door of the bar.

"Oi!" she cried. "Anybody home?"

"Amanda!" Sweeney tugged the woman away from the door. "What if there is someone there? What's your plan?"

"Plans are for losers," Amanda said. To Sweeney's horror, the door suddenly popped open a few centimeters and the silhouette of a man's face appeared. He seemed to assess the women briefly, eyes glittering in the dark.

"Two?" he asked.

Sweeney was frozen. She marveled at Amanda, who nodded confidently.

"Yep, two tonight, my good man. Just two."

"It's five each for newbies. Four for members. You're not members, are you? I haven't seen you before."

"We just joined today," Amanda said. "This morning."

Sweeney wiped sweat from her brow. The thought crossed her mind that Amanda knew what was going on here, had known all along. But as the man shifted the door, Amanda put a hand out, palm up, like she expected to receive something. Only Sweeney noticed the gesture. Amanda dropped her hand as the man turned and gestured into the bar.

"Let's go." Amanda grabbed Sweeney's arm.

"What is this? What's going on?" Sweeney gave a harsh whisper as they walked into the dark.

"I don't know. But it sure is exciting!"

"It's totally inappropriate," Sweeney said through her teeth. "We need to get out of here and call backup."

"Backup is—"

"For losers?" Sweeney whispered harshly. "You know what's not for losers? Surviving the night. Living to old age. Dying in your sleep in a warm, comfy bed and not on the floor of a shitty dive bar."

"This way." The man led them to the bar, where a row of three candles cast a dim glow over the bottles and glasses there. Sweeney began to commit the young man's face to memory, his height, details about him—the navy suit and silver ring on his finger, the bump in the bridge of his nose. His face was passive, almost bored. He reached down and opened a panel in the floor behind the bar, showed the ladder leading into the dark with an open palm.

They descended into the empty keg room. Again three candles provided the only light. It was only now that Sweeney could hear the thumping of music, obscure, voiceless droning. An underground nightclub? Sweeney knew there were speakeasies popping up in Brisbane and Melbourne like this, secret bars behind the rows of bottles in convenience store fridges or behind bookshelves in seemingly ordinary coffee shops. As the man pulled open a thin painted wooden panel on the concrete wall, a room lit with red lights appeared and the music rose. She could hear the sound of voices inside talking, cheering, groaning.

"Fight club," Amanda said, the two women standing steeped in anticipation in the dark keg room. "That's my guess. What's yours?"

"I don't have one," Sweeney said.

"Witches' coven," Amanda said. "You can have witches' coven as your guess. Loser buys dinner."

They emerged into a cellar so large it petered into darkness, makeshift rooms divided from the central space by the use of velvet-draped partitions. The centerpiece of the main space was a semicircle of plush leather sofas, three in all, a scattering of fur pillows and throws hanging from chair arms or fallen to the floor. There were people here in various states of undress, some fully naked, kneeling or bending over the arms of the sofa, some entangled on an enormous black fur rug that looked as though it might have once been the pelt of a giant bear. People stood watching the slithering, grinding, and gripping happenings on or around the sofas, twinkling glasses in hands, cigarettes pinched between fingers. The room was utterly crammed with people, couples embracing against the walls or moving from one velvet-lined room to another. Sweeney glimpsed a complicated pulley system rigged in one room as the curtain door was pulled back. She looked up and saw black ropes feeding through a hook in the ceiling above the partitions.

"Oh my god," she was saying. Sweeney only realized her mouth was moving, words were tumbling out, as her volume began to increase. "Oh my god. Oh my god!"

Amanda's mouth hung wide open, her jaw muscles flexed. While Sweeney shielded her eyes, Amanda stood pointing, arm out, agape.

"We have to get out of here." Sweeney shoved Amanda's arm down.

"THIS IS AMAZING!"

"Amanda." Sweeney grabbed the girl's arm as a man wearing a plastic mask of a doll's face shifted by them, heading toward a small bar erected in the corner near the door. "Let's go. Let's go."

"What are you doing here?" Claudia Flannery was suddenly all that Sweeney knew, a great dark bird glittering with black jewelry swooping out of nowhere into the path between her and the door. "Who let you in? This is a private residence! Get out! Oh my god, get out!"

Sweeney was shoved into Amanda. The air was hot and heavy with the sweat of the bodies filling the room. The music was so loud her own voice seemed immediately lifted up and carried away.

"What the hell is this place? Who are these people? Why didn't you tell us about this?"

Claudia disappeared through the flap in the door without answering. Sweeney struggled to keep up, slipping and almost falling as she followed the woman up the stairs, Amanda at her heels.

"You have no right to be here." Claudia turned on Sweeney again in the quiet of the empty bar, her eyes wild. "No one admitted you. Outside of hours, this business is a private residence, and anything that happens here is a private matter. You're trespassing. You're—"

Amanda's eyes were closed. She stood with a solemn hand on her heart, her other palm pressed close against her lips as though trying to restrain the words that came in a shuddering rush.

"That was the greatest thing I've ever seen," Amanda murmured. "A pleasure den. A secret pleasure den. Sweeney, I swear to you, by the hair of Gandalf's beard, I would never have guessed that. Not in a million years."

Claudia had summoned the doorman, issuing reprimands at him as she dragged him toward the two investigators.

"Get them out of here!" Claudia screeched. She and the doorman both shoved at the women together, bustling them through the front door of the bar. "Get them out! Out! Out! Out!"

On the porch of the Barking Frog, Sweeney stood watching the rain pattering onto the wisteria flowers, tapping onto leaves, making them dance. Things she had seen in the hidden cellar but not processed in the seconds she stood watching the goings-on came back to her. Slick, oiled bodies. Complicated lace lingerie being pulled down by rough hands. Candles. Sexual implements she didn't recognize, in chrome and black rubber, a group of people sitting in armchairs in one of the velvet partitioned rooms, the curtain hanging open, exposing them. They had been men in heavily made-up masks, their bodies strapped and squeezed awkwardly into latex suits hung with enormous, bulbous breasts. Sweeney watched Amanda taking off her heels, preparing to mount her bike again.

"What in the name of all that is holy is a pleasure den?" Sweeney asked.

"You've never encountered one?"

"Not in Holloways Beach," she sighed. "We don't even have an adult shop."

"Well, pleasure dens, they differ," Amanda said, holding a hand out, feeling the rain on her palm. "Some only cater to certain tastes. But from the looks of that one, they were set up for a variety of needs. You go to pleasure dens because they're safe, fun, nonjudgmental environments where you can explore your sexuality and your fetishes and all that sort of stuff with people who like the same things you do."

She walked down the porch and over to her bike, hooked her shoes on the handlebars again. The rain was easing.

"Bondage. Slave and master stuff. Role-playing. Pain games. Swinging. You do it there. Pleasure dens provide catering, too, sometimes," Amanda said. "A bar. Drugs. You can go there to watch or fuck or participate, or you can just hang around friends with your guard down. Those guys in the masks, they're called Maskers. They wear prosthetic woman suits, masks, make like they're real dolls. You pay a membership fee to the establishment and they run these events regularly. It's a much safer way to do that sort of thing . . . if that sort of thing is your *thing.*"

"I can't believe you know about all this," Sweeney said.

"A girl in Brisbane Women's told me about them," she said. "She and her husband used to swing. They'd meet couples online and invite them over to their house to share partners. A guy turned up to their place once and he hadn't brought his partner like he promised he would. Big no-no. Really pissed the husband off. He'd really been looking forward to it, I guess."

"What happened?"

"They tortured him. They were thinking about killing him but the dude got away through a back window. Estelle, the girl I knew, she said she hadn't wanted to do it but her husband was pretty insistent. She got twenty years. If they'd just gone to a pleasure den it could all have been avoided. But her husband didn't like the crowds."

Sweeney watched as Amanda mounted the bike, her bare toes curling around the edge of the steel pedals.

"I'm going home," she said, and raised a hand to high-five Sweeney as she pedaled off. "That's enough excitement for me for one night. Woo!"

"I've been developing a plan of attack over the past couple of days," Sean said. I could hear the anger and frustration in his voice, a clipped, unnecessary precision to every word that came through the phone. "We'll wait until the episode airs tonight, and then we'll file our suit. It's already drafted. It's ready to go."

I stood on the grass in the morning light, at the edge of the road not far from the Barking Frog. Once again my pursuit of the case was being interrupted by my tangled, barbed life, its relentless vines creeping, creeping around my ankles, my wrists, trying to drag me back.

"Can't we just file something to prevent them from airing the episode?" I asked Sean.

"That's not going to work, Ted. Not at this stage."

"So the damage has been done. It's going to go out."

"The damage was done when someone at *Stories and Lives* leaked to the rest of the press that there was a new accusation on the table. Don't worry, we'll find out who that was. We are going to take them all down, Ted. Erica fucking Luther and fucking Channel Three and Melanie Springfield."

"Do we know if Melanie Springfield has been in contact yet?"

"No, but I'll be putting in a request for the interview she did with the show. The full transcript. Apparently, the little snippet of Melanie they showed you during your interview was just going to be a taster to lead the viewers into a full episode with her that's already been filmed."

"Where is the sister in all this? Where's Elise?"

"No one knows. She's gone to ground. Won't take phone calls."

"I want to see that transcript as soon as you get it," I said. "I just don't understand how they could have done this, Sean. It's not true, any of it. Shouldn't *Stories and Lives* have corroborated Melanie's story? Wouldn't they have known we'd sue right away?"

He sighed, inhaled deeply, and set about trying to explain it all to me in layman's terms. Technically, the *Stories and Lives* producers didn't have to fully corroborate Melanie's claims as long as they presented it in such a manner that they weren't seen to be professing that it had actually happened. They'd say they were just reporting the accusation, not trying to say it was true. In order for our suit against the show and the network to be successful, we'd have to prove that they'd assisted in damaging my reputation by airing the content. And they'd argue, no doubt, that such a thing was impossible at this point. Even if *Stories and Lives* lost a lawsuit against me and had to pay for it, it was worth the risk. The whole country would be tuning in to both Melanie's and my interviews. It would smash any other program on at the same time out of the ballpark.

It was Melanie who should really have been sweating over a lawsuit. I presumed she didn't have the kind of legal pull and piggy bank that *Stories and Lives* did. In order to defend herself against my defamation suit, she'd have to present a defense that what she'd said was true. It's not defamatory if it's true. And how could I ever prove that what she was saying about me hadn't happened? Two decades had passed since the days she was talking about, those hazy summer afternoons at her house, the nerve-racking, dreadful responsibility of having a "girlfriend" for the first time. How could I prove I hadn't touched her sister inappropriately? Was she even saying I touched her?

I listened to Sean's strained assurances and felt a great pressure growing in my skull.

None of it made sense. Why would she do this to me? I knew money could be a motivator. Melanie would have been paid big bucks by *Stories and Lives* for her interview detailing new allegations against me. What she was paid was probably in the hundreds of thousands, like the fee I'd accepted for mine. But my decision to talk to the show for the money had been with the secure knowledge that I wasn't going to hurt anyone, except possibly myself. Had Melanie thrown me to the wolves just for cash? There was no telling; Melanie and her sister had gone to ground. Surely when they'd decided to release the allegation, they'd been prepared to back it up to the police and to my lawyer. Were charges being arranged at that very minute? Was I about to be arrested? How could Melanie think she could tell lies about me to a national current affairs program and simply walk away without having to defend what she'd said?

A searing hangover headache was pulsing at the back of my eyes. I'd lost track of what Sean was saying.

"I'm talking big money, Ted," Sean said. He was almost seething. I hadn't heard him swear since my trial. He was generally a very refined, considered man. "This is bullshit. Utter bullshit."

"We'll see what she says when she pops up," I said by way of parting. "She'll have to say something."

Amanda had asked me to pay a visit to the houses behind the Barking Frog to see what information I could gather. She'd said only that one of the houses had contained a "scary recluse woman" who wouldn't talk to her, and that in the other was a dog who wanted to eat her. I'd started in the middle of the row but found the house shut up, seemingly with no one home. I wandered along the road to the northmost house, building up a good sweat by the time I reached it. I guessed I was half a kilometer as the crow flies from the back door of the Barking Frog.

The terrifying, man-eating dog Amanda had described was indeed there. But her owner Lila, a young woman in yoga tights and a sports bra dragged the animal away and locked it in a bedroom, allowing me to come inside.

"It's all very sad," she said briskly, crouching and rolling her yoga mat up on the floor. "I read it all in the paper. Two young kids. Well, not *kids*, exactly. Young people."

She looked uncomfortable suddenly, brushed at her sweat-damp hair, shielding her eyes. I got the sense that she knew exactly who I was, thought she'd put her foot in it by mentioning children. I'd introduced myself as Collins at the door, but that was hardly mastery of disguise. It was more than likely that the local newspapers had heard about my and Amanda's involvement in the investigation and printed a short article about my case.

"Did you want a coffee or something? I've got this really amazing matcha. Change your life."

The dog was scratching at the door of the bedroom.

"Oh no. I'm fine," I said, taking the seat she offered at the kitchen counter. "I won't stay long. I know my colleague Amanda asked you some questions about what you heard the night of the murders. I just had some follow-ups."

I ran through some general questions about her life, her interactions with the bar. She had a spiky, annoyed kind of response to the place. She didn't like all the rubbish left lying around behind her back fence from drunks wandering through the rainforest to and from the bar, and the place got noisy on a Saturday night. She'd visited once and found it too dirty for her tastes. Lila's house was the exact opposite of the dusty, rugged bar I'd visited on the morning after the murders. Her kitchen counters were almost bare, spare for the complicated-looking machine that made her matcha and a small cluster of succulents in pots the size of egg-cups. On the fridge, a single glossy magnet read "If it doesn't challenge you, it won't change you."

Lila sat stiff and rigid in the stool on the other side of the counter, her hands clasped tightly on the countertop. She listened to my questions and gave her responses like she was being interviewed for a job, her face grave with nerves.

"I found a syringe back there once," she said, her lip curled in disgust. "I was walking McKinley back there, you know, along the stream. And there it was. Cap off and everything. I've heard junkies frequent the place. That there are drug deals, maybe."

"Oh." I looked concerned. "Well, it could have washed up the creek. You never know. We haven't substantiated anything about drug deals at the bar yet."

"It's so dangerous," she said distantly. "I hate junkies. If you want to waste your life, don't try to waste mine, too. I could have stepped on it and caught who knows what. Or the dog might have stepped on it. Or some kids playing in the—"

She caught herself. Looked at me, her eyes wide.

The foot, once again firmly in place.

"It's . . ." I struggled for words, my face growing hot. "It's fine, Lila."

"Oh, no." She put her hands to her mouth. "I didn't mean—"

"I get it." I smiled. "It must be awkward."

"*So* awkward," she sighed with relief, leaned forward. "I don't know how you *stand* it. It's like a big fat elephant, following you around the room, everywhere you go! It's like when someone's got a huge scar down the middle of their face and you don't know whether you should mention it or not. You know what I mean? I'm rambling now. I should stop. It's just, I feel bad for you. I didn't know who Amanda Pharrell was the other day or I'd have probably felt the same way when she came to question me. Her being a murderer—that's even worse, isn't it?"

I had no words.

"I guess that's why you guys hang out, right?" She winced. "Safety in numbers. Everywhere you go, people know who you are. What happened. Or didn't happen! I mean. Oh. I'm so sorry."

I stood, folding my notebook shut. "Thanks for your time, Lila. I'll let you know if anything else comes up." I tried to hold a smile as I made for the door. She walked me out, hanging her head the whole time in shame.

I stood in the street and looked up at the canopy, tried to breathe. I made a promise to myself that if I was going to do one thing that day, I was going to work on the investigation I was hired to without my past getting in my way. Without someone getting distracted by the huge scar down the middle of my face that no one knew whether or not they should mention. I trudged to the middle house in the row and knocked again, but again no one was home. I was exhausted by the time I reached the furthest property, a run-down house with a warped roof ticking in the heat of the day.

Something brown and furry scampered away into the long grass as I approached the front door. I could hear a television playing loudly inside. I knocked and it switched off, and a woman answered. She was rotund and dressed in a pink cotton nightie sprinkled with little black flowers. She observed me for a few seconds without speaking, tugging at the already stretched collar, exposing her fleshy upper chest.

"Oh, I'm sorry." I looked at her bare feet. "I seem to have caught you at a bad time."

"No you haven't." She smiled, exposing yellowed teeth. "Come in."

I paused, seeming to have lost my grip on the situation, the order of things. I glanced toward the road.

"I'm, uh. I'm Ted Collins. I'm here with the investigation into—"

"Come inside! I'll get you a drink!"

One witness who couldn't ignore who I was. One witness who didn't seem to care at all who I was. I was in a fairy tale, the wolf going door to door, threatening and friendly in turns, uncovering secrets and trying to decipher riddles.

I entered the house, skirted a heap of damp newspapers in the hall, walked cautiously into the cluttered living room. There was no telling which television had been blaring the show, as four old-fashioned ones in wood-veneer boxes had been stacked in a tall tower before a window covered with a sheepskin comforter. On a low table before an armchair covered in quilts, an army of ants was slowly dismantling a pile of yellow corn chips. I was sweating profusely within seconds, the blankets over all the windows creating a bubble of heat expanding beneath the ceiling.

The woman walked to the fridge and poured me a glass of chocolate milk in a scratched plastic glass. I held it thankfully, not willing to do much more. As she turned and went back to her armchair, I stood rigid in the doorway. There seemed to be nowhere for a guest to sit unless they were willing to brush stuffed toy animals off the many low side tables or perch on the top of a stack of sewing magazines.

"I was wondering if—"

"You can sit down if you want," she said. She gestured to the carpet at my feet. I glanced down the short hall to the front door, trying to decide how best to get out of the quicksand of a situation I found myself in.

"Do you know anything about the murders at the bar behind this property?" I asked. "A couple of nights ago, there were some shootings. I believe police have come and chatted with you, but from what I've been told you haven't really, uh. You haven't been willing to say much."

"Do you have a girlfriend?" the woman asked. Avoiding eye contact, I noticed a stack of envelopes on the floor in the corner. They were addressed to Ms. Mona Wallgreen.

"You're Ms. Wallgreen, is that right?" I asked. "Were you home on the night of the shootings?"

"I don't leave here very much," she said brightly, taking one of the remotes beside the chip bowl covered with ants. There were five of them. I looked around for the fifth TV. A puzzle piece missing. "I don't have a boyfriend. I could go out on dates if I had a boyfriend. We could go to the movies and hold hands."

I decided I was underqualified for interviewing Mona. I went to the kitchen doorway, putting my glass of chocolate milk on the edge of the sink.

"Mona," I said. "I'm going to go. I'm running late for an appointment. But I might send back another officer. I hope you'd be willing to—"

The click of a gun. I froze, my hand on the glass, half my body in the living room, half in the threshold of the filthy kitchen. The sound was unmistakable, yet it didn't make sense in the absurd environment in which I stood. I tried to convince myself that Mona had simply turned the television on, my hand still frozen on the glass, ants wandering up from the sink top toward my fingers. As I let the glass go and turned slowly back around I saw that Mona had a gun pointed right at me. A huge chrome magnum revolver, a Desert Eagle, I thought, though I could barely look at it, the terror was so fast and heavy in my chest. Mona held the gun out from her body like a practiced gunslinger, her flabby arm outstretched.

"Bang, bang!" She smiled. I jolted at the words, sweat now pouring down my body beneath my shirt, making the fabric stick to my back.

"Mona," I said gently. "Is that thing loaded?"

She still had the remote in one hand. She turned the television on without looking at it. I half expected the "Do You Feel Lucky?" scene from *Dirty Harry* to come on. She had this calm, cheerful look to her face. But a portly man with a shiny bald head was simply reading the economic forecast. Mona put down the remote and picked up another revolver from the table on the other side of the armchair, out of my view. Another revolver, a snub-nosed Smith & Wesson. She pulled the hammer back and pointed the two guns at me.

"Mona," I said, trembling. I was having flashes, not for the first time that week, about what an investigation into my murder would entail. Whether anyone would ever even bother prosecuting this woman for it. Whether Kelly would come to my funeral. "Please put the guns down."

"Watch this," she said. I braced for impact, a slug in the guts or chest, tearing through bones and organs. But instead, the barrels of the guns flipped. She twirled the two revolvers on her index fingers expertly, her tongue wedged between her lips, giving each a dozen or so spins before jamming them simultaneously down the sides of the armchair cushion as though inserting them into holsters. I watched as she quick-drew them again, spinning them out to aim them both at me, then spinning them back into the imaginary holsters.

"Pretty cool, huh?" she asked.

I nodded. She performed the trick a couple more times, sending shocks of fear down my body whenever the aim of the guns came up to me, her greasy hair waving at the sides of her plump face as her body worked the weapons. She pointed the guns at the television sets, pretending to pop off rounds at her reflection in the gray glass. "Pow, pow, pow."

In time, I inched over and asked her as softly and calmly as I could to hand the guns to me. She did, and I clicked their barrels open.

They were fully loaded.

I stood in the sun outside Mona Wallgreen's house for a couple of hours giving the story of what had happened inside to hostile, uncomfortable officers of every level while her property was searched. Sweeney arrived and heard my tale, taking furious notes to back up her recording. Mona had given permission for her property to be searched, so a warrant wasn't needed. But I got more and more uncomfortable with the situation as officers began bringing clear evidence bags out of the house and loading them into the back of a truck. There were dozens and dozens of guns. Inside the house I could hear Mona mumbling and shuffling about as she directed the quietly shocked officers to another cache of weapons, and then another, and then another. She had long, antiquated rifles and sawn-off shotguns and small, ornate derringers with ivory handles. The officers coming in and out of the house kept exchanging flabbergasted looks with one another, wondering, it seemed, when the collection would end. The guns were coming out from beneath couches and down from on top of shelves and from behind lumps of meat in the freezer that appeared to have been there for decades.

"Two of my officers came and visited her the other day," Sweeney said. "And she gave them nothing. Wouldn't let them in. And Amanda said she had the door slammed in her face. But you"—she squinted at me—"she let you right in? Why?"

"I think she might have liked the look of me," I said uncomfortably. "There were hints about the position of boyfriend being available."

Sweeney wiped her mouth, and I couldn't tell if she was stifling a laugh or not.

"What do we know about her?"

"She's Mona Wallgreen." Sweeney flipped a page of her notebook. "Forty-seven. She was being cared for by her father until he passed away a couple of years ago. That's all anyone really knows. I assume the guns were his. We'll have to run them all, see where they came from."

"Right."

"What do you think?" Sweeney glanced toward the trees through which the Barking Frog stood. "She goes over there wanting to perform her gun show and pops them both?"

"Would explain the money on the roof," I said. "Doesn't look like Mona needs or wants cash."

"Doesn't explain how she knew to lie Keema and Andrew on their bellies, hands clasped behind their heads. That's classic law-enforcement behavior, directing them to do that."

"Maybe." I shrugged. "Maybe we're assuming too much. Maybe they just got down and did that. Instinct. Something they'd seen people do in the movies."

"Hmm." Sweeney nodded.

"Although I reckon we're up to about thirty guns come out of that house so far," I said, watching a pair of officers trying to fit the magnum into an evidence bag. "And not a single nine millimeter yet."

Sweeney's chief arrived, and after a brief hello to Sweeney, ignoring me, he wandered into the house. Mona came out the front door, accompanied by a short patrol officer, and bent at the waist, pointing to something under the house. The officer looked weary. I felt his pain. There was a lot of paperwork ahead for these guys.

"I'm, uh." I debated whether to step in or not. "I'm getting a little worried about this."

"About what?"

"The search."

"Why?" Sweeney glanced up at me. "She gave her permission."

Mona had indeed acquiesced to the search after I'd suggested to her that it was a good idea to let officers in. As her imaginary boyfriend, she'd taken my word.

"But she's clearly got some mental problems." I gestured toward Mona in her pink nightie. "The defense will argue she couldn't give consent for the search and anything you find will be tossed out. I've seen it happen."

"Oh." Sweeney nodded. She looked vaguely embarrassed. "Of course."

"If you find the murder weapon now, you risk it being—"

"I get it, Ted. I get it," she huffed. Her chief wandered back over, and Sweeney straightened like a soldier coming to attention, her lips taut.

"I think we should halt the search," Sweeney said before her chief could open his mouth. "There may be an issue with Ms. Wallgreen's capacity to consent to a search. It was a mistake to go in. I'm going to give the order to pause here, and we'll get an emergency warrant rushed through."

"Right," Chief Clark said. "Exactly as I was about to say. The woman looks like she's lost her bloody marbles. I'll tell the guys inside, and you can spread the word out here."

Sweeney nodded and went to the officers near us to spread the message. I went along with her, feeling guilty.

"Pip," I said and caught her arm when we were out of earshot of the others. "I didn't mean that to sound patronizing."

"No, no," she sighed. "It wasn't patronizing. It was correct. I just wish I'd known it myself. I'm just out of my depth here."

"I spent most of my time as a cop completely out of my depth," I said. "I think it's in the job description. You're fine, Pip. You're right where you need to be."

She laughed a little and rubbed my arm, taking off to continue stopping the search. I don't know if she really believed me.

Getting home was a relief. Dale wasn't there. I'd let the geese out before I left and they had gathered in the shade under the porch. I crouched before them and Woman hissed at me in greeting.

"I nearly got shot dead today by a crazy shut-in with cowboy skills," I told her. "What did you guys do?"

The geese waddled out from under the porch, inspired by my presence, and started pecking at the lawn. Woman walked with me behind the main group, listening while I updated her on the Barking Frog case. We came to the wire fence and stood for a while side by side, man and goose, looking for signs of danger on the surface of the water. When we found none I went to the little tub of goose food I kept on the porch and unclipped the lid, filled a cup with the mixture of grains, pellets, and dry grass. The geese mainly lived on the fresh grass of my lawn, but this mixture kept them fat and happy, and it was a good tool to get them to go where I wanted them to if I had to herd them back into the playhouse or up onto the porch quickly. I shook the cup and they came waddling toward me as fast as they could, all except Woman, who wasn't so easily driven into a frenzy. As I walked the cup of mixture back down to the lawn, I saw Dale Bingley appear from around the side of the house, sweaty like he'd been out walking in the heat.

We said nothing. The crackling tension of the night before wasn't there, but I knew it could swell to cyclonic levels in an instant. He stood beside me as I scattered the lawn with the mixture, the geese huddled before me, pecking and sifting through the grass.

"Do they have names?" he asked.

"Yes," I said, clearing my throat. My face was reddening. "But they're not. Uh. I mean, I'm the only one who lives here so I named them things only I really understand."

He stared at me.

"That's Squishbird," I admitted, pointing to a bird. "She always used to end up squished in the huddle when they'd sleep at night beside their mother. Sometimes all the other birds would pile on top of her, covering her completely."

"Squishbird," Dale said. I thought I marked the tiniest flicker of a smile at the corner of his mouth. This was humiliating.

"Bitey Bulger." I pointed to another bird. "Like the gangster. Whitey. Whitey Bulger."

"He bites?"

"Not hard." I put my hand out. As usual Bitey rose up and started biting the side of my hand and wrist, snapping my fingers in short, tugging nips. "He's always done it. I don't know why. Maybe it feels good."

Dale watched as the bird returned its attention to the grass. I looked at the cup half full of mixture in my hand.

"Here," I said. I put a hand out. Dale stared at the hand. I waited. Our long shadows in the morning sun were sentient on the grass before us.

Dale put his hand, palm up, on mine. I tipped some mixture onto his palm. He crouched, and the birds flocked to his hand, long necks shivering with excitement, ducking and pecking at the mixture in turn, great gobbling beakfuls.

I thought I heard Dale laugh.

Dear Diary,

I walked to Penny's front door with the dog in my arms like a fairy-tale peasant come to put an offering before the queen. I remember the feel of her, warm and struggling against my chest, a young dog who just wanted to explore the new sights and smells of the front of the house. I thought she'd have plenty of time to do that. I thought I was bringing her to where she'd belonged all her small and miserable life, the pencil drawing of the dog made real as though by magic.

Penny's mother, Andrea, opened the door, and it all went wrong in a matter of seconds.

"I live next door," I explained after the initial smiling pleasantries, the white dog licking my ear. "I know this is a bit weird but my . . . my sister owns this dog here, Princess, and she's taken off to England with her husband. I know your daughter—Penny, is it?—I know she's wanted a dog for a while now, so—"

"I'm sorry." Andrea shook her head once like she was struggling to understand. Her expectations of what I'd come to the door for turning, flipping. "What's going on? Your sister . . ."

"My sister's abandoned this dog." I laughed, and knew it sounded

forced. Tried to reel it back. "She's kind of dumped it on me. She's in England now. She went with her boyfriend. Her husband."

"Is she coming back?"

"No."

"I'm sorry, I don't understand how I can help."

"Well, I know your daughter has wanted a dog."

"How do you know my daughter?" Andrea pulled back, her mouth hardening. This wasn't going the way I'd planned. I could feel the muscles in my neck and shoulders pulling tighter and tighter. I dropped the dog at my feet, maybe too hard.

"We talk over the fence," I said, pointed to the back of the house. "I'm Kevin. Your next-door neighbor."

"Well, Kevin, I don't know how I can help." Andrea glanced down at Princess, the cold bitch eyes of a woman without a soul. "We can't have a dog here. I work. There'd be no one to take care of it during the day. And Penny's not old enough—"

"Penny is very responsible," I snapped. "She's a very mature person."

"That may be," Andrea said carefully, eyeing me with the stillness and caution a person reserves for a madman on the street. "But Penny is not having a dog. Not this dog. Not any *dog. If your irresponsible sister has dropped this animal on you and gone away, I suggest you keep it yourself or you take it to the pound."*

Princess was straining on her lead, trying to sniff the flowering bushes to the side of the doorway. I yanked her back to my feet. The dog yelped. Andrea took a step back in the doorway, holding on to the jamb.

"Don't you think it's important," I said slowly, "to listen to what Penny wants? She wants a dog. This is the perfect dog for her. It's not hard to care for a dog. You feed it. You pick up its shit. It'll bring Penny untold fucking joy. What kind of a mother are you?"

Andrea stiffened. I'd gone too far. I felt sweat breaking out on my temples. I needed to rescue the situation before it got out of control. Before I got out of control.

"I'm sorry." I wiped the sweat on the collar of my shirt. "I'm really sorry. I just—"

"Take the dog to the pound," Andrea said. "And don't talk to my child anymore."

She slammed the door in my face.

Claudia Flannery arranged herself in the chair in the interrogation room at Crimson Lake police station and sighed, watery eyes wandering disdainfully over every scuff mark and stain on the bare white walls. It was a mystery to Sweeney why the room seemed to inspire such disgust in the bejeweled old crone. She remembered the sour smell of burning oil and human sweat hanging in the air of the cellar beneath the Barking Frog, the occasional unmistakable whiff of Vaseline. She could only imagine what that smelled like when the lights were up, what stains and marks the candlelit darkness hid.

Amanda took a long while finishing up an explosion of friendly chatter with Sweeney's chief outside the interrogation room door. The friendliness seemed distinctly one-sided. Chief Superintendent Damien Clark had indeed been around when Amanda had committed her murder, and had made it clear to Sweeney that he wanted the bubbly investigator out of the station as soon as possible. Sweeney had assumed that, when Chief Clark discovered she had been working with the private investigator, she would be yanked into his office and given a roasting, and that the lean old man would have insisted Amanda be removed from the investigation altogether. But it wasn't so. Not yet, anyway. Perhaps the hard-faced, softly spoken man knew that Sweeney felt lonely and intimidated in her role as the station's only detective-rank inspector. Like a father who tolerates his child's bad friend, he'd staved off Amanda's blathering with minimal civility, huffed off to his office, and slammed the glass door, leaving the two to interview the bar owner together.

Amanda watched the preparations of the recording for the interview like a fascinated child. When Sweeney identified herself as Detective Inspector, Amanda gave her a little congratulatory bump in the shoulder with her own, obliterating any air of officialdom Sweeney had managed to gather in the room until that point. Sweeney set her pen to her interview sheet and wrote Claudia Flannery's name at the top of the page.

"Ms. Flannery," Sweeney said, "I'm obliged to inform you that we intend to pursue a range of charges against you arising from what Ms. Pharrell and I witnessed last night."

Claudia yawned.

"The first charge," Sweeney insisted, her voice hardening, "will be lying to the police. You told us your establishment, the Barking Frog, would be closed yesterday evening. That was not the truth. And you failed to mention the sizeable basement connected to your establishment, thereby preventing our forensics officers from including it in their processing of the crime scene."

"No one asked me about the basement." Claudia rolled her eyes. "Perhaps if you'd wanted to search it, you could have told me it was considered part of the crime scene."

"We never knew it was there!" Sweeney said.

"Then it looks like *someone* should have checked the building plans to ensure they covered all of the establishment," Claudia sneered. "Who exactly is in charge of this investigation?"

"Sweeney!" Amanda pointed. "You're in charge! It was *you!*"

Sweeney kicked Amanda's shin under the table.

"We suspect that the release of the sprinkler system that damaged the crime scene at the bar yesterday morning was not an accident,"

Sweeney continued. "I put it to you, Ms. Flannery, that you deliberately tampered with a crime scene in order to prepare your establishment for the events of last night."

"'I put it to you.'" Amanda closed her eyes, sighed, as though remembering an old, cherished song. "I was waiting for you to say that. I love it when cops say that."

"Lying to police, overtly *and* by omission," Sweeney continued, glaring at Amanda. "Tampering with a crime scene. Attempting to pervert the course of just—"

"I understand what you're saying, Detective Inspector Sweeney." Claudia gave a bored sigh.

"Then there are drugs charges," Sweeney said. "Amanda and I saw people in that room engaging in the use of illicit substances. A search of the establishment will surely render positive results for evidence of drugs on the premises. And I suppose none of the substantial income you receive from events like the one you hosted last night shows up on your income tax statements."

"Detective." Claudia put a withered hand meaningfully on one of Sweeney's. "None of those charges are ever going to be pursued. So why don't you just dispense with the threats and ask me what you want to ask me?"

Sweeney reeled in her chair, glanced at Amanda to see if there was something the investigator knew that she didn't. Amanda was examining her chipped black nail polish.

"What are you talking about?"

Claudia fiddled with a huge red stone on a pendant on her spotted chest. "What you saw last night was a well-established, very popular gathering. A very exclusive meeting of very particular people who pay a premium charge to engage in activities of a specialist taste."

"*Well-established,*" Amanda crooned deeply, imitating the woman across the table. "*Particular people. Premium charge. Specialist taste.* I like the way you talk, Clauds. You should work in advertising."

"My establishment caters to activities that my clients like to keep private," Claudia said. "I keep secrets. People come to me from all across the state, sometimes from the other side of the country, with unique requests. I do what I can to fulfill those requests. Someone wants to drink human blood, or have someone cut them, shave them, burn them during an intimate act, well, there's only one place in the whole state where you can experience that in a safe, secure, professional environment."

"I'm not sure I need to know all this." Sweeney grimaced.

"Last year I had someone come to me who wanted to experience being eaten. Only in part, of course. I don't deal with murder. But I was able to find that person a partner, and at one of my parties the two went off together and enjoyed that experience."

"Are human beings red or white meat?" Amanda asked.

"Could we just stick to the point, Ms. Flannery?" Sweeney snapped. "We've got a double murder on our hands in an establishment that you fully admit caters to dark, twisted tastes."

"Dark, twisted tastes!" Claudia slammed her hands on the table, her palms spread, as though bracing for an earthquake. "That must be the most ignorant thing I've heard in a long, long time."

"I don't know if it's ignorant but it's certainly politically incorrect." Amanda nudged Sweeney, waggled a finger in her face. "People can drink each other's blood if they want to. No one's forcing you to go watch."

"*You* forced me to go watch last *night*," Sweeney hissed, blocking the microphone beside her. "We could have been walking in on *anything*."

"We did walk in on anything." Amanda smiled. "Anything and everything!"

Sweeney unblocked the microphone. "Claudia Flannery, did you arrange for someone to murder two young people in your bar as a part of the sexual or . . . or experiential services you provide?"

"I did not."

"Do you have knowledge of why these young people were murdered in your establishment that you're keeping from police?"

"No, I do not."

"Did you arrange this experience, and then have the person who paid you for it make the whole thing look like a robbery? Did you have them throw the bar's takings up onto the roof for you to retrieve later? Did you try to tamper with evidence of the crime by releasing the bar's sprinkler system and destroying the crime scene?"

"No, I did not." Claudia Flannery hung an arm draped in glittering fabric over the back of her chair. "And now that I've told you that I didn't, you need to put the whole matter to rest, Detective Inspector Sweeney. Because I guarantee you, those are the only answers you're going to get, and banging your head against the issue for much longer is only going to diminish your obviously vibrant soul."

"What are you *talking about*?" Sweeney looked to Amanda again. "Ms. Flannery, you're facing serious charges here. You need to just—"

There was a tapping on the glass panel in the door to the interrogation room. Amanda jolted in her seat as though stung. It was Chief Clark, curling a finger, beckoning Pip into the hall.

As the door closed behind Sweeney, the tall, immaculately dressed man began to speak. His tone was one of reverence. Quiet, and calm.

"Thank Ms. Flannery for her time and send her out," he said. "Call her a cab and give her a cab voucher."

"What?"

"You heard me. Pack it up, and ship her out."

"Why?"

"Because I've just had a call from the premier's office, that's why," he said. The two officers stared at each other. Claudia's words came back to Sweeney in a sickening rush.

A very exclusive meeting of very particular people . . .

"Oh, Jesus Christ." Sweeney turned and kicked the wall beside the interrogation room door. It was all she could do not to scream. "Are you serious? Are you fucking serious? I don't care who's going to these underground weirdo sex parties or how fucking important they are. I'm trying to find out who murdered two kids!"

"Well, word is getting around to the very important people that the hostess of their 'underground weirdo sex parties' is giving an official interview, and that is going to cause mass panic if we don't shut it down right now." Chief Clark's whisper was hard and low, like a snake's hiss. "I'm not going to field calls from magistrates and celebrities and fucking politicians all day long reassuring them that their dirty little secrets aren't going to be on the cover of the paper tomorrow just because you don't have any other leads."

"I have other leads!"

"Great. Drop this one and get on to them instead."

Chief Clark tugged open the door to the interview room.

"Cooked it with garlic and olive oil?" Amanda was leaning over the table, mouth agape, embroiled in gossip with Claudia Flannery. "Did you taste some? What was it like?"

"Get out, Amanda." Sweeney jerked a thumb toward the door, defeat making her limbs seem heavy as lead. "Ms. Flannery, you too."

When I left the house, Dale was sitting on the porch in the sun staring idly at the list of convicted sex offenders in the area of his home, shifting the pages slowly, eyes wandering over the faces there. It seemed a dangerous thing to leave him doing. He'd been shocked to learn the number of registered offenders in his local area, and I didn't think that shock was eased by the fact that of the twenty-one people listed in the fifty kilometers from where Claire was abducted, only two had been convicted for sexually assaulting a child. In the collection were men who had raped or molested adult women, their wives or an acquaintance usually, but in one case a woman at a nursing home where the offender worked. There was one female offender on the list, a teacher who had been convicted of sexually molesting a teenage boy. The rest were made up of child pornography charges.

I'd watched Dale looking over the pages for a little while, knowing exactly the kind of dark thoughts that were swirling through his brain. It's a shock to learn for the first time that there are far more sex offenders around in polite society than the newspapers report. Gang rape and child rape make the national news, but a man's drunken rape of his neighbor after a house party doesn't. It's shocking to learn that they exist at all, and then shocking again to learn that they some-times go on after serving their time in prison to live relatively ordi-nary lives working at the local store or sitting down with a friend to coffee on the front porch, or walking their kids to school.

I thought about explaining to Dale that some of the offenses on the list went back decades, and not all of them might be true. But then I imagined a man who I wasn't completely sure hadn't raped my daughter trying to explain to me that the world wasn't such a bad place and I dropped the issue. I'd tried to broach the issue of my new accusations with him, but he wouldn't look up from the pages.

"I need to know how you feel about them," I said, struggling to find the right tone. "I mean, you can't be feeling nothing."

"I'm trying to get my daughter's case solved," he said. "This is about Claire. This is about finding the man who hurt her. I can't focus on anything but that right now."

"So you're just using me," I said.

"Yes." He glanced at me. "You think I actually care if you're a good person or not?"

"Well . . ."

"What did you think?" he asked. "If I found out you were innocent we were going to be best buds? Go to the pub together and grab a schnitzel? Watch the game?"

"No."

"The day we find out what happened to Claire, that will be the last day we'll ever see each other. Maybe it'll be the last day you'll see anything at all."

"What does that mean?"

"What do you think it means?"

I stood uncomfortably, watching him slowly turning the pages of sex offenders over, working his way down the list, reading the details. I left, my stomach in knots, and made a phone call in the car.

Dr. Val Gratteur answered her office phone after only a couple of rings.

"I was just going to call you," she said.

"Oh, really? Why?"

"No, no. You go first. Mysteries annoy me." I heard her exhaling, imagined her blowing cigarette smoke. The medical examiner smoked like an old Russian gangster.

"I need a friendly ear. I'm in a bit of trouble." I told her about Dale Bingley's haunting presence in my house. The subtle death threat he had just burdened me with.

"Amanda knows he's there," I said. "But I feel like someone else needs to know he's hanging around me in case, I don't know . . ."

"In case he does away with you," Val said.

"He's been close a couple of times."

"Well, I'll make a note of it," she said. I heard paper shifting against paper, the click of what must have been a pen. "I'm writing it in my logbook this very instant. Ted Conkaffey . . . murder . . . equals Dale . . . Bingley . . . I drew a little picture of a knife for good measure."

"Thanks," I said.

"Are you in the car?"

"I am."

"Turn it towards Cairns," she said. "I was going to call you because that murdered boy's girlfriend is on her way here. She asked to see the body."

"Oh?"

"Yes," Val said. "Struck me as odd. Thought you might like to watch."

"I'm on my way," I said.

"Don't freak out," I said as I entered the medical examiner's office, the small, frail-looking Val Gratteur turning from her cluttered workbench to greet me. Val had been an early supporter of mine, an unexpected friend in need when I'd turned up at her offices looking for some information about Amanda's and my first case together.

Back then I hadn't been accustomed to being recognized in public, and she'd sat me down and told me without frills or fuss that she knew who I was and wasn't convinced of my guilt. Since then she'd proved a good listener when I was afraid or stressed, a solid sounding board for my theories and, of course, an excellent goose babysitter when I went away.

"Oh, crap," she sighed, noting what remained of my black eyes, the stitches. "You didn't tell me you'd actually been in fisticuffs with the guy."

I launched into the placations of a boy who had been in a scrap to a worrisome mother. She sat me down and tested my cracked ribs with her firm hands, looked in my eyes with a little torch. Val was, among all else, my only safe form of medical care since my accusation. She inspected the stitches Amanda had put in me with pouting, thoughtful lips.

"These aren't half-bad, you know." She stood back and appreciated my face. "I'd hire her as an assistant if I wasn't so concerned with how much fun she'd have in here."

"Are you going to take them out?" I felt the stitches.

"Couple'a days."

"Will it scar?"

"Oh you'll have a devastatingly rugged scar." She smiled. "But the 'chicks dig scars,' so they say."

She gave my shoulder a few hard pats like a mother proudly testing the solidity of her grown-up son.

"So what's so odd about a young woman wanting to see her dead boyfriend off? Aren't you supposed to view the body for closure?"

"Just an odd tone to her voice," Val said. "I thought it would be prudent to have someone else present, just in case. How are my birds?"

"They're good," I said. "I'm looking forward to having time to keep working on their house."

"Once you get the ghost out of yours," she said.

"Mmm."

"Are they going to be safe in Mr. Bingley's company while you're away?"

"He doesn't seem to mind them," I said. I tried to explain what it was like living with a man who one minute was prepared to put his hand in mine, and the next minute threatened to kill me. Val stood with a palm on the steel autopsy table, hip cocked, watching my face with concern.

"When are you going back down to Sydney?" she asked.

"I thought I'd take off this afternoon," I said. "I don't want to be anywhere I'm known to frequent when the show goes to air."

I'd told Val about my guilt at not being able to stay and continue the case with Amanda and Sweeney, that I had to head back down to Sydney to make an official statement on Melanie Springfield's accusation. At precisely seven that night, *Stories and Lives* was going to air my interview, complete with the snippet about a "predatory relationship" with her eight-year-old sister and my response. I'd glanced at my watch a hundred times that day already, counting down the hours until the next chapter of my nightmare began.

In time Val wheeled out Andrew Bell's body from a room behind two huge swinging doors. A couple of friends and family members who couldn't make the funeral had decided to come and view the body, so Val had asked the funeral director to come in early and dress Andrew. He was dressed in a neat black suit with fine pinstripes, expensive. The tie was an oddly joyful floral print, pink and red. The director had done what she could with his head, but the back of Andrew's skull had been obliterated during the shooting and she had been forced to shave the rest of it to document the injuries. In stark contrast to his suit, Andrew was wearing a Brisbane Broncos football team beanie, the rearing horse emblem pulled low on his smooth forehead. As per custom, Val took a white sheet from the shelves beside a rack of tools and spread it over the body only seconds before a buzzer announced Stephanie's entry.

The receptionist brought her in. Stephanie walked weakly, her steps shorter than usual, the hesitant tread of someone struggling under the physical weight of grief. She burst into tears at the sight of the figure on the gurney, hardly seeming to question my presence in the room at all.

I went to her and held her. It seemed the only real option when I realized Val wasn't going to. Val had probably realized long ago that hugging the families of her victims wasn't worth the emotional toll it would take on her later as she lay awake at night, remembering their shoulders shuddering in her arms, the intimate feel of their gasping breath on her skin. They tell you not to hug victims in your initial training in the police. When you hug you cross the professional barrier, the one that's supposed to keep you safe from the horrors of your job.

"Are you sure you need to do this?" I asked. "There are other ways you can say goodbye to Andrew."

"He's not going to look how you're used to him looking," Val said. "It might affect your memory of him when he was alive."

"I want to see," Stephanie said, drawing away from me. She let a few sobs escape her thin lips, pushed back a lock of sweaty hair. She was not taking care of herself, this girl, and that worried me. There had been no one supporting her at the crime scene except Michael Bell, and no sign that her parents were going to come from interstate to help her get through her loss. Here she was again, alone. I knew Sweeney had put two officers on Stephanie, but she'd likely not insisted it be twenty-four hours a day or involve more than parking in the street outside her house while she was inside.

Val pulled the sheet back to Andrew's waist. Stephanie looked for a few seconds then turned and shoved her face into my chest.

"It's okay," I lied. I waved at Val and she covered the body again. "This is . . . This is all going to . . ."

What was there to say? This was all going to be over soon? This was all going to go away? Neither of those things was true. I was hardly focusing on the girl crying in my arms, trying to think back to when I was fifteen. My mother had died of breast cancer. There hadn't been much to say then, either. Lots of uncomfortable looks. People turning away from me at school, going to play with other kids, leaving me with my weird, incomprehensible grief. I hadn't even cried at first. It seemed impossible to accept, her being gone, for either my dad or me. We'd avoided each other for weeks afterward, neither of us wanting to be the one to break the standoff. I was so lost in these thoughts when Stephanie spoke that I hardly heard what she said.

"I did it," Stephanie cried. I rubbed her back, my hand thumping up and down over pointy bones.

"You didn't do anything. This was a horrible, horrible thing. It doesn't matter that—"

"I did it, Mr. Conkaffey." Stephanie drew away from me, wiped her face. She looked up at me, her mouth trembling, a downturned line. "It was me. I did it."

Dr. Valerie Gratteur was at the head of the gurney, about to push Andrew's body away toward the double doors. An unlit cigarette hung from her bottom lip, her mouth open in shock. I stared at the medical examiner, trying to put my thoughts in order. Stephanie's hand came up to my arm, and with a weight that didn't seem to fit with her tiny figure, she gripped me, as though hanging on against a terrible current.

"I was there that night," Stephanie said. "I killed them."

Val gave me a look that said "I told you so" and began wheeling the gurney with Andrew Bell's body on it away to give us time. I took a chair from Val's workbench and dragged it to where Stephanie stood. She eased into it like she was favoring fresh wounds.

"I'm going to turn on the recorder on my phone," I told Stephanie. "Is that okay? I really think we need to . . . uh . . ."

"It's fine. It's okay." Stephanie nodded, wiping tears. "I know you have to do what you have to do."

The girl had become stiff, numb. Val crept into the room and stood leaning against a spare gurney near us. I brought up the voice memo app on my phone and started recording.

"You're not obliged to say anything at all to me," I said. "You're here of your own free will. No one's threatening you. No one's pressuring you right now. Would you agree?"

"Yes," Stephanie said, nodding.

The hand that held the phone was shaking. I tapped the screen, made doubly sure the seconds were being recorded.

"I'm Ted Conkaffey," I said. I'd forgotten the old scripts I used to use for interviews, the ones that ensured the confession was useful to Sweeney and her team. My career as a police officer seemed a million years ago. "I'm in the presence of Dr. Valerie Gratteur of the Cairns Hospital's Forensic and Scientific Services office, and Stephanie Neash. Stephanie, you've . . . you've just said something to me and I think it might be a good idea if you say it again for the recording."

I stated the date and time, having almost forgotten to, struggling to decide if this was appropriate. She was over eighteen, legally an adult. I wasn't obliged to wait until she had a lawyer or a parent or guardian with her. The recording I was about to make might not stand up in any courthouse. But exhilaration and terror were coursing through me, and all I knew was that I wanted to capture what she was about to say even if it meant it would be legally problematic.

"I killed Keema and Andrew," Stephanie said. She blurted the words between sobs, eyes fixed on the floor before her. "I was there that night. I knew about the affair already. I found out weeks ago. I was so mad I just killed them both. I was so mad, so humiliated. I'm so fucking humiliated."

Stephanie held a fist to her eyes, seemed to want to beat at her forehead with it. Val lit the cigarette she'd been intending to have and started sucking hard on it, blowing smoke over her shoulder. I felt a sudden impulse to ask her for one, to do the same.

"Can you go back for me?" I asked. "When did you discover the affair, exactly? How did you find out about Andrew's relationship with Keema?"

"I don't know when it was exactly. You could look it up, probably. I sent her a message. He had been acting weird," Stephanie said. Her voice was tiny. I held the phone toward her. "He was attached by a fucking string to his phone. It went everywhere with him. Even into the shower. My girlfriends said that that's when you know—when they start taking the phone to the bathroom with them instead of leaving it hanging around the house. So I went through it. The only time I could get at the phone was when he was asleep. All the messages were deleted. All the texts. All the Facebook chats. I saw this girl I didn't know in his list and I sent her a message."

"Who this?" I said. Stephanie lifted her eyes to me.

"Yes. That was the message."

"She didn't answer."

"No."

"When did you know definitively that they were having an affair?"

"I went to the bar one night while they were both closing up." Stephanie wiped tears from her cheeks, drew a long breath that came out shuddering. "I saw her get into his car. She should have left before him, but the two of them left together. He must have driven her home. He got back to his dad's place an hour later. I was sleeping over, in his bedroom. He said they'd had a customer stay late."

Val Gratteur eased a long stream of smoke through her lips. She tapped the end of the cigarette into a petri dish she'd taken from a refrigerator and folded her arms, eyes wandering over the girl in the chair.

"I was so embarrassed." Stephanie's voice rose high as the sadness crashed over her again. The humiliation seemed to be the hardest part. "I didn't even tell anyone. Not Andrew. Not his dad. I just didn't say anything. I pretended. Maybe I thought if I kept pretending, it . . ."

"It wouldn't be real," I finished for her.

She hung her head in her hands.

"I went there again," Stephanie said. Her voice had lost all emotion now. It was cold and worn, a beaten thing. "That night. Tuesday night. I saw them together. They were laughing and singing as they packed up the bar. He grabbed her around the waist. They kissed."

Val and I waited. Stephanie didn't speak.

"Where did you get the gun?" I asked. "Where is it now?"

Stephanie struggled. She looked around her as though awakened from a dream, eyes wide.

"Maybe it was Andrew's?" Val offered. "His dad's?"

"Try not to suggest any information." I raised a hand. "She's got to give us these details herself."

There was a growing unease in my stomach, something about Stephanie's wandering glance, her restless hands. She looked distressed. Uncertain. Now and then I could see the anger crossing her face like clouds drifting across the moon, darkening everything, making her still. The tears were still rolling down her cheeks. She swiped at them too hard, stretched her skin as she did, a girl who'd known very little comfort in a long, long time.

"I don't remember much before or after. The clearest part is being there, watching them. The gun—I think it must have been Michael's," she said. "I don't know what I did with it. I was walking around in a sort of haze. I still am. I haven't slept."

She fell into sobs for a while. Val and I watched her rocking gently in the chair, one knee jogging, ankle tendons straining under her loose cotton pants.

"I'm so tired," she moaned.

"Okay, we're done." I shut off the phone recording. "I'm going to make some calls. We'll go see Detective Inspector Sweeney. She can get you a bed set up at the station and then we can talk about all this later."

Stephanie stood, her arms clasped tight against her chest. She seemed to stand there wondering if I'd hold her again, if things had changed now that I knew that she'd taken two lives, that she was a damaged and dangerous creature. I wrapped an arm around her and held her to me. She was so small and cold, untouched by the warmth of my body.

"It'll be all right," I said, though I had no basis for knowing if that was true. "It'll be all right."

Dear Diary,

Even as I write this, I can see how futile words are. How impossible it will be to express what happened on paper, how I felt. I can describe physically what happened to me as I turned away from Andrea's closed door and headed back toward the ute, tugging the dog along with me. My body temperature skyrocketed. My teeth locked together. A pressure swelled in my brain so fast and so heavy that my eyes were clouded with green exploding spots and splashes of red color. I almost forgot about the animal altogether. Got into the car without it, found the lead, yanked it up by the neck and threw it onto the passenger seat. The mutt's howling made things worse. I couldn't breathe. I drew the car away from the curb and roared down the road.

People talk about blacking out with anger, acting without knowing what you've done. Yes, there was some of that. I drove, going nowhere, faster than I could help but not fast enough, apparently, to attract any attention. I got onto highways. Got off again. But for the most part, I was there watching, as something, some black and swirling collection of smoke, another body, climbed into mine and I willingly let it take control. I surrendered, and the fury drove. I was helpless to do anything but crawl into a corner of my own being and scream about how perfectly it had all been about to be, and how viciously it had been stolen from me, my dream. My one.

Penny. Penny. Penny. Penny.

Did Andrea know how long I had been looking for Penny?

She was too stupid. People like that can't comprehend that a soul could search for another soul beyond time, beyond physicality, beyond Earth. To get in between the meeting of two souls was the worst crime. The most vile and evil crime. I shook with it. Outrage. I was demented. The dog crawled into the footwell of the passenger seat and whimpered, panted. I ignored it. I drove and drove, my body hard as a rock in the driver's seat, rigid with pain.

Only the sight of her drew me out of it. A flash, a shock of white at the corner of my vision. I reeled in my seat, glimpsed her out of the back window standing alone at the bus stop kicking dirt. Like a bubble bursting, the anger rose and split and I was flooded with relief. So fleeting, the distraction. All my muscles relaxed. I gulped air, turned the car down a side road and crept back toward where I had seen her. There was a strip of bush behind the bus stop, thick brambles, tangles of wild unflowering bougainvillea covered in thorns. I got out of the car and stood looking at her through the brush.

She could have been Penny with that hair. A hand curled at her side, slender white fingers picking at the belt loops on her jeans. When she turned and glanced up the road I saw that she was not Penny at all but a pointier, frailer version. Straight, skeptical eyebrows. Big lips. I hardly got the details. The fury was climbing again. Rising, rising. I was shaking. I watched cars whizzing past.

I was beginning to understand what I would do. Had known all along, really, from the moment I pulled off the road. Maybe it had been there longer, the plan. Maybe it was there when I wanted to buy the van. Maybe it was there when I was a teenager, dreaming. It was only fully formed now. The thoughts were coming clearer. Coming with words. With cautions. With whispered promises.

A car pulled over next to the girl suddenly. I watched, shaking violently, as a big man got out, balked at the sight of the girl standing there. The two examined each other. I crouched, gripped the trunk of a nearby tree with one hand, my mind screaming.

The big man fiddled with his car as more cars whizzed past on the road. Said something to her. Her voice tinkled back, too soft to be much more than baby-bird murmurs through the bush. The big man raked a hand through his black hair, waved goodbye and left.

The highway was empty. I went back to the ute, grabbed the leash and pulled hard. The dog fell, squealed, began limping on a front paw. Good. I had to move fast now. I tugged the dog toward the bush, grabbed it by two hanks of white fur and threw it into the bramble.

The dog yelped. Struggled. Limped.

I watched.

She'd turned away from the road. Blue eyes searching the bush, finding the dog there, trapped, injured, the bright red collar twisted up in the branches. I hid behind a tree. Listened as she neared, her soft voice coming over the screech of cicadas in the trees all around us.

"Oh, puppy!" she said. "Poor puppy!"

My ex-wife called me as I sat in the boarding lounge at Cairns airport, hiding behind a magazine. Whenever she calls these days I get a stab of pain in the chest, knowing it can only be bad news. Kelly doesn't call to shoot the breeze. I answered, still shielding my face from the rest of the waiting passengers with a copy of *Empire*.

"What's up?"

"Are you coming down to Sydney tonight?" she asked.

"Yeah," I said, my nose inches from some celebrity I didn't know brandishing a laser gun. "I'm going to give a statement about the allegations tomorrow morning. I also said I'd drop in and talk to those people. The *Innocent Ted* people."

"You didn't tell me you were coming."

"I didn't really tell anyone I was coming. Last time I came down I had Khalid and his boys trying to take care of me. I'm hoping he doesn't find out about the *Innocent Ted* thing."

"Well, I wouldn't have told him," Kelly said. "Your secret would have been safe with me."

"I thought it was probably too short notice to set up a supervised visit with Lil so I didn't bother," I said. "Unless you think we can sort something out? I'd love to see her."

"Oh, um." Kelly clicked her tongue, thinking. "Probably not. But you could just come to the house."

"I don't think that's a good idea." I laughed.

"Why not?"

"I'm in enough trouble at the moment. I don't need to be upsetting the court by violating my visitation provisions." I paused as a flight announcement murmured overhead. "And going to the house might be hard. For me. I haven't been back there since . . ."

Since I packed my things and fled like a fugitive, my life in tatters and the people baying for my blood, I thought. *Since I tried to decide if I would leave my wedding ring on the dresser or take it with me, my wife having not looked me in the eyes across the courtroom in weeks.* Kelly hadn't been there to say goodbye. She'd been staying with her mother. The house had been cold. Too quiet. All the things suddenly not even half mine, not mine at all—pictures of Lillian as a newborn only just framed and hung on the coral-pink walls.

I imagined myself going back there now, seeing my old books taken from the shelves and boxed up, Jett's things on the table on my side of the bed. New things Kelly had done or changed around the place. Had she replaced the old cracked stair off the back door? I winced, the desire to cry prickling painfully in my nose.

"Maybe we could see each other," Kelly said.

I dropped the magazine in my lap. Remembered myself when a woman across the aisle glanced at me.

"What for?" I asked.

"What for?"

"Uh . . . yes?"

"Jesus, Ted." Kelly gave a humorless laugh. "That hurts. You make it sound like I hate your guts."

"I know you don't hate me, I just . . ." I shrugged, as though she could see me. "Look, I'm not thinking straight. I just heard a murder confession and gave a girl her last car ride in the free world. I dropped her at the police station. It's been a bit crazy here."

We hung on to the line, both us of silent. Another flight announcement came and went.

"Can we just see each other?" she asked.

"Okay," I said.

INNOCENT TED, EPISODE 9A:
EMERGENCY SPECIAL EDITION

Content warning: *Innocent Ted* contains adult themes and violence. Some content may be distressing to listeners. It is not intended for all audiences. Listener discretion is advised.

<INTRO MUSIC>
<SLICE IN SOUND EFFECT>

FABIANA GRISHAM: *Welcome to* Innocent Ted, *a true crime podcast about the 2016 abduction of thirteen-year-old Claire Bingley and the wrongful arrest of Ted Conkaffey, father and drug squad detective with the New South Wales Police Force. You're listening to episode 9A, a special edition mini-cast addressing recent developments in Ted's case. I'm Fabiana Grisham, lead crime reporter for the* Sydney Morning Herald *and true crime expert.*
　　Innocent Ted *listeners will know that, three days ago, Channel Three's* Stories and Lives *began previewing an upcoming episode in*

which Ted answers reporter Lara Eggington's questions about the case. Although it was initially billed as a tell-all about the abduction and Ted's wrongful prosecution, online newsrooms soon began circulating suggestions that new allegations of sexual misconduct against Ted will be revealed in the interview.

<CHANNEL THREE NEWS AUDIO>
And in other news tonight, *Stories and Lives* reporter Lara Eggington has refused to address rumors that an upcoming episode of the current affairs program will contain new sexual assault accusations against disgraced former detective Ted Conkaffey. Eggington revealed only that the episode will be "explosive," and that the terrible case that captured the nation's attention last year may not be over yet.

FABIANA GRISHAM: *Here at* Innocent Ted *we have stood by Ted Conkaffey from the beginning and will continue to do so as these events unfold. We believe wholeheartedly that Ted was wrongfully accused of Claire Bingley's abduction and sexual assault, and that her real attacker is still at large. We've done the best we can here week by week to examine the details of Ted's case and try to find answers to those unanswered questions about Claire's attacker, and determine how he can be brought to justice. Next week, as scheduled, we'll be interviewing Trevor Fuller, the secret witness who was never heard during Ted's trial. You'll hear Mr. Fuller recount seeing Ted on that fateful day, minutes after the alleged abduction of Claire, at a nearby 7-Eleven.*

As these new accusations about Ted emerge, we'll be on the ground reporting to you on what may be yet another devastating miscarriage of justice leveled against an innocent man.

In an exclusive event for selected Innocent Ted *subscribers only, Ted will address the new allegations and questions from the audience tomorrow. Of course, for Ted's protection, we'll release the location of the event to attendees only, but the event will be Sydney-based. If you'd like to be a part of that limited live audience, please go to the Innocent Ted website and click through to the applications page. On the night, we'll be streaming on Facebook Live for those who cannot attend.*

That's all for now. Keep tuning in, keep contributing, and stay in touch via Twitter, Facebook, and our homepage.

Remember; if it could happen to him, it could happen to you.

Thanks for listening, everybody.

Dear Diary,

Chaos. It was sheer chaos. I don't know how my mind kept order-ing my body to do things, but somehow, while black waves of hate and fury crashed and broke inside my brain, my limbs worked. I took the dog. Got in the car. Drove away from where I'd left her after it was over. Headed back onto the empty highway and turned east toward the coast. Somehow I ended up on the verge of an aban-doned parking lot outside a closed-down factory, I didn't even know where it was. Blistering sun baking the asphalt. Dead grass and old brown bottles smashed and scattered. I sat on the edge of the lot and gripped my head. Rocked. Made noises. I couldn't bring my breath-ing rate down. My heart was hammering in my neck and temples, the sheer force of my blood thrumming through my veins making my skull feel like it was being squeezed. With every beat the thought came.

I killed a girl. I killed a girl. I killed a girl.

There was a crushing inevitability to it. A kind of relief. I'd al-ways known that one day it was going to get out of control. Maybe not this out of control. But perhaps that had been my mistake—I should have let it out in little gasps, pressure released from a shudder-ing, shaking, blistering hot valve. Now a girl was dead. I sat on the ground and felt the world turning under me, tried to get a grip.

When the grip came it was just that—a foothold after frantic hours of floundering, drowning in the dark. I had to be smart now. I looked at the car, the animal curled in the passenger seat, visible through the open driver's-side door. Time to be measured. Careful. Whatever happened next, it needed to be on my terms. No one was going to take control from me again. I had to think.

Get rid of the dog. Kill it.

No, I wouldn't kill it. I couldn't kill again, not now, not with ex-haustion rapidly taking over from the fury. If I hurt the thing and it got away from me, someone would find it, might find it even if I could bring myself to finish the deed. I'd drop it at the RSPCA. It wasn't far. They didn't ask questions. The sun was setting. They'd be closed now. Simple. Easy. No mess.

I dumped the dog and drove back toward home, didn't even look at Penny's house, turned my head right away, shielded my eyes as I ran to the front door. Chloe was in the living room, the television on, uni papers spread all over the floor. She slammed a textbook closed at the sight of me.

"Jesus Christ!" She tried to take my arms. The scratches. The girl had fought hard. "What happened?"

"I got a flat tire on the ute." I tore away from her, headed for the bathroom, tried to keep my voice level. "I stopped by the side of the road and slipped. Fell down into a ditch."

"Oh my god, are you—"

"I'm fine, Chloe! Fucking hell, would you just leave me the fuck alone! Every time I come in the door you're all over me!"

I slammed the bathroom door in her face, spat more vitriol at her from the other side of it as I washed my slashed arms and neck. My thoughts were still racing. The flat tire story. That wasn't smart. She'd expect a new one on the ute now, the unused spare. I'd have to wait until she went to bed, go out and change it, puncture the old one. The *ute. I should get rid of it. I'd parked behind the bushes when I first saw the girl, but it's possible someone saw me drive off after I'd knocked her out and loaded her into the back. Maybe someone saw me crossing the back roads. I shouldn't get rid of it too quickly or without warning. We'd only just obtained it. Nothing suspicious now. No stupid moves. I had to be careful. They'd be looking for someone who talked about the case a lot. Someone who changed their appearance suddenly. Acted weird.*

Chloe was upset, sulking at my outburst. Good. I'd let her be mad at me for the rest of the evening, blessed silence. I'd make out like I had a concussion from rolling into the ditch. I'd crawl into bed and stay there.

The night seemed to pass in years. Chloe came and went. Said things. I didn't listen. Lay on my side of the bed pretending to sleep, counting off the times my mind repeated the hellish words.

I killed a girl. I killed a girl. I killed a girl.

I awakened from a half sleep the next day at noon, forgetting all about the tires. Nightmares. I'd had to explain the fever, the sweats, the twitching by saying I was suddenly sick. Chloe bought it. Of course she did. She returned in the afternoon, slamming the screen door like she always did, probably coming home from being up the street buying me chicken soup ingredients. Doing her best to care for me like I really was sick. I didn't move. Listened as she switched the television on, the blanket pulled up over my head.

. . . found alive this morning by a driver traveling on the Hume Highway at Menangle at around six a.m. Police say they're searching for a man in connection with the child's abduction and sexual assault, and are appealing to members of the public to . . .

I shot upright in bed and ran to the door to the lounge room. Images of police cars, an ambulance, an empty field lined by wire. Some small blond guy and his wife now in a police conference room, both crying, shaking, giving thanks to police for searching for their little girl through the night. Relief and terror. The girl's parents.

She was alive.

Amanda had been banned from participating in the official interview of Stephanie Neash at the Crimson Lake police station. That was fine. Amanda had been banned from things all her life. In Year 5 a bunch of girls had banned her from sitting on the sandstone ledge outside the library where she had liked to pore over *Where's Wally?* books in the sunshine, because they'd decided they liked to use the ledge as a stage to practice their dance routines. All the cool girls seemed to be enrolled in dance classes, but Amanda knew not to bother with that sort of thing. Her sense of direction was all twisted up. Sometimes she would see the ball coming at her during a game, when she was forced to do sport, and while her brain willed her toward the ball her legs would, of their own volition, turn and move in the opposite direction. Amanda thought sometimes she belonged in an upside-down place, somewhere identical to the one she lived in now, only where left was right and right was left and people felt cheerful when their hearts were broken. Big smiles spread on bright faces in mortuaries, people laughing over graves.

She'd stood in the foyer of the police station with Ted after he'd brought Stephanie in, Sweeney seeing the young woman to a waiting room and getting her a tea to calm her nerves. Ted had been twitching, nervous, pacing restlessly as he conveyed his tale about the confession.

"How 'bout that," Amanda had said brightly. "If this turns out to be the truth, we'll be all wrapped up by tea time."

"Not me," Ted had said, lowering his eyes as a patrol officer walked through the glass doors, giving him a glowering look. "I've got to head down to Sydney. I told those podcast people I'd come speak to them."

"Oh, what?" Amanda said. "Why the hell did you do that?"

The big man sighed heavily. "I don't know. They're on my side, I guess? The *Innocent Ted* people, they're my supporters, and I may be in desperate need of supporters if this second accusation doesn't go away. If I have to go to trial again I'm going to need to hire Sean, and Fabiana mentioned something about being able to raise money through the podcast to help with that. I don't want Kelly and Lillian going without because of me. And besides all that, I have to go and do the appearance, because I may need them and because I said I would. I don't like to let people down."

"You're a man of your word."

"I try to be." He looked at her. "But I'm sorry. Because I also gave you my word that I'd be here for this case."

"You've got dramas." Amanda waved dismissively. "Maybe one day I'll have dramas and you can cover for me."

Amanda saw her partner off through the doors of the police station with a sinking feeling. She knew it was not only because of the dire situation he faced. A part of her was wondering if it might be the last time she saw him here in Crimson Lake. As he walked to his car, she felt something tugging her forward to the doors, a desire to watch him go for as long as possible lest he should never come back.

But that was silly. Of course he would come back. He belonged here now.

She stood on the other side of the two-way mirror and watched as a fragile Stephanie Neash took her seat beside the recorder, and Chief

Clark and Pip Sweeney set up the tape. Chief Clark had reluctantly granted Sweeney's request to allow Amanda to watch the interview after Sweeney cited Michael Bell's insistence that in order for him to trust the police, he wanted his private investigator involved as much as possible. She mentioned nothing about wanting or needing Amanda's assistance herself. Sweeney had told Amanda sharply to "behave" herself before the observation room was unlocked for her. Amanda had looked around at the empty plastic chairs in the otherwise bare room and wondered what trouble she could possibly get into here.

After some initial chatter and the reading of the cautions, Clark gestured to Sweeney to go ahead. It was her show.

"Ms. Neash, you've said already that you do not want to have a lawyer present with you at this time, and you've been made aware that you are well within your rights to have that happen."

"I don't want a lawyer," Stephanie said.

"Okay." Sweeney lifted a sheet of paper and directed Stephanie to look at it. Her shoulders rose as she took a deep breath. "Then, Ms. Neash, I direct you to a transcript of a recording made by Edward Conkaffey earlier today before he brought you to these premises. I'll read aloud the conversation as it's presented here for the tape."

"Okay," Stephanie said. She listened as Sweeney read out the words Stephanie and Ted had spoken at Cairns Hospital, recorded on Ted's phone.

"Would you agree this is a full and fair representation of exactly what you said?"

"Yes."

"So you admit that you did kill Andrew and Keema at the Barking Frog Inn that night?"

"Yes." Stephanie nodded.

"Can you take us through what happened?"

Stephanie recounted the evening of the killings, arriving home from work herself, waiting for Andrew to come home in the early morning hours, being unable to sleep. It seemed that usually when he was staying over he would come into the house, shower, and slip into bed with her, sometimes not even waking her. This night was different. Fed up, Stephanie had driven to the bar and watched the lovers through the open front doors of the establishment, sitting in her car parked across the road in the dark.

"And what happened next?"

"It's hard to remember it all exactly. It's not . . . It's not clear."

"Just try your best," Chief Clark said.

"I can see myself going to the front doors of the bar and kind of walking in without making any noise," Stephanie said. She rubbed her eyes. "I think they saw me when I got to the counter, outside the kitchen."

"Did you have the gun with you at this time?" Sweeney asked.

"I must have grabbed it when it was in the car." Stephanie shook her head slightly, as though trying to sort through racing, colliding thoughts. "It must have been on the seat beside me."

"So you brought it with you from home?"

"I guess so."

"You can't remember?"

"The past few days have been really crazy," Stephanie said. She took a couple of tissues from the box she had been given and wiped her cheeks. "I was so angry at the time that I think my brain just didn't record certain things. It's like I can see myself now, standing in front of the two of them in the bar, but I can't see anything about the gun. What I did with it after I used it. Where it came from. It's like those parts of my memory are just gone. Blank."

Amanda leaned on the two-way mirror and studied Stephanie's face closely.

"Have you ever used a gun before?" Sweeney asked. "Do you know how to use one?"

"I know how to use one but I've never used one before, no."

"So what happened next, after you walked into the bar and Andrew and Keema saw you standing there?"

There was a long pause. Stephanie held the tissue up to her mouth.

"I think I said something like . . ." She sniffed. "Like 'How could you?' or 'Why?' or . . . I'm not sure. I can see them looking at me, and I'm holding the gun out like this."

She held her arm out, pointed it at Sweeney's face. The hand trembled, two fingers pointing out, the barrel wavering.

Amanda pushed the intercom on the wall beside her, making Clark and Sweeney jump in their seats.

"This is bullshit," Amanda said.

The two swung around as though they could see her through the mirror.

"Who is that?" Stephanie asked.

"Amanda Pharrell, would you kindly butt out?" Chief Clark snapped, his eyes wandering blindly over the mirrored glass. "I'm noting the interruption of private investigator and notorious pest Amanda Pharrell for the tape. She has not been invited into this interview and was permitted to watch from the observation room, *silently*."

"This is not silent." Amanda pushed the button again, her sudden voice making Sweeney jolt again. "This is me saying this confession is bullshit. Rather loudly, actually. This thing is hideously loud. Is there a volume control?" Amanda experimented with the buttons on the panel beneath the speaker. One produced a high-pitched squeal.

"Interview suspended at three forty-five p.m.," Sweeney breathed, shutting off the tape as her chief marched out of the room, throwing open the door. She followed at a run, locking the door behind her, sure she was going to see the big man holding Amanda by the throat as she turned into the observation room.

"Am I going to have to have someone escort you from the building?" Clark panted with rage. "You do *not* just chime in to an official police interview like you're a fucking sports referee!"

"How ungrateful!" Amanda balked. "I'm trying to save you time. Well, I'm trying to save me time, really, by getting Sweensy Peensy out of there so we can get back to the case." She gestured to Sweeney. "Stephanie is turning your police station into a filthy whorehouse of lies, Chief. Why would you want to waste your time on that? Time is money, chump."

"The interview has been running for, what, ten minutes?" Clark snapped. "You're saying she's lying? You know that? Already?"

"Amanda is right, uh . . ." Sweeney bit her lips as Chief Clark turned on her. "She's right about some of the things Stephanie has said so far. We believe that Andrew was startled by his attacker outside the pub, possibly out the back, before the shooting, for example. That doesn't wash with Stephanie's account that she walked into the front of the bar and the two only saw her when she reached the counter. That, at least, I'm in support of Amanda about."

"The whole thing's bullshit." Amanda glanced at Stephanie through the glass. "Look at the size of her. You think she's going to hold up a pistol for the first time with one hand, arm extended like Dirty Harry? No way. It'd be far too heavy for her. And okay, sure, *maybe* she could have got a kill shot in after she got them both on the ground. Doing Keema would have been easy. But it took multiple shots to kill Andrew and they all hit their target as he moved. There's no way that girl got used to the recoil so fast."

Amanda took her wallet and keys from the table like she was preparing to go.

"The kicker for me was her account of what she said," she snorted. "*How could you?* or *Why?* Yeah, sure. That's what I'd have had her say if this was an episode of *Days of Our Lives*. But this is the real world. If she was that hepped up on blinding, murderous rage she'd never say something as lucid and calculating as *How could you?* She probably wouldn't have said anything at all."

"She said she took the gun with her," Chief Clark said. "So there's been no talk of blinding rage. It was premeditated."

"No, she said she *can't remember* taking the gun with her." Amanda pointed a finger in the air. "She said, and I quote, 'I was so angry at the time that I think my brain just didn't record certain things.'"

Chief Clark looked through the glass at Stephanie, who had hidden her face in her hands, the scrunched tissues peeking out from between her fingers.

"You ask me, it's a false memory or she's covering badly for someone," Amanda said.

Sweeney felt the air leave her lungs in a long, sickening sigh. She had been so exhilarated to bring her first homicide to a close. The first notch in what would surely be a long row before she found her confidence in the role, before she would believe that her colleagues over in Holloways Beach weren't laughing at her for taking the placement so early out of patrol. But she acknowledged now the tiny seedling of doubt that had started growing in her the moment she saw Ted Conkaffey walking Stephanie up the steps of the police station that afternoon. Not Stephanie.

"She's tired." Sweeney cut into a low stream of Chief Clark's threatening and grumbling at Amanda for interrupting their official interview with her wild theories. "Stephanie. She's tired and guilty and grief stricken. Confused about how angry she is at Andrew that he had the affair and how sad she is that he's gone. She hasn't had a stitch of emotional support since the thing happened, except from Andrew's father, who's grieving himself. Maybe she . . . I don't know. She's constructed a memory in which she killed Keema and Andrew and rolled it around and around in her brain enough times that she now thinks it's true."

Chief Clark folded his arms, stared Sweeney down. She could almost hear his thoughts. His quiet calculation of how he was going to get her out of his police station, this fuck-up, this trainee detective who'd brought him nothing but unusable witnesses.

"I'm not ready to release her." Clark gave a dismissive wave of his hand. "Maybe she is tired and confused, but she's all you've managed to dig up so far. Get her into a cell, get her to sleep and when she wakes up put her straight into a room with a psychologist. Search her house. I'll organize a warrant. And you"—he turned on Amanda— "you're banned from this station. I don't want to see you unless you're under arrest for something."

"Ooh." Amanda smiled, clapped the chief on the shoulder as she passed him, making for the door. "Don't tempt me, Clarky. You know I'm a naughty girl."

Amanda was standing on the steps of the police station when Sweeney emerged from the glass doors. The strange investigator was standing stiffly, facing away from the building, her elbow out at an awkward right angle from her body. As Sweeney approached she noticed an enormous multicolored butterfly walking the length of Amanda's forearm, wings upright except for the occasional pause when it spread flat, seeming to want to blend with the vibrant tattoos crowding Amanda's arm. Sweeney felt the humiliation and dread of the past few minutes shift slightly, not completely lifted, but resisting a definite push from the sight before her. Amanda turned her arm as the butterfly strolled over her wrist, onto her palm and settled there on the bare pink flesh, stark against the rest of her colored skin.

Amanda looked at Sweeney and shrugged, offering no suggestion for how the creature's visit had occurred, or why.

"Do you think Stephanie's covering for someone?" Sweeney asked, watching the insect on Amanda's hand.

"Dunno," Amanda replied with another shrug. "If she's just confused, trying to question her further on why she's confessed would be a waste of time. You'll only tangle her mind into impossible knots. Leave it to the shrink."

A taxi pulled up to the curb before the police station and a man and a woman exited, immediately presenting themselves as outsiders to the Cairns region. The woman was far too heavily dressed—long sleeves, and impractically formal in a silk shirt and slacks, dark patches emerging beneath her arms and at the center of her chest from the humidity. As the man got out of the taxi, the fronds of a short palm tree at the edge of the lawn brushed the back of his neck. He swiped irritably at the plant.

"Keema's parents," Sweeney said.

Amanda saw that Keema's mother had the same immaculate, caramel skin and slightly upturned eyes. Sweeney swallowed hard, took a couple of steps down to intercept the parents on their march toward the door.

"Brian, Sefina," Sweeney said, cringing slightly. "I'm Detective Inspector Pip Sweeney. I didn't think you'd be here until tomorrow."

They shook hands. Sweeney shared her commiserations. Amanda leaned on the concrete banister nearby and tried to keep a straight face as the butterfly walked up the back of her arm and onto her shoulder, where she lost sight of it, barely able to feel its tiny, hairy legs as it traversed the side of her neck.

"The leads we have thus far are very promising," Sweeney lied. "I'll take you inside and we can sit down with my chief for an overview."

"I have to tell you at the outset that I'm distressed that we've had to come here," Sefina said. Received Pronunciation. Amanda liked the sound of it. Felt a strong desire to burst into an impression. "Could we possibly organize an extended meeting at the hotel where it's more comfortable?"

"Oh, ah," Sweeney struggled for words and glanced at Amanda, almost looking for assistance. "I could . . . It's possible we could—"

"When Keema said she was going to tour Australia, I envisioned Sydney," Sefina said. "Melbourne. I've been to Melbourne. Really lovely, some of the best coffee I've ever had in my life. Here? Here, I mean." The woman gestured helplessly to the road, the distant mountains. "Our taxi was delayed on the way from the airport because a gigantic bird was dashing all over the road. Some prehistoric man-eating thing. I didn't see it, but the whole bloody road had been shut down. I was terrified."

"A cassowary." Sweeney blushed. "Yes, sometimes they get themselves trapped inside the road barriers. It's best not to try to carry on when that happens. If you hit them it's . . . They're quite large. An endangered species, actually."

Amanda listened intensely. Grief again, yet another form, this one the micro-focus type. She knew that grief sometimes made people focus on minute or unimportant things as a distraction from what was at hand, the huge and foreboding burden that was loss. It made people keep their appointment with the hairdresser on the evening of the day their spouse was killed. Focus on tasks. Focus on objects. Anything but the horrible truth.

She thought she might actually be feeling something, a sad little stirring, encouraged by her analysis of Keema's parents' grief. But the butterfly stepped across the threshold of her ear canal and Amanda laughed hard, just once, a sort of exhilarated cough. The three people standing on the stairs turned toward her. She waved at the creature and it fluttered away.

"Let's go inside." Brian Daule put an arm around his wife. "We'll get this over and done with."

There were a couple of aggressive incidents on my way down to Sydney this time. Fewer than I expected, actually. While I used the self-service check-in kiosk at Cairns airport, a couple of young men with backpacks stood nearby watching and sniggering threateningly, and when I passed one of them shouted, "Kiddie-fucker! Piece of shit!" There were some dirty looks on the plane, no *vive-la-résistance* wine and cheese this time. A few people stopping in their tracks and pointing as I made my way through the terminal at the other end. As I got into a taxi a woman in the queue yelled "Hey! Hey!" trying to get my attention. I slammed the door without responding and we drove off, but I did catch her mouthing something that didn't look particularly friendly at me.

When Kelly was working, before Lillian, she used to manage a gym in the CBD, the kind that takes in polished men and women in corporate getup and spits them out glossy and half-naked, their taut bodies strapped into colorful Lycra. It gave me a little boost of self-esteem that she hung around these beautiful, powerful people doing impressive sorts of things all day—lying on gym mats putting their feet behind their heads while making multimillion dollar deals on

Bluetooth earpieces—and at night she came home to me, the drug squad meathead. Sure, there was intelligence and cunning in what I did for a living. Sometimes I used world-class surveillance and intelligence-gathering techniques to nab some of the most dangerous criminals in the country. I'd been a part of teams that ordered private jets out of the sky, that sealed diamonds as big as garden peas into evidence bags, that posed cheekily for pictures with confiscated gold-plated AK-47s.

But then again, sometimes I burst in on filthy apartments looking for dope, and some drug dealer's girlfriend threw a day-old plate of fish fingers and mashed potato at my face.

When I would meet Kelly for dinner in the city sometimes, we'd go to a tiny Chinese place off Goulburn Street called Emperor Duck. When she suggested we go back there this time I was torn. The food at Emperor Duck was incredible, and I hadn't been anywhere near the place since long before my incarceration. But as I walked along George Street from my hotel toward the restaurant, I sensed dread emerging between my thoughts, an almost-angry stirring at what had been taken from me since I last walked these streets, my wife's hand in mine. When I slid open the glass door to the dim, small res-taurant I found Kelly sitting at a table just inside the door, our usual spot, where she could watch youths walking up the hill from China-town in their crazy flashing shoes and studded belts, the girls with fluffy rabbit-fur handbags dyed in impossible colors. It hurt to be here. The big, milky-eyed barramundi hovering dismally in the green-tinted tanks behind the counter could have been the same creatures I'd seen when I last paid the bill over two years earlier.

The dread deepened when Kelly stood to greet me. She was wear-ing a cute little black dress and playful red heels. Her calves were like something out of an athlete's health magazine. I hadn't showered since that morning, and my shirt was rumpled from the plane. I'd planned to have a quick dinner with her, get back to the room and watch my interview on *Stories and Lives* alone. I was saving the shower for what I predicted would be such an excruciating, cringing shame after the show aired that I would need to steam off the surface of my skin with an hour or so under the fount.

"So," she said as we sat down. "The big day."

"Mmm," I groaned, smoothing out the paper tablecloth. "I can't say I'm looking forward to it."

"Are you absolutely sure you don't want me to watch it with you?"

"Positive," I said. "I know how it goes. It's terrible."

"I'm just thinking about you all alone in that hotel room with no one to support you."

I thought about how long I'd spent in a prison cell, all alone, with no one to support me. I was going to mention it, but guessed it was a bit soon for prison talk. She'd ordered wine. I poured myself some.

"I brought you these." She pulled some photographs from her handbag and slid them across to me. They were happy snaps of Lillian. Joy punctured the dread. I grinned and laughed, flipping through them slowly, careful not to leave prints on the images with my grimy hands.

"Look at this." I stopped at one of Lil in the bath, her hair all soaped up, molded into a shark fin on top of her head. I glanced up and noticed that Kelly was looking at my bare finger, the spot where my wedding ring used to be. I'd taken it off and left it on the bedside table in the hotel room. I folded my hands closed and she noticed that I'd noticed her staring.

The arrival of the appetizers saved us. I picked up chopsticks from the metal canister by the window.

"You don't know how to use chopsticks," Kelly said.

"You wanna bet?" I pinched her on the knuckle with them, picked up a dumpling and dipped it in soy sauce.

"Who taught you to do that?"

"Amanda."

"Huh," Kelly said. She didn't seem hungry. I had assumed Kelly had invited me here to talk about the divorce, about getting the paperwork moving again. Perhaps there was something she wanted to tell me about Jett, that it was getting serious maybe. But as she watched me eat, she told me instead about the emergence of Lillian's speech, how worried she'd been when our child stalled at "Mama" and "Nanna" and seemed determined not to say more before bursting, almost overnight, into small sentences.

"My mother's minding her right now. Not Jett."

"I wouldn't have minded if Jett was taking care of her," I said. "He seems like a reasonable guy. A dick. But a reasonable dick."

"I know," Kelly said. "It just must be hard, that's all. I do realize that it must be painful, you know. I'm not ignorant to everything."

"Of course it is." I was about to go on, talk about how undermining and emasculating it was for me to see another man providing for my child, whether it was care, money, or affection. But Kelly cut me off.

"It is for me," she said.

I was momentarily confused. I drank my wine.

"Seeing you getting on with other people, I mean," Kelly said. "Other women."

I waited for an explanation. There wasn't one.

"Oh, you mean Amanda?" I laughed. "Oh no. There's nothing between Amanda and me."

Kelly scoffed.

"There really isn't."

"You're telling me you guys have spent the amount of time you have together and there hasn't been *something*?" she asked. "Come on. Didn't you save her life?"

"I'm not sure I really saved her life," I mused. I'd carried Amanda up a hill in the rainforest after she'd been mauled by a crocodile and fought the thing off. The newspapers had described the event gleefully. Amanda had regaled journalists from her hospital bed about going for the animal's eyes with her fingernails. "She was probably just resting after the attack. I wouldn't have been surprised if she'd dragged herself up the hill on her own if I hadn't managed to find her. She's tough as nails."

"Ted," Kelly sighed.

"She's not a sexual person," I said. "At least not around me. It would be a complete stab in the dark for me to guess what the hell she's attracted to. It's like that, trying to decide on anything at all about her. She's completely without reason."

"What do you mean?"

"Like . . ." I sat back, shook my head, watching the barramundi watching me. "Like, for example, if she's not on a case, every Saturday afternoon, at three o'clock on the dot, she smokes a single cigar and watches *GoodFellas*."

"*GoodFellas*?"

"With Robert De Niro."

"I know the movie," Kelly said. "Why that movie?"

"No idea."

"Are we talking every Saturday afternoon?"

"Every single one," I said. "At three o'clock. You can't call her on the phone when it's on. She won't come to the door even if she knows you're standing there knocking. You have to wait for it to finish. It's one hundred and forty-five minutes long, in case you were wondering. I don't think she'd leave the building if it was on fire."

"What's wrong with her?"

"I don't know," I said. "I don't know that there's anything wrong with her at all. She just has her way and that's that. Some of the things she does, I kind of like. She's sort of impervious to the horrors of the world. Like an alien."

"She's an alien?" Kelly laughed incredulously.

"If I found out she was an actual space alien I would not be surprised at all," I said.

Our mains arrived. She groaned and gasped over it, made a big deal, the way she used to when we were together. She doled out my serving. Put the chili paste on the side, the way I liked it. Our smiles faded, and I wandered back into dangerous territory.

"I'm curious to know why it would be hard for you," I said carefully. "Even if I was in a romantic relationship with Amanda."

Kelly toyed with her food. Wouldn't meet my eyes. When she spoke, eventually, her voice was small.

"I know it probably seems like I just stopped loving you when I shut off contact with you, Ted," Kelly said. "But I didn't. I really didn't. I just put my feelings for you on hold. And they've been on hold this whole time. Until now."

I swallowed a piece of calamari that was too hot. I felt it sear its way down my throat, chased it quickly with wine.

"What?"

"I've listened to the podcast," Kelly said. "I've gone back through the trial documents. I've talked to people. Sean. Your lawyer. He was very good to listen to me, to answer my questions. Very patient."

The dread was returning. A sharp pain in my gut, high up, near my heart.

"I may have made a mistake," Kelly said. She put her fork down. We stared at each other.

"I made a mistake," she corrected.

"This is . . ." I began. My thoughts were racing. I shoved more pieces of calamari into my mouth, stalling for time. Washed them down with more wine. "This is very kind. I appreciate it."

"Oh, Ted."

"No, no, I'm serious," I said. "I'm not being sarcastic. It's kind of you to put it into words. You didn't make a mistake—you followed your instincts, and at the time that meant backing away from me. There was no right or wrong way to handle it. It hurt. It still hurts. But Kel, you didn't walk away from me for fun, or because you enjoyed it, or because you wanted to punish me. I've always known that."

She dabbed delicately at her eyes with a napkin from the holder beside me, trying to save her makeup. My throat was tight. I watched the people walking by outside the windows, young people texting on screens encased in big rubber phone cases shaped like teddies or bunnies. When Kelly took my hand she drew me out of a downward spiral into nervousness over my television appearance. Only an hour to go until it all began again.

"Maybe we can fix it," Kelly said.

"We can fix it, sure." I squeezed her fingers. "There's not much to fix. Kelly, I'm not angry at you."

"No, Ted, I don't mean our friendship. I mean our marriage."

I drew my hand away. Felt flashes of anger. Confusion. Longing. I scratched at my throat, where the muscles were still tightening. Tried to press the ache out of my eyes, the desire for tears.

"Come home," she said. "Come home and be with Lillian and me. She needs you. I need you."

Dear Diary,

I witnessed my own death. Twice.

The first played out in my plans. In the days after the attack, I made a mental list. I'd get the car detailed. I would sabotage it, maybe cut the timing belt, empty the radiator fluid, and run it to smoking, report it to Chloe, suggest that perhaps we'd bought ourselves a lemon. Then, a week later, I'd sabotage it again, throw a tantrum and demand we sell it. If the car had been seen, I figured police would be looking for cars bought and sold in the days after the attack. They'd be looking for a panicked offender. I wouldn't panic. I refused to panic.

I'd go out and spend some time with the boys at the pub. They'd be looking for someone acting weirdly, wanting to talk about the case. Evasive. I'd go to an internet café and keep an eye on the leads both on the police media sites and in the forums. It would be stupid to keep googling it from home. If there was so much as a whiff of me, a good composite sketch or a partial license plate, I'd end it. Prepare the apartment, write my note, wait for Chloe to come home. No sense leaving Chloe around to put words to it all. She'd never explain properly.

She was too simple. She'd make me look like a monster. I'd do her quickly, then do myself.

I saw us aligned neatly on a plastic sheet on the living room floor, holding hands maybe, something gentle. The door unlocked and slightly ajar, waiting for that inevitable someone to find us. One of my mates coming round to grab a jacket left here over the weekend. Chloe's mum. The unsuspecting postman. I'd make no apologies in the note. This was not my fault. Not a decision. Not something I could have helped. I'd tell my mother I loved her and sign off. Neat.

And then I was sitting with Chloe, watching but not watching one of her stupid shows, when a news update told me someone had been arrested for the attack.

It took everything I had not to move, not to speak. I wanted to scream. And then, over the coming days, I watched my death again. Only this time it wasn't a slow, sorrowful imagining of my demise at my own hands. It was a thrilling, maddening, frenzied death played out by another man.

I learned his name was Ted Conkaffey. The big, black-haired man from the roadside, the one who'd stopped beside her.

I watched him tumble and twist as he fell, mystified, feeling the wind passing over him shred at my skin at the same time it did his. There were proud portraits of him in his cadet uniform, chest puffed and chin high, the peaked cap almost comical on his square head. Bright-eyed youth playing dress-up games with a bunch of other grinning boys. I dug and dug, each time bringing up new tragedies from within the bowels of the internet. Ted on his wedding day, his elderly father bent and smiling, a good foot shorter than the big broad cop. The enormous specter of him in black riot gear standing at the cordon of some drug raid or another. Heading to court in a suit to give evidence against Khalid Farah, drug lord and suspected murderer. Here Ted was the street-grimy Clark Kent, his superhuman strength and goodness obvious through the awkwardly buttoned shirt. From drug trials to his own trial, one side of the courtroom to *the other, his tie looking too tight, choking him, a public hanging already happening long before the verdict.*

I watched him wither and pale as the world screamed at him. Dying, dying. This would have been me, jail-starved and beaten. Disgraced and running, trying to hide in the tangled wilds of some arse-fuck suburb on the edge of nowhere.

I became fascinated by Ted. How the treacherous north had darkened and toughened his skin; seeing him appear, bearded and black-eyed, in reports of mobs gathering at his broken-down home. Months passed without word. I flicked through reports about him and his new partner, Amanda Pharrell, the killer. The other me, born again, ruggedly handsome and wounded on flashy, sensational ads for Stories and Lives.

I became obsessed. Not only had I witnessed in grotesque detail round-the-clock coverage of my own demise, but I'd seen my own redemption, too. A part of me knew it was all a fantasy. That this Conkaffey guy obviously possessed incredible qualities in order to survive it all. But then, it was so easy to see my face on his, the downcast eyes, the pained grimace. He pressed on. On and on through life, defiant of the shame the world heaped on him. Refusing to be buried alive.

I listened to a podcast about him, sitting rigid on the couch, eyes wide, ears pricked. There was mention, all of a sudden, of an appearance. Ted himself. In the flesh.

I grabbed my phone and opened the episode, clicked the link at the bottom of the page. My hands were shaking.

Amanda and Sweeney sat at the bar, two dejected souls, whiskey at their fingertips, chins low. Amanda was simply mirroring Sweeney's body with her own. She'd read somewhere that a lot of empathy was exhibited physically. If she wanted to feel what Sweeney felt, she should act as Sweeney acted. The new police detective rapped the side of her glass with her fingernails, now and then wincing slightly as embarrassing or undignified thoughts crossed her mind. Amanda looked along the bar to the kitchen area, where the chefs wandered back and forth, flashes of raggedy black aprons dusty with glove powder and flour.

All evidence of the murders had been cleaned and bleached away. Amanda was puzzled by that. Of course she didn't believe that Claudia Flannery and her employees should have left the reddish brown smears left by Andrew's struggling feet on the tiles. The print of Keema's jaw and chin, red and round, perfect beneath the uneven droplets and puddles all around it. But surely there should have been *something*, otherwise how might the thing be remembered?

For Amanda's own crime, it seemed very important to friends and family of the girl that her murder be remembered. Amanda had read in the newspaper in prison about the five-year anniversary. *We must never forget what happened to Lauren,* her mother had said. And yet, as far as Amanda knew, there was nothing to mark the spot where she had stabbed Lauren to death in the rainforest. No cross, or briskly informative plaque: *Here is where Lauren Freeman was stabbed to death. Her killer didn't mean it. She was trying to get someone else. May she rest in peace or whatever.* Amanda had noted this strange contradictory insistence on both remembering and forgetting in other cases she'd heard about in prison. For a brief time one of her cellmates was a woman who had drowned her three children. The woman had commissioned memorial tattoos from another inmate. Yet the house where the babies had died had been sold immediately, bulldozed, replaced with a small park. The houses on either side of the park had changed their numbers to confuse the casual murder voyeur as to the house's original location.

"Why didn't I have someone pick them up from the airport?" Sweeney groaned suddenly, distracting Amanda from her thoughts.

"Would that have helped?" Amanda asked. You were supposed to ask questions when you were being a good listener. "I'm not sure cassowaries curb their behavior for police cruisers."

"It's not about the cassowary," Sweeney sighed. "It's about consideration. I left them to get a bloody taxi. How rude. I'm fucking this up. I'm fucking it all up. I feel like shit."

"You're a cop," Amanda said. "I think that's part of the job description."

Sweeney smiled. "Out of my depth and feeling like shit. Both in the job description."

Amanda shrugged.

Sweeney said, "Doesn't this kind of work ever bring you down?"

"Nah," Amanda sniffed.

"Not even when . . ." Sweeney seemed to be treading carefully. "Even when you know very intimately the effect that a sudden, unexpected death can have on a family?"

Sweeney watched Amanda carefully. The noise of the bar swirled around them.

"Sweens, are you trying to tell me something?" Amanda asked.

Sweeney couldn't find the words. Yes, she guessed. She was trying to tell her something. She was trying to share, for the first time in more than a decade, what she had done. Because something was telling Sweeney that Amanda would be the only person who could possibly understand what Sweeney felt about her father's death. About her refusal to help him. The guilt. The shame.

And yet, at the same time, she knew there was every chance Amanda was incapable of understanding at all.

"Why don't you just choose your penance," Amanda suggested.

"Huh?"

"Whatever it is you did," Amanda said. "Whatever it is you've been tiptoeing around me for days with—why don't you just decide on a penance and serve it, and get on with your life."

Sweeney swallowed hard.

"I was lucky, see," Amanda continued, sipping her whiskey and smacking her lips. "Someone gave me mine. I went to jail. It was a pretty good penance, as far as they go. I had a great time there. A really great time." She laughed to herself, smiled at her drink as though watching some long-ago prank being played out on reflections in the tea-colored liquid. "But when it was done, and I walked out, that was it." She dusted off her hands. "Doneski!"

"Okay." Sweeney nodded.

"Whatever your crime was . . ." Amanda appreciated her partner for a second, shook her head. "No. I'm not going to try to guess. Whatever it was, go ahead and pick a punishment for yourself that you think is befitting. Do it. And then, move the fuck on."

"Move the fuck on?"

"Yep. You don't have to forget it completely," Amanda said. "Cut one of your fingers off, maybe. Then it'll always be there, every time you look."

"I'm not going to cut one of my fingers off!"

"Well, I don't know! Say a thousand Hail Marys. Chop down a

tree with a pair of scissors," Amanda said. "I told you—I didn't have to come up with mine, I don't have any great ideas!"

Sweeney watched the investigator. The television above the bar flashed colors over her face, the yellow of a rose tattoo on her neck. The red of an anatomical heart poking out above the neckline of her shirt. Sweeney heard a promotion for Ted's appearance on *Stories and Lives*, but she didn't look at the screen. All over Amanda, the scars of the croc attack sliced through the tattoos like lightning, carving the once beautiful face of the portrait of a geisha on her bicep into a grotesque, cracked-mirror image.

"Is that what the tattoos are about?" Sweeney asked. "Were they penance?"

"No."

"Like a reminder?"

"No."

"Can you tattoo over these?" Sweeney asked, drunk enough on the whiskey to reach out and touch the nearest scar. Amanda slapped her hand away.

"No touching! Rule one!"

"Sorry, sorry." Sweeney had encountered Amanda's rules already. Rule fourteen was the most amusing to date. No use of the word "bulbous," ever. Under any circumstances.

"I won't tattoo over these." Amanda pulled at her bicep, examined the scar there. "They're too badass. Who else do you know who has teeth marks on their butt?"

"No one."

"No one," Amanda confirmed. "Me? I've got heaps. He really munched me."

"Must have been some tasty butt," Sweeney said.

Amanda choked on her drink, laughing. Sweeney felt uplifted for the first time that day. That was Amanda. Sweeney felt the constant pull of tension around the woman, the terror that she would break out and do something inappropriate or weird in front of a victim's family, her colleagues, members of the public. Mingled with this in the perfect storm of emotions swirling within her was the awareness, all the time, that this woman had killed. That she was capable of killing. And what a weariness that brought in Sweeney, because she saw herself reflected there, the woman who carried on like nothing was wrong despite the death that forever stained her. And now, the storm broke with sudden irrepressible joy. Pip finished her whiskey. Yes, Amanda was exhausting. But every night this week Pip had gone to sleep and fallen into welcoming blackness, something she hadn't done since she was a teenager. It was like Amanda absorbed her pain. A magnet constantly pulling invisible forces from her.

A scuffle behind them near the door to the bar, glasses toppling. They turned, and there was Michael Bell by a table of seated men, staggering drunk. Sweeney found herself standing, her hand going to her belt, searching for the gun she had left at home.

"You come and drink here," Michael was wailing, his arm out, pleading, gesturing to the kitchen. "My son was murdered in there. This is where he died."

"Should we . . . ?" Sweeney glanced around the faces in the bar, some watching the fray, others refusing to look, cringing, hands over eyes. When she looked at Amanda, the woman was picking her teeth with a bent straw.

"Nah," she said. "Better to let the boys get it."

As Sweeney watched, the men at the table ushered Michael outside, arms around his broad shoulders, patting hard. A few hostile looks were thrown Sweeney's way as she turned back toward the bar. The town wanted this solved. They wouldn't wait much longer before they started looking for ways to issue their own brand of justice. People liked a cause in places like this. A reason to band together, to be angry. Injustice would bring them crawling out of their hidey-holes like spiders sensing a tugging on their webs.

"I let Stephanie Neash go," Sweeney said. The bartender glanced at her, a young spiky-haired redhead who might have been covering a shift originally meant for her friend Keema or Andrew. The girl had been eavesdropping while racking and polishing glasses. Sweeney kept her voice low, leaned in to Amanda. "She didn't do it."

"You search the house?" Amanda asked.

"Yeah," Sweeney said. "No sign of a weapon. No gunshot residue. Not that that would have proven anything anyway, but we did check, and we checked the Bell place, too. All there was at Stephanie's place was a bunch of unwashed dishes in the sink and a sad, neglected cat that didn't appear to have been fed in a while."

"Huh." Amanda examined whatever she had picked from between her teeth.

"In the bedroom there were photos of her and Andrew," Sweeney said. "Letters from when they were in high school. Passing notes, having conversations. He used to call her Little Love and she used to call him Big Love."

Sweeney cleared her throat, rubbed the bridge of her nose.

"Are you crying?" Amanda asked.

"No, I'm not crying." Sweeney sniffed. "It's just sad. That's all."

"The high school stuff?" Amanda shook her head. "But it's been years since they were in high school. I don't understand. Why is that sad?"

"Never mind," Sweeney said.

"Hey, what'd the shrink say about the false confession?" Amanda asked.

"Oh." Sweeney sniffed. "She said they're more common than you think. Coerced false confessions happen a lot—you know. The cops keep someone in too long, muscle them a bit maybe, suggest that they might have forgotten what they did. But non-coerced ones do also appear every now and then. The lack of sleep, the grief, the isolation."

"Right." Amanda nodded.

"Stephanie is riddled with guilt. Initially her idea was that maybe if she'd said something about the affair, confronted Andrew about it, he could have come back to her. Avoided shifts with Keema. Not been there that night," Sweeney said. "The guilt and the anger grew and grew and then she started worrying, *Maybe there's another reason I feel so guilty.* A story started to form in her mind."

"The human brain is so weird and awesome." Amanda smiled.

"Is that, uh . . ." Sweeney glanced at the eavesdropping bartender. "Is that kind of how it was with you?"

"You mean when I gave my false confession?" Amanda raised a conspiratorial brow. "When I told them I'd killed Lauren on purpose?"

"Yeah." Sweeney leaned in. "I mean, how come you didn't . . . you never said . . ."

"Sweeney," Amanda whispered in the other woman's ear, "stop being so nosy."

They both laughed. Sweeney had felt the hairs on the back of her neck rise as Amanda's breath tickled the rim of her ear. The bartender was frowning. Sweeney gestured to the back and Amanda followed, skirting the kitchen area and heading out the back door. A chef on a cigarette break spotted them as they arrived in the dim light, ducked back into the kitchen, guilty. Sweeney smelled dope on the wind.

The creek bank was alive with the call of night creatures, the barking and coughing of reptilian life punctuating the high-pitched strumming of insect wings. As they stood listening, looking at the lights of old Mrs. Songly's house across the creek, a movement caught Amanda's eye.

"Oh!" She grabbed Sweeney's forearm. "Poss-poss!"

A brush-tailed possum the size of a large housecat had reached the base of a nearby eucalypt. The two women stood frozen as it began ambling toward them with the wide, awkward tread of a creature unaccustomed to making its way along the ground. It came to within a couple of meters of them and stood sniffing the air with its pink nose, its pointed ears twitching.

"I don't have any food, buddy," Sweeney said. Amanda was searching her pockets. She produced a single cashew nut and held it up in the light.

"It's your lucky day, mate," Amanda said.

"What are you doing walking around with nuts in your pocket?"

"Nut, in the singular," Amanda said. She offered no further explanation, simply crouched and held the nut for the possum to take. It reached out with a tiny, furred hand and took the nut, turned and sprinted off into the dark. Sweeney realized she was grinning. They were both grinning. When Amanda turned toward her, Sweeney felt a heavy thump in the very center of her being, almost like the push of an invisible hand from behind.

She drew herself up. Waited for the strength to do it.

But she resisted. Her feet remained planted. She felt the smile on her face wither away, and in time Amanda's had too as the other woman's mind drifted off, her eyes wandering over the forest surrounding them.

I sat on the edge of the stiff bed in the hotel room and took a deep breath, let it slide softly out of my lungs, the television remote on my knee. Before me, an unnecessarily large blank screen. Two more slow breaths, and then my mind swirled back into the turmoil of the last hour as I finished up dinner with Kelly and walked back through the rain to the room, causing my breath to quicken, to catch.

We can fix it.

Come home.

I need you.

Anger swelled, reached breaking point, cracked and fell away, leaving confusion in its wake. I'd spent so long fantasizing about Kelly saying those words to me that when she had, I'd almost mistaken it for a daydream. In the months since my accusation, I'd learned to coax myself to sleep at night by running a story through my head. Me standing on the doorstep of my home. Kelly opening the door, welcoming me in, noticing my confusion and panic. Me trying to explain to her everything that had happened, Claire Bingley and my arrest, my time in prison, the hateful, vengeful public. Kelly telling me none of it had been true. No time had passed. It was still that fateful Sunday morning. We hadn't fought. I hadn't ever left to go fishing. I could still stop it all from happening.

There hadn't been anything to say to Kelly's offer at the restaurant. Was it even an offer, or was it a plea? I'd mumbled something about not knowing what she meant, about not really understanding how she could want that. But, of course, we both knew what she meant. How she could want it. Our marriage had been great. Yes, there had been arguments, the occasional walkout. But we'd made a great team. We made each other laugh every day. We'd been right in the middle of that blessed, exhausting, exhilarating time of a new baby—struggling to adjust but knowing that we would, celebrating every triumph, every struggle, every milestone. We'd been on the edge of wonderful new territory for the two of us. Parenting. And then it had all fallen to pieces.

She wanted me to come back so that we could resume that dreamlike state. Of course it wouldn't be the same. But it would be good. We both knew it would be good. She'd have to teach me things about baby girls. My baby girl. I'd have to relearn Kelly's language, adjust to her routine. We'd presumably get to see each other's new bodies for the first time. I'd investigate her new edges, curves. She'd see scars I'd obtained in my new life as an accused criminal.

I gripped my head and tried to breathe. There was no time to think about that now. Dale Bingley was pushing into my mind, a coiled black snake encircling my entire life back in Cairns, threatening to squeeze. He'd be sitting down to watch what was about to happen on national television. Everyone would. Kelly was probably racing home to be with Jett right now. Lillian in bed, two glasses of wine on the coffee table. Sean would be watching it in his chic apartment in Potts Point with his partner Richard trying to talk the angry lawyer down from ranting at the screen. My colleagues. My old friends and neighbors. With gritted teeth, I forced myself to lift the remote and push the red button at the top of the device.

A lengthy introduction. Plenty of words that made me wince.

Vicious. Shocking. Predator. Punches to the heart between rounds of barely comforting concessions. *Accused. Alleged. Unproven.* Suddenly I was on the screen looking surprisingly handsome. I felt ill, couldn't tear my eyes off the screen to go and be sick. Minutes passed while I waited for that terrible moment, for Lara to sigh meaningfully, tilt her head in that severely skeptical way and turn my attention to the laptop with Melanie's message on it. Ad breaks came and went. I was drenched in sweat and plucking at the front of my shirt as the minutes ticked down, my phone conspicuously silent.

And then Lara was on the screen standing alone, telling me *Stories and Lives* would be following the case closely and that more information on me could be found on their website. I sat rigid as more ads came, and then the thumping rock-music theme of some dance show.

I didn't even look at the screen when my phone rang. I forgot to say hello.

"Are you there?" Sean said.

"Yeah, I'm watching," I said. Happy youths were throwing one another about and posing as their names flashed on the screen. "The Melanie part must be up next."

"It's over. The show's over. They didn't air it."

"But they said—"

"They didn't air it, Ted."

I watched a lean, toned female host introducing a panel of strangely dressed judges.

"But what does that mean?"

"I don't know!" Sean laughed, disbelieving.

"Is there a late edition of the program? Maybe it's on there."

"There is no late edition. There's nothing on the website, either. I'm on the home page. Nothing. It's not there. The accusation is not there."

We held on in silence, Sean clicking on his computer, typing things. Me watching some guy in a silver top hat talking to some very nervous kids in leotards.

"Is it a mistake?" I asked.

"Let's hope not," Sean answered.

Dale Bingley sat in the kitchen of his daughter's accused rapist, a small television he had found in the front room now plugged into the wall beside the man's battered toaster. The Ted on the screen was a far cry from the man he'd watched carefully over the past days. He knew a hollow-cheeked, tired-looking man with eyes constantly drawn to the horizon across the water as though he could see an unreachable paradise there, an over-the-rainbow place where his troubles meant nothing. He was charismatic on the screen. Handsome. But that was everyone's favorite thing to hate about him, wasn't it? That he was undeniably likeable. Not the monster of fairy tales.

Half listening to Ted's measured protests on the set, Dale turned to the papers before him, the laptop with pages open, one showing utes, one open on Ted's email account.

There were Ford Falcons registered to owners who lived in the area of Claire's abduction, some of them within the model range of 1988 to 1992. But none of them were blue. Dale looked at the cars on the screen and felt the familiar sting of fatherly shame he'd never shaken since Claire's attack. He knew it was ridiculous. Sexist. But a part of him felt that, however irrational, if he had been a better *man*, a stronger, more masculine man, a tougher man, he'd have been able to prevent what had happened to his daughter. It was probably some ancient caveman thing, a stupid instinct from history. A real man's duty was to protect his child, and that meant knowing somehow when she was not safe. It meant knowing about cars and weapons and investigative police work. It meant being able to match Claire's attacker physically when the time came, to beat him, to conquer him.

Ted's sheer strength the night before had brought all those feelings back. The man had picked him up off the floor like a child and thrown him through a door. Dale had watched idly as Ted reattached the door after their fight, drunkenly trying to fit the screws into place, fumbling with the screwdriver, the geese still muttering angrily in their house on the lawn. Was Ted a better man than Dale? Would he have been able to protect her? There were suggestions in the evidence before him that Claire's attacker, if it wasn't Ted, was twenty-five years old or close to it. Was he strong? Did he know about models of cars? Did he have a child?

He exhaled. There were too many variables. Dale didn't know if the color of a vehicle, when it was changed, had to be updated on the registration form. Was that something the motor registry insisted on? Or was it just encouraged? Could any of the Ford Falcon XF utes on the papers before him actually be blue?

Dale rapped on the edge of the laptop, then glanced at Ted's email inbox.

He opened the email from Khalid Farah, curious. Dale had seen the short, arrogant gangster in the news from time to time—expensive-looking suits, immaculate, slicked hair.

Coffee, you gotta answer my texts, bro. I know you're gonna find this guy. You better think about what it'll be like for you if you hand him in and he gets eight years. We can help you do better, yo. We can help you do right.

Dale read the message from start to finish a few times over. The television program ended, no sign of the new accusations. The keys to Ted's car were sitting on the countertop in a little wooden bowl.

Dale clicked "Reply." When he'd finished writing, he stood and took the keys in his hand.

Heavy. A crushing heaviness infecting everything, liquid lead coating my throat and chest, rolling in waves down my legs. I woke on top of the bed, my arms sprawled out, still naked from the shower I'd finally managed to drag myself into after the *Stories and Lives* program. I had inexplicably slept the deep and dreamless slumber of the dead, but I was awakened by a splinter of light from the edge of the curtains covering the hotel window and found myself too weighed down to move. It was midday. I turned my head as my phone started buzzing. I was faintly aware that it had been buzzing for some time.

Kelly, of course. And before her, two calls from Sean and one from Khalid Farah. There was a small collection of unidentified numbers, probably journalists and swearing, threatening crazies who had dug up my phone number somehow, I guessed from experience. I didn't return the calls of anyone who had called me. Instead I flipped through the numbers until I found Sweeney and held the phone to my ear with an aching arm.

"Ted?"

"Hello," I said.

"Are you okay? You sound terrible."

"I need—" I drew a difficult breath. "I need something to do. Something mundane. I'm not feeling the best."

"Okay." I heard Sweeney pushing some papers around, adjusting the phone against her ear. She was at the station. I recognized the low grumble of cop voices in the background, a security door buzzing open and a phone ringing. "I've got stuff you could do. We're widening the search. I suppose you read my message about Stephanie's confession not stacking up? Michael Bell's clean. I'm going through a list here. All the past and present staff of the Barking Frog, some people who have admitted to being at the pleasure-den parties."

"The what?"

"Just—never mind. I've got a collection of names. I'm going through bank accounts, social media profiles, criminal records."

"Perfect," I said.

"Family and friends of—"

"Give me them, too."

"How about I just send you a big ole list of names?"

"Thank you." I rolled away from the light. My laptop was on the bedside table. Without shifting upright I dragged it toward me and pushed it open. Sweeney had fallen silent, clicking on her own computer, emailing me.

"Shouldn't you be feeling a bit better?" she asked hesitantly. "The new accusation. It wasn't on the program last night. I'm sorry. I . . . I watched."

"Everybody did."

"So that's good, isn't it?"

"I don't know."

"Oh."

"My wife—" I began. But how to explain? I curled up and listened to the police station in the background of Sweeney's call. Her gentle breathing. "I don't know about that, either."

More clicking. Someone, a man, laughing.

"Maybe you should call Amanda," Sweeney said suddenly.

"Why? What's happened?"

"Nothing," Sweeney said. "She just, uh . . . She just makes me feel . . ."

I waited. Sweeney sounded like she regretted starting her sentence and now didn't know how to end it.

"She just makes me feel better," she admitted, after a time. "That's all."

I took her advice. Amanda answered on the second ring.

"Listen to this," she said. I listened, heard nothing.

"What was it?" I asked.

"Nature," she said proudly. "I'm in the forest. Trekking around looking for clues. Are you wallowing in your own sorrow? You sound like you are. I've warned you about wallowing, Ted."

"What happened with Stephanie?" I asked. "You're sure she didn't do it?"

"No, she just went whacko with grief, that's all."

I thought I understood the feeling.

"Where did the Mona Wallgreen lead go?" I asked.

"Not far," Amanda said. "We found a pair of tradesman's boots in her house which we couldn't rule out as being worn by the killer. We couldn't find a single nine millimeter pistol, but that doesn't mean she didn't dump it somewhere in the rainforest and the search teams just haven't found it yet. She's not talking to police, or to me, so we're at a bit of an impasse for now. She's got a relative down in Sydney who's going to fly up and convince her to surrender some DNA samples, maybe tell us what she knows."

"Hmm," I said.

"Yes, indeed, hmm."

"And what's all this about a pleasure den?"

"Oh my GOD," Amanda crowed. "That's right, you never heard about that." She proceeded to tell me all about her and Sweeney's adventure below the Barking Frog. As Sweeney had predicted, I felt a little smile growing on my face as Amanda jabbered on.

I stared at the phone screen when she hung up. A picture of Lillian on the wallpaper, peering out from behind an app. Devious, gummy smile.

Beyond the phone, on the table beside the bed, was my wedding ring. I put down the phone, pushed aside the laptop, and reached for it.

Amanda sat down on the creek bank and pulled off her pink Converse shoes, slipped her toes into the water. Tangled in the reeds was the detritus of the night before, chip packets pulled out of the bins behind the bar and scattered by possums and other opportunistic night creatures. Despite the trash, the water was good. She wiggled her toes in the creek, the water rushing against her ankles, swirling and making eddies.

A day had passed since she had stood nearby with Sweeney behind the Barking Frog, looking up and seeing the stars between the tree canopies peeking through at the creek. Sweeney had emailed her part of a list the day before and Amanda had started working through it, but the monotony of the clicking and dragging at her computer in her office had driven her almost insane. Computers were difficult for Amanda. They hummed and glowed and zinged, bubbling with life suddenly without warning, messages appearing from nowhere, sent by no one. Though they were inevitably about her passwords or updates or her connections, Amanda never shook the feeling that, one day, one of these messages might be something sinister. Bad things had a way of popping unexpectedly into her life, a bubble rising invisibly, exploding, consuming everything. Very rarely had anything bad ever come from a distance, announcing its intentions like the smell of a storm on the wind. The noises and bleeps of computers bothered her. She'd abandoned the list before long.

Instead she'd spent the previous day wandering, thinking, head down, watching the asphalt pass beneath her feet. She'd walked through the list instead of researching it on the zinging, singing machine. She'd walked to Michael Bell's house and watched him through the windows. He must have sent all his helpers away, as she found him sitting on the couch alone, staring at the blank television set, a piece of some cloth she didn't recognize in his fingers. Maybe a T-shirt of Andrew's. Amanda knew that grieving people liked to fondle the clothes of their lost loved ones. She didn't know why. She'd wandered to Stephanie Neash's house and tried to look through the windows there at the young woman, but she was gone. The rooms in the house were dark.

Amanda walked home, and then took her bike to the house of the young chef who'd cooked the last meals at the back of the Barking Frog that night, and his kitchen hand who had put away the plates and polished cutlery, minutes ticking down until Andrew and Keema died. She rode to Claudia Flannery's house, a terra-cotta bungalow perched on the edge of Crimson Lake, not far from Ted's. The old woman had been sitting at her kitchen table when Amanda arrived, forking halfheartedly through a plate of pasta. She was wearing those big, heavy earrings and necklaces still, folds of chiffon hanging on her spotted arms.

Amanda wasn't so arrogant as to think she'd be able to divine the killer of Andrew and Keema simply by looking at their face through a window. But she'd longed to feel something as she rolled from house to house, a ghost in the cold looking in on living people, admiring their warmth. She'd wandered all night from home to home, no real pattern to her movements, finally stopping when all she found were black rooms and drawn curtains.

In the morning she'd taken her bike and turned it toward the Barking Frog. The place where it all began.

She stood now and wandered a few meters down the creek, crouched and plucked a few smooth stones from the bottom. Tiny yabby-like creatures fled from her grasp. The bottom was sandy. She dug down, twisted her hand back and forth. New perspective. New feeling. It was warm down there with watery life.

She wondered if she might have been able to tap into that weird spiritual thing Claudia Flannery liked to talk about, to listen to the bar and the creek and the forest and hear them whisper cosmically to her about what happened to the murdered bartenders. But the jack-hammering from the Songly house began and made her wince with shock. Amanda opened her eyes and looked at the house across the creek. The fence with the new blond paling of untreated wood stuck in the row of old palings like a gold tooth.

She walked up the bank toward the house, peered irritably through the cracks in the fence. She could see old Mrs. Songly's legs lying on the footrest by a couch, the slippered feet flopped apart. Amanda wandered around to the front of the house. Perhaps the old woman was worth talking to about her ghostly gaze, the eye she'd swept over the men and women connected to the Barking Frog. Maybe Mrs. Songly knew something about Claudia and her pleasure parties, even if she hadn't heard or seen anything specifically on the night of the murders. Amanda knew it was useful sometimes just to be in the presence of old people when a puzzle presented itself, though she couldn't account for exactly why. The old timers in prison, the lifers, had always brought her calm. And besides that, they invariably smelled good.

She stopped at the corner of the front of the property, where the side fence was partially hidden behind some bushes. A fence paling was missing. Interesting. The fence was newer here. Blond, untreated wood. Amanda reached up and touched the new, shiny nail, twisted and bent, the paling yanked off around it, it seemed.

Amanda rounded the end of the fence and walked through into the backyard, to the back fence, where the blond paling had been re-nailed into the gap in the side facing the Barking Frog Inn. Amanda pushed on the paling. It didn't budge. She stood back and kicked the paling as hard as she could, dislodging it, sending it flopping to the grass on the creek bank.

A new perspective. She could see directly through the gap in the fence to the back door of the Barking Frog. And presumably, she thought, someone standing there could see directly through the gap to where she stood. She understood. Almost saw Andrew standing there that night at the back of the pub. The paling had not been in place. Andrew had stood across the creek and looked through the gap to where Amanda now stood in the mottled shade, the heavy sun beating down above the trees.

Whatever he'd seen had made him run.

But what had he seen?

Amanda turned around just in time for a closed fist to smash her in the side of the head.

Sean and Frankie were waiting for me in the reception area of the Parramatta police headquarters, standing an awkward distance apart, Sean pretending to look through his phone. I'd finally answered the phone to Sean early that morning, having spent the entire previous day languishing in bed like a slug, the laptop on my chest, the police files of strangers scrolling before my eyes. Working on the Barking Frog case was a welcome dark tunnel to fall into, little tendrils of the lives of the people surrounding the murders leading me this way and that through an underground maze, well away from my tumultuous world. I tracked down the social media accounts of the young men and women who currently or had recently worked at the bar, and worked backward. Their present talk led me to believe that none of them were anything but shocked and saddened about the killings, but there was the odd interesting tidbit of less-than-sympathetic talk on the social media messages. The girls didn't like that Andrew had been cheating on Stephanie. And the guys wanted to believe it could never have happened to them.

TIKO: Its really really bad and all that but I cant stop thinking like if I was gonna rob the place id have picked Andys shift too man.

MATT: You reckon?

TIKO: Yeah man he was fuckin loose as shit. He didn't give a rats about the place. Ive taken shifts with him and he has one or two customers at the bar and he fucks off into the kitchen to spin shit for like half an hour. Leaves the register wide open. He was never gonna put up a fight.

MATT: You think it was a customer? Someone thought Andy would be easy pickings?

TIKO: Well they didn't come on my shift did they?

I'd taken the side entrance to headquarters, having spotted press on the front steps of the towering concrete building. I wondered if someone in Melanie's camp had leaked that I would be giving a police statement, or if one of my old colleagues had got wind of it and told the media. The entryway I took was reserved for notorious killers and rapists coming to give evidence, undercover cops and informants. Now me, the most hated man in Australia.

I hadn't seen Little Frankie since the morning I was arrested, the few agonizing hours she and my workmates had been given to shout at me in the interrogation room, express their horror and disgust. It hadn't been an official questioning. They'd just needed their time to ask me directly if I'd done what I was accused of, to look me in the eye and see if I lied to them.

Short, stocky Frankie, with her heart-shaped face perpetually turned upward. She'd always had to stand on a milk crate when we took squad photos so that me and the guys didn't tower comically over her. We'd graduated from the academy together. Sean strode forward when I appeared and shook my hand.

"Melanie Springfield is coming in to give her statement today," Sean said. He clapped me on the shoulder. "But we'll be in and out before she arrives."

"So she is coming," I said. "She is going through with it."

Sean didn't answer. Or maybe he did, and I didn't hear it. I was reeling. Frankie took a stiff step forward and cleared her throat, professional distance, protecting her heart. She'd always been a crier, Frankie, but she wasn't crying now. Her eyes were red and her lips were a thin, hard line, but she wasn't giving in.

"I'll take you up to the interview room," she said.

"Level five?" I asked. My old level.

"No, seven," she said unevenly. "We thought . . . It's just that Davo and Morris are here, you know, so . . ."

My drug squad brothers. I understood. It would be more than reasonable to expect either of them to take a swing at me, given the chance. Our other colleagues probably expected it, in fact. I followed Frankie and Sean into the elevator and we emerged on a long hall of empty interview rooms. We took one and Sean and I sat quietly on one side of the table while Frankie set up the things we would need, official police statement sheets and paper. She went and retrieved coffee, which I thought was nice. She wasn't obliged to do anything like that. She kept her eyes steadfastly away from mine, which was facilitated by her floppy black hair constantly falling across her brow. She'd never been very confident about her hair. She had been frequently cutting it all off when I knew her, regretting it then trying to grow it out. She poured the coffee and put a packet of sugar down next to my cup, slid the milk over to me. She remembered how I liked it. After everything that had happened, she still knew me. I wanted to tell her, like I had on the phone, that *she still knew me.* This was proof. But instead, other words rose.

"Do you still see Kelly?" I asked her suddenly. Frankie looked at

Sean as if for help, didn't dare look at me to see if it was a casual question or a challenge.

"I haven't seen her in a long while," Frankie said. "I text now and then."

She's asked me back, I wanted to say. *If I say yes, we're going to pretend nothing ever happened.* Would Frankie be a part of that, too? Would assuming my old life mean I could have some of my friends back? That *they'd* have *me* back? The accusation had deleted me from the lives of my colleagues, too. From Kelly's life. I'd not only lost her but she'd lost me, and now she was finally feeling that loss. If I decided to go back, I'd be leaving Amanda. Val. The house on the water. The geese. It was a silly thing to contemplate, but suddenly the tree on Redemption Point flashed into my mind. The vines would come up and strangle it to death in my absence.

The silence was ringing. Sean and Frankie took out identical stapled sheaves of paper, Sean sliding his across to me.

"I thought we'd respond directly to the issues raised," Sean said.

"Oh, this is it?" I said. I took the pages with shaky hands. "This is the transcript of Melanie's interview with *Stories and Lives*?"

"There it is, in full." Sean sighed, revulsion clipping his words again. I read the pages while they watched me, my eyes dancing over the cold, printed lines as shockwaves of dread came again and again. I had to read some lines several times over. It was hard to focus.

LARA: *When did you first think something was wrong?*

MELANIE: *Ted started asking whether Elise had a boyfriend. I said of course she doesn't, she's eight. Like, I felt weird myself, you know? Ted was my first boyfriend. But he was very advanced. It struck me at the time that he'd probably had other girlfriends before. He was always wanting to touch, to kiss. He wanted to play Truth or Dare, and that's kind of how he led me into sexual things. And he wanted to involve Elise.*

"This isn't true." I was trembling all over. I wiped my sweating brow. "None of this is true."

"Let's take it a step at a time," Sean said. Frankie started the tape and did the introductions. Sean put a hand on my shoulder. It was all I could do not to shrug it off. "Tell us about your relationship with Melanie."

"It was nothing like this." I gestured to the papers. "Nothing at all like this. I was not *advanced* and there was no sexual kissing or touching. Melanie *was* my first girlfriend, and I was very nervous. I just about broke it off because I couldn't bring myself to kiss her. I was embarrassed—we were close with another teen couple and they kissed all the time, in front of us, like they were showing off."

"So you never kissed?"

"No." I put my head in my hands. "I tried. I put an arm around her a few times, for photos and things. But I was a really awkward teenager. Tall and goofy, you know?"

A flicker of a smile from Frankie. Maybe she wanted to say she had known me to be like that. I'd been the biggest person on the drug squad and she the smallest. We made fun of each other for it. But Frankie's smile was a flash if there at all. The words on the paper before us were stark, like a death warrant, almost painful under my fingertips.

"So it wasn't until you were at university that you became sexually active?"

"Yes."

"And who was that with?"

"Oh, just a girl." I shifted uncomfortably in my seat. "I don't want to bring her into this unless it's absolutely necessary. It was just a girl from one of my classes. I took criminology and criminal justice, thinking I'd be a cop or a lawyer. I didn't make the grades for lawyer. Too much drinking, partying. It was really the drinking at uni that broke me out of childhood. It gave me the confidence to talk to girls for the first time."

"Did you date anyone between Mel and the girl at uni?"

"No. It wasn't even as though Mel and I were dating," I said. "We just said we were going steady, and we held hands when we were at school. I sent her love letters and she wrote me poems. That was it."

"You and Melanie—were you sexual at all? Even if not, all the way into intercourse?"

"No," I said. "Not at all. And if I couldn't get up the guts to even kiss her, I don't know how she thinks I was going after her little sister."

"So you're saying she's completely making it up? Fabricating the entire claim?" Frankie said.

"Yes. And she's doing a bloody good job of it," I said. I read over the words before me. There was sweat beading at my temples. "I mean it's . . . It's very convincing."

"For a pack of lies," Sean murmured.

"It's like she's taken the story from somewhere. Like she's mistaking me for someone else."

"How so?" Frankie asked.

"When she talks here about this Truth or Dare business. Yes, kids my age played Truth or Dare and Spin the Bottle, but *we* never played it. Melanie and I."

"It's a very specific detail," Frankie mused. "She's actually naming a game that would initiate sexual experimentation, even bargaining that might lead easily to sexual abuse."

I nodded.

"She's not just saying you led her into sex," she added. "She's telling us *how* you did it."

"Well, I didn't do it," I said. "I don't know who did, but it wasn't me."

Frankie seemed to catch herself musing, wandering out of her role as interrogator and over to the territory of being my colleague again. She straightened.

"She says here that you would lead Elise into touching games by bringing her treats." Frankie pointed at the page before me. "Clinkers chocolates, which you knew were her favorite."

"How would I know that?" I asked.

"Try not to ask questions," Sean warned me. "Just answer the accusation, firm and straight. Just like in your trial. No unnecessary speculation."

"I did not lead Elise or Melanie into any 'touching games,'" I said. "I did not bring Elise any treats. I did not act sexually toward her in any way, or encourage her to act sexually toward me."

"Did you ever touch Elise affectionately?" Frankie asked. "Like, with Melanie, you said you went so far as to put an arm around her shoulders. Did you ever hug her sister? Wrestle with her or grab—"

Frankie's phone blipped on the table beside us. She looked at the lit screen, frozen, her hand in the air above it. I watched her pick up the phone, open the message and read it. She gave the proper statement officially pausing the interview, reading the exact time off her watch and repeating the date. She clicked off the tape. I glanced at Sean, disbelieving.

Frankie made her apologies and left, closing the door quickly behind her. I put my head in my hands.

"What now?" I groaned.

"I don't know, mate." Sean thumped my shoulder. "But whatever it is, I'm right here, and we'll handle it together."

We sat in silence. Fifteen minutes passed. I read Melanie Springfield's statement over and over, trying to understand how she could possibly have said the things about me that were printed there. I had very few memories of Melanie's house. It had been bigger than mine, I knew that. Melanie's parents had been what my dad called "posh." They'd had a pool table and an old pinball machine in the basement that Mel and I liked to play with. A saltwater pool that was so deep at the end it made my ears hurt to plunge all the way to the bottom. Elise had hung around us as much as she could until her sister got annoyed and banished her. I remembered the little girl at the top of the stairs to the basement pool room, sulking, trying to eavesdrop. The girls in Melanie's year had carried around big binders with all their exercise books in them, covered in special glittery stickers. I remembered telling her, very maturely I thought, how lame sticker collecting was. Melanie being hurt by the comment. Me going out the next day to get her some from the newsagent.

I knew how sexual abuse interrogations went. I'd suffered through them after Claire's assault, but I'd also been trained in them in the academy. I'd sat and watched a couple of them during my early years. Frankie would come back into the room and continue on at a helicopter level, circling around and around my and Melanie's and Elise's relationship from above, coming down slowly, level by level. Soon, I knew, she'd begin discussing what my particular sexual interests were. What turned me on now. What had turned me on as a teenager about Melanie. What I'd liked about Elise. Her personality. Whether I'd ever thought anything sexual about Elise, even if I'd never acted on it, even if only in my mind.

Slowly, slowly winding down, heading for a gentle, feather-light landing, Frankie would try to see if she could get me to say it. That I'd been that boy. That predatory boy.

And, of course, telling her that would be telling her that I was that predatory man, the one everyone said I was. Maybe it would be a relief to her. I didn't know.

When Frankie returned, there was a woman with her who I didn't recognize. The woman was dressed all in black, a thin hoodie and jeans with tattered hems. The two women stood outside the door talking animatedly. Frankie gestured toward me. The young woman looked. Nothing had twinged in me the first time I saw her, but as she turned toward me, her mouth open, almost frantic, I recognized her as the little girl Melanie and I had spent our brief relationship trying to avoid.

I'd stood and walked into the hall without realizing it. My heart was hammering.

"Elise."

It was Elise Springfield. The little girl at the top of the stairs, pouty lip and heavy, clopping leather school shoes bought a size too big so she would grow into them. I'd thought I remembered little about her, but as I looked at her I realized there was plenty there—I remembered the way she'd wailed when her sister had pulled her hair, and I remembered that she'd had a real nail-chewing problem, apparently still did. I remembered her room now, as I stood looking at her, her white pet mouse and the plastic hanging beads strung over the windows. My first girlfriend's sister. Someone who should have had the right to fade completely from my life, and me from hers, a fleeting, meaningless connection formed and broken decades ago, a brief passing without pain. All I could think as I looked at her was that this was unfair. Her being dragged here was unfair. She should have remained the funny, pouty little girl in my memory.

"Look at you," I said, for some reason. An absurd tingle of joy or novelty or something had struck me. She was all grown up. But then the crashing reality of it all hit me. My mouth was suddenly dry. I was desperate. "Elise, you know I didn't . . . I didn't . . ."

"Ted, I'm so sorry," she said. She was wringing her hands. "I'm so sorry about all this. We haven't known what to do. We were going to ask for a press conference, but we wanted the police to be there, to . . ."

"Who?" I asked. "Who's 'we'?"

"The family," she said. "Melanie. She made a terrible mistake, Ted."

Sean was standing at my side. I felt the heat of his body suddenly, as though his fury was literally burning him from the inside.

"Mum and Dad and I," Elise stammered on. "We . . . We didn't know she was going to do it. Any of it. We thought that after *Stories and Lives* didn't show the accusation a couple of days ago that maybe it would all blow over. But it hasn't. It's getting worse. *Stories and Lives* won't answer the phone to us. We've spoken to Mel and she's agreed to read a statement for the press retracting her interview."

"So she . . ." I could hardly speak. I looked at Sean, who was blank. Stunned. "Melanie, she—"

"She lied," Elise said. "She's sorry."

———

The story emerged in frantic stops and starts. Elise began crying in time, wiping her eyes on the backs of her hands. No one seemed game to go into the interview room and sit down, to move out of the hall, in case Elise and her words evaporated into thin air as quickly as they had appeared.

Melanie had suffered from an undiagnosed mental illness for years. Elise wondered if she was bipolar, but it was difficult for her and her parents to get her older sister to go to specialists or take any medication, so a treatment plan when doctors did make an attempt at diagnosis was unmanageable. Though the relationship between the two women was strained, Elise had called Melanie when she first saw me on the news after my arrest for Claire's abduction, remembering me from when we were kids. She'd received some texts from Melanie in the months afterward, always about the case. Elise had worried that her older sister was following the case too closely, that it might become one of her "obsessions." Melanie had, at times, become fixated on the activities of American presidents, climate change, and the occasional murder cold case. But my arrest had really captured her imagination. And then, one devastating day, Elise's mother had called after visiting Melanie's apartment. She told Elise she had found something worrying.

"Mum didn't know what it was," Elise said. "But when I looked at it, I knew. It was an appearance contract. It was signed by the producer, by the network heads, by Melanie. It stipulated money that Mel was going to receive for her interview with them, with *Stories and Lives.*"

"Why didn't you stop her?" I asked.

"Mum found the contract last week." Elise sobbed. Her mascara was smeared. "It was too late. She'd already given it."

"The network didn't call you at all to check Melanie's story?" I asked. "They didn't call your parents?"

"It was the *money*, Ted," Elise pleaded, glancing at Sean. She must have known from Sean's face that he was with me. My lawyer was slowly purpling from the neck up. "Melanie wanted the money. She told them she was the only one who could account for your . . . what you wanted to do to me. She said she never told our parents, and that she'd asked me and I didn't remember. She wanted that money. And the show, they wanted the story."

Sean snorted. His jaw was so tight I could see muscles moving in his temples.

"I'm sorry." Elise reached out. Seemed to want to take my hand, but stopped herself. I was untouchable. "Mel is sick. She's sick, and she's secretive, and we would have stopped her if we'd just—"

"Don't get sucked in by this crap, Ted," Sean said to me. "Mentally ill or not, she systematically, strategically, and with deliberate fore-thought set out to ruin any trace of a good reputation you had left in the world. If you ask me, she probably thought she had struck gold when she saw you'd been arrested for Claire's abduction. There are people who are like that. They come wriggling out of the wood-work when they smell opportunity."

Sean gave Elise a searing look. The young woman actually cow-ered, neared Frankie, the sleeves of her hoodie almost in her mouth.

"Your sister thought she could drop the accusations on national television and then run off with the money like she didn't have a care in the world," Sean said. "Who was going to question them, right? The whole world knows this man's a fucking monster!" Sean slapped me in the chest. I winced. "And then suddenly the police are involved, she's chickening out with a fucking mental illness sob story. What a heartbreaker. No worries, then! All's forgiven!"

"No." Elise stiffened with a moment of boldness. "She—"

"We're suing," Sean snapped. He went back into the interview room and slammed down his briefcase, started stuffing papers into it. He came back to the door. "We're suing your sister, Ms. Springfield. We're suing the producer. We're suing the network. *Stories and Lives* hasn't answered the phone to you because they're holding damage-control meetings. I suggest you and your family do the same."

Sean charged past Elise, his shark eyes locked on her downturned face until the last instant. The best lawyers can do that. Reduce you, so that you can't even look them in the face, the strength drained right out of your legs and your stomach threatening to force itself up into your throat. I knew that from experience.

Frankie followed Sean down the hall, leaving Elise and me alone. I was too exhausted to even feel awkward. I leaned in the doorway, watching my lawyer go, his rants bouncing off the narrow walls as Frankie tried to calm him. Elise took her hair out of its ponytail and put it up again, an unconscious resetting, pulling the hair too tight, still sniffling. She nibbled her nails. When she dared to meet my eyes, she found me watching her and looked away, burning with shame.

"I can't imagine what all this has been like," she said.

I couldn't think how to describe it, so I didn't try.

"Did you read the transcript of the interview?" I asked.

"Yes."

"Those accusations," I said. "They were pretty specific. The treats. The games. You have to wonder if she adapted what she said from something real that happened to her. Or you."

Elise wiped a tear and shook her head.

"We'll get her back into treatment," she said. "She's sick. Very sick."

Elise hitched her handbag on her shoulder, fiddled with the strap, little gestures to tell me she was about to go. That this was the time to say what a man in my position should say, perhaps what we both knew—that the press conference and the denials weren't going to help. That the damage had been done. Ten years from now, people would still know me from Claire's abduction. I was never going to shake that accusation. But if they ever had any doubt about me, if they ever wondered if I was just an innocent man living through everyone's worst nightmare, they would half remember some other accusation that might have been covered up or suppressed before it ever met the light of day in full.

Maybe I'd never been going to live a normal life again after Claire. But what Melanie had done had made absolutely sure of it.

"You must hate us," Elise said eventually. I thought about it. I guess I deserved to. But Elise Springfield, the little girl all grown up, looked as tired as I felt just then, standing in the hallway of the police headquarters, her eyes puffy from tears. In the end, I told her that she was wrong. I didn't hate her, or her family. Maybe it helped her, or me. Before she left, she gave my hand a brief squeeze.

At first, there was only light. Then colors came, red and green, smashing into each other in explosive starbursts against the backs of her eyelids. Pretty. She was being dragged by the wrists. Amanda had only been knocked out by a punch once before in her life. She'd copped a stray fist trying to break up a fight in the visitors' center of Brisbane Women's Correctional, mainly because the guy going to town on his ex-wife had totally disregarded that the woman was holding a baby against her chest. Amanda didn't usually mind the odd prison fight. She found their spontaneous appearance in her otherwise ordinary day as refreshing as finding a surprise ten-dollar note on the pavement. But not that time. The big lughead in the visitors' center had fractured her cheekbone.

Nothing felt fractured now, as far as she could tell, except her conception of time. Just when she thought she was coming to, it seemed she slept a little more, on her chest on the dust-coated floor, long enough for her hand, trapped under her hip, to become numb. In time, voices came to her. She lay still and listened.

". . . any more of your pussy-arse shit. We need to get this done. Go into the other room, if you have to. I'll just pop her."

"It's over. Come on, Jay. Come on. We need to cut our losses and go. We can't make this any—"

"I'll just pop her, mate. Bran, move. *Move.*"

There were shuffling footsteps. Cursing. Amanda tasted concrete dust and blood in her mouth.

"A cop is different."

"She's not a cop. Look at her."

"She told me she was a cop or an investigator or something."

There was a pause. The grind of boots on grit on tiles. Amanda felt her wallet wrenched from her back pocket. Her phone was already long gone. She struggled as one of them took her wrists, began winding tape around and around them. She fought, and they were surprised by her sudden wakefulness. She slid awkwardly onto her backside, looked up at them.

Two young men, the same ones she had encountered the first morning after the murders, at the front of the Songly house. Damo and Ed. Or Bran and Jay, as she now knew. Two dark-eyed, rough-bearded men, distinguished by the shapes of their faces. One wolfish and lean, the other box-headed and brutish. They stared down at her, measuring, as she was measuring them. Amanda felt blood running down the side of her neck from her ear.

"Which one of you arseholes punched me?" she snapped.

The men looked at each other. One had her wallet, the wolfish-featured man, his eyes dancing between the item and her.

"Amanda Pharrell," he said, reading her credit card. "You a cop or not?"

"Last time I checked they frowned upon neck tattoos and violent homicide in the academy," Amanda said.

"Homicide?" the wolf scoffed.

"Look me up." Amanda spat blood on the floor. "I've killed. But I won't kill you. I'll just smash your face in. One for one, that's how I like it."

"Jay, this bitch is crazy," the wolf said.

"My ear is *throbbing*," Amanda wailed.

Jay bent and took a pistol from his back pocket. He pushed the slide back and pointed the barrel at Amanda's face.

"Girl, your problems aren't limited to a punch in the fucking head," Jay said. He was the mean one, Amanda could tell. There was always a mean one. One ideas man and one easily led man. One brain, one brawn. This would be the man who hit her. She was sure of it. "You better forget about who punched you and think about whether you want to die fast or slow."

"Don't." Bran nudged his partner with his boot. "We need to talk about this. We might need her as leverage. She'll be missing from somewhere, mate. Someone will come looking for her."

Jay and Amanda watched each other. Amanda knew the man before her was looking for her fear. But there wasn't any. Wouldn't be any. Fear was one of the things that Amanda felt most rarely. It was an impossible equation to solve in her brain, a puzzle that now and then partly assembled itself before the pieces inevitably fell away.

"I'm gonna break your nose," Amanda said. Jay frowned and got to his feet, followed his partner into the other room.

Dear Diary,

I'm so excited, I need to get this down right now. I can't do any-thing else. I haven't even left yet. I'm sitting in my car. My god. My hands are shaking.

I met him.

I had to meet him. Since I was a kid I've known there was some-thing different about me, something bad. I've lived my whole life feeling that awful absence of hope, that whenever the real me was exposed, my life would be over. There was no coming back from it, from public knowledge of my true nature. I'd confessed as a kid to my shrink, who'd helpfully passed it on to my mother. But Mum had of course shrugged that off as a teen being weird and never told another living soul. As I grew I knew a single drunken slipup, a half-sure sighting of me staring too hard at someone's kid or talking inappro-priately about pedophiles, sympathizing, reasoning: that would plant the seed. The seed that grows and grows, that no amount of pulling or poisoning can destroy. Every human interaction held the potential for it. Every word. Every movement. Every handshake. Every hug.

I was a balloon wobbling and rolling around everywhere, knowing any second everything could spill. My sickness. My virus.

Deadly exposure.

Ted Conkaffey. He'd been through the fires and come out alive, a broad-shouldered hero emerging in slow-walking silhouette from the flames. Supervillain. My great white hope. Yes, he was scarred, war-torn. The Ted Conkaffey who I'd watched, transfixed, on Stories *and* Lives *wasn't the fresh-faced, grinning guy of the uni graduation photos the press so loved to bandy about. The man I'd seen so briefly on that fateful day exiting his car, approaching my girl. He was de-flated. But he was alive. I wanted to be in his presence, even if it was just to look gratefully into the eyes of the man who had endured my death for me.*

Of course, I was nervous. The more nervous I am, the earlier I ar-rive at a place. So I got to the Lord Chesterton Hotel just as lunch was finishing, when Ted's appearance hadn't been slated until three that afternoon. There had been the necessary provisions to make. The podcast, which of course I've listened to extensively, asked listeners to go into a lottery to be allowed to attend the meeting. I knew I couldn't risk that. With hundreds of thousands of listeners Australia-wide, I'd never make it, and I didn't want my name on some list of attend-ees in case it ever came around to bite me. A deep-web contact was able to get me the address and the meeting time. It's very useful to have people on the internet who can break into places and get you what you need like that, the same kind of people who can source you special de-lightful things that might get you into trouble if you went through the more obvious channels.

The Lord Chesterton Hotel was a good choice, I thought. Cozy, chipped sandstone and old fireplaces, long tables downstairs evoking the heyday of establishments like these full of shipmen from the harbor down the hill yelling and slamming down beer glasses. Big portrait of a proud-chested blond man in a military uniform in the main room—hands on hips, surveying the battlefield. Narrow carpeted stairs led past framed relics from the pub's history to the planned meeting place—a small private room off the side of the empty fine-dining restaurant. I crept, rigid with anticipation, up the stairs and along the creaking floors, deciding I'd get a look at the room before everyone arrived, plant myself before those who would check names off a list closed the room to gawkers. I didn't for a moment expect Ted to be there this early. But there he was. Sitting alone at the little bar. I knew the outline of the back of his head, the thick skull and big hand gripping a polished rocks glass of some honey-colored liquid.

I was so nervous I could hardly move. Here he was! The other me. The man I would never be, could never be. Both so much more than I was, in strength, in quiet resilience, and so much less than me. So far out of reach of the sacred darkness in which I kept my secret. Exposed man. Ted Conkaffey was everything I'd ever feared. When he turned toward me, and his eyes met mine, I felt a stab of exhilaration in my chest.

I haven't had many opportunities to celebrate anything over the past year or so. But as I sat alone in the bar at the Lord Chesterton, I decided it was time. The lovely owner, an older ginger-haired woman with ancient hands that had probably poured millions of beers, had settled me in the quiet room. She was obviously a "sympathizer," an *Innocent Ted* partisan. When she'd asked if I wanted anything to drink while I waited, my first instinct had been that I didn't want to lose my edge for my first dreaded public audience. But then, since leaving the meeting with Frankie, Sean, and Elise, I'd enjoyed the delightful sensation of a huge weight sliding off my shoulders. I ordered a Wild Turkey and sat sipping it as she left me to my thoughts.

The online newspapers were already picking up on Melanie Springfield's imminent press conference. I put my phone on the fuzzy bar runner and opened the top hit, the bourbon warm in the back of my throat.

CONKAFFEY SHOCKER: *STORIES AND LIVES* DUMPS ACCUSATION CONTENT, EX-GIRLFRIEND RETRACTS ACCUSATION

In a move that has bewildered Australians following the Ted Conkaffey case, Sydney woman Melanie Springfield has released a public statement retracting accusations she made in an interview with Channel Three's current affairs program *Stories and Lives* against the disgraced former detective. Five million viewers tuned in two nights ago to see new sexual misconduct claims against Conkaffey that were never aired. Springfield plans to give a press conference later today retracting the claims, which she apparently made to *Stories and Lives* producers in an exclusive interview, that Conkaffey molested her younger sister 15 years ago. Springfield had claimed that the abuse occurred while she dated Conkaffey in high school. Springfield's sister, Elise, and her parents will be in attendance at the press conference, along with representatives of the New South Wales Police.

Of course, there was no cause for me to go dancing in the street. Whatever Melanie's reason for accusing me—whether she was mentally ill, wanted the money or notoriety, or simply had always held a grudge against me for ending our brief little teenage romance—the damage was done. If the Australian public thought that the chances of a man being falsely accused of something like child molestation could happen once, they certainly wouldn't believe it could happen twice. People would think Melanie balked at the prospect of repeating her claims in a courtroom. Or that one of my apparent drug dealing compatriots had paid her off, or threatened her life. But a late retraction was better than no retraction at all. I raised my glass to myself and smiled.

Along with my success at the station, I'd managed not to run into my old squad brothers and get myself whomped again, and I liked to believe something had shifted between Little Frankie and me. She'd seen Sean out and then come back to me on the seventh floor, where I'd been sitting alone trying to think through Elise's revelations. When Frankie found me I'd just poured myself a cup of that coffee and was staring into it, lost.

"Your lawyer is mad as hell," she'd said.

"I pay him to be," I'd said back.

Frankie couldn't trust me now, not after my arrest for Claire Bingley's attack. But maybe seeing an accusation against me turn up false had given her hope. As I'd tried to point out to her on the phone in Cairns, she didn't have to trust me to help me, and by helping me, even when there was a chance I was guilty, she'd always know she'd done everything she could to stay loyal and true to the old Ted she had once known, the one she liked, her teammate, even if he was dead now. Maybe that's why she put a folder of papers down before me in the interview room and stepped back into the doorway, physically and emotionally distancing herself once again.

"These are copies of the Crime Stoppers calls about Claire Bingley's abduction," Frankie said. "When the AMBER Alert went out, the call center started getting flooded with sightings, so the first few pages are just that. But then after she was found, and it was announced she'd been assaulted, people started ringing in with leads about the culprit. Obviously, they sort of fizzled out after we arrested you."

I'd weighed the papers in my hands, watched her standing there in the doorway.

"Is anyone on the case right now?" I asked. "Is there anyone I can talk to about current leads?"

"The case is in holding," she said. She couldn't look at me. I knew why. "In holding" meant the case had been shelved pending new evidence. As far as the brass was concerned, they knew who had raped Claire Bingley. They just couldn't prosecute him for it.

I'd glanced briefly at the papers in the taxi on the way to the Lord Chesterton, but Elise's appearance at the station had got my mind so tangled up, I hadn't had time for much more. The folder was now in my backpack on the floor beside my stool at the bar. The owner of the pub came by after a while and refilled my glass without asking, and I noticed a young man standing in the doorway of the room.

The hairs on my arms and the back of my neck stood on end. I put the bodily reaction down to nervousness at my speaking commitment, at the strange faces that would soon fill the room, wanting to know every intimate detail of my horrific past year. I smiled at the young man anyway, and he gave a nervous smile back.

"Are you here for the—" I gestured at the empty room behind me "—the thing?"

"Yeah."

"You're a bit early," I said.

"So are you."

I nodded and turned back to my drink, my face burning. At first I'd thought he was a bit young to be off work in the middle of the work day, coming to check out the star of his favorite true-crime sob story, but I guessed podcasts were a young person's sort of thing. He took a stool at the bar two down from mine and put his arms on the counter. The owner had ducked away again, thinking I'd be the only person in the room for a while and wanting to give me my privacy. The young man was dressed neatly, like he'd just left the office to come down here. Deliberate short stubble and pomade in his hair. The quintessential hipster at work. Neither of us spoke, though I felt him watching me and tried to ignore it. I flicked through stories on my phone about Melanie Springfield, sent a text to Dale Bingley.

How's the car hunt?

He got back straightaway.

None of the guys on the sex offender list had Falcons. Thinking some of these Falcons might have been sprayed at home or color not updated on rego. Losing faith.

The "losing faith" line made my blood run cold. If there was one thing I needed, it was for Dale to keep his faith that we could find Claire's attacker. If he decided that her attacker was, in fact, me, there was no telling what he might do to my house. My birds.

Don't lose faith, I wrote. *He is out there. We will find him.*

Dale didn't answer.

Did you see this? I sent him a link to the story about Melanie Springfield's retraction. If he knew I wasn't guilty of that, perhaps it would help.

He didn't answer.

Are you still at my place? I asked.

"I'm Kevin, by the way," the young man said. He reached across the space between us awkwardly and offered a hand. When I shook it, it was limp. Cold.

"Ted," I said. "But you knew that."

"Yeah," he said with a laugh. He was wringing his hands on the bar top, nervous, rubbing his fingers together too hard. "There's so much I want to ask you. About it all. You know. How you could have . . . How you could have survived it, I guess."

"Well . . ." I stared at the bottles on the shelves behind the bar, found myself lost for words. He'd asked the one thing I really didn't have an answer for. How I'd survived it. How I kept going on. "I suppose you'll get your chance . . ." I gestured toward the room, letting him know I thought I should probably keep question time for the audience when they arrived. He nodded vigorously. I felt bad for shrugging his question off. I was about to offer him something when two huge figures appeared at the edges of my vision and Linda and Sharon pulled out stools on either side of mine, groaning as they heaved their bulky bodies onto the creaking, struggling wood.

"Oh god." I put my head in my hands.

"Thought you could give us the slip, eh, bro?" Sharon said.

Kevin looked alarmed at the end of the bar.

"How did you know I was down here?" I asked, reaching for my drink.

"Khalid hears everything, eventually."

"I bet he does."

"It's a dangerous thing you're doing here." Linda jerked a thumb toward the room. "Any of these creeps could have it in for you."

"Well, I feel very reassured by your presence," I said. "Thanks so much for coming. Try not to crush anyone before you know they're really a threat."

"Uh-huh."

"Is everything okay here?" a voice asked. Fabiana Grisham was standing in the doorway, looking stunning, as usual. She'd cut her hair into a short, deep red bob, and her gray dress was tight over her severe, hardened figure. Linda's and Sharon's stools creaked as they leaned back to get a proper look at her.

"It's okay." I got up and went to her, hugged her, got one of her sharp pecks on my cheek. "They're associates of mine."

"Thank you so much for doing this, Ted," she said. "I know times are tough right now. But, like I said on the phone, this is really critical to maintaining the podcast. You have to appear supportive. People want to know that *you know* they're on your side."

"It's an odd feeling," I admitted. "I mean, I don't know these people. Why *are* they on my side?"

"Because they want to see justice done," she said. "Everybody does."

I wondered what that meant. Was justice to these people simply me having my name cleared? Or would the podcast perhaps be responsible one day for catching Claire's real attacker? The show was called *Innocent Ted*. Though I couldn't bear to listen to it, I wondered if perhaps I should. Fabiana had dug deep, deep into my life and the events surrounding Claire's ordeal. I was about to sit in a room with a bunch of people who knew things about me that I couldn't possibly guess.

"Thanks for setting this up," I told her, despite my reservations.

"Well, we're almost ready to get rolling." She patted me on the shoulder. "It's time for your close-up, Mr. Conkaffey."

Amanda didn't need them to tell her what had happened. She knew from the house around her, could see the story in their eyes. She lay on the floor and watched it happening in her mind, almost like a film, the minutes ticking by and the house darkening behind her eyelids.

It had been a loud night. Creatures squawking in the trees, rustling along the creek bed, now and then a curious possum squeezing through the gap in the fence, an old paling rotted and fallen away.

Victoria Songly had been doing what she did every night. The television, the tea, her crossword book for the ad breaks and the old couch, the one by the glass doors, the one Tom had favored before he died that smelled a little like him. Through the doors, across the yard and through the gap in the fence, she could just make out the golden rectangle of the back door of the Barking Frog on the opposite side of the creek. If her eyes had been better she might have seen the light blinking now and then as people moved before it. A chef running here and there.

Victoria fell asleep in the chair as she often did, snoring peacefully as the chef disappeared, and the cars in the lot rolled away, the very last one taking Darren Molk, the postman, off into the night. The last man to see them alive. Andrew Bell had emerged at the back door of the Barking Frog. The red dot of his cigarette wavered as he paced. Pack-up time. The long, boring haul toward the moment they could shut the doors and drive off themselves, he and the glamorous British girl counting up the beer stock at the end of the bar.

2:45 a.m. Had they knocked at the front of the neat little house, or had they simply walked around the back, slid open the glass door, and stood over Victoria Songly as she slept? Amanda knew only that when Jay and Bran arrived there that night, the old woman had not reacted as they'd planned. Instead of quietly answering their questions, she'd fought. Withered fingers grabbing and slapping, thin wailing voice ripping through the air. It was almost certainly Jay who'd hit her. The mean one. He'd watched her stumble out into the yard, still howling, blood running in rivers down her white nightie and spindly legs. He'd finished her off on the lawn with one of the big, square rocks from the fish pond.

Jay had looked up when it was finished and she'd finally fallen silent. Up through the gap in the fence, almost as though he'd sensed himself being watched. He spied the glowing doorway of the pub across the creek. A young man in silhouette, walking forward as though in a dream, his eyes wide in the dark, struggling to process what he had just witnessed through the narrow gap.

Amanda wondered if Jay and Andrew had locked eyes. It had been a bright night. The moon high. She wondered who had run first. Andrew twisting back toward the pub, catching his foot in the damp earth, falling on his hands. Jay sprinting around the side of the house, down the bank, leaping the tiny creek in his panic. Bran shouting for him, horror-struck, standing over the body of Victoria Songly sprawled on the lawn, no idea where his partner had run off to, not until he heard the gunshots. Amanda wondered how the conversation had gone outside the pub after the deed was done, Jay perhaps smoking one of Andrew's cigarettes, playing it cool while Bran berated him.

How could you do this? How could you do this? This wasn't the plan. You said no one would get hurt!

Relax. I know what to do. The pub will look like a robbery. Take this. A little bonus for our troubles.

She could see Bran throwing the cash bag up onto the roof of the Barking Frog just to spite his trigger-happy partner. Bran was like that. Spiteful. Wimpy little tantrum-throwing bitch who hurled things when he was mad. Jay hadn't worried about the tantrum and the perfectly good cash thrown away. They were about to be deep in a whole lot more. And he didn't need to fight Bran on this. Bran had only agreed to this whole thing because Jay had promised no killing. And now they were three victims deep, too far in to ever hope of turning back.

Oh, Amanda had been dumb. She had stood at the door of this house the very next day and looked at the face of the one named Bran and not known anything was amiss. She'd not looked down at his workman's boots. She'd gobbled up their pathetic stories about being Victoria's grandsons. She had seen Victoria Songly sitting in the orange and black recliner just inside the door and not known the woman was dead. Yes, it had only been a slice of her visible from the doorway. An elbow on the armrest, not enough of a view to measure for life, or the absence of it. Victoria had been positioned there deliberately, the tea beside her a real artistic touch. The men had later moved the dead woman, put her by the glass doors so that just her feet could be glimpsed over the fence by any of the curious cops who happened to take a peek. Socked feet and slippers that would hide the lividity in her skin, the swelling, as she decomposed. Amanda should have known something was wrong. Even the thinnest blood didn't warrant socks and slippers in Cairns.

Keeping her body there in view of the cops had been daring, creative, cunning. She had to give them that. Because dumping her body would have created a liability. A body could be found, particularly with all the land and creek searches being held nearby for the gun. If the old lady appeared to be at home, present and comfortable, then there was no need for questions. All they'd had to do was fend off the cops. Ah, yes, she'd spoken to an officer—they didn't remember the name. She'd said she didn't remember anything, hadn't heard anything. Oh no, no, she couldn't talk now, she was asleep. She was confused. She was busy. Come back later. Maybe tomorrow. Everything's fine. There were enough men and women on the investigation to support the bluff. Detectives had been pulled in from as far away as Brisbane. All the two men had to do was stay vague, stay casual, stay happy. Victoria had Alzheimer's. What good was she to anyone anyway?

Amanda had been so stupid. The vintage car in the driveway—that was another giveaway she'd completely overlooked. Clearly not in use, the car belonged in the garage. The gun, too. Cheap and cheerful, easily obtainable 9mm Browning pistols. As Ted had rightly said, they were not the kind of guns career robbers tended to buy. They were a gun for a single job. A gun that wouldn't raise any eyebrows.

But all was not lost. It brightened Amanda's spirit to know that these two men were also, apparently, not very clever. Cunning and creative, yes. But while they discussed her possible demise, she had been left in the space before the front door, the living room off to the right of her, the garage and bedrooms to the left. Though her hands were taped, they'd not gagged her. She could, at any minute, start screaming her head off. But she wouldn't. Not yet. There would likely be no one at the bar across the creek this early to hear her, and her best plan of action now was to earn the men's trust.

The second thing counting against the men in Amanda's assessment of their intelligence was the state of the house. They were not renovating, of course, but that story had been a good cover for the noise. She could see through the distant doorway to the garage, where the concrete floor had been ripped to shreds over the days since the murders, the smooth finish now an uneven sprawl of rocks and jagged holes cut by the jackhammer. The men had hedged their bets that what they were looking for may not in fact have been hidden in the concrete floor by knocking holes in all the drywall. Before Amanda in the entrance hall, a series of holes had been smashed through the apricot pink surface, the drywall pulled forward, powdered and papery and hanging, exposing hollow interiors. With still no luck in their search the men had torn up the carpet in one of the bedrooms and flung it onto the floor of the living room, where it now lay in a slashed heap, staples poking out from ragged edges.

Curious, Amanda shimmied along the short hall on her backside, not confident in standing with her arms pinned and her head still ringing from Jay's punch. She reached the living room and peered in, wrinkling her nose at the smell of decomposition, human waste. Mrs. Songly was still in the chair by the glass doors, most of her hidden from view by the curtain, her limp legs stretched out on the couch's footrest. The top half of her body had been wrapped clumsily in a white sheet now stained with various bodily fluids. A sad mummy sagging forward slightly, her thin arms in her lap deadly shades of oyster blue and gray. Beyond the view of the glass doors, the men had trashed cupboards and shelves, tossed books and ornaments on the floor. There were glass shards twinkling on the kitchen tiles, the backing of cupboards ripped out and strewn across the counters. A pile of mail had slipped from the countertop and fallen near where she sat.

Amanda shimmied forward again and pinned one of the unopened envelopes with her bare foot, dragged it back with her as she headed toward the front door. It was awkward going, but she positioned the envelope by the front door, turned and flopped onto her side. She rubbed her head and face against the envelope, trying to smear some of the blood from her ear onto the surface. When she had made some suitably dramatic-looking streaks of bright red she got to her knees and sat down again, pushed the bloody envelope under the crack in the front door and onto the step just seconds before the men emerged from their conference in the bedroom.

"Have you decided if you'll kill me or not?" Amanda asked.

"You really are one weird little bitch, aren't you?" Jay shook his head, strode forward and grabbed a handful of Amanda's hair. She spied the gun hanging by her face as he yanked her toward the living room.

"Because if you've decided to kill me, I'd advise strongly against it."

"Oh yeah? Why's that?"

"Ow! That's attached, you fucker!"

Jay shoved her onto the floor in the living room. Bran had walked to the glass doors and ripped the curtains closed, his face grave. Amanda sat on the floor, looking up at the man as he prepared to end her life.

"I know what you're looking for," Amanda said. "And I know where to find it."

Dear Diary,

What an insane thing it was, to sit in the middle of something that I created. This must have been what it was like to have a child. I'd never really thought of having one myself—too dangerous. But this overwhelming sense of achievement was something I could probably get used to. Every single person in that room at the Lord Chesterton was there because of me, because of what I had done. I took my place at the back of the room when the journalist arrived, hoping when Ted introduced her to his "associates" she'd misunderstood that label to include me. I didn't know who the big hairy beasts who had turned up to support Ted were, but his shoulders seemed to have relaxed a little, now that they were here. Fabiana did her important fluttering around, setting up the Facebook Live feed and directing her podcast helpers to check identities as people arrived through the door. I watched Ted retreat to the end of the bar, flanked by his keepers, unable to decide, it seemed, if he should smile with embarrassment at people as they came in or pretend to be distracted by the view out the small window.

I had the whimsical sense that these people were all actors in my own play, that my hero, Ted, was standing there and breathing and trying to control his nerves simply because I had put him there with my devastating act; I had decided his fate. And no, look—I don't want to sound like I think that what happened to Claire was justified because it created all this, this activity, this energy. *But isn't everything that is born, born of pain and suffering? It was because I suffered my affliction that I'd acted, and because Claire had suffered my actions that this had all come about. It was almost musical. I felt a real desire to know intimately what Ted had suffered in prison because of me. We could share pain with each other. That's what people don't understand. Sometimes pain can be as magical and productive as joy.*

Ted took his place at the head of the room, and Fabiana did her cringingly narcissistic introductions, her shiny dark red bob picking up the lights at all the right angles, liquid ink. And then, before I knew it, Ted was speaking, taking us through that day again. He was agitated. Not a public speaker. Turning his wedding ring around and around.

When it came to question time, the audience erupted with hands high—the wrinkled arms of middle-aged ladies and the tattooed trunks of huge, muscled men. There was a teenager in the room, a boy in the front row with his mother. Fabiana decided who would get to ask their questions.

Urgh, what a bunch of sops they were, too! Half driven to prove their own unique emotional investment in the case, half determined to show Ted unparalleled demonstrations of sympathy, they prattled on with their theories about who had attacked Claire. A known rapist living in the area. A South Australian serial killer, inactive since 1975, reemerged somehow back into the killing fields, a row of ghost girls trailing sadly in his wake. When a woman at the back suggested someone from the drug-dealing underworld might have committed the deed to frame Ted, the big lugs in the corner bristled and huffed like disturbed crows, rattling the enormous gold chains at their necks. These people so badly wanted a piece of evidence to suggest that Ted was innocent, a simple answer that would come shining down out of the sky like the beams of an alien ship. There was a heavy lady in the back row waggling her arm back and forth who just about looked like she was going to suggest some X-Files-style solution to the problem. I shifted as far away from her as my seat would allow.

The scariest thing I heard that day was a question from the first couple of rows, the arm of a young man I couldn't see.

"Ted, have you or the police followed up at all on the leads Amanda Pharrell gave you? The ones about the blue ute and the white dog? I think it's in episode seven of the podcast . . ."

I had heard, of course, in episode seven, the mention of Ted passing on some leads to Fabiana Grisham about the ute and the dog. The details were vague, and the two weren't mentioned again. I hadn't been worried, as I understood that Amanda Pharrell, the woman who had dug up the leads in the first place, was crazy. There was no license plate mentioned. No witness corroboration, no composite sketch. And in the mixture of hundreds upon hundreds of leads mentioned across the podcast, the blue ute and the white dog were indeed true, but didn't seem to be given more attention than the rest of them. It helped that the podcast stated that the CCTV of me was blurry and unusable, the RSPCA hadn't identified me or my car, and that the ute they were looking for was a Ford Falcon XF. That was good.

"We're looking into a couple of things with that," Ted said. "I'd rather not go too deep into what's happening with the investigation right now."

Bullshit, in other words. The ute and white dog leads were bullshit. Ted didn't have a thing on them, and neither did his weirdo friend Amanda.

The final question from the audience was a real bleeding-heart case, a true eye-roller, but I guess I should have expected something like it to top off the sycophantic display of Ted-love the audience had shown for the entire event. A woman put her hand up and asked, "Whatever happened to the white dog?"

Ted was taken aback. "Um"—he searched the ground for an answer— "I don't actually know. We didn't trace the dog after it was dumped at the RSPCA."

"I hope it's okay." The woman's voice was smaller now, sad. I think I threw up in my mouth a little. These people had done a mad scramble to show Ted they cared deeply about him and the case in the hour they'd been given, to demonstrate how incredibly sensitive they all were. As the journalist woman called the event to a close, there were still questions to be answered. Ted looked exhausted. I thought about leaving, joining the slow shambling queue of people heading out the doors.

But I had to let him know what he had done, I guess. I had to speak to him again. Because what's coming now is because of him.

The question-and-answer session with the *Innocent Ted* people was draining. I'm not the world's best public speaker. It was worse somehow that the strangers gathered here obviously felt so deeply for me, that they wanted so badly for me to find the answer and fix my life. Give them the happy ending they expect from tales as miserable as this. I'd got used to rooms packed full of hateful stares and whispered insults, the disappointed sigh of people I'd let down. There were older men and women here, more than I'd expected, who looked on me with the parental hurt one feels when their child is being picked on by a bully.

After the session, those who had not been game enough to raise their hand during the allotted time stood around me at the bar asking their own queries. The owner gave me a consolatory look and put another bourbon on the runner by my hand. I had to be careful I didn't have too many, start to get loose-lipped. But the people wanted to know personal stuff now. How it was with Kelly. Whether or not I'd had any contact with Lillian since my arrest. Did prison leave me with PTSD? Had I had counseling? A woman put a peach-colored, filigreed business card into my hand. A psychiatrist. I was to call her any time, day or night.

I noticed, at the back of the crowd, the first one to arrive, Kevin, loitering. As he'd been there in those initial excruciating moments while I prepared for the room to fill with strangers, I guessed we had a kind of camaraderie now. He'd seen me through my ordeal from start to finish. He gave an understanding half smile, a shared jibe at the people peppering me with questions.

An old, bent-backed man in a plaid cardigan was the last of the crew to reach me. The others had moved off to Fabiana to tell her how good the event had been, to congratulate her on her work for my cause. The old man was licking his lips, squinting as he meticulously checked through his thoughts before he spoke them.

"A Ford Falcon XF ute, you were saying?" He pointed a gnarled finger at the chair I'd left abandoned at the front of the room. "See, I haven't listened to episode seven. I have to have my granddaughter play them for me. She was the one who got me into the whole thing, the radio shows. Radiocasts. Podcasts. Whatever they're called. You said it was a Falcon you were looking for?"

"Uh-huh." I nodded. "The ute we were searching for was a Falcon XF. Pale blue. We know they never came in blue as standard, so we're looking into that, checking to see if we can find some that were sprayed commercially."

"Well, you know, it's interesting," the old man said, nodding, "because, back in the late 1980s, I seem to recall that Ford was engaged in a kind of rebadging arrangement. And it might have included their Falcons."

"A what, sorry?" I asked. Kevin was nearing us. "Rebadging? I'm not terribly good with cars."

"See," he said, eyeing Kevin warily as he encroached on us. "At the time, back then, Australian car companies were trying to ward off sales of foreign-designed vehicles. So they would—"

"Sorry to break in here." Kevin put his hand on the old man's shoulder. "Would I be able to borrow you for a second, Ted?"

The elderly man took the cut-in kindly, wandering off with his squinting look, his theories obviously still bubbling. I didn't like the interruption, watched the man go, thinking I'd catch him and hear whatever he was talking about before he left the pub. He'd come a long way to see me. Put in a lot of effort. The guy didn't even know how to play a podcast by himself. He deserved to be heard. But I didn't want to offend anyone, so I gave Kevin his time.

"Thought I'd save you." He smiled. "Old kook might have tied you up for the rest of the day."

I gave a halfhearted laugh.

"What did you think of the gig?" he asked. "Some crazy theories, right? That South Australian serial killer—how funny. Guy's first murder was in 1965. Even if he'd started as a teenager, he'd have to be a billion years old by now."

"Well, I'll hear any theory," I said, sipping the bourbon. The room had steadily emptied. I felt again that weird rush of sensitivity over my arms and neck, a chill, like a cold breeze through an open window. I shrugged it off, turned and leaned on the bar. I got the sense that this guy was trying a little too hard to be my friend. This was a sick kind of celebrity I was experiencing.

"You seem down," he said, mirroring me, his arms on the bar.

"I'm all right."

"Don't let them get you all emotional, man. That woman about the dog."

"Well. She's right," I admitted. "I never found out what happened to the dog."

"It's just a dog," Kevin snorted. "It would have been fine. RSPCA would have taken it in, fixed it up, sent it on to someone else. They're good like that."

"Yeah." I nodded, chewed my lip in what I hoped was a distant, disinterested way. "Anyway, I guess I'll go thank Fabiana. I've got a plane to catch."

"Look, Ted," Kevin said, putting a hand on my shoulder. "It's been really good to meet you. You're a true inspiration."

"An inspiration?" I frowned.

"I know. It's weird. But, like, having met you I feel kind of . . . free."

"Free to do what?"

He dropped his eyes, shrugged, didn't seem to be able to explain.

"Look," he said instead. "I want to show you something."

He pulled out his phone. Linda and Sharon were in the small doorway to the hall, making eyes at me, wanting us to get rolling. I guessed they were going to be my ride to the airport, whether I liked it or not. Kevin took out his phone and flipped through it, showed me a picture of a young girl. I winced, thinking it was Claire. But it was another pale blond creature on the edge of teenage-hood, one of the ghostly beings who flittered through my nightmares on the roadside at the bus stop, the dust rising from my car tires. She was wearing a maroon and blue school uniform. The picture was embellished at the bottom with a school crest.

"This is my Penny," he said.

"Your daughter?" I frowned.

"No, no. My, uh . . . my sister."

"She's beautiful," I said, taking a step back toward the door. I was experiencing a strong urge to retreat. "Nice to meet you. I've gotta go."

I turned and left him there in the empty room with the empty chairs, clutching his phone and looking down at the screen, the picture of his Penny. Afternoon sun was catching dust motes swirling all around him, microscopic fairies dancing off his shoulders, tumbling down his arms.

In the car on the way to the airport, I realized I was sweating only when it dripped off the edge of my jaw. Through the CBD, up William Street, into the Eastern Distributor, nothing. Then it hit. Fever heavy. Sharon was frowning at me in the rearview mirror.

"Bro, you all right back there?"

"I don't know." I wiped my face. I felt cold, shaken.

"Don't throw up in the fucking car." Linda turned in his seat, glared at me. "It's just been detailed."

"Pull over," I said.

Sharon turned the enormous black vehicle onto the grassy strip of land before the Sydney Airport sign, causing a row of cars behind us to grind to a halt, honking. I got out and bent over at the waist, my hands on my knees, struggling to breathe. Linda came around and stood watching me, hands on hips.

"What did you eat?"

My mind was spinning. Frantic, electric thoughts zapping and zinging. Linda stood beside me, his face twisted, terrified that I might be sick on or near him.

"I think I just . . ." I said. I couldn't catch my breath. I straightened, thumped my chest. "I was just . . . The dog . . . He said . . ."

"Talk straight, you fucking idiot!" Sharon yelled from the front of the car.

"He said the dog would be 'fixed up,'" I explained. "The guy at the bar, Kevin. He said the dog would be fine, the RSPCA would take it in, fix it up, and adopt it out. What did he mean, *fix it up*? How did he know the dog needed *fixing*?"

I'd never told anyone that the white dog, the one surrendered to the RSPCA at Yagoona by a man in a blue ute, the one used, perhaps, to lure Claire Bingley from the roadside, had been surrendered with a broken paw. Amanda had taken the report from the RSPCA. She'd passed that report on to me. I'd passed some of it on to Dale Bingley. So only Amanda's contact at the RSPCA, Amanda, Dale, and I should have known the dog needed "fixing up." Maybe it was nothing. Maybe he meant wash the dog. De-flea the dog. Put a new collar on it. "Fix it up," the way you might "fix up" an old house.

But maybe he meant actually fix it. Fix it because it was broken.

I tried to call Amanda. Her phone went straight to voicemail. In my desperation, I tried to explain the situation to the two goons watching over me.

"He probably just meant fixing up, like . . . like . . ." Linda held a big hand out, glanced at Sharon for help. "Like a good wash and uh, clean . . ." He fell into Arabic. They shouted a stream of it at each other, Linda wanting to reason with me, Sharon needing him to get me in the car.

"No." I sucked air in through my nostrils, tried to stop the shaking in my limbs. "He meant fix. I know it. He meant *fix*. I got a creepy vibe from the guy as soon as I laid eyes on him. He showed me a photo. I . . . I can't . . ."

I staggered to the car, put a hand on the warm black side panel. A plane roared overhead, making my ears pulse.

"It was him," I said. "It was him."

"She don't know shit." Jay turned to his partner. "Go outside and fix the fence before one of the coppers sees it. I'll finish this off."

"I know where to find what you're searching for," Amanda said. "Just the way I know *what* it is. The signs are all around you. I can't believe you've spent days tearing this house to shreds when it's so close."

The two men looked at each other, looked at the woman on the floor before them, the blood running down her neck, between her breasts.

"Let me spell it out for you." Amanda took the lead when they wouldn't come along with her. "You're here for his money. Tom Songly. His buried treasure."

Jay gave a barely convincing snort of derision.

"It isn't hard to work out." Amanda licked blood off her lip. "Not looking at the two of you. You're definitely not brothers. Different eyes, different skin tones. Different hands. But you both stand the same. You got the same length stubble, meaning you shave at the same time. And you wipe your noses on the back of your wrists the same way. Not because you've got runny noses, not in this heat. But because you've developed a nervous tic. How do two guys develop the same nervous tic?"

Bran opened his mouth to answer.

"In prison," Amanda said. Bran's eyes widened.

"You spend every second of the day together for a couple of years, you pick up each other's habits. You met in prison. That's how you knew to put them on their stomachs to incapacitate them, fingers interlocked. You've done it plenty of times yourselves under the order of guards. You, you're the weak one." Amanda tried to point with her shoulder toward Bran. "You were probably in for identity fraud. Burglary. Possession of stolen items. Nothing face-to-face. You don't have the gumption for face-to-face crime. You were going to be dead meat in the can and you knew it. You needed someone strong. Experienced. You were lucky you got him for a cellmate." She looked at Jay. "You were in longer. You've got more shitty tatts. And that ugly collection of scars in the crook of your elbow—that's from heroin. Not neat little track-mark scars. That buckshot look is the kind you get from using on the inside where you can't get needles, so you use a shaved-down bike pump spike. I've seen it before. You came in a heroin user. Which probably means you were a thief. You've got to steal to feed that habit. That's how you knew to wipe your prints from the safe. And the extra time, that means it wasn't just burglary. It means you were probably in for a violent cri—"

Jay's face had reddened steadily. Before Amanda had finished talking he grabbed her by the throat and pinned her.

"You've got a big fucking mouth," he snarled, lifting her by the neck and banging her head against the floor. "But you're not telling me what I want to hear."

"About the money." Amanda struggled to sit up again when he let her go, then reeled as the room spun. "You heard the story after you became cellies. A smart crook would have kept something like that to himself. But you both heard it at the same time. Sticking close to each other for protection. Someone chatting to you in the chow hall.

Talking shit. Talking about corrupt cops in the 1970s. Maybe it was an old lifer. Someone convincing. Someone who was there. They told you about Police Commissioner Tom Songly, the top dog. How all the money flowed upwards from the beat cops on the street, and he was one of the few people to come out of the train wreck of a royal commission unscathed."

Amanda looked across the living room at Victoria Songly's body, the reeking, stiff half-mummy with the blue hands.

"It would have been a lot of money. He was in power during the key years. And a couple of his lieutenants, they might have asked him to take care of their shares while they went away so they didn't have to leave it with their wives. A big honey pot that no one believed in, no one was brave enough to go after. They told you the old man was dead. That he'd become paranoid in his twilight years and concreted his cash into the garage floor. They told you that there were millions waiting for the right person to come along. Nothing standing in your way except a sick old lady. An easy job."

"Who told her this?" Bran whispered harshly, grabbed his partner's arm. "Jay, she knows. She fucking knows. And if she knows, someone else knows."

"She doesn't know it." Jay spat on the floor. "She's guessing. A good fucking guess. If she'd known it she wouldn't have come here alone."

"It's hardly a guess when there's so much evidence." Amanda frowned.

"Right." Jay shoved Amanda's shoulder with his boot, knocked her over hard. "So where the fuck is the money?"

"Well, it's not concreted into the garage floor." Amanda gave a bloody grin as she righted herself again.

"We fucking know that!" Bran snapped. He gritted his teeth, growled. "For fuck's sake, woman. He's going to kill you. This man here is *going to kill you.*"

"No way," Amanda said. "He wouldn't dare. Jay's smart. Aren't you, Jay? You're not going to kill me until you get what you want."

"So tell us!" Jay screamed.

"No way," Amanda said again. "What do you think I am, an idiot? If I tell you, you'll kill me."

Jay snapped. He grabbed Amanda by the hair.

I called Pip Sweeney. She answered in a couple of rings.

"Where's Amanda?"

"I was just going to call and ask you the same thing," she said. "I haven't seen her all day. Her phone's off. She's not at the office. Are you okay?"

I hung up and got back into the big black car. Linda followed, confused.

"Where to?" Sharon asked.

"Just drive," I said, tapping on my phone. I opened the email from Frankie giving me access to the motor registry database, but my hands were so shaky and sweaty I could barely go further, and I didn't know what to search for in any case. I had a name. Kevin. I applied the search for Ford Falcon XF utes registered in the area of Claire's abduction on that date and brought up the list of names, scrolled painfully through them. No Kevins. The car might have been in his girlfriend's name. His mother's. Anyone's. There was probably CCTV footage of Kevin at the Lord Chesterton Hotel. But the police weren't going to put out a bulletin for him, not on my word alone. And the media weren't my friend right now. I called Fabiana.

Linda was turned in the front passenger seat, watching me. When Fabiana answered her phone, I started speaking before she said hello.

"I need you to go through your list of attendees for today's event," I said. "Tell me Kevin's surname."

"What?"

"Please." I held on to the handle above the car window, closed my eyes, forbade myself to scream at her. I repeated my request. Heard papers shuffling.

"There are no Kevins on this list," Fabiana said helplessly. "What do—"

I hung up. Sharon was driving us east, toward the beaches. I went back to the car search. Stared helplessly at the names.

Doherty, Richard. Mount Annan. Ford Falcon XF Ute. 1988. DDB 451. White.

Dubbs, Matthew. Camden. Ford Falcon XF Ute. 1987. SHF 111. White.

French, Anna. Woodbine. Ford Falcon XF Ute. 1988. AL 29 EE. Red.

The list went on and on, little buttons at the bottom of the page taking the search out wider and wider from my selected location, Mount Annan. I adjusted the dates for my search. Nothing. Fabiana tried to call back. I ignored the call. Trying to search on my tiny phone was giving me motion sickness. Sharon pulled the car over on another grassy strip and I climbed out. I felt helpless, furious. A text came in from Kelly asking when my flight was leaving. I had a flash of myself in my old house, Lillian in my arms, Kelly at my back, everything that had been stolen from me. I screamed and kicked over a road marker, threw the phone onto the grass.

"Bro, calm down," Linda was saying. I grabbed him, just to have something to grab on to, my fingers biting through the fabric of his suit jacket. It was a mistake. I smelled his heavy cologne as he pushed me up against the side of the car with the effort of a man subduing a child, knocking the wind from my chest.

"Chill, bro. Just fucking chill. What did the dude say?" Linda held me pinned against the car with a single hand against my chest. It was impossible to move. "What did he look like?"

"He was young," I said. I squeezed my eyes shut. Twenty-five, I guessed. Closer to thirty maybe. I had a flash of Dale Bingley in my kitchen in Crimson Lake. His words coming out of my mouth. The description of the man who had adopted the white dog from the British couple on the day of Claire's abduction. "Young man, maybe twenty-five. Neatly dressed, brown hair. Polite."

How can he be twenty-five? Dale had pleaded. *These people are telling me the guy who raped my daughter is twenty-five years old.*

Linda let me go. Cars were whizzing past us on the road. A golf course split down the middle, cyclone fencing. I retrieved my phone, went to the diamond wire and held on to the fence. I watched old men meandering across the immaculate greens, their long, pressed trousers.

"He interrupted the old guy," I whispered.

"Huh?" Linda was behind me. I turned.

"The old guy. At the pub. What was he saying? Did you hear? He was talking about Ford Falcons. About . . . badges. Car badges? Kevin came and interrupted him, cut him off. The old guy was saying the . . . the Aussie car companies had been trying to fight off foreign . . . foreign car sales?"

"Rebadging," Sharon said from the car, his arm over the back of the passenger seat, watching us. I ran to the open door.

"What?"

"The car's badge is the little picture on the front and the side." He pointed to the bonnet of the car. I looked and saw a silver shield with red and yellow blocks. "Sometimes companies, they used to swap designs of cars. Saves time, money. They just take the same car and put their own badge on it."

I was trembling all over. I looked to Linda, who seemed as confused as I was.

"So two cars can look exactly the same but be different brands?" I said.

"Yeah," Sharon sniffed.

"Oh Christ." I went to my phone, struggled to find the internet browser. "Oh Jesus. Then maybe it wasn't a Ford Falcon. Maybe it wasn't a fucking Ford Falcon. Maybe it was something else."

I searched *Ford Falcon XF 1988 rebadge.*

The Nissan ute was a badge-engineered version of the XF Falcon utility sold by Nissan in Australia from August 1988 to 1991 . . .

"The Nissan ute." I opened my email. Followed the link to the database search engine. My fingers were making damp prints on the screen. The keyboard wasn't working. "The Ford Falcon was the same as the Nissan Ute."

Carroway, Chloe. Glen Alpine. Nissan Ute. 1988. REN 555. Blue.

"Blue." I shoved Linda in the chest. "Blue! Blue! It's fucking blue!"

The beating was short, but hard. Amanda tried to curl into a ball, but Jay kicked her in the back, legs. She shuffled across the floor, trying to escape him. She could barely hear Bran in the background, his voice moving as he paced.

"Come on, man. Oh Jesus. Come on, bro."

When there was a pause, Amanda rolled onto her knees. There was glass on the floor here, small pieces of it working their way into her exposed arms and legs.

"What kind of a pussy," she huffed, "beats a woman with her hands tied?"

That really broke him. She could hear the breath coming out of him in low, heavy growls as he pounced on her.

"Oh yeah? Oh yeah?" He was frantic, flipping her and ripping the tape off her wrists. "I'll show you a fucking pussy!"

His hand on her skull, a death grip, banging.

Pip stood on the bank of the creek behind the Barking Frog Inn, looking at a pair of pink Converse sneakers sitting, side by side, on the soil. She'd begun to grow concerned with Amanda's silence on the phone at around midday. The two had planned to meet at the Shark Bar, Amanda in the seat she owned, Sweeney trying to distract her from the day's many newspapers. There were good leads she wanted to follow up on. Conkaffey had passed on some interesting criminal links he'd discovered in the backgrounds of a couple of the bar's regulars. She wanted to bring Amanda in to reinterview the men at their houses. Then there were the shell casings found in the forest a kilometer from the Barking Frog. They were waiting on analysis of them. Michael Bell had asked for another meeting. There was much to do, and Pip felt invigorated after a good night's sleep. But Amanda was missing in action. She might have pressed on without her weird, unpredictable little partner. But Amanda had become like her magic feather. She felt more confident, more in control with the woman by her side. She'd wondered as she dozed off the following evening if a partnership between her station and Conkaffey and Pharrell Investigations might be possible. Maybe through Pip, the hostility of the Crimson Lake force toward Amanda might be lessened. Her colleagues might be able to truly see Amanda's value. Anything seemed possible.

Pip had gone to the office on Beale Street and looked in the window at the cats lying in the sunshine. When they'd noticed her standing there, a couple had pawed at the glass, meowed angrily. Were they hungry? She'd knocked, called, received no answer.

A part of her was worried that Amanda was gone because of their meeting at the bar a day earlier. That moment, as they'd stood almost where she stood now, and Pip had felt her whole body infected with urgency. Driven to move. She'd looked into Amanda's eyes. Had Amanda known what she was thinking?

She looked down the length of the creek. Back toward its source. No sign of Amanda. But these were, unmistakably, her shoes—mud-spattered from bike riding, grass tangled in the laces. There was relief now mingling with the concern. Sweeney looked up and saw that a paling was missing from the fence across the way. The unmatched one, snapped in half, lying on the opposite creek bank. Puzzled, she crossed the creek. A sound from the house, a crashing. The renovators. Amanda might have gone to requestion them. A good idea. Pip walked around the side of the house to the front door and raised her hand to knock as the sound of paper crumpling came from beneath her boot.

I stood at the wire, watching the golfers, and called Frankie. Didn't explain anything, just told her the name of the girl and asked for the number. She could hear how disturbed I was. How frantic. She didn't ask questions, just logged in to her computer and accessed the phone company databases, extracted the number, read it to me as I typed it into my phone.

I called. Both goons were in the car now, watching me as I paced back to them, then to the fence again, my head down and shoulders aching with tension.

"Hello?"

"My name is Ted Collins. I'm a member of the New South Wales police," I lied. There was no time to explain the truth of who I was. "Is this Chloe Carroway?"

There was a pause. I tried to breathe.

"Mal, is that you?"

"Listen to me very carefully," I said slowly. "Is this Chloe Carroway?"

"Yes."

"Well, I'm Senior Sergeant Ted Collins." I could hear a tremor in my voice. I tried to talk slowly. "I'm from the *New South Wales police department*."

"Okay . . ."

"I need you to answer some questions for me."

"Right now?"

"Yes, right now."

"It's the police." She'd turned away to talk to someone in the background, muffled the mouthpiece with her hand. "He says he's the police!"

"Can you please tell me," I said, "if last year, on April tenth, 2016, you were the owner of a Nissan ute? A blue one?"

"Um. April? Yeah, that's right. But I don't own it anymore. We sold it."

"Do you have a person in your life named Kevin who had access to that ute at that time?"

"Yes, that's my ex-boyfriend." She muffled the phone again. "Oh my god, he's asking about Kev."

"Chloe, tell me Kevin's last name," I said.

"Driscoll," she replied. "Is he in trouble?"

"Driscoll? Kevin Driscoll?" I turned toward the car. Saw Linda and Sharon exchanging a look with each other. "Can you spell that? D-R-I-S-C-O-L-L? Chloe, how old is Kevin?"

I reached for the handle of the open back passenger door but it shut before I could grab it. Linda had pulled it closed from the inside. I watched him shut his own door, glancing at me, emotionless. I reached for the handle again but the car was moving. They sped off without me.

"Hey!" I ran a few paces after the car. "Hey!"

I stood by the side of the road, confused, the phone hanging in my hand. All of a sudden, the road had emptied of cars. I could see an intersection in the distance. I started running, putting the phone back to my ear.

"Hello? Are you still there?"

"Yes," I huffed.

"He's twenty-five," Chloe said. "No, he'd be twenty-six now. Is he in trouble?"

"Do you know where he lives now?"

"No, I . . . We broke up."

A flash across my mind, the girl in the picture, Kevin holding the phone, looking down at her like there was no one else in the world. Something in me had stirred, some primal recognition of the danger of this man, of the ruin he had wreaked on my life, on Claire's life, on Dale's life. I'd sensed his badness. His hand on my fate. And now all I could think of was that little girl in the picture in his hand, the face in his fingers. She'd looked so much like Claire. Jesus. She'd looked like her twin.

You're a true inspiration.

Having met you I feel kind of free.

Free to do what?

"Where do his parents live?" I asked Chloe.

"His *parents*?" The girl laughed nervously. "Is this a joke?"

"His sister. Kevin's sister. The little blond girl. He showed me a picture on his phone."

There was a long pause. I got to the intersection, waved madly at a taxi. It sailed past me.

"Kevin doesn't have a sister," Chloe said.

Amanda's plan had worked. Stupid boys. Prison boys, still strung out on the incredible bravado they'd had to display on the inside, a door opened on a world of animalistic instinct that they could never close again. Jay had ripped off the duct tape on her wrists. Amanda waited for a pause in the punches raining down on her before throwing herself upward and wrapping her arms around him, entangling him like a snake. She bit. Her nails tearing into his shoulders. Her heels digging into his legs. Her teeth biting into the tender flesh at the side of his head. She got what she was aiming for. The warm, salty, hard flesh of his ear. Her own ear thumped with the pitch of his scream. When he tried to pull away, she gripped on harder, followed, let him drag her with him. They rolled together like lovers, and when she was on top Amanda rose up and balled her fist, brought it down hard on his nose. The bone crunched.

"I told you!" She laughed as he gripped at his broken face. "You fucking arsehole!"

Bran had her by the arms and was dragging her back. Jay rolled, fumbled for the gun that he'd discarded by the couch when he started to beat her. Amanda tried to lunge forward, to reach for it at the same time, but Bran's arms held firm. As Jay's fingers came within inches of the barrel they froze at the sound of a wail.

"Nobody move!"

Sweeney was in the doorway to the back garden, having slid the glass open silently, her gun at the ready. No one breathed.

"Back the fuck up!"

Her aim was on Jay. The man with the bloodied, crooked nose was sprawled on his stomach, fingers hovering unsteadily over the barrel. Sweeney was panting now, her eyes wild. "Don't even think about it!"

Jay backed up. Amanda wriggled out of Bran's arms and flopped onto the floor, grabbing the pistol from the pile of glass where it lay.

"Sweeney," she said, laughing. "You're an absolute—"

A bang. Amanda screamed. In the fraction of a second Sweeney had taken to glance to her left at the corpse in the chair by the door, Bran had grabbed his gun from the back of his jeans and shot her.

Amanda watched Sweeney fall, one hand clutching the front of her shirt.

A taxi finally came, but I had nowhere to direct it to. All I knew was that I needed to be moving, needed to know that I was in pursuit of Kevin Driscoll. It seemed as though hearing his surname increased the burning hatred twofold. He was suddenly more than a concept. A real person. I held the phone and watched people flash by the car, couples walking along the footpath, motorists in other cars. Kevin Driscoll had, for a time, had a girlfriend. He was twenty-six. He did not have a daughter, or a younger cousin, or anyone in his life that Chloe could think of who was small and blond and school-age. All she could tell me was that when they were together, he'd struck up a sort of friendship with the little girl next door in the house where they previously lived. Chloe had seen them talking over the fence. I'd tapped the address of their old house into my phone with painstaking care, Chloe on speaker, the confused rumblings of her friends or whoever was in the background of the call now and then distracting her, causing her to pull away. Chloe didn't know where Kevin lived now. He'd unceremoniously dumped her, giving her little reason, a few months after Claire's abduction.

Did Kevin Driscoll have a new girlfriend now? I gripped the

seat belt at my chest, squeezed it until my fist shook and ached. Were Kevin Driscoll and his new girlfriend planning on getting married? Having babies? Buying a house? Kevin Driscoll had stolen my life. A ludicrous impulse I couldn't deny kept surfacing in my mind, that when I found him, I would take my life back from him. He had it, like a talisman, a physical object. I would get it. I would steal it back. I would hurt him. I would kill him.

The taxi driver was distinctly uncomfortable at the look of me. Had been since he pulled over, got a closer look at the man at the road-side, smelled the sweat. He probably thought I was a junkie, a mad-man. With few words I directed him west, toward my old suburb, the sprawl of farmland and little residential settlements outside Sydney.

I could find Kevin's new address easily enough. Now that I had his full name, I texted Frankie. I didn't trust myself to speak, not with this kind of fury raging in my veins. She would check her police data-bases, come up with an address. Did I trust myself to go there and not kill Kevin Driscoll? My whole body was ticking and twitching with rage. I would at least beat him. I knew that. I would beat his brains out. There was a wild lion inside me, a furious and beaten thing, a creature reduced to its instincts only. I could see myself killing him. Smashing his face with my hands. Losing all control. I'd get the ad-dress, go there, and end him.

But as I waited for the reply from Frankie to come through, I looked at the other address, the one Chloe had given me, the rental house where she and Kevin had once lived. The image of Kevin kept flashing before my eyes, standing in the bar, holding his phone, look-ing at the picture of the little girl. He'd lied. She wasn't his sister. Was she the neighbor child, the one he'd spoken to over the fence? The chances were slim. The world was full of pretty little girls, his for the taking. But she had looked so much like Claire. White-haired and slim, a perfect beauty on the edge of adolescence. His words whis-pered back to me as I stared at the address.

You're a true inspiration.

I feel kind of . . . free.

Free to do what? Was he going to hurt a child? Was he going to hurt *that child*? I tried to remember the school uniform colors. The letters on the crest. It was impossible. My mind was racing, details and names and addresses crashing into one another, now and then everything being obliterated by a crashing wave of red-hot fury.

I knew I had to go to the old address, the one with the neighbor girl. As much as I wanted to go directly to Kevin's house, to find him, to get my hands on him, I was a cop. I had once been a cop, anyway. This wasn't about me. It had never been about me. It was about that girl in the picture, about Claire, about however many girls Kevin had hurt before, however many he might hurt in the future if I didn't stop him now. I needed to make sure that girl was okay. A quick detour.

I gave the driver the address Chloe had given me. Every stoplight was an agony. Frankie wasn't responding. Kelly called. I rejected it, wiped the sweat off my phone onto my jeans.

When the taxi turned into Kevin's old street, I spied patrol cars. Two of them, parked haphazardly in a V-shape on the front lawn of a small house, blocking the footpath. My heart twisted. I had been right. My instincts, whatever it was that made him keep coming back into my mind, standing there staring at the picture. He had come here. Before I knew anything about what was happening at the house, I knew, in my soul, that he had come here.

"Stop! Stop! Stop!" I beat on the back of the driver's chair, threw notes at him as he ground to a halt. I got out and sprinted down the street. It felt good to be running, not sitting idly waiting for the horror to unfold before me. Already, neighbors were coming out of their houses, stopping on the corners, pointing. I turned the corner of the picket fence, ran up the stairs and through the open front door.

There was a woman talking frantically somewhere up ahead inside the house, the huge leathery presence of cops in the small kitchen. I stumbled down the hall, searing with dread, past photographs on the walls of the girl from the picture. The very same girl. Penny. White hair. Big eyes. Penny was Claire. I could see it now. The waiflike figure hanging upside down from monkey bars, pirouetting on a big empty beach. The cops in the kitchen twigged to my presence immediately. I was met at the doorway to the kitchen with an open palm, some young beat cop with his other hand on his gun.

"Whoa whoa whoa! Stop right there!"

"Is she okay?" I kept coming, forced the cop to back up. I saw him unclip the buckle on the gun. "Is the girl okay?"

Four cops, all on high alert. Shouting. I looked into the kitchen. There at the table, a woman sitting with the girl, Penny, in her lap. The girl was curled against her chest, red-faced, wailing, the uncomposed, growly crying of a child. The mother looked as though she'd been doing some wailing of her own. She hardly noticed my presence. Her words were rushing together, panicked.

". . . said he just wanted to talk to her. He kept saying it. That he just wanted to talk. He shoved the door open. I was screaming. No one would come!"

"Where did he go?" I gripped the frame of the door to stop myself from rushing forward and grabbing the woman by her shoulders. "Kevin Driscoll—where did he go?"

The mother looked at me. She knew the name. Kevin.

"Conkaffey." One of the street cops had clued onto me now, recognized my face. "Jesus fuck! What are *you* doing here? Get out! Get him the fuck out!"

"That's Ted Conkaffey!" someone gasped.

"Is this the guy? Is that the guy who came here?"

Two hands pushing me out, one hand grabbing the shoulder of my shirt, trying to drag me back. The mother protested, bewildered. I wasn't the guy who had attacked her, barged into her house, tried to talk to her child. I was let go, pushed down the hall, trying to listen to her words over the snaps and barks of the cops manhandling me.

". . . some big Middle Eastern guys . . ." the mother said.

I planted my feet, straining to listen.

". . . just grabbed him and hauled him out. I don't know where they went . . ."

"Oh god," I whispered. I recalled the look that Linda and Sharon had exchanged as I stood outside the car, when I had spoken Kevin Driscoll's name. They'd been waiting to hear it. A name was all they needed. They'd got here before me, before the cops, right on Kevin's tail. Khalid Farah was a powerful man. Far more powerful than the police. Within seconds of knowing Kevin's full name, Khalid probably had some dodgy contact or other punch the name into a system, track his phone. Khalid could find people. No one escaped him. He made a living from it.

That's why they had left me. Linda and Sharon. They'd abandoned me at the roadside because they knew, as Khalid knew, that I'd never sanction it, never allow them to abduct Kevin Driscoll right off the street the way the young man had done to Claire Bingley. That's why Khalid had put his men onto me. For my protection, yes. But because they knew—knew in their bones—that I'd find him. That I was always going to find him. And Khalid wanted Kevin. He'd told me himself at the airport that first day. He wanted that man. He wanted to be the one responsible for putting him down, for taking another predator off the streets.

The moment I mentioned Kevin's full name, Linda and Sharon had what they'd been waiting for. And now Khalid and his men had beaten me to my quarry.

"Get the fuck out, pervert piece of shit!" The cop behind me shoved me hard in the shoulders. I staggered out of the house, stood on the lawn as they berated me. My whole body was cold. I still had my phone in my hand, gripped in my fist like a weapon. The cops wanted to know where I had come from. Why I was here. How I knew the child and her mother. I couldn't answer. Couldn't speak. I wandered away from them, ignoring their threats, a big crow avoiding swooping myna birds. The neighbors were staring, murmuring to one another. A woman leaned over her front fence and asked me what was going on, no idea, it seemed, who I was. I looked at her like she was an alien thing, incapable of putting it all into words.

I walked along the footpath in no direction at all, mere meters, before I stopped at the sight of a set of keys shining in the last of the day's sun. I crouched shakily and took up the keys. I knew without any kind of clue that they had been dropped by Kevin as he was wrestled toward a big black Escalade by Linda and Sharon. I knew this, saw it before my eyes, as though it was being shown to me by a divine force. When I turned, I saw the car the keys belonged to. A dark gray Commodore, parked adjacent to the keys. I walked toward the car, Kevin's car, and opened the front door. Got in. I don't know why I did these things. I was operating now on pure automation, my brain filled with thunder and noise.

There was a thin journal and a pen on the front passenger seat. I looked at the book. Didn't touch it. Gripped the steering wheel and breathed in the smell of him.

My phone, in my lap, rang with an unknown number. I knew who it was before I accepted the call.

"Conkaffey," Khalid said. "I'm goin' to give you an address."

It was faster than she thought possible. Like the crashing of a wave, energy surging upward, tipping, falling uncontrollably. Amanda lifted the gun, turned, scraped her knees on the floor, actioned the weapon as her eyes met Bran's. He was shocked by what he'd done. The weak one finally having the strength to do what was necessary. His mouth was open, hanging. Amanda fired twice, hit him somewhere in the mid-section, shoving him backward into the kitchen bench, the wall beside it. He slid down. Jay grabbed at her. She butted him hard with the gun, slammed his head with suddenly frantic movements, the un-coordinated fending-off of a wild cat.

Maybe she screamed. Amanda didn't know. At the edges of her vision she saw something she hadn't seen in decades. The bare dirt at the rim of a small clearing in the rainforest, the gaping mouth of an open car. For a second, she was back there, back at the site of her first murder. She felt once again the transition from human to animal fighting to survive.

And then it was gone. Jay had slumped against her legs, Bran doubled over by the kitchen, gripping at his stomach, groaning. Amanda went there, took his gun, thought about finishing him off.

But the visions were gone now. She was here, in the old lady's house, one man unconscious, one man dying, two guns in her hands.

She went to Pip. The brand-new detective was lying on her back on the grass, her feet hanging over the edge of the glass door into the living room. Amanda crawled to her side, dropped the guns, put a hand on her partner's blood-soaked hands, the warm, slick fingers covering the hole in her chest.

"Jeepers," Amanda said. "This isn't good."

"No," Pip panted. "It's not."

The women held the bullet wound together, their hands becoming soaked, rising and falling with Pip's rapid breaths.

"I guess this is—" Pip's voice caught over blood in her throat. "My . . . my penance."

"Yeah." Amanda nodded. "I guess so, huh? You didn't get to choose yours, either."

Somewhere in the distance, the sound of a siren was beginning to grow. Amanda couldn't tell how far away help was. One ear was blocked with blood. Sweeney must have called for backup before she burst in. Amanda was aware that an older cop, a harder cop, would have waited until her colleagues arrived before trying to tackle the situation herself, even if she heard her friend's anguished cries from inside the house. But not Sweeney. It was because of Amanda that Pip was dying. For once, there were no words.

"I should have . . ." Pip said. Unconsciousness was already pulling at her. She refocused on Amanda, squeezed the other woman's fingers. "I should have acted, but I didn't."

"Oh Jesus," Amanda sighed. She grabbed Pip's face and bent her lips to the dying officer's. The kiss was hard. Hot, filled with pain. All the pain Amanda had seen in Sweeney's face as the cop stood beside her that night behind the Barking Frog, obviously fighting with her own heart. It seemed to last a lifetime, but it ended, Amanda pulling away fast.

"Happy now?" she asked.

Amanda thought she saw a flicker of a smile cross Sweeney's lips before her head fell back against the grass.

It was raining. A light misting rain, the same that had been falling on that day as I stood before her at the roadside, the little girl whose life was about to be ruined, along with mine. Of course. I drove Kevin Driscoll's car through the streets, hardly able to follow the directions my phone whispered to me through my clattering thoughts. I took wrong turns, sped to the end of blocks, my teeth gritted, cursing myself. The horizon was pink, then red, then black, and soon enough it became speared with the aerials and chimneys of ancient factories and warehouses. I slowed down, rolled over gravel and glass, between wire fences pushed open into the dust. There was a light on, finally, gold glimmers around a slice of corrugated iron. I turned and stopped at the sight of my own car. The car I had left at my house in Cairns.

There was only one man who could have taken it and driven it here.

My email, open on my other laptop, the one in my kitchen where I had left the vengeful father. He would have contacted Khalid through my account. Together, the two of them colluding, knowing I was coming here. Knowing I would lead them right to their victim.

I walked unevenly from Kevin Driscoll's vehicle, leaving the door open, the interior lights on. I went back, wiped my fingerprints from the gear stick, door handle, the steering wheel and keys, then stood dumbly, trying to think what to do. How to stop it all unfolding. But I was an actor on a stage, unable to do anything but follow the script. I went to my car and looked it over, ran my hand over the hood, as though to affirm it was really there and not a prop. Out of the darkness beside me, Linda emerged from stage left. I heard his heavy, nasal breathing before I saw him.

"When you're ready, bro," he said.

When you're ready. Like an usher seeing a gentleman to his seat in a crowded theater, his voice quiet to avoid upsetting the patrons already seated. It was all so organized, so routine. But this is what they did, after all, these people. Khalid's men. What I was about to see, to experience, was his everyday work. A little evening production pieced together carefully, a pet project.

Linda pushed open the door, led me forward. They were all there. Sharon watching, his arms folded, impatient to continue into the next act. Khalid standing off to the side, a supervisor, production manager. His suit almost luminescent in the glow of a hastily acquired lamp. Dale Bingley was standing with his bloody, grazed fists clenched, watching me enter. And there, among them all, was Kevin Driscoll, the young man I'd spoken to what felt like minutes earlier at the Lord Chesterton Hotel.

He was sitting lopsided in a plastic chair. He had been beaten badly. The smooth, handsome face I'd barely taken in before was now bloodied, swollen, the mouth gaping and running with blood. One eye looked me over from head to toe. I watched as a flash of recognition caught his damaged features. An almost friendly look, the glance of a wounded fellow soldier. *We're in this together, brother.*

"Did you call the police?" Khalid asked me. I didn't answer. Didn't need to. He knew that, while I'd never have wanted to be a part of this, a sick curiosity about their plans had drawn me here. I wanted to see. I needed to see my revenge fantasy playing out, even if it was only for a moment of delicious real life. How many times had I imagined this as I lay awake in my prison cell? In my empty house, away from my family? Claire's true attacker bound. Beaten. Pleading with me as I did whatever the illusion required to get me to sleep that night, made him pay for what he had done to me, to Claire, to all of us.

Now that I was here, now that I was seeing it, smelling it, the blood on the dusty warehouse floor, I'd had enough. A moment was all it took. Only minutes earlier I'd felt the certain and crushing desire to beat Kevin Driscoll to death with my bare hands, a magnetic pull toward his house promising me how good and natural it would feel to kill him. A perfect crime. But now that he was before me, bound and bloodied, that hot fury was nowhere to be seen. I was empty, shivering.

"Okay," I said. "It's over now. This has to stop."

Sharon sniggered. Khalid's smile was thin, the cheerless leer of a snake.

"We can't do this. I'm calling the police now." I took my phone from my pocket. No sooner had it met the air than Linda had it from me, and was pushing the power button, switching it off, sliding it inside his coat.

"Is there anythin' you want to say to him?" Khalid asked, gesturing to the beaten man in the chair. "You don't have very much time left."

Kevin was watching me. Of course I had things to say. I'd said them in those nighttime fantasies as I beat him, long, streaming descriptions of everything he had taken from me. But now as I tried to speak, my throat tightened, strangling the words. How could I say anything? How could I put what this man had done into words? Kevin was watching me, waiting for me to tell him about my pain. I'd glimpsed him at the back of the Lord Chesterton with all the strangers who had come to hear me, wanting me to lay it all out, every wound, every embarrassment, every longing ache. Kevin and I watched each other. He knew. I could see it in his eyes. He knew what he had done to me, and he wasn't sorry. He had the look of a man surveying his creation. The master of ceremonies. Because, in the end, we were all here on this bloodied, darkened stage because of him. We were all his puppets. Well, it would stop now. I was not going to spout the lines he had written for me. I was not going to let him die in the final act and cement this cruel life, this nightmare he'd created for me.

"No," I said. "I don't have anything to say to him."

Dale was trembling with rage. He strode forward, mechanically, at Khalid's glance and took a pistol from his hand.

"But this can't—" I said. I looked at Linda and Sharon for help. "This can't go on."

"Ted, this is all outside your control." Khalid put a hand up, calm. "You may not be happy about this right now, but it's happening. This. Is. Happening. It's going to be good for you in the future, when you think back on it. Just trust me, bro."

"Dale." My voice was rising, echoing off the walls of the vast, dark space. "You can't let this happen. This is what he wants. This is what they want. Dale? Dale! Stop! You can't do this. Dale, you can't!"

I took a step toward him. No more than one. Linda's great arm swept around my neck and tightened, dragging me back. I grabbed at the arm. Slippery fabric. Impossibly hard muscle underneath. "No! No No No!"

Khalid was untying Kevin's hands. The young man fell onto the floor. Dale, so much bigger now than I'd ever known him, thicker, wider, full of fire. Every muscle in the man's neck and jaw was standing out, straining, as he kicked and stomped on the man on the ground. I tried to shake Linda off. Sank to the ground. He sank with me, putting the pressure on, cutting off my air, making my eyes pulse.

"Please, no!" I cried. "I need him alive. *I need him alive!*"

I'd come here to get back everything I had lost. I didn't care about Kevin. I didn't care about Khalid and his men. I had defied all the terror and all the hurt of the past year to face the man who had ruined my life, to look into his eyes and know that *his* nightmare, the one he deserved, was just about to begin. I'd come here to change the game. Take back control. If he died now, none of that would be possible. I'd never be completely exonerated without his confession. Kevin himself would be gone again, as swiftly as he had come, blessedly free of the judgment, the punishment, the suffering that he deserved. The justice.

This was not justice. I did not want this.

But I wasn't the man with the gun. Dale Bingley was. He raised it to the face of the young man on the floor and thumbed the hammer down with a sickening click.

"How does it feel?" Dale asked. Kevin didn't answer. He just closed his eyes.

Dale fired.

He fired a number of times. How many, I didn't know. The gun was big, flashy. Full of kick. Linda was squeezing my neck too hard in his excitement, so that the sounds of Kevin's death were mere thumps in my oxygen-starved head. Linda let me go and I fell on my hands and knees, gasping for air. When I looked up, Dale was pointing the barrel of the pistol at me.

Khalid didn't move. Didn't say anything. Neither did his men. And I knew then, in their stillness, that it had always been about Kevin for these men. They'd wanted to vanquish a monster. To be responsible for another death. They wanted the credit. To be the ones who had given a vengeful father this brutal kindness, to be the ones that could be counted on to provide that kind of justice. Dark heroes. They didn't care about Dale, or me. Dale's eyes were empty, as depthless as the single black pupil of the gun. Linda had moved away from me, leaving me to Dale, if he wanted me. I exhaled my last breaths, watching, waiting for this man full of fury to unleash some more of it on me.

He didn't. I watched, shaking, as he let the gun lower.

Khalid and his stagehands were moving now, the time having come to close their show. Linda dragged me to my feet. Sharon took the gun carefully from Dale's fingers, struggling to unlock his white knuckles. Khalid was strolling to the body on the floor, a cigarette packet emerging from the salmon-colored silk lining of his jacket. He tapped a cigarette loose and waved it toward me, hardly taking the time to look my way.

"Get him outta here," Khalid said.

Amanda sat on a smooth decorative piece of sandstone at the front of the Songly house, one elbow on her knee, watching the red and blue lights of the five patrol cars before her going around and around. If she focused on them for a few seconds, stains of their colors remained when she looked away, zinging and swirling in the dark at the edge of the rainforest. All around her there was activity. Police walking in and out of the house, taking pictures, measurements, video of the crime scene. They came in a trail like ants, endless trips back and forth, going in with empty hands and coming out with brown paper bags of evidence. Few paid attention to her sitting there watching, an elvish statue drenched in blood. Some ambulance officers came after the first round of pickups, the transportation of Pip's body, Bran's body, Jay dazed and groaning on a stretcher. They crouched by Amanda, tried to fuss over her, their rubber fingers already probing. She waved them off. Rule one. No touching.

When the early hours were approaching, and the number of people going in and out of the house had sufficiently thinned, she stood and stretched her neck. Chief Clark was just inside the doorway of the house, looking over it all, his hands hanging by his sides. Grief. The lazy, sloppy kind. Amanda saw it tugging on his features like a thick clay mask as he turned toward her.

"I killed again," Amanda said, gesturing halfheartedly to the spot where Bran had lain only hours earlier, gurgling out his last breaths. "Sorry."

"Amanda, you . . ." The chief's words trailed off. He tightened his lips, sucked them in, seemed to have trouble containing them all, or finding any, Amanda didn't know. She watched, waited. But in time the chief only sighed and walked away from her, shaking his head. Now that she was back in the house, the few officers here were glaring at her. One had tears in his eyes. She wiped her blood-stained palms on the front of her T-shirt, drew a deep breath. It seemed they all were waiting for her to say something. She hoped, when she said it, that it came out right.

"She was a great copper," Amanda said, raising her chin importantly. "And a great kisser."

They all took this in for a moment. Then, one at a time, they got back to their work. Amanda waited, but no one responded to her claim. She supposed the lack of rebuttal was a good thing. When an officer passed her, coming from the garage, she asked him politely for a plastic bag for her wet shoes down at the creek. He bumped past her without acknowledging her request, so she just went to the dead old lady's kitchen and got one for herself.

The bag was not for her shoes. Amanda had nine identical pairs of pink Converse shoes. The ones by the creek could wait. Instead, she took the garbage bag and wandered out the front door and around the side of the house, down the darkened passage by the bushes, past the spot where the paling was missing. She went to the darkest corner of the empty yard, far beyond the reach of cameras flashing inside the house, sparkling behind the curtains. She glanced around, and when she was sure it was safe, Amanda knelt by the fishpond.

Bran and Jay, killers and thieves, had been stupid on many levels. But not seeing that the fishpond was clearly where their treasure lay was a real clanger, Amanda thought. Cash, hoarded and saved over decades, would not be concreted into a garage floor. The old man faced hefting a jackhammer up with his spindly arms and nearly giving himself a stroke just to get at it. Because what was the point of saving wads of cash like that, a childless old couple doing the grocery shopping, waiting for pension day, saving their receipts in case of misappropriation? To view, of course. To hold. To know. Because Tom Songly had been a corrupt cop. One of the biggest, the most powerful. He'd managed to scrape through the hellish consequences of the corruption inquiries of the 1970s and 1980s unscathed. He'd gotten away with it. He was not going to bury his takings. No way.

There would be people out there, disgraced cops who had gone to prison after the inquiries, who would want their money back when they got out. And there would be rumors, of course, of his having the money that circulated among men who were not cops and who had never been. Jailhouse gossip. Old Tom Songly would have wanted the money accessible so that he could give some of it out if he was ever threatened. Pay his own ransom. Keep the hounds away from his door, if they were ever so brazen to come.

So the garage floor was out. The idiots had been through the walls, the roof, under the house, under the tiles, under and over and through every surface of the old couple's possessions. But Songly would never have hidden the money inside the house. A search warrant by local cops wanting to try their luck with a shakedown would turn up the money too quickly. Tom's hiding place needed to be not the second, or third, or fourth place they looked, but the very last. A place so obscure that it would take time to think of. Too much time for a quick smash-and-flip search.

It also had to be somewhere Victoria would never find it, not with her obsessive cleaning, her restless retired boredom driving her in ever-spiraling circles around the house with her mop and broom and brushes. It was never going to be hidden at the back of a cupboard she might clear out, behind a loose panel she might discover. The house was out.

Amanda could see old Tom Songly out here in the yard with his garden spade and sun hat, now and then peeking over his shoulder into the living room where Victoria sat watching her shows. The garden. His domain. Amanda could see him wiping the soil from the spade, leaning over the pond carefully, dipping the spade into the water between the lily pads, fishing around between the fishes, until he found the edge of something. She imagined him lifting the iron grille, the stones that held it down at the bottom of the fish pond sliding way. Tom Songly seeing the edge of the clear plastic wrapping down there in the water, spotted with bright green algae. And between the algae, beyond the plastic, the patterns and textures of hundred-dollar bills.

Amanda didn't use a spade. She reached into the water as she had at the creek behind the Barking Frog and, in the dark, carefully prized up the slippery grille. Bubbles rose to the surface, disturbing a goldfish darting from one side of the pond to the other, slithering, slick, past her naked arm.

"Watch it, fishy." She smiled.

The first package, when it came up, was as big as a loaf of bread. She shook it a little, making raindrops for the fish, then put the brick of wrapped cash into the garbage bag beside her. When she'd prized the second money loaf up, the level of water in the pond had dropped significantly. She replaced the grille, and the stones, and folded the disturbed lily pads back onto the surface.

Amanda picked up the bag and tied a knot in the end. Bran and Jay. They'd been so close. Just not close enough.

"Idiots," she said.

Amanda hefted the bag over her shoulder and walked down the side of the house, into the dark.

EPILOGUE

The property was vast but barren, a bald patch in the otherwise lush farmland of Taree, near the Queensland border. A few years of camp fires just off the back porch, cattle wandering here and there across the dirt, and the regular crisscross of trucks and cars had deadened anything green that might have braved the immediate surrounds of the small house. Where there might have been flowers in ancient wood-lined beds along the side of the building, there were discarded beer bottles, an old tire, a milk crate full of rusting engine parts. I glanced over at the phone on the passenger seat of my car, checked the address I had been given was exactly right, before creeping steadily to a halt beside a corrugated iron carport.

The morning sun was making the iron tick. I got out, and immediately a cloud of wriggling, writhing chocolate-colored bodies swirled around my legs. Border collies, six of them, barking, snuffling my shoes. He'd been expecting me, had calmed the dogs as my car breached the distant front fence. Had held them back only long enough for me to get out, at which point the dogs came rushing, sniffing, barking. He was standing at the edge of the porch wearing flip-flops, black and white. His toes were dry and cracking, his face broad beneath a faded cap.

"Ted, eh?" He jutted his chin at me as he came down the steps. I smiled, offered my hand, braced for recognition of my face. There was none.

"That's me," I said. "Thanks for seeing me, Al."

"No problem, mate." He scratched his chest. He was ruddy faced and sunburned, what looked like a homemade haircut hidden beneath the cap. "Bit of a weird story, I gotta tell ya. I half decided you were havin' me on."

"Nope," I said. "God's honest truth."

"Right." Al slapped away the nose of a border collie who was snuffling at his crotch. "Well, she's round 'ere, mate. Wouldn't expect her to greet you at the car, that's for sure. She's a lazy bitch, I'll give her that."

He led, and I followed, up onto the porch, where the shade was a relief. There was a small plastic child-safety gate to keep the border collies off the stairs. A coffee table made from old pallets sat before mismatched cane lounges sunken with the shape of bodies now gone. At the very end of the porch, lying on its side on a hair-covered blanket, was a pure white dog.

She lifted her head, got to her feet as we approached. She was fat. Sadly fat, the sagging belly and thick neck of an unhappy creature who gorges on whatever passes beneath her nose. The dog had a cheerful face, though. Pointed at the nose, broad at the forehead, a mingling of perhaps dozens of breeds. I smiled at the triangular ears pricked, sharp, like two cupped hands.

"So this is her, huh?" I said. The white dog didn't come to me, which I thought was odd, given the doggy smile about her lips. But as I crouched, hands out, in greeting, she took a couple of steps forward and I noticed the limp. The right front paw. The one that had been broken when she arrived at the RSPCA in Yagoona. I pretended the limp was a shock. "Oh dear. What's that all about?"

"Yeah, she's had it since we got her," Al said. "These fucking rescue dogs, mate. You never know what you're getting. It's a lucky dip."

"Is it permanent?"

"Aw, look, I wouldn't spend the money finding out, you know what I mean?" He gestured to the dog. "When we got her, the RSPCA said she had recently recovered from a break. Needed rehab. Told us how, and all. I tried to tell her, Renni, my girlfriend at the time. Tried to talk her out of it. A rescue dog with a medical problem? You fuckin' serious? But no, no, no. She wanted her *own* dog. Had to be a tragedy, something she could feel good about."

"Right," I said. I smoothed the white dog's cheek and neck. She wagged her tail.

"I breed the collies, you see," Al continued. "Those beautiful, intelligent things you saw back there at the car. The pups are two K each. When I was with Renni, we had seven bitches and seven sires and we were two weeks off having a new litter of six or more. Nope, wasn't enough for her! Can you believe it?"

I didn't answer. Didn't need to.

"She wanted something special. Heaven help me. She goes and brings back this bag of problems." Al gestured to the dog. "Jay-sus. Honestly. Women."

"Yup."

"So anyway, tell us more about the crime, mate." Al slapped my chest. "You said on the phone it was an abduction? Down in Sydney, was it?"

"Look, it's not something I can really go that deep into."

"Right."

"It's a complex investigation."

"Uh-huh." Al nodded vigorously, looked back at the animal at our feet. She was sitting looking up at me, the cupped ears swiveling, listening, failing to understand. "Nah, I get it. I get it, mate. Look, I'm happy to help. Anything you want to know about her, I'll tell you. There's not much to say, really. She's a piece of shit mongrel with a gimpy leg. When my girlfriend left, she didn't even take it with her. Thing doesn't even catch a ball. Were you gonna take pictures of her, or . . . ? You never really said on the phone what you wanted."

I hadn't known exactly what I wanted when I'd called a day earlier from my hotel room in Sydney. It had been a struggle to get the information out of the RSPCA, without police credentials, on exactly where the dog had gone after she was dumped at the gates by Kevin on that day. I'd held the receiver, winced at the silence on the other end of the line, wondering if the administrator was about to tell me the dog had been humanely euthanized.

The white dog had been on my mind for a while. In the week since it had all come to an end, as I sat alone in my room drinking Wild Turkey and watching the traffic on the street below, she had returned again and again to my mind. I'd been almost too afraid to make the call.

Leaving Sydney, driving northwest along the inland highway, I still hadn't known what I wanted. But now I knew. Standing with Al the border collie breeder on his battered, sun-dried porch, looking down at the white dog, I knew.

I reached into my back pocket and drew out my wallet.

Rumbling along the highway, my window down, air shuddering in and out of the vehicle. The white dog sat upright on the passenger seat, mouth open and tongue foaming, panting as she watched the road ahead, that bad paw slightly raised, all her weight leaning on the good one. I let the phone in the center console play what it wanted through the radio, a wandering streaming channel, hits from the 1980s. The musty, acrid smell of unwashed dog was strangely nice. I crossed over to the coast road just to draw out the journey with her. I think she might have liked to stick her head out the open window beside her, but her balance wasn't good.

I stopped somewhere near Byron Bay and bought a couple of sausage rolls at a little roadside service station, stood outside the car looking in at her looking out at me while the pastry cooled. When I offered her the roll she didn't even sniff it. Just took it into her jaws in two gulps. Gone. Impressive.

Near Burleigh Heads I noticed a flea crawling in the hair on my arm, pinched it and put it out the window. The dog lifted a paw, acquiesced as I reached over and examined her belly. She was crawling with them. Flashes of black between the strands of white. I gave her a rub on the head, reached down and lifted the battered tag from the front of her throat.

"Pig," I read aloud. The dog's ears swiveled, mouth drawing closed, ready for my command. I gritted my teeth, tugged the tag. It came right off the tattered old collar.

"Sorry, honey," I told the dog. "'Pig' isn't gonna work for me."

I chucked the tag out the window. We rode together in silence.

Near Mackay, a song came on the radio. Celine Dion's "Think Twice." I jolted at the sound of the dog's howling, having forgotten she was there. The dog looked at me. Paused. Lifted her head and howled again, a low, sad, lilting sound perfectly in keeping with the song on the radio.

I drove and watched. The dog sang and sang. And when Dion's song was over, the animal beside me fell quiet, that pink tongue appearing again, jiggling with the vibrations of the car.

"Is it just that song?" I asked the beast, taking the phone from the center console. I typed into the search bar as I drove. Something by Ronan Keating had begun to play. I cut of it off to play Celine Dion's "The Power of Love."

I watched the dog. Nothing. And then, just when I'd turned back to the road, she lifted her chin and began to howl. She sang and I grinned.

"'Celine' it is, then," I said. I fell into long overdue laughter.

She came in the afternoon, not bothering to announce her intentions in any way, just walking around the side of the house and leaning her bike against the fence like she usually did. I was standing with my shirt off, the humidity such that even the menial task of painting was making me sweat. I'd decided green was best for the goose house. I didn't want it to stand out too starkly from the rainforest surrounds of my property. The birds were sitting all around me on the grass, beaks tucked into backs or feathery breasts, round, featureless stones. I'd finished the sides and stood dabbing paint onto the front façade of the playhouse when I heard the unmistakable tread of squeaky sneakers on the lawn behind me.

Two weeks. But already some of the bruises and grazes Amanda had come away from her ordeal with were easing, sinking back into her colorful flesh, swallowed by the flowers and portraits and leaning, curving buildings on her skin. If there was one thing Amanda did well, it was heal. She still had two black eyes, but those eyes were smiling, as always. I glanced at her, raised my brush in greeting. She stood and watched my work for a while, squinting in the sun, before Celine raised her head from where she lay curled in a ball among the birds, a camouflaged creature revealing its true form.

"Oh lord!" Amanda grabbed at her chest. "That was a good trick."

"I think she thinks she's one of them," I said. Celine had indeed integrated with the birds, but it hadn't been smooth sailing. As I'd knelt by the bathtub, pouring warm water from a jug over the stiff-legged dog, I'd heard the indignant slapping of webbed feet on the floorboards behind me. The soapy water was swirling with dead fleas. I'd turned and spied two geese jabbering in their strange language, instinctual confusion at the sound of the water in the bath and the distinct lack of Neil Diamond in the air. The birds had eyed the intruder dog, clicking, tittering. Celine had barked and they'd fluttered away, a frenzy of panicked wings. Over a couple of days, the animals had come to some kind of silent agreement. It became obvious to the birds, I supposed, that Celine was too fat and too awkward to chase them. And to Celine, perhaps, that Bitey Bulger was going to bite no matter what she did, but it wasn't all that hard.

Amanda had left me alone for the time I'd been back. She'd found out somehow, in her almost supernatural way, that Kelly had asked me to come home. It didn't take me or Kelly to tell her that. Amanda might have heard it, the anguish in my voice when I called to tell her what had happened to Kevin Driscoll. When I'd told her, Amanda had joined the small, select crew of vastly different characters who knew. To the rest of the world, what happened to Kevin was unclear.

There were clues, of course. Police had found Kevin in the warehouse, slumped on his side, minute by minute cooling as his body adapted to its filthy surroundings. Beside Kevin's body they'd found a man, someone resembling, but wholly different to, the Dale Bingley who'd existed not long before. Dale had been sitting with his knees drawn up, his arms hanging loosely around them, calm. The gun was gone. In the dust nearby, there were shoeprints, some of them very large, some of them very expensive.

Outside the warehouse, police had found Kevin Driscoll's car with the driver's side door open, the cabin light on. No prints. On the passenger seat, a journal and a pen, long scribblings in a heavy hand. A diary.

I'd seen Dale Bingley on the news only the night before, standing with his wife on the steps of a police station. He'd shaved. The shirt he was wearing was immaculate. Rose Bingley was holding his hand. All around them stood important people, people I didn't recognize. Lawyers. Detectives. Specialists, probably. I didn't know. He'd made bail.

The man who'd stolen my life was dead. In time, the media would release details of the diary, and that would go some way to exonerating me, at least for people who wouldn't go so far as to believe that Kevin and I had acted together and that he'd deliberately kept me out of his writings. The police had kept me in Sydney for a week, wanting to talk about Dale, Khalid Farah, Kevin. Why I'd been at a house the police knew Kevin had been at only hours before he had been murdered. Why I'd called his ex-girlfriend, and what we'd spoken about. Whether or not I believed Dale Bingley had set out to murder Kevin, and whether or not I'd been there when he did. I'd brought Sean to the interrogations and enacted my right to silence. There was no case against me. The police couldn't put me at the scene of the crime. I'd reported my phone stolen and thrown out my shoes, and no witnesses had seen me or Dale driving there that night. The case against Dale also had major problems. There was no gun found at the scene or anywhere near it. Dale wasn't talking. His lawyer was one of the country's top QCs. If he got into trouble, there would always be a provocation defense. Temporary insanity. Self-defense. Whatever they liked. I didn't think the case against Dale would hold up. Or that he would care if it did.

Amanda knew that my wife had offered to give me back something of what I had lost. In the week I'd been in Sydney, I'd seen Lillian again, this time alone with Kelly at a McDonald's, Jett nowhere to be seen. She'd asked me again to come home. I'd given her my answer.

Knowing all these things, Amanda stood beside me saying nothing, chipping old paint off the cubby beside her with her thumbnail. Maybe she was afraid to ask if I was going back. I didn't know what fear was like for her, my strange little partner.

"I'm sorry about Sweeney," I said. Amanda turned toward me too fast, betraying the terror I knew was there. I dipped the brush in the paint. "I know you liked her."

"I did like her." Amanda nodded. I saw her glance at my bare ring finger, quick as a flash. She looked away again. Cool and distant, or trying to be.

"They'll be angry at us," I said. "The Crimson Lake cops."

"Mmm," Amanda agreed.

"On the next case, we'll have to keep our heads down," I said.

I felt Amanda watching me. Tried not to smile. In time, the stiff, upright strip of color that she was in the corner of my vision seemed to slouch. She was leaning against the cubby, smiling, looking at the animals on the grass, feathers and fur gleaming in the dying sun.

No, I wasn't going back to Sydney. To my wife. I loved Kelly still, of course. She was the mother of my child. But the woman that she had been before the fateful day that changed our worlds was gone now, and a new woman had taken her place. She was battered, bruised, and strained by what had happened. Her heart was broken, and her trust was gone. It wasn't her fault. It was Kevin's.

What Kevin had done had changed me, too. I wasn't the same man. And to think that Kelly and I could go back, two completely different people trying to love each other in the same way we always had was a decision that was destined to fail. I didn't want to have to leave that house again, packing my bags, saying goodbye to my daughter, starting over with that awful loss and loneliness newly heavy in my chest.

I belonged here. A different man with a different life. Displaced, but defiant, resolved to grow. I would work it all out eventually; how I could still be in Lillian's life the way I needed to be. How I could form a new relationship with Kelly, if not as her husband, as her friend. How I could accept never being free of my accusation. I'd just work on it, one bit at a time. I wasn't alone. There were people in my new life who would help me.

"The dog," Amanda said, drawing me away from my thoughts. "What's her name?"

I put down my brush, slipped my phone from my back pocket. I was already laughing as I brought up the music player.

"Watch this," I said. "You're gonna love this."

ACKNOWLEDGMENTS

As always, in acknowledging the people who helped me reach this point in my writerly life, I must mention the creative writing teachers in my past who armed me with the necessary tools of my trade. Those wonderful scholars were James Forsyth, Dr. Gary Crew, Dr. Ross Watkins, Dr. Roslyn Petelin, Dr. Kim Wilkins, Dr. Camilla Nelson, and Dr. Christine De Matos and their colleagues. Without you all, I would never have become what I am.

I will forever be indebted to the founding members of Team Fox, those sassy ladies Gaby Naher, Bev Cousins, Nikki Christer, Jessica Malpass, and Kathryn Knight. Thank you for listening to me, believing in me, and putting up with me. I admire you all more than you will ever know.

To those other wonderful publishing people all across the world who have joined the team, I owe you just as much. Some of you include Lisa Gallagher, Lou Ryan, Jerry Kalajian, Kristin Sevick, Linda Quinton, Michaela Hamilton, Thomas Wortche, Susan Sandon, Selina Walker, and the rest of you know who you are.

Thank you to my fellow author buddies Adrian McKinty and James Patterson for always being ready to lend an ear.

All my love and thanks to my readers all over the world, who never leave me feeling lonely or unappreciated. I have treasured every review, letter, and comment, and it has been so wonderful meeting some of you in real life.

And as always, to my wonderful Tim. Thank you for being there whenever I needed you, word by word and page by page. You are a true delight in my life.